THE TRAP

Kimberley Chambers lives in Romford and has been, at various times, a disc jockey and a street trader. She is now a full-time writer and is the author of seven novels.

Also by Kimberley Chambers

KIMBERLEY CHAMBERS

The Trap

HARPER

Harper
An imprint of HarperCollins*Publishers*
77–85 Fulham Palace Road,
Hammersmith, London W6 8JB

www.harpercollins.co.uk

A Paperback Original 2013

7

Copyright © Kimberley Chambers 2013

Kimberley Chambers asserts the moral right to
be identified as the author of this work

A catalogue record for this book
is available from the British Library

ISBN: 9780007435036

Set in Sabon by Palimpsest Book Production Limited,
Falkirk, Stirlingshire

Printed and bound in Great Britain by
Clays Ltd, St Ives plc

In memory of all our brave soldiers who have lost their lives in action including my own grandfather "Gunner Thomas Henry Caunter"

Acknowledgments

A big thank you to my lovely editor Sarah Ritherdon, and to all the team at HarperCollins for their hard work, advice and dedication. It is truly a pleasure to be part of a company who has so much faith in me.

Thanks also to the best agent I could wish for, Tim Bates, and my brilliant typist Sue Cox. To Rosie de Courcy for helping me to get where I am today, and to Lady Heller for cheering up my working day with her truly dysfunctional text messages.

I had never been one for social networking until I became a writer, and it is only through Facebook and Twitter that I have got to know and become fond of so many of my readers. What a great bunch you are! And I can't thank you enough for all the loyalty and support you have shown me. Writing can be a lonely old job at times and your posts and tweets certainly do brighten up a dull day..........x

If you trap the moment before it's ripe,
The tears of repentance you certainly wipe.
But if once you let the ripe moment go,
You can never wipe off the tears of woe.

William Blake

Prologue

Autumn 1965

Unable to make himself heard above Sandie Shaw belting out 'Long Live Love', Donald Walker made his way over to the Wurlitzer jukebox and turned down the volume.

'Don't do that! You know I like Sandie,' Mary Walker said, as though she knew the singer personally.

'There's somebody knocking at the door,' Donald informed his wife.

Mary walked over to the door and unbolted it. She was greeted by a sturdy-looking woman standing there in a dark-grey overcoat. At a guess, Mary thought she was probably in her mid fifties, but it was hard to be sure because of the curlers and hairnet on her head. 'Hello. Can I help you?' Mary asked, politely.

'No, but I can help you,' the woman replied, barging her way past Mary and into the premises.

Donald and Mary knew very little about the East End or its natives. They were North Londoners, having lived in Stoke Newington for many years, but this café in Whitechapel had been far too cheap to turn down, which is why they had decided to up sticks and move.

'Hello, I'm Donald and this is my wife, Mary. As you have probably already realized, we are the new owners of the café. We officially open for business tomorrow but would you like a cup of tea or coffee?' Donald asked.

Shaking her head, the woman held out her right hand. 'I'm Freda. Freda Smart. I live just around the corner.'

'And how can you help us?' Mary enquired. She had a feeling that Freda was about to ask for a job, but there was no chance of that as she and Donald had spent every penny they had refurbishing the rundown café and were in no position to employ staff just yet.

'I can help you by telling you why this café has been empty for eighteen long months before you bought it and why you probably got it for peanuts,' Freda spat.

Mary gave her husband a worried glance. This café had been half the cost of any others they had looked at and the only one in their meagre price-range. But this woman seemed unhinged somehow and Mary wondered if she perhaps held a grudge against the previous owner.

'Would you like a glass of water?' Donald asked. He had noticed that the woman's forehead had beads of sweat forming which had now started to drip onto one of his brand-new melamine tables.

'No, don't want nuffink. Just come to let you know the score. No-one else round 'ere will tell you. They're all too bleedin' well frightened of 'em, but I ain't.'

'Frightened of who?' Mary asked, perplexed.

'Frightened of the Butlers. They own that snooker club just around the corner. Old Jack who used to own this café, they killed his son, Peter. Broke his wife Ethel's heart it did and if you don't abide by their rules, they'll rip the heart out of your family too. I saw you move in. You got two little kids, ain't ya? Well, if you just do as I say, you'll be OK. Albie's the dad. He's a piss-head, a proper waster. The mother is the brains of the family. Hard-looking old cow called Queenie. Her sister is Vivvy, she has a mongol son, and Queenie's kids are Vinny, who is the worst out the bunch, Roy, Michael, and young Brenda. When they come in here, look after 'em. Serve 'em before any other customers and don't charge 'em for food or drinks, you get me?'

Seeing the distressed look on his wife's face, Donald was extremely annoyed. Opening their café tomorrow was meant to be one of the best moments of their lives and yet this madwoman was here, upsetting his Mary and threatening to spoil the joyous occasion. 'I can assure you, Freda, that Mary and I will not be giving free drinks or food to anybody and our customers will also be served in the order they arrive in. Now, if you don't mind, could I please ask you to leave? Mary and I still have lots of work to do before we open tomorrow and we have very little time left to accomplish that task.'

Absolutely furious that her sound advice hadn't been listened to, Freda stood up, stomped towards Donald and poked him in the chest. 'Dig your own grave, what do I care? But, don't say I didn't warn you. The Butlers, remember the name. They catch people in their trap, just like spiders do,' she yelled, as Donald escorted her out of the café.

'Oh my God! What have we done, Donald? And who the hell are the Butlers?' Mary asked, when her husband had locked the door.

Donald took his wife in his arms. At six foot, he towered over Mary's five-foot frame. He was the man of the family and protect her he would. 'Do not worry yourself, my darling. Freda is obviously the mad local scaremonger. And even if that Butler family do come in here, we won't have any problems with them, I can absolutely assure you of that.'

Nestling herself against Donald's broad chest, Mary

3

breathed a sigh of relief. Her husband's instincts were never wrong.

Five minutes later the jukebox was back on and Mary and Donald worked happily side by side. They sang in unison to the Beatles' 'Help', but what they didn't realize was that in the not-too-distant future, they would be needing help themselves. Every word that Freda Smart had spoken happened to be the truth. She wasn't mad, nor was she a scaremonger. She was just a realist who had done her utmost to warn a decent family of the perils of moving to Whitechapel.

CHAPTER ONE

'There's two people waiting outside, Daddy. Can we open the door now?' asked young Nancy Walker.

Urging his eleven-year-old daughter to come away from the window, Donald smiled as Nancy skipped towards him. Nancy was like a miniature version of her mother: petite, blonde, with blue eyes and a cute button nose.

'How're we doing for time, Donald?' Mary shouted out.

Holding his daughter's hand, Donald led her into the kitchen. 'We have twenty minutes until our business officially opens, my dear,' he said, proudly. He had worked two jobs for many years to secure his and Mary's aim of a better life for themselves and their family. He had even worked at weekends while Mary brought the children up nigh-on single-handedly, but it had been worth it now they had achieved their dream.

'Look, Dad. I buttered all that,' Christopher said, pointing towards a stack of bread.

Donald ruffled the hair of his eight-year-old son. Christopher looked nothing like his mother and sister. He took after his dad with his brown hair and his chocolate-coloured eyes.

'Can you put that cake in the display cabinet for me,

Donald? Oh, and turn the jukebox on as well,' Mary ordered.

Donald raised his eyebrows to the ceiling at the mention of the jukebox. He had been totally against purchasing such an object. He had finally relented when Mary explained her exact reasons for wanting one. 'I don't want ours to be like some grotty old transport café, Donald. I want it to be vibrant and modern. If we buy the jukebox outright, just think of the extra income we will earn with people putting all their pennies in. We don't want a café full of old-age pensioners, do we? We want to attract a younger crowd that have money to spend, and music is the best attraction of all. That new band, the Rolling Stones, would liven up a graveyard,' Mary insisted.

Donald sat down on one of the posh plastic shiny red chairs that his wife had fallen in love with. She had an eye for décor, did his Mary, and Donald had to admit she had done a bloody good job. Red and white had been her colour theme and apart from the picture of James Dean that sat proudly on the wall opposite the jukebox, everything was a mixture of those two colours. Thinking how trendy and also how very American it all looked, Donald smiled, stood up, and walked into the kitchen. 'I can't wait any longer. Let's open the door now, shall we?'

'Can I open it?' Christopher shouted, grabbing his father's arm.

'No, I want to do it,' Nancy said obstinately, pushing her brother out of the way.

'Behave yourselves, please. Seeing as your mother designed this and buying a café was all her idea in the first place, it will be her that opens the door to the public.'

Eyes shining with excitement, Mary picked up the scissors. Donald had put a piece of red ribbon across the outside of the door this morning and once that was cut, their

6

wonderful café was open for the whole wide world to see. 'To happiness and success,' Mary said.

Queenie Butler stared at her mother's grave and crouched down next to her sister. 'We've tidied you up, Mum, and we're off now. Love you. God bless,' Queenie said, kissing her fingers and placing her right hand against her mother's headstone.

'Yep. God bless, sweetheart,' Vivian added, solemnly.

'Don't our flowers look beautiful?' Queenie commented, linking arms with her sister.

Vivian nodded. 'Best-looking grave over here by miles. At least we have respect for the dead, unlike some people,' she said loudly, as Old Mother Taylor walked past.

'Stop it, Viv,' Queenie laughed.

'Well, her old man's grave is an eyesore. How the hell can she visit him regular and stare at those weeds? It ain't bleedin' normal. Lazy old cow,' Vivian said, loudly.

'Whatever is your Lenny doing?' Queenie enquired.

Marching over to her nine-year-old son, Vivian clipped him around the ear. 'What have I told you about pissing over 'ere, eh? If you wanna do a wee-wee, you ask me and I'll take you to a toilet. You don't get your dingle-dangle out in public, understand? It's naughty.'

'Sorry, Mummy,' Lenny said, grinning.

As her nephew skipped on ahead of them, Queenie chuckled. 'I'm sure he only does it to wind you up, Viv. He laughs every time you have a go at him. Sod all wrong with his brain. Smart as a button, he is.'

Vivian batted her eyelids. Lenny was her only son, she adored him, but it wasn't easy bringing up a child with disabilities. Lenny had nearly died when she'd given birth to him. She had gone into labour at home and when the doctor finally arrived, he hadn't been able to get her son out at first. Lenny had been in the breech position and it seemed like an eternity before he finally entered the world. Queenie had been with her throughout, holding her hand while she screamed blue murder and both of them had thought little Lenny was a goner. He lay motionless on the bed for a good few minutes before the doctor managed to find signs of life. The relief she felt when she heard that first cry come from his lips, Vivian would remember till her dying day.

Lenny's dad was an East End Jack-the-lad called Bill Harris. Bill was working his way up the criminal ladder and had felt humiliated being associated with a son who wasn't born perfect. It was common knowledge locally that Bill was knocking off the tarty barmaid in the Blind Beggar and when Vivian finally learned of his betrayal, she had packed his clothes in a couple of sacks, marched inside the pub with Queenie alongside her, chucked them at the barmaid, and told her she was welcome to her no-good husband. That was over three years ago now, and Vivian had never clapped eyes on Bill Harris since. Rumour had it that he'd moved to Barking and set up home with his new tart. Viv hoped this wasn't true, as she would much prefer the bastard to be six feet under and covered by earth.

'Your Lenny looks more and more like my Michael every day. Wouldn't Mum have loved him now?' Queenie said, wistfully.

Vivian nodded. Their poor old mum had died last year and had adored young Lenny. She'd had a stroke and was found dead in her armchair with her knitting on her lap. She was only fifty-seven, no age at all.

'Shall we pop in and see the boys in the club on the way back?' Queenie asked. She was dead proud of her two eldest sons for recently setting up their own business. It was officially a snooker club, but it was common knowledge locally that it was really an illegal drinking and gambling den.

Queenie wasn't daft. She knew Vinny and Roy had pulled off a robbery or two to afford such an establishment, but it didn't bother her. She wanted her sons to live the good life and if that meant swindling the odd person or company along the way, then so be it.

'Yeah, why not. They might find Lenny some jobs to do this afternoon which will give me a break. Old Jack's café re-opens today, you know. Fat Beryl saw one of them juke-boxes being delivered there, so it sounds posh. Let's be nosy and have a cuppa there first, then we'll pop in to see the boys.'

'Oh, I dunno, Viv. Say all Old Jack's customers are back in there? He was ever so popular, was Jack. My Vinny swears blind he had nothing to do with young Peter's murder, but I don't fancy walking into a furnace. Perhaps we should pop in there when it's been open a couple of weeks? Bound to be packed today.'

'People are always gonna spread bloody rumours. Your Vinny's got good morals, you know that. Peter was a pervert, that's a fact, and if it was Vinny that topped him for touching up that poor child, then he deserves a bleedin' medal. Let's walk in there with our heads held high. You are Queenie Butler, no bastard would have the guts to say anything bad to you, would they? Or me, for that matter, and if somebody did get a bit lippy, we'll just walk round the corner and tell the boys.'

Knowing how feared her two eldest sons were, Queenie couldn't help but chuckle. 'Sod it then. Let's go and be nosy.'

Donald and Mary had been rushed off their feet all morning. Donald was in charge of the cooking in the kitchen and Mary was out at the front taking customers' orders and making teas, coffees, sandwiches and rolls. Even young Nancy and Christopher had worked flat-out. They were in charge of the washing and drying up, with the promise of some extra pocket money.

At the first lull in the day's activities, Donald left the kitchen to join his wife at the counter.

'The interest that jukebox has caused, you would not believe. Everybody who has come in has had a look at it. Told you it would be good for business, didn't I?' Mary said, treating Donald to a smug expression. Her husband could be a domineering man at times, but Mary had learned to stick up for herself over the years. Nancy always sided with her, and Christopher with his father, but overall they were a happy, well-balanced family.

'You most certainly did, my dear. I can't believe how busy we have been, can you? Perhaps it's a bit of a novelty as it's our first day, but if things continue in the same vein, we will have to look at taking on a member of staff, Mary. The kids start their new school next week, remember? And there is no way I would have had time to wash and dry up this morning as well as cook all the food.'

'Let's see how things pan out. Perhaps we can take someone on part-time to help us out in our busiest period?' Mary replied. She and Donald had planned to open from seven in the morning to seven in the evening to begin with.

Donald didn't answer. He was too busy watching the reaction of his seated customers to the two bleached-blonde women and dark-haired child who had just walked in. They were being treated like royalty. Because there were no spare tables, at least three different people had leapt up to give them theirs and one man had even offered to buy them their food and drink.

'This has to be members of that Butler family that Mad Freda warned us about,' Donald hissed in his wife's ear.

10

Mary smiled broadly as the young boy ran over to the jukebox and the two women approached the counter. 'Hello, I'm Mary Walker and this is my husband, Donald. We are the new owners of this establishment,' Mary said, for about the fiftieth time that day.

'Music, Mummy. I wanna dance,' young Lenny shouted at the top of his voice.

''Ere you go, boy,' an old man in a flat cap said, handing Lenny some coins.

Queenie held out her right hand. 'Pleased to meet you. I'm Queenie Butler and this is my sister, Vivian. My sons own the snooker club just around the corner and that young man over there is Lenny, Vivvy's boy.'

The volume on the jukebox wasn't overly loud, but as Lenny started singing and bopping away to the sound of Buddy Holly's 'That'll be the Day', most of the people in the café fawned over him, then clapped in unison.

Mary joined in with the applause.

'Rock and roll mad, he is. Dunno where he gets it from. Nobody else in the bleedin' family likes it,' Vivian informed Mary.

'Right, we'll have two cups of rosy and I'll have one of them scones with thick butter on it,' Queenie said.

'I'll have a scone too and a can of pop and an iced bun for my Lenny,' Vivian added.

Remembering Mad Freda's warning about the Butlers not paying, Mary was relieved when Queenie handed her a pound note, then thanked her as she gave her her change.

Mary followed Donald out into the kitchen. 'Well, that Freda was obviously mad. She said the boy was a mongol and even though you can tell he is a bit backward, he certainly isn't one of those. And even though the women seem a bit rough and ready, they were polite enough and paid for their order.'

Donald kissed his wife on the forehead. 'I told you every-thing would be fine.' There was no way Donald would worry his Mary, but he really hadn't liked the look of those Butler women. The atmosphere in the café had been normal before they'd walked in and he could tell people were only offering them their tables, fawning over the child, and gener-ally falling over backwards out of some kind of fear. Donald wasn't stupid. Those Butlers had danger stamped all over them.

Vinny and Roy Butler grinned as they divided up the previous evening's takings.

'Blinding! And another good night was had by all,' Vinny said, as he handed his brother a pile of notes.

Roy chuckled. 'You sticking the other pile back in the kitty?'

'Yep. We gotta speculate to accumulate,' Vinny replied, in a sensible manner.

At twenty, Vinny was two years older than his brother Roy, and between them they were on their way to becoming a force to be reckoned with. A container-load of TVs they had stolen had paid for them to buy the rundown snooker club, and even though it had taken six months to save enough money to refurbish it to their lavish taste, it now looked very classy.

Unlike a lot of young East End wannabes, Vinny and Roy had gone down the clever route of keeping themselves to themselves. Their father Albie was an arsehole. He was also an alcoholic, and watching him make a complete prick of himself over the years had put the boys off ever frequenting pubs.

Neither Vinny nor Roy was a complete teetotaller. Both lads enjoyed the odd Scotch on the rocks here and there, but they only ever drank in front of friends and family, or on their own premises. In their line of business, both lads always liked to have their wits about them. Being clever was part of their image.

One of the reasons Vinny and Roy had decided to buy the club and turn it into the headquarters of their empire was that they hadn't wanted to tread on anybody else's toes. The East End was littered with villains, with the two most frightening families being the Mitchells and the Krays.

The Mitchells were based in Canning Town and were heavily into pub protection. They were a family firm, run by the old man, Harry. He pulled the strings while his three sons, Ronny, Paulie and Eddie, terrorized people into handing over their hard-earned cash.

Then there were the Krays. They were local lads who had made a real name for themselves. They were virtually beyond the reach of the law now. Earlier this year they had escaped conviction for nightclub extortion. They'd even been given an interview on TV after that and hung out with film stars and celebrities.

Vinny didn't know if being that famous was a good thing or not, but he was determined to be feared, well-respected and rich. As a lad, he had idolized both the Mitchells and the Krays for what they had achieved in life and he was hell-bent on topping their glory. Wanting to be the best was part of Vinny's nature.

'Who is it?' Roy shouted, as he heard a knock on the door.

'It's the bleedin' woman who gave birth to the pair of ya,' Queenie yelled.

Vinny grinned as Roy unlocked the metal door and Lenny ran towards him. 'All right, Champ? What you been up to?' Vinny asked, lifting the boy off the ground and swinging him around in the air. Vinny adored his cousin, all the family did.

'Been Nanny's grave, then I went dancing in the café,' Lenny replied, sporting a big grin.

'Dancing in what poxy café?'

'Old Jack's café. It's re-opened today. New people have taken it over and it's got one of them jukeboxes in there. I wouldn't swing him around too much. Three iced cakes the greedy little sod has eaten and he's bound to be Tom Dick at some point,' Vivian explained.

Not wanting sick over his brand-new shirt, Vinny sat Lenny on a chair. 'So, what do you think of the décor, Auntie Viv? You haven't seen the leather chairs and sofas yet, have you?'

Vivian grinned. She loved her nephews. Unlike a lot of young men these days, Vinny and Roy had impeccable manners. They still referred to her as 'Auntie' and probably always would. Viv sat down on one of the burgundy sofas and stroked the quality leather. 'Oh, it's beautiful, boys. Looks like a palace now, eh, Queenie?'

Queenie felt as proud as a peacock as she nodded her head in agreement.

Roy stood up. 'I'll get you and Auntie Viv a glass of sherry,' he said, gesturing for Vinny to follow him.

'What's up?' Vinny asked.

'Why don't we tell her now? Seems as good a time as any,' Roy whispered, when his brother joined him behind the bar.

'Nah. Not in front of Champ,' Vinny replied.

'Well, we gotta tell her soon. I hate seeing Dad take the piss out of her like this. He's such a bastard.'

Vinny nodded in agreement. Breaking the bad news to his mother was not going to be easy, but it had to be done. 'We'll find a way to tell her in the next couple of days. And don't worry about Dad. That treacherous piece of shit will be dealt with, I promise.'

Noticing the dangerous glint in his brother's eyes that he had seen many times before, Roy felt his stomach knotting. 'What do you mean by dealt with? I know he's a prick, Vin, but we can't do anything bad to him, he's still our dad.'

Leaning towards his brother's ear, Vinny spoke loudly and clearly. 'I wouldn't care if he was the King of England. Nobody makes a fool out of our mum and I mean fucking nobody. Our dad will pay for the liberty he has taken. Trust me on that one.'

CHAPTER TWO

Albie Butler lit up a Salem cigarette and sighed blissfully as the nicotine hit the back of his throat. There was nothing more pleasurable than a fag after getting your end away, unless you counted the first drag of the morning.

Judy Preston was a twenty-five-year-old mother of one. Her son Mark had just turned three and instead of marrying her like any decent man would have, Mark's father had dumped Judy on learning she was pregnant.

Judy knew she was gossiped about and frowned upon in the street where she lived. Her neighbours were all older than she was and Judy knew they thought it disgusting that she had given birth out of wedlock. Judy didn't care about their narrow-mindedness. Her mum helped her bring up Mark and nobody would dare say anything to her face for fear of retribution from her brother, Johnny.

Having an older sibling who just happened to be a face certainly had its benefits, and when her relationship with Albie did become common knowledge, Judy knew she would get little grief from his family thanks to who her brother was.

When Judy made another grab for his already over-worked pecker, Albie Butler leapt out of the bed. Judy

Preston was by far the prettiest of the half a dozen or so lassies he'd had flings with since marrying Queenie, but the look on Vinny and Roy's faces yesterday evening when he had popped in the snooker club told Albie that they knew he was at it again. If they told Queenie she would chop his bollocks off and feed them to next door's dog and that wasn't a chance Albie was willing to take.

'I'm really sorry, Judy, but I think we're gonna have to call it a day. My boys are onto us and I can't risk her indoors finding out. I love you, you know that, but all good things must come to an end,' Albie said regretfully.

Judy stared at Albie with her mouth wide open. Did he honestly think he could come round for one last bunk-up and then casually dump her like a bag of old rubbish? Because if he did, he had another bloody think coming. Thankful that she had kept the news she had known for the past six weeks to herself, Judy grinned. 'I'm afraid walking away from me isn't an option, Albie. I'm pregnant and it's yours!'

Vinny poured himself a Scotch on the rocks and sat down in his office. Roy had begged him not to rough up their dad and in the end Vinny had reluctantly agreed. Tomorrow, he was taking his family out for lunch and that was when he planned to expose his father's infidelity. His mother was no shrinking violet and Vinny was sure that once she knew what his arsehole of a father had been up to, she would batter him to Bow and back herself.

Smiling at the thought of his mother smashing her frying pan around his father's head, Vinny stared at the picture of her that sat proudly on his desk. She and Vivian were side by side on a sofa holding Brenda. It had been taken over a decade ago when his sister was just a baby. His mother and Viv looked more like twins than sisters, and Vinny couldn't

17

help but notice how much they had aged since. Both still dressed smartly and had beautiful smiles, but the wrinkles they now sported told a story of the hardship they'd endured throughout their lives.

Vinny had been a mummy's boy for as long as he could remember. His dad had been, and still was, a two-bob con merchant and had never really been there for him and his siblings. He earned his beer money by selling cheap imported booze and fags and had never had a proper job in his life. Vinny's mum had. She had two cleaning jobs for years just to put food in her children's mouths and had only given up work last year when Vinny had insisted that he was now wealthy enough to support her.

Remembering how elated his mother had been when she had told both of the petulant rich women she worked for to shove their jobs up their arses, Vinny grinned and stared at the photo of himself standing in the middle of his two brothers. All three of them had inherited their father's jet-black hair and green eyes, and when stood together, they made a striking-looking trio.

At six foot two, Vinny was taller than Roy and Michael, but only by an inch or so. Both he and Roy wore their hair slicked back with Brylcreem and they often got mistaken for Italians. Vinny found that a big compliment, as he knew that in their expensive suits, accompanied with their swagger, he and Roy could pass for members of the Mafia. Michael wouldn't though. He was a Mod and the only suit he ever wore was a tonic one. Tomorrow was Michael's sixteenth birthday and Vinny and Roy had clubbed together to buy him the moped he had been harping on about for months. His brother had no idea of the surprise coming his way and Vinny couldn't wait to see his face when he got it. Shame his birthday would be spoilt by learning his father was an untrustworthy piece of shit, Vinny thought sadly. It couldn't be helped though. Harbouring the truth from his mother had left Vinny with a guilty taste in his mouth.

Vinny sighed. He had always been under the impression that there was no love lost between his parents. They rarely slept in the same bed. His drunken father usually crashed on the sofa. However, his mum was still bound to feel aggrieved, which was why Vinny had decided to wait until after Michael's birthday lunch to tell her the sordid truth. Michael would still have a top day, whatever happened. At least his moped would soften the blow.

Hearing the doorbell sound, Vinny took the envelope out of the drawer and went downstairs. It cost him eighty quid a month to keep the Old Bill off his back, but it was worth every penny. 'There you go, George,' he said, handing the envelope to the chief inspector.

'Any chance of a brandy to warm the cockles? Bleedin' taters it is,' George said.

Vinny led him inside and poured him a drink.

'So, how's it going?' George asked, before knocking it back in one and holding out his glass for an immediate refill.

'So-so. It's like any other business, George. Some weeks are busy, some quiet. It's been dead the past couple, but I suppose it would be with Christmas creeping up on us. People have no spare pennies this time of year, do they?' Vinny said, in his most sincere voice. He wasn't going to inform George that ever since he had started having strippers on at the weekend, the club had been packed to the rafters and he had been raking it in. George Geary loved a pound note and would most certainly want an increase on his bung if he knew that.

George eyed the furniture and décor. There were four snooker tables at the back, which wasn't many considering the joint was meant to be a snooker club. The rest of the place was kitted out with glass tables, burgundy leather chairs and sofas to match. There was a stage, with spotlights above it and big speakers. And in the centre of the club, an expensive-looking chandelier hung proudly from the ceiling. The bar was shiny aluminium and there was every optic known to mankind behind it.

Holding out his glass for yet another refill, George smirked. He knew Vinny was lying. A colleague of his had watched the comings and goings at the club last weekend and had reported back that it was jam-packed.

Nothing escaped George's attention, he had been biding his time like a viper waiting to strike and knew now was as good a time as any. 'We have a big problem, Vinny. The powers above know that you've been illegally serving liquor in here and they now expect me to do something about it.'

Vinny felt the colour drain from his cheeks. If he couldn't continue serving alcohol, he had no business left. 'But I thought you said I'd be fine. What have I been fucking paying you for if you can't square it for me?' he demanded.

'Hold your horses. I've already had a word in a couple of people's shell-likes. It will cost you, but I can definitely get you a liquor licence.'

'How much?' Vinny asked.

'Fifteen hundred quid and a drink on top for me,' George said, even though he had already put five hundred on top of the grand he had been quoted.

'How much! That's fucking extortion, George. I haven't got money like that lying around. I've spent virtually every penny I've earned so far on doing the place up.'

'I tried to knock the price down for you, Vinny, but my contact wasn't having none of it, I'm afraid. Surely it's better in the long run for you to go legal? And I will drop my fee to fifty pounds a month, rather than eighty.'

'Why have I still got to pay you if I'm properly licensed?' Vinny asked.

'Because you are illegal in other areas, Vinny. I know you have strippers in here and I know that people gamble. You haven't got an entertainment or gambling licence, have you?'

Vinny leant his elbows on the bar and put his head in his hands. George had him by the short and curlies and Vinny knew it. Trouble was, there was nothing he could do about it, except cough up. 'Come back next week and I'll have the dough for ya.'

Albie Butler was sitting in the Blind Beggar, staring at his pint, in a stupefied trance. He was in shit, deep shit, and he didn't have a clue what to do about it.

'You all right, Albie?' shouted out Sid, who was perched on his regular barstool.

Albie didn't even bother answering. He was anything but bloody all right. Cursing the day he had ever set eyes on Judy Preston, he sank his drink and called over to the barmaid to pour him another. Why hadn't he used a rubber even though that lying cow had sworn she was taking that new contraceptive pill?

Taking his empty glass back to the bar, Albie returned with a full one. After Judy had informed him she was up the spout, he had spent ages begging her to get rid of it. He had even offered her a nice lump of cash which he had planned to borrow off Vinny or Roy, but the selfish bitch was intent on ruining his life.

Keeping a bit on the side secret was one thing. Keeping a fucking baby who belonged to you secret was another. Vowing to think with his brain in future rather than his pecker, Albie tried to fathom a way out of the difficult situation. Judy's brother was a handy bastard and at his age, Albie was no match for an up-and-coming wide-boy like Johnny Preston. Vinny and Roy were though. They could more than hold their own against anybody.

21

Albie sighed worriedly. Judy needed the frighteners put on her to force her to get rid of the child and if admitting his sins to his two eldest sons was the only way to make that happen, then admit his sins he would. They weren't going to be best pleased, especially Vinny, who had threatened him over his wandering eye in the past. But what choice did Albie have? None.

Finishing his pint, he stood up and nervously made his way towards the snooker club. His boys would have to help him in his hour of need, wouldn't they? He might have fucked up big time, but he was still their bloody father.

Queenie Butler took the birthday cake out of the oven and grinned at her sister. 'Well, what do you think?'

'Ah, it's beautiful, Queenie. Best cake I've seen in years,' Vivian replied, truthfully.

'Can I have some?' little Brenda asked.

'No, sweetheart. We can't cut it up until tomorrow, otherwise Michael won't see the beauty of it,' Queenie replied.

'Awww,' Brenda whined.

Queenie stared at her offspring. Brenda was eleven now and could be an obstinate little mare at times. Unlike the boys who favoured their father with their black hair and chiselled features, Brenda looked more like her side of the family. Her hair was mousy brown, the same as Queenie's and Viv's natural colour, and she was a skinny little thing even though she had the appetite of a horse.

'Please, Mum?' Brenda tried again.

Vivian laughed. 'You help me carry the cake to my house so our Michael don't see it and I'll give you a nice iced bun. Deal?'

Queenie smiled when Vivian and Brenda left the house. Family was the most important thing in the world and she loved hers with a passion. Albie was a tosspot, she knew that, but he had given her four beautiful children, for which she would always be grateful to him. She didn't love or respect him any more. What woman could love and respect a bone-idle drunk? But he never pestered her for sex these days and even if he did, she would never leave him. He was the father of her children and for that reason alone, she would always see it as her duty to suffer him.

'Oh, I do love being two doors away now, Queenie. It feels like we live together, don't it?' Vivian said, letting herself back in with her own key.

Queenie laughed. It was her Vinny who had secured Vivian the council house next door but one. It had become available a few months back when old Ada had passed away and Vinny had offered the man at the council a backhander to ensure it went to Viv. He had bragged when he had come home that the man was so petrified, he had refused to take the money, but had given Vinny the keys anyway. 'My reputation precedes me once again, Mum,' Vinny had chuckled.

'Is that my little soldier I hear coming down them stairs?' Vivian said, when she heard Lenny's familiar flat-footed walk. He had been tired earlier, so had gone for a lie-down on Queenie's bed.

'Can I watch *Mr Ed*?' Lenny asked excitedly. The programme featuring the talking horse was his current favourite. Before that, it had been *Flipper*.

'Yep, course you can,' Queenie replied. Both she and Vivian now had posh TVs. They had been Christmas presents last year from the boys.

'I love *Mr Ed* too,' Brenda said, following her cousin into the lounge.

Queenie locked eyes with her sister. 'Ain't we lucky with our little lot, eh? I know we've had hard times, but kids don't come no better than ours, you know,' Queenie said contentedly.

Vivian grinned. 'We're blessed, Queenie. Truly blessed.'

After George had left earlier, Vinny had spent the rest of the afternoon shagging his prettiest stripper, Karen. Unlike his brothers, who were both girl-mad, birds didn't bother Vinny as a rule, neither did sex.

Apart from his mother and aunt, Vinny was no big fan of women in general. He found girls his age silly and annoying, so why he had bothered ramming himself inside Karen again, who was already asking him questions such as 'Am I your girlfriend now?' He did not know.

Vinny got out of bed and quickly got dressed. He had only ever had one proper girlfriend in his life and the slag had broken his heart. Fifteen, Vinny had been when he'd first set eyes on Yvonne Summers. She was two years older than him, but the age gap hadn't mattered as he was very mature for his age. To say he had treated Yvonne like a princess was putting it mildly. Even back then, he knew how to earn a bob or two and he was forever taking her to the pictures and buying her nice presents. Had she appreciated his adoration and kindness? No. The whore had two-timed him, then run off with a lad five years his senior. Rumour had it, she'd moved to Leeds.

Vinny had been distraught at the time and didn't know how he would have got over it if it wasn't for his mother. She had held his sobbing body, wiped away his tears and made him feel worthy once again.

'So, am I your girlfriend now?' Karen repeated, desperation in her voice.

The doorbell saved Vinny from insulting her. 'Get dressed and go out the back way. I've got business to deal with,' he said, coldly.

Wondering if George had come back to try to extract even more money, Vinny took the stairs two by two. He flung open the big metal door only to see his father standing there with a sheepish expression on his face. 'What do you want?' Vinny asked, unable to hide the bitterness. He didn't want to let on to his dad he knew about Judy Preston before tomorrow. He wanted to watch him squirm when he announced his infidelity at the restaurant in front of his mother.

Unable to look his son in the eyes, Albie stared at his shoes. 'I've got a bit of a problem and I really need your help,' he mumbled.

'What do you want? Beer or Scotch?' Vinny asked, leading him into the club.

'Scotch please, son.'

Vinny poured two large Scotches on the rocks, then sat down at a nearby table. 'Fire away then.'

With his hands clasped together, Albie twiddled his thumbs. There was no sign of Roy which was a shame as Roy had a lesser temper on him than Vinny. He also had a more understanding nature.

'Where's Roy?' Albie asked.

'Gone to collect Michael's moped.'

Albie stared at his hands. There was no easy way of saying what he had to say, but he wanted to find the right words. 'I've got meself in a bit of a pickle, boy. I know I promised you I would never stray again, but I had this bird come on to me. Only young, she is, and being a weak man, I was flattered if you know what I mean?'

'Oh, I know what you mean all right. And I know who the tart is. You've been shafting Judy Preston, haven't you? So, what's happened? Has her brother Johnny found out and now wants to chop that diseased little cock of yours off? You make me sick, Dad, do you know that?'

'I'm sorry. I know what I did is wrong, but your mum don't want me in her bed no more. It was just too good an opportunity to turn down. I ain't getting no younger, boy, and I was just flattered I suppose. I do love your mum though. You know that, don't you, son?'

Unable to stop himself, Vinny sank the rest of his drink, then brought the glass down so hard against the table, it smashed into a thousand fragments. 'Do not fucking sit there telling me you love my mum when you stick your cock in anything that moves, and do not ever call me your son again. You are nothing to me. I despise you,' he snarled, standing up.

Albie looked back down at his feet. 'How long you known for?'

'A week or so. Was gonna confront you tomorrow in front of Mum at Michael's birthday bash. I'm still telling her, so don't think you're fucking getting away with this one. I warned you before after I found out about that Maureen bird that if you did it again I would grass you up.'

'You can't tell her, boy. I'll never do it again, I swear on the Bible, but please don't tell your mother.'

'You can go to hell, Dad. Unlike you, I'm a man of my word and tell her I shall. She's bound to kick your sorry arse out, so what you gonna do then? Gonna set up home with your young bit of skirt, are ya?'

Absolutely petrified that his whole world was about to fall apart, Albie stood up and banged his fists against the glass table. 'You can't tell her, Vinny. I know I don't deserve it, but you really need to side with me for once on this. I need your help, boy.'

Vinny chuckled. 'Why? 'Cause Johnny Preston is gonna give you a good fawpenny one? Good! Saves me from fucking doing it.'

'It ain't Johnny. He knows about me and Judy and he's OK about it.'

'Well, what is it then?' Vinny asked, his lip curling into another snarl.

'Judy's in the club and she's keeping it. I accidently got her pregnant.'

Vinny leapt up, grabbed his father by the neck in disgust and rammed his body against the wall. 'You fucking what?'

'It weren't my fault. She said she was taking that tablet thingamajig. She lied to me,' Albie said, panicking.

Unable to stop himself, Vinny did what he had wanted to do for years. He beat his father senseless.

CHAPTER THREE

Bored with doing the washing up and spending their lives confined to the café, young Nancy and Christopher Walker begged their parents to allow them to go out to play.

'You're to go no further than a short walk away and you are to be back here by five at the latest,' their father ordered them.

Missing her friends from Stoke Newington dreadfully, Nancy tagged along reluctantly behind her brother. All day, Christopher had been harping on about the rich men with the posh cars whom he had seen the previous day when he had taken a trip to the sweetshop, but Nancy wasn't car-mad like her brother. She wouldn't have been able to tell the difference between a Sunbeam Tiger and an Austin Healey.

'This is it,' Christopher said, plonking himself down on a doorstep opposite the snooker club.

'But there ain't no rich men here, nor is there many cars,' Nancy complained.

'Well, there was yesterday. That Jaguar Sedan is the car that I want when I'm grown-up.' Christopher pointed to the shiny black car that belonged to Vinny Butler.

Nancy took a strawberry bonbon out of the paper bag

and popped it into her mouth. 'What do you want to be when you grow up, Christopher? I think I would like to be a hairdresser and do famous people's hair like Twiggy.'

Sucking on a Kola Kube, Christopher wanted to laugh, but didn't. Twiggy would never have let his sister near her hair, but it was good Nancy had dreams, because he was determined to fulfil his. 'I'm gonna be a policeman and catch people like Jack the Ripper. He killed loads of women round 'ere, you know.'

'What's that man doing, Christopher?' Nancy asked, bemused.

Christopher had no idea who the Italian-looking man was, but when he punched a nearby wall and then glared at him and Nancy, the boy's intuition told him it wasn't safe to be there. He grabbed his sister's hand. 'Come on, let's go back to the café.'

Michael Butler entered his mother's house wearing his trademark green parka and a big grin on his face. 'Urgh. What's that smell?'

'Lavender bags. Dotted them all over the house, including that stinking bedroom of yours,' Queenie informed her son.

Michael screwed up his nose and plonked himself on the Dralon sofa. His mother was the most house-proud woman that he knew. Years ago, their lounge had looked like anybody else's. But since Vinny had been earning good money, it had had a complete transformation. The new floral wallpaper now matched the mustard three-piece suite, and the rest of the room featured dark teak furniture, a posh rug and floor lamps, a modern round coffee table and, his mother's pride and joy, a glass ornament cabinet which was now full to the brim with expensive pieces of china that Vinny was forever bringing home.

'So, how was Carnaby Street?' Vivian asked excitedly.

She had never been there herself, but knew it was all the rage at the moment for the youngsters.

'Yeah, hip. Met a nice bird, and Kev got himself a well ace pair of two-tone shoes. If my brothers give me money for my birthday, I wanna go back up there and get a pair too,' Michael replied.

Knowing full well that Vinny and Roy had clubbed together to buy Michael his much-wanted moped, Queenie winked at her sister. 'Don't know what they are giving you, son, you'll just have to see what tomorrow brings.'

'I wish I was going to be sixteen tomorrow. I hate being eleven. It's so boring,' Brenda piped up.

'I wish I could be eleven all over again, sweetheart, and know what I know now. I certainly wouldn't make the same bleedin' mistakes again,' Vivian told her niece.

'By saying mistakes, she means my dad,' Lenny said casually.

Michael looked at his mum and aunt. Knowing that a truer statement had never been spoken, all three burst out laughing.

Roy was shocked to see Vinny sitting on the concrete steps of the club looking extremely dishevelled. 'Whatever's happened?' he asked, staring at his brother's ripped blood-splattered shirt.

Vinny took a long drag from his cigarette and flicked the butt onto the kerb. 'I've given Dad a good hiding,' he admitted bluntly.

'What! You fucking promised me that you weren't gonna touch him, Vin. I thought we'd agreed that we was gonna confront him together at the restaurant tomorrow?'

'That's before I knew he'd got his young bit of skirt up the spout,' Vinny spat.

Gobsmacked, Roy sat on the step next to his brother.

'For fuck's sake. Mum's gonna go off her rocker when she finds that out. Where is Dad now?'

'Lying on the floor in the club. Mum can't find out that it was me who done him over. We tell her nothing now, do you hear me?'

Roy nodded. 'What about the bird he's knocked up? I take it she is getting rid of it?'

Vinny stood up. 'Me and you will have to pay her a little visit to help her make her mind up.'

Roy followed Vinny inside the club and bolted the door. 'What about her brother, Johnny? He's meant to be a bit handy, ain't he?'

'There's two of us and one of him, but that's another reason why everything that's happened just stays between me and you now. You say nothing to no-one, not even Michael, because if Johnny Preston does start playing up, we might have to get rid of him.'

'I'm in agony. I think I'm dying. I can't breathe properly,' Albie Butler cried out.

Roy gasped when he saw the state of his father. His face was covered in blood where his nose had caved in and Roy could tell immediately that his right leg was broken below the knee as the bone was poking through his skin. 'Fucking hell, Vin. You shouldn't have done that much damage to him.'

'Help me, Roy. Please help me,' Albie begged.

Ordering his brother to phone an ambulance, Vinny crouched down next to his father. 'You got jumped by four lads outside the club who were after this, OK?' Vinny said, taking the wallet out of his father's pocket and putting it in his own.

In terrible pain, Albie started to cry. 'I know I deserved a clump, but I can't believe you broke my leg. How any lad could do that to his own flesh and blood is beyond me.'

'You just wanna be grateful that I never broke your fucking neck. If the Old Bill question you, you say I heard a commotion, came outside, the boys had already legged it, and I dragged you in here, OK? Then in return, I'll make sure Mum don't find out your dirty little secret.'

'You're not a nice person, Vinny. You are one callous bastard,' Albie spat.

'And you are a dirty old pervert. Now, do we have a deal or not?'

Knowing that he had no option other than to agree with his violent offspring, Albie nodded his battered head.

Queenie was dishing up the sausages and bubble and squeak when Vinny and Roy let themselves into the house. 'What's the matter?' she asked, putting her spatula on the worktop. Both of her sons looked ashen-faced and serious.

'Look, don't panic 'cause he is gonna be OK, but Dad got jumped outside the club by a gang of lads. They took off with his wallet,' Vinny explained.

'Well, I bet there weren't much in that,' Vivian mumbled, unfeelingly. She was no fan of Albie Butler and felt her sister could have done much better.

'Is he OK? Where is he now?' Queenie asked, her face etched with concern.

'At the hospital. The ambulance man said they thought both his legs might be broken,' Roy replied, feeling awkward.

'Gordon Bennett! What is the world coming to if men like your dad are getting mugged? You better take me to him now,' Queenie ordered.

'Eat your dinner first, Mum, then Roy will take you up there,' Vinny replied.

'Ain't you coming as well?' Queenie asked, surprised.

Not wanting to be anywhere near his arsehole of a father,

Vinny shook his head. 'Roy'll look after you, Mum. Someone has to be at the club, don't they?'

Queenie eyed her eldest child with suspicion, but said nothing. Both Vinny and Roy had virtually blanked Albie during dinner the other day and Queenie wasn't stupid. She could tell Vinny had fallen out with his father. Now all she had to do was find out why.

Humming along to Petula Clark's 'Downtown', Mary smiled as the woman she and Donald had nicknamed Mad Freda approached the counter. 'Hello. What can I get you?' This was the first time Freda had visited the café since the day she had knocked at the door to warn them about the Butler family.

'Mug of tea and a piece of that fruit cake, please. So, how's it going?' Freda enquired.

'Ever so well, thanks. Donald and I have been run off our feet again today.'

'Met the Butlers yet?' Freda asked.

'Two ladies who came in the other day introduced themselves by that name, but they were lovely, ever so polite,' Mary replied, desperate to avoid getting involved with tittle-tattle.

'Huh. Brady and Hindley was probably lovely and polite people too,' Freda said sarcastically, referring to the couple who had recently been arrested for murdering children on the moors.

Thankful when Freda plonked herself at a table over by the door, Mary called her son over to the counter. Unlike his sister, who had been helping Donald in the kitchen all day, Christopher had done nothing but sit on his backside and read his *Roy of the Rovers* comics.

'Two burgers and chips,' Donald shouted out.

'Get the plates off your dad and take them over to that table next to the jukebox, Christopher,' Mary ordered her son.

Christopher stood transfixed to the spot with his mouth wide open. The rich-looking man with the posh Jaguar car who he had seen punching the wall earlier had just walked into the café.

Albie Butler felt terribly sorry for himself as he lay flat on the hospital bed with both legs up in traction.

'Jesus, Albie. Whatever happened, eh?' Queenie asked, marching into the ward with Vivian behind her.

'Got jumped by a gang of lads for me wallet,' Albie mumbled.

'Why ever did they jump you? Everyone who knows you is aware you ain't got a pot to piss in,' Vivian replied, her voice as cold as ice.

Albie glared at his wife's sister and, instead of calling her a fucking old trout like he wanted to, managed to bite his tongue.

'I bought you some pyjamas up, and made you a ham sandwich,' Queenie said, plonking a carrier bag on the bed next to her husband.

'I can't get pyjama bottoms over the plaster and I can't eat nothing. I'm in too much pain. A small bottle of brandy wouldn't have gone amiss though,' Albie muttered miserably.

'Ungrateful old bastard,' Vivian mumbled under her breath.

'I've just spoken to the doctor. They reckon you'll be in here for a while, you know,' Queenie informed her old man.

'Thanks very much. Cheer me up, why don't ya?'

'So, what exactly happened? Have you spoken to the Old Bill yet?' Queenie asked.

'Yeah. Not much I could tell 'em. It all happened so quickly, I didn't get a clear view of any of the lads. Where's Vinny and Roy?'

'Roy and Michael are waiting in the corridor. The nurse

said we could only come in two at a time, so I'll send them in next. You had a fall-out with our Vinny and Roy?'

'No. What makes you ask that?' Albie asked defensively.

'Because I've sensed a bad atmosphere the past few days. What's going on, Albie? I ain't some silly old fool, you know, and I will find out, so you might as well tell me now. What you done to upset them?'

Albie looked at his wife with pure hatred in his eyes. Here he was, with two broken legs and three broken ribs, confined to a stinking hospital bed for Christ knows how long, and instead of concern, all Queenie was worried about was her precious sons. Was it any wonder he strayed at the drop of a hat?' I ain't done anything to upset the boys, OK? Now, please go and get me a bottle of brandy to help me with the pain. Killing me, my ribs are. I would give you the money, but the bastards who attacked me nicked me wallet.'

'The doctor said you were on strong painkillers. You ain't meant to drink with them, Albie. You might keel over and die in the night,' Queenie advised him.

Hoping that her sister's warning just might come true, Vivian put her hand inside her handbag. 'Poor sod's been right through the mill. I'll treat him to a bottle.'

Knowing full well why Vivian had made such a kind gesture, Queenie had a fake coughing fit, then dashed out of the ward before Albie could realize she was laughing.

Little Christopher Walker was mesmerized by the dark-haired man in the charcoal suit.

'Stop gawping at people. Go and collect any empty plates and cups,' Mary hissed in her son's ear.

Another person who had her beady eyes on Vinny was Freda Smart and when Christopher approached her, she couldn't help but speak her mind. 'Should be strung up by the balls, the lot of 'em. Bloody murderers,' she said in a loud voice.

Vinny smirked. Freda had been extremely friendly with the café's previous owners and was the only person in the East End who would have the nerve to accuse him of killing Old Jack and Ethel's son. She was spot-on actually. Fifteen-year-old Peter had had a habit of exposing himself to young girls and had one day made the fatal mistake of touching up a neighbour's eleven-year-old daughter and forcing her to touch him in an undesirable place. Absolutely fuming, Vinny had decided to rid Whitechapel of such an unsavoury character and a few weeks later Peter was found at the bottom of the Thames.

Vinny turned around in his seat. He loved winding the old battleaxe up. The café wasn't packed, but Vinny could see the worried expressions on the other diners' faces. 'Spouting cock and bull again, are you, Freda? Can't be long now until they cart you off to that funny farm,' he said.

'Sod all wrong with my marbles. I know exactly what yous Butlers are and unlike everyone else round 'ere, I ain't bleedin' frightened to tell you either. You can do me in next for all I care,' Freda yelled, stomping out of the café.

Vinny chuckled and raised his eyebrows to fellow customers. It didn't bother him that Freda accused him of being a murderer in public. In fact, she was doing him a favour as it just made people fear him more.

With no-one waiting to be served, Mary darted out into the kitchen to fill Donald in on what had just happened.

Aware that the young boy's eyes were on him once again, Vinny smiled at Christopher. He had already recognized him as the one who had been sitting opposite the snooker club earlier. 'Can you show me how to use your jukebox?'

Christopher ran over to the Wurlitzer. Vinny put on

Roger Miller's 'King of the Road', which happened to remind him of himself, then handed the child half a crown.

Absolutely ecstatic at the unexpected gift, Christopher ran out to the kitchen to show his parents.

'Who gave you that?' Donald asked, his face reddening with anger, knowing only too well who it was likely to be.

'The man in the suit gave it to me because I taught him how to use the jukebox,' Christopher explained.

'Can I have some money too, Daddy?' Nancy asked, tugging her father's sleeve.

Donald was fuming. He wanted no involvement with this Butler family and he had always forbidden his children to accept money or gifts from strangers. 'What have I told you about taking money off people, eh?' he said, dragging Christopher out of the kitchen by his arm.

'Stop it, Daddy. You're hurting me,' Christopher said, bursting into tears.

'Donald, stop overreacting for goodness' sake,' Mary urged him. She didn't want to upset or make a scene in front of their customers.

Vinny had just dotted his cigarette out and was about to leave when Donald marched up to him with Christopher in tow. 'Is this the man?' he asked his son.

The little boy was sobbing. He not only felt embarrassed, he wanted to keep his half a crown. Nodding his head, Christopher stared at his feet in shame.

'Excuse me, sir. It was very kind of you to give my son this money, but I'm afraid I have brought my children up not to accept gifts off people they do not know, so I insist you take it back.'

Vinny stared Donald in the eyes and immediately disliked him. He could tell he was one of life's do-gooders. 'It wasn't a gift. Your son earned it by showing me how to use the jukebox,' Vinny replied casually.

'Well, Christopher won't be accepting it all the same,' Donald said, putting the coin on the table and dragging his son away.

About to tell Donald that he should get off his fucking moral high horse, Vinny saw Christopher's distraught little face glance around and decided not to bother. The old man was obviously a twat, so what was the point of upsetting the kid even more? Slipping the half a crown into his pocket, Vinny nodded politely at Mary, and quietly left the café.

CHAPTER FOUR

Determined that their father being hospitalized wouldn't spoil their younger brother's sixteenth birthday, Vinny and Roy got up with the larks the following morning and walked around to their mother's house, pushing the moped between them.

Both Vinny and Roy had stayed at the club again last night and Roy had just suggested to his brother that they have the upstairs decorated properly so that they could live there permanently.

'I dunno. We've got to pay that conning bastard Geary fifteen hundred quid next week, which will leave the coffers a bit lean, Roy. Not only that, I like to keep a daily eye on Mum and Auntie Viv and make sure Champ is OK. Leave the idea with me and I'll have to think about it.'

Due to the freezing December temperature and the lack of heating in his bedroom, Michael decided to skip having a wash until after he'd had a cup of tea to warm himself up.

Queenie sang 'Happy Birthday', as her son galloped down the stairs.

'Thanks, Mum. Is there any tea in the pot? Bleedin' taters, I am.'

'It's just started snowing, boy. Told you yesterday the

39

sky looked full of snow, didn't I? Bet you're glad you took this week off work, eh?'

Michael nodded. He had left school earlier in the year and was working as a trainee mechanic in a local garage. He loved the job as he loved tinkering with cars and bikes, but the money was crap, and the garage was freezing cold this time of year.

'I'm gonna pop up the hospital and take your father his toothbrush and razor before we go out for lunch. Do you wanna come with me so he can wish you happy birthday?' Queenie asked.

'Yeah, I'll come,' Michael replied without hesitation. Unlike his brothers, he was actually very fond of his father. He often went for a pint with him on Sunday lunchtimes and he was upset that his dad had been set upon by those bloody yobs.

'Many happy returns, bruv,' Roy said, giving Michael a manly hug.

'Is it present time yet?' Queenie asked excitedly.

'Sure is,' Vinny grinned.

Ordering Roy to go and get Vivian so she wouldn't miss out on the fun, Queenie handed Michael a parcel. 'That's from me and your dad. Your brothers picked it, so if you don't like it, blame them,' she chuckled.

Michael was thrilled when he unwrapped the paper and saw the blue Fred Perry polo shirt. 'That's well nice, Mum. I'll wear it today,' he said. Fred Perry shirts were really in for Mods at the moment. His best mate Kev had two of them.

'Happy birthday, Michael,' Lenny said, running into the house with a handmade card in his hand.

Michael hugged his cousin to his chest. 'Cheers, Champ.'

'Right, you ready for mine and Roy's present?' Vinny asked.

'Yep.'

'Follow me then,' Vinny ordered.

Queenie and Vivian followed the boys out the front and clapped their hands with glee when Michael caught his first glimpse of the trendy moped.

'Oh my God! It's a Lambretta! Is it really all mine?' he asked, his eyes shining with excitement.

Vinny threw him the key. 'Yep, it's all yours. Me and Roy have got another surprise for you as well, but you won't find out what that is until we get to the restaurant.'

'Bloody hell! This is the best birthday ever,' Michael exclaimed, throwing his leg over the saddle. He already knew how to ride a moped. Kev had got one over a month ago and had let his friend ride it many a time.

'Be careful because that bleedin' snow's settling,' Vivian yelled, as Michael fired the engine up.

'So, what other surprise have you got for him?' Queenie asked Vinny and Roy.

'A mohair suit. We want him to come and work with us at the club. He's old enough now,' Vinny replied casually.

'But he's already got a job and you know how he has his heart set on being a fully qualified mechanic,' Queenie reminded her sons.

'Yeah, and he's on shit money and spends half his life covered in grease and making the tea for that prick he works for. That ain't a job, it's a piss-take, Mum. From now on, he works with me and Roy.'

Determined to see Vinny again in the hope that he might still give him the half a crown, Christopher Walker bribed his sister with a bag of sweets so she would sit in the doorway opposite the snooker club with him.

'Dad is gonna go mad if you take money off that man,' Nancy said, taking her aniseed twist out of her mouth so she could speak properly.

41

Christopher glared at his sister. He hadn't wanted to bring her to the club, but his parents were adamant that he could only go out to play if he took Nancy with him. 'Dad won't find out, will he? Unless you're gonna tell him, of course.' 'I'll tell you what. If Vinny gives me the money, I'll share it with you. But, you must promise me you won't say a word about us coming here to Mum and Dad,' Christopher said.

Unlike some of their friends back in Stoke Newington, neither Nancy nor Christopher had ever received much pocket money. They were given the odd penny or two sporadically to get some sweets or a comic and both were desperate to feel the jingle-jangle of coins in their pockets.

Nancy grinned. 'OK, I promise.'

Judy Preston lived in a one-bedroomed council flat in Forest Gate. Her mum usually popped in most mornings to help her look after her son Mark, and when the door-bell rang, Judy just assumed that her mum had forgotten her key.

At three years old, Mark was into everything and after Judy flung open the front door, she immediately ran into the kitchen to scold her son for chasing and terrorizing the cat. 'He's been a little bastard this morning, Mum,' she shouted out, as she smacked Mark on his bottom.

Hearing no reply, Judy turned around just as the door slammed. Seeing the two men in suits and Crombie coats, she let out a piercing scream.

Vinny grabbed Judy and put his hand over her mouth. 'Take the little 'un into the lounge while I have a chat with Mummy dearest,' he ordered his brother.

'Come on, little fella,' Roy said, picking up young Mark.

'Don't you dare hurt my baby. If you lay one finger on

him, my brother will kill you,' Judy spat, when Vinny moved his hand slightly to enable her to speak.

'It ain't your son I've got a problem with, it's you, ya slag. Now, I'm gonna take my hand away from your mouth properly, so we can have a nice little chat. Open it and scream and I shall put my fist straight down the back of your throat, understand?' Vinny asked, his eyes gleaming dangerously.

Judy nodded. She had now guessed her intruders were Albie's sons and wasn't so frightened any more. 'What do you want? Has your father sent you around to terrorize me?'

Vinny stared at his prey. She wasn't bad-looking in a common, tarty kind of way and he wondered what the hell she had ever seen in his father. 'For your information, my old man doesn't know I'm here. He is currently residing in the London Hospital with three broken ribs and two broken legs. He had a very unfortunate accident, you see.'

Wondering if Vinny was winding her up, Judy shrugged. 'Nothing to do with me, I'm not seeing him any more.'

'Sensible girl. But what about the baby? You'll need money to get rid of it.'

'I'm not aborting my baby. My Marky would love a little brother or sister to play with and I'd then qualify for a council house with a nice garden. Your dad can go to hell for all I care, but I'm keeping his child.'

Grabbing Judy by her throat, Vinny shoved her roughly against the wall. 'You ain't keeping it, you silly whore. I'll give you a fortnight to get rid and if you don't, I shall fucking get rid of it for you. Now, do we understand one another?'

Suddenly feeling frightened again, Judy nodded lamely. Vinny had mad eyes and she found him quite scary.

Vinny took his hand away from Judy's throat, pulled fifty pounds out of his pocket and handed it to her. 'That should cover your heartbreak, darling,' he said.

Judy took the money and was relieved when Vinny called his brother.

Roy came out of the lounge with a giggling Mark in his arms and handed Judy her son. 'Cute kid,' he said, as he followed Vinny towards the front door.

'I'll be back to see you in a fortnight,' Vinny shouted, glancing back at her.

Judy said nothing. She would keep the fifty pounds and let her brother deal with Vinny and Roy. No-one was going to make her get rid of her baby, that was for sure.

When the snow started to come down more heavily, Nancy begged her brother to come home with her.

'I will in a bit, but let's just wait another half an hour, eh? Vinny always gets here by midday,' Christopher explained.

About to demand that they go home that very second, Nancy spotted a posh car driving slowly towards them. 'Is this him?' she asked hopefully.

Recognizing the Jag and and the number plate, Christopher stood up and urged Nancy to do the same. 'As soon as he pulls up, I'm going to walk over the road and apologize for Dad's behaviour. You stay here.'

'No, I'm coming with you,' Nancy insisted. There was no way she was going to chance her brother keeping the money for himself.

Vinny and Roy were still chatting about their father's bit of fluff when they pulled up outside the club. Both agreed that they should carry at least a knife on them for the foreseeable future, just in case there was any comeback from Judy's brother.

'Do you think we should pay Johnny a little visit? Explain the situation, like,' Roy asked.

Vinny shook his head. Even though Judy lived in Forest Gate, Johnny Preston was a South London boy. He had recently started to hang around the Richardsons like an unwanted dog and liked to tell anyone who would care to listen that he was now part of their firm. Vinny knew that this wasn't the case. Eddie Richardson was in partnership with Mad Frankie Fraser. They were in the gambling business, owned most of the fruit machines and one-armed bandits in pubs and clubs all over London, and Vinny had heard through the grapevine that Mad Frankie Fraser thought that Johnny Preston was nothing more than a two-bob cock. 'Nah, Roy. South London ain't our territory, so we'll bide our time and let silly Johnny come to us,' Vinny said, sensibly.

'You might as well wait 'ere while I run in,' Roy said, changing the subject. They had only stopped at the club to pick up the mohair suit they'd had specially made for Michael in Savile Row.

Vinny picked up his newspaper and seconds later was aware of somebody hovering nearby. Recognizing Christopher, he opened his window. 'You all right, boy?' he asked.

'Yes, thank you. This is my sister, Nancy, and we came to apologize for my dad's behaviour, sir,' Christopher said, solemnly.

Vinny grinned, stepped out of the car and ruffled Christopher's hair. He'd been a bright kid once himself and he could sense that Christopher was hoping to get his hands on the money he had offered him the previous day. 'No more calling me sir, it's Vinny to me mates,' Vinny replied, taking a ten-shilling note out of his wallet and handing it to the boy.

Nancy and Christopher both stared at the note with their mouths wide open.

'Take it, then. It's to share equally between you,' Vinny urged.

Christopher snatched the note and nudged his sister.

'Thank you, Vinny,' Nancy said, feeling suddenly shy.

'Yeah, thank you very much, Vinny,' Christopher added.

Watching the two children run away excitedly, Vinny grinned. That was his good deed done for the day.

Michael's best friend Kevin had a Jamaican dad and an English mum and as the two young men walked into the Rib Room in Belgravia, both were aware of the nudges and whispers from snooty onlookers.

'My brothers will be here in a minute. We're a bit early,' Michael said, awkwardly. He was well aware that the two posh old trouts on the table behind were looking down on Kevin because of his colour.

'Is they talking about me because I a Negro?' Kevin asked, imitating a heavy Jamaican accent.

Michael burst out laughing. Kevin had been brought up in Mile End and was as cockney as he was. His dad had gone back to Jamaica when Kevin was just a baby and Michael always joked that the only other black man Kevin had ever met was the coal man when he was covered in soot. 'Can you imagine the crumpet we'll pull when we go out for a spin? We can go up Carnaby Street whenever we want,' Michael suggested.

Kevin grinned. 'I reckon we are gonna have the time of our lives now we can get out and about properly.'

Michael raised his glass and clinked it against Kevin's. He adored his best pal, his family, his job, and now he finally had his beloved Lambretta, life was all but perfect.

'Bleedin' posh round 'ere, ain't it? Talk about how the other half live,' Vivian said to Queenie. She had never been to

46

this part of London before and it was certainly more wealthy-looking than Whitechapel. Where they lived, the air was polluted by the rotting fruit in the market, and women were on their hands and knees scrubbing their doorsteps daily. Vivian couldn't imagine the women of Belgravia even knowing what a scrubbing brush was.

Vinny had chosen the restaurant as a treat not only for his brother, but also with his mum and aunt in mind. The Rib Room had the reputation of selling the best beef in London and Vinny knew how partial his mother and aunt were to a decent piece of steak. 'We're nearly there now. Harrods ain't far from here, you know,' Roy said, pointing in the direction of the famous store.

'I wanna do a wee-wee,' Lenny said, holding the crotch of his trousers.

'I think I'm gonna puke,' Brenda complained, clutching her stomach.

Knowing how travel-sick his little sister had been once before in his car, Vinny pulled over immediately. 'You know where the restaurant is from here, don't you, Roy? Walk down there with Mum, Auntie Viv and the kids while I find somewhere to park.'

'How's she getting on with that girl at school now?' Vivian whispered, as Brenda leapt out of the car and began to retch onto a nearby kerb.

Brenda had started secondary school only a few months ago. In her old school she'd had lots of friends, but in her new one, she had made very few and the only good friend she did have, she'd had a fight with earlier in the week. 'She was glad I let her have today off to come out with us, but she'll be OK. You know what kids are like. They hate one another one minute and are best mates again the next. What about Lenny? You told him he's going back to school after Christmas yet?' Queenie asked.

Vivian shook her head. Lenny had always attended mainstream schools, but the teachers had recently struggled to cope with him. They said he needed to go to a school that would be more equipped to cope with his needs. Vivian had been furious at the time and had given the headmaster what for. She wasn't stupid, she knew her son was different, but she hated hearing other people say it. The local council had come to her rescue when Vinny had gone up there and had a strong word with them. Lenny would very soon be picked up every morning to be taken to a school in Aldgate that had much smaller numbers in the classrooms, more teachers, and most importantly catered for children with learning disabilities. Now Vivian had got her head around the fact her son would be attending a special school, she was quite pleased. Lenny needed more one-to-one tutoring and she wanted him to be able to read and write properly. She hadn't told him about his new school yet though. She knew what Lenny was like. He would worry and ask her thousands of questions, so she'd decided to tell him only a day or two before he started there.

'Here we are,' Roy said, nodding towards an opulent-looking building.

Queenie and Vivian glanced at one another approvingly. They were both thinking exactly the same thing. Vinny and Roy were certainly going up in the world and long may that continue.

The lunch was a roaring success, but by the time the dessert arrived, Vinny had started to become pissed off. For the past ten minutes all Roy, Michael and Kevin had discussed were girls they'd copped off with or fancied and not only did Vinny think that this was an inappropriate conversation to be having in front of his mum, aunt, Brenda and Lenny, he was also angry as he would rather be talking business.

In Vinny's eyes, earning big bucks was and would always be far more important than some dopey slag of a bird. Yvonne Summers had taught him that lesson.

Watching his mum and aunt egg Michael on to tell them more about the girl he had recently dated with the massive boobies, Vinny had a sudden urge to smash his glass against the table.

'Whatever's the matter?' Queenie asked, as young Brenda and Lenny both nigh-on jumped out of their skins.

Roy knew exactly what the matter was, but said nothing. Whenever he met a girl he liked, he always played it down to his brother because he knew he would get the third degree otherwise. Not once had Vinny ever liked a girl he had courted and Roy dreaded the day he met the special one whom he wanted to spend the rest of his life with, as he knew that it would cause murder. All Vinny was interested in was money, notoriety and violence. Anything with tits and a fanny did not come into that category and Roy could never see Vinny getting married himself. He just wasn't the type.

'You haven't answered me. I asked you what the matter was?' Queenie repeated.

Vinny did his best to disguise his temper. Michael's birthday had cost him a bloody fortune and had he known beforehand that George Geary would swindle him out of fifteen hundred quid for a licence to serve poxy alcohol, he might not have gone so overboard. 'I haven't brought this family to a top-class restaurant so we could spend the day talking about women's body parts. If I wanted porn, I would have gone to Soho. Brenda and Champ don't want to listen to such garbage, do they? Young ears an' all that.'

'We were only having a laugh, Vinny. Nobody said anything bad,' Vivian said sternly. She was shocked by her nephew's uncalled-for outburst, to say the least.

'It's my fault. I started the conversation, so I'll take the blame,' Michael admitted sheepishly.

Looking at his brother's sorrowful expression was enough to snap Vinny out of his temper tantrum. 'No, it's not your fault, it's mine. I overreacted because I'm just dead excited about your other surprise. That is why I wanted to change the direction of the conversation and I'm sorry for snapping at everybody.'

''Ere you go, bruv,' Roy said, handing Michael a large brown bag.

Thinking how lucky his pal was to get so many wonderful presents, Kevin looked over Michael's shoulder as he opened it. 'That's well ace! It's real mohair,' he exclaimed.

Michael couldn't believe his luck. The Lambretta had been his best present ever and on top of that he had now been given an amazing suit.

'That's to wear for work,' Vinny said, grinning like a Cheshire cat.

'Christ, I won't be getting oil and petrol over this. I'll stick with me overalls for work, thanks,' Michael chuckled.

Queenie felt her stomach churn. Vinny had a strange way of dealing with matters at times. Surely offering Michael the job and waiting for his response would have been more appropriate than telling him he had a new job?

'You ain't working at that shitty garage no more, Michael. Me and Roy popped down there this morning to inform your boss that you won't be coming back. He was fine about it. He understood that you needed to move onto bigger and better things,' Vinny explained.

Lenny and Brenda were happily chatting amongst themselves and had no idea of the importance of the adults' conversation. Queenie, Vivian and Roy did though. The glances exchanged between the three of them said it all. Kevin had always been wary of Michael's older brothers, especially Vinny, so not wanting to get involved in a family dispute, he just stared at his hands.

Michael stared at his brother in total disbelief. There was a programme on TV called *Candid Camera* that Bob Monkhouse presented. It set up situations such as the one that he currently found himself in, where a camera was hidden in the premises. Then, all of a sudden a man would pop out of nowhere and reveal that it was all a big joke. 'Is this some kind of a game? You are winding me up, aren't you?' Michael asked, in a voice that didn't sound very much like his own.

'Course I ain't winding you up. You're sixteen now, Michael. You're a man, not a boy, and you can't spend the rest of your life working as a glorified teaboy. That's why me and Roy decided that the time was right for you to come and work with us at the club. We need an extra pair of hands and you'll be on loads more money than you're on now. In time, all three of us will become equal partners.'

'But I don't want to work at the club, Vinny. I want to be a mechanic. It's always been my dream to be a mechanic, ain't it, Mum?'

Unable to look her youngest son in the eye, Queenie nodded, then turned her attention to Lenny and Brenda. This was nothing to do with her, it was boy's talk and she didn't want to get involved in taking sides. She loved all her sons, so how could she?

'Once you start at the club and you've been there a week or two, you'll love it, Michael. No more freezing your nuts off while lying on a concrete floor,' Roy joked. He could tell by the look in Vinny's eyes that he was getting annoyed by Michael's lack of gratitude and he didn't want the atmosphere to turn sour.

'Look, Roy, Vinny, I really appreciate what you're offering me and all the lovely presents you've bought me, but I don't want to work with you. I love my job in the garage and one day my dream is to own a garage of my own.'

Vinny laughed sarcastically. 'And my dream was to be the next Jimmy Greaves and bang in goals for Spurs, but it never happened, did it? I'm sorry and all that but me and Roy really need you to come and work with us now. We can't employ strangers, we don't trust 'em enough, and as our brother, you owe it to us to link up with the family firm. We're Butlers, and like it or not, us Butlers stick together. It's not up for negotiation; it's your duty, Michael. You start first thing Monday morning.'

CHAPTER FIVE

Nancy Walker lowered her eyes when her teacher introduced her to the rest of the classroom. Everybody was gawping at her, so much so, she felt like one of those strange-looking people who appeared in freak shows.

When Nancy was allocated a desk next to another girl with mousy brown hair, she was relieved when the girl smiled at her.

'It's horrible starting a new school, isn't it? But don't be nervous. You can hang out with me in the playground,' the girl said kindly.

Thrilled that she had already made a new friend, Nancy grinned. 'What's your name?' she whispered.

'Brenda. Brenda Butler.'

Michael listened miserably while Vinny and Roy explained the workings of the club to him. He already missed the smell of oil and petrol and the excitement he felt tinkering about with different makes and models of cars and bikes.

'So the bulk of our profit comes solely from the booze. We buy that for peanuts off a guy called Ted, and in return, Ted gets treated like royalty every time he sets foot in here, which is most weekends,' Vinny explained.

'So, what will I actually be doing then?' Michael asked, his voice devoid of any enthusiasm. He still thought his brothers were bang out of order.

'You'll just be doing the same as me and Vin. All we do of an evening is chat politely to the customers, keep an eye out for trouble, and generally make sure the place is ticking over nicely. My mates Pete and Paul work on the door making sure that only members come in. Don't look so glum, Michael, you'll love it when you get in the swing of it. It's the good life, bruv,' Roy said.

Sick of his brother's lack of enthusiasm and sullen expression, Vinny stood up and grabbed Michael by the lapels of his new mohair suit.

'What you doing, Vin? Leave him be,' Roy ordered, when Vinny pushed Michael roughly towards the wall.

Vinny ignored Roy's advice and gave Michael some home truths. 'You are one ungrateful little cunt, has anybody ever told you that? It is about time you started acting your age and pulling your weight for this family like me and Roy have had to for years. Who do you think supports Mum, Brenda, Auntie Viv and Champ, eh? It ain't our useless fucking father, that's for sure. You owe it to us to chip in and that is what you shall do, so the quicker you put a smile on that miserable fucking face of yours and show a bit of spirit and gratitude, the better.'

When Vinny let go of him, a shocked Michael sat on a nearby sofa and put his head in his hands. Nobody argued with Vinny, including him, so there was no way out of the situation. He knew he was going to hate his new job, but he would just have to grin and bear it. What other choice did he have? 'I'm sorry, Vinny. I'll work hard for you, I promise,' he said, meekly.

Feeling a bit guilty for obviously frightening his younger sibling, Vinny walked over and ruffled his hair like he used

54

to when he was a child. 'We don't need you back here until tonight, so why don't you shoot home, take your suit off and go out on your moped, eh? You've got your test next week, so you need to get some practice.'

Grinning falsely, Michael thanked his brother and left the club.

Mary Walker wasn't having the best of days. She had got two customers' orders wrong, dropped a plate of food and then scalded her hand with boiling-hot water.

'Why don't you have a sit down and I'll bring you over a nice mug of tea?' Shirley offered.

Mary smiled.When Shirley had asked for a job on Friday, the café had been that busy that Donald had asked her to start immediately. Shirley only lived a few minutes' walk from the café, and therefore knew most of the punters really well. 'OK then. I could do with resting my feet for ten minutes. I shall be a bundle of nerves until they get home, you know,' Mary said, referring to her children's first day at a new school. Christopher hadn't been too bad this morning, but she had overheard Nancy crying in the bathroom, which had worried her terribly. The junior school that Christopher was attending was only five minutes from Nancy's new school and the children had been adamant that they wanted to walk to and from school together. Mary had wanted to take them, but both children said it would make them a target for bullies if they turned up with their mother in tow.

Mary plonked herself down at a nearby table and was just about to start reading the newspaper when Queenie and Vivian Butler walked in with little Lenny.

'Hello, sweetheart. How long you been working here?' Queenie asked Shirley.

Pretending to read the paper, Mary carried on

ear-wigging. It soon became obvious to her that Shirley knew Queenie and Vivian very well. Furious when somebody gave little Lenny money to put in the jukebox because it left her unable to hear the conversation properly, Mary scuttled out the kitchen to tell Donald the latest.

When Judy Preston got a bee in her bonnet, she found it very hard to shift it and the more she thought about Vinny and Roy Butler turning up at her house and barging their way in, the more irate she became. Her brother Johnny had been livid when she had told him and he was going to sort out Vinny and Roy for her. That wasn't enough for Judy though, which is why she had decided to pay Albie a visit in hospital and give him a piece of her mind as well.

'Come on, Mark. Get in your pushchair,' Judy urged her son.

'We going Nanna's house?' Mark asked excitedly.

'No, we are going to see the cowardly tosser who has impregnated me.'

After having lunch in the café, Queenie and Vivian went to visit their mum in nearby Bow Cemetery, then parted company on the way back because Queenie felt it was her duty to visit Albie.

'I would say give the old bastard my regards, but you know I don't mean it,' Vivian said, putting her headscarf on to stop the drizzle getting to her hair.

After telling her sister that if she hadn't have suffered the misfortune of marrying Albie, she wouldn't be visiting the old bastard herself, Queenie waved goodbye, then made her way into the London Hospital. As she reached her husband's ward, she heard his name mentioned and her ears pricked up. Pretending to go through her shopping bag as though she was searching for something, Queenie surreptitiously looked out of the corner of her eye. There was a young blonde girl with a child in a pushchair, asking the nurse for directions to Albie's bed. Wondering who on earth the tart could be, Queenie cautiously followed her into the ward.

As usual, being the miserable old bastard that he was, Albie had the curtains drawn around his bed. Queenie crept up to the neighbouring bed and put her forefinger to her lips to warn the senile old Mr Perry not to say anything. Surely her Albie hadn't found himself a young bit of fluff? Queenie hadn't fancied the dirty, disgusting old drunk for years, so how could anybody else?

Albie had been fast asleep until he felt a violent prodding on his right arm. Expecting it to be Queenie, Albie nearly had a cardiac arrest when he locked eyes with Judy Preston. 'You can't come here! What do you want? My Queenie'll be here soon. You're gonna have to leave,' he said, his face twitching with anxiety.

'Well, you should have thought of that before you got me pregnant, then sent your sons round my house to threaten me in front of Marky,' Judy spat.

Unable to stop her legs from buckling, Queenie took a tumble and fell on top of old Mr Perry.

'Get your hands off me chopper! Nurse, nurse,' the stick-thin fragile ninety-four-year-old wailed, as he put his right hand on his private parts to protect them.

Pulling herself together, Queenie took a couple of deep breaths, picked up her umbrella and flew through Albie's curtain like a bat out of hell. 'You dirty fucking old bastard,' she screamed, as she began to smash her brolly over her cheating husband's head.

Judy stood rooted to the spot. Queenie was a typical, no-nonsense, hard-faced East Ender and just by taking one look at her, Judy knew she would rather fight Vinny and Roy together than her.

'Get off me, woman. You're hurting me. I'm sorry. I'm a weak man and I made a silly mistake. It's you I love,' Albie swore, covering his already throbbing head with his hands. If he hadn't had two broken legs, he would have bolted out of the ward as fast as a greyhound coming out of its trap at Walthamstow.

'A silly mistake! I'll give you silly mistake, you dirty, disgusting old toad,' Queenie yelled, continuing her violent assault.

Old Mr Perry clapped his hands on his knees with joy when the nurse pulled back the curtain. He hadn't had this much excitement for years. 'Yee-haw,' he shouted in glee.

'Whatever's going on?' asked the appalled nurse, as she tried to stop Queenie hitting Albie with her umbrella.

Realizing that her son was screaming blue murder and not wanting to be Queenie's next brolly victim, Judy decided to make her getaway.

Queenie had eyes like a hawk and immediately clocked Judy slyly trying to depart the fracas. 'And where do you think you're going? You brazen little hussy. I ain't even fucking started with you yet,' Queenie said, chasing Judy up the ward.

'Yee-haw,' Mr Perry yelled again.

'Look, I'm really sorry, but please don't hit me in front of my son. He's frightened enough as it is. I know I shouldn't have got involved with Albie, what with him being a married man and all that, but I swear to you it is all over between us,' Judy said, with tears in her eyes.

Queenie put her brolly and bag on a nearby chair, then stood with her hands on her hips and studied Judy Preston. She was bit tarty-looking, but was certainly not ugly, and how she could ever fancy Albie, Queenie would never know.

'Oh, you're welcome to him, darlin'. I've had years of putting up with the drunken, potless bum. But what's all this about you being pregnant and my sons paying you a visit? And don't fucking lie to me, 'cause I'll smash you all around Whitechapel with this brolly if you do.'

Judy lowered her eyes through guilt. She had never once given Queenie a thought when she had been screwing the arse off Albie, but now his wife was standing in front of her, Judy felt terrible about the whole thing. 'It is true that I'm pregnant and your sons Vinny and Roy did pay me a visit. They ordered me to get rid of my baby and even left me money to pay for an abortion, but I can't do it. I am willing to bring the child up with the help of my mum and brother. I don't want your Albie or anything from him. I just want to keep my child and my Marky to have a little brother or sister.'

The thought of Vinny and Roy knowing about their father's deceit and keeping it secret from her made Queenie feel more sick than Albie's affair itself. She had never really loved her husband, not in the way she had loved her precious children, and she couldn't believe her two eldest sons had betrayed her in such a way.

'Are you OK? Shall I get you some water?' Judy asked, when Queenie all but fainted onto a nearby chair. The woman looked deathly white and Judy was suddenly scared that she might die on her.

Lip curling into a snarl, Queenie managed to find the strength to stand up again and point her scrawny forefinger in Judy's face. 'You can have Albie. When he is discharged from here, he can live with you, but I forbid you to have that baby. I will not have my sons and daughter having no half-brother or -sister. You get rid of that unborn brat, or else. Now fuck off. Go on, fuck off.'

Petrified by the deranged look on Queenie's face, Judy

grabbed the handles of her screaming son's pushchair, and legged it down the corridor.

Unable to relax all day, Mary Walker was relieved when Nancy and Christopher came home from school with beaming smiles on their faces. 'Donald, they're home,' Mary shouted out.

'Well, how did you get on?' Donald asked, wiping his hands on a teatowel.

Both excited about meeting new friends, Christopher and Nancy spoke over one another and neither could be heard properly.

'One at a time. You first, Nancy,' Donald ordered.

'I have a new best friend. Her name is Brenda and she is really nice. My teacher was lovely as well, but she is really fat,' Nancy explained.

Mary chuckled. 'Well, I wouldn't be saying that about your teacher at school, darling. What about you, Christopher? Did you meet any new friends?'

'Yep. Tommy is my new best mate. He wants to be a policeman just like me,' Christopher said proudly.

Donald grinned and ruffled his son's hair. Christopher had only had the fixation about becoming a policeman for the past few weeks. Before that, it was an airline pilot, then prior to that, a racing-car driver.

'Can me and Christopher go out to play? My friend Brenda only lives five minutes away and Christopher's friend Tommy lives in the same street. We all want to play hopscotch together,' Nancy said, her voice brimming with excitment.

'No, not today. Your mother and I haven't met these friends of yours yet and we would like to ensure they come from good families before you go off street-raking with them,' Donald said, in his usual prissy manner.

Her husband generally wore the trousers in their household, but for the second time just lately Mary felt compelled to put her foot down. 'Don't be such a stick-in-the-mud, Donald. It's wonderful the children have made new friends on their first day at school and if they want to go out and play with them while we tidy up in here, then they shall.'

Donald wasn't used to being undermined. 'OK, Mary. But, I want them back by five for their tea and if they get themselves into any mischief, be it on your head.'

Vivian was busy scrubbing her doorstep to ensure it looked more pristine than anybody else's, when she heard a terrible howling noise coming from behind her. Wondering what on earth it was, she stood up and was amazed to see Queenie clinging to the gatepost. 'Whatever's wrong?' Vivian asked, dropping her brush and getting up off her hands and knees.

'It's Albie. Something terrible's happened,' Queenie sobbed.

Having had it hard for most of their childhood and adult lives, neither Queenie nor Vivian ever really cried. The last time they had done so was when their dear old mum had died but, bar that, Vivian couldn't ever remember her sister shedding tears since girlhood, other than those of joy, when her children had been born. 'Oh Queenie. Let's get you inside. Has Albie died, love?' Vivian asked, silently praying that he had.

'I wish the old bastard was dead,' Queenie spat, as Vivian sat her down on the sofa.

Pouring Queenie a large glass of brandy, Vivian listened in bewilderment when her sister explained exactly what had happened at the hospital.

'I know it's hard to swallow, but you'll be far better off without him, Queenie. After the initial shock of finding out about my Bill's affair, I've never been happier since I slung the old bastard out. You don't need Albie. He's a drunken fucking bum and I'm gobsmacked that he even managed to pull himself some young bird. I wouldn't want him if he was the last man left on earth.'

'I ain't worried about fucking Albie. That dirty old goat can rot in hell as far as I'm concerned. It's my boys lying to me that has cut me to pieces. I've no idea if my Michael knew as well, but Vinny and Roy most definitely did. How can they keep something like that from their dear old mum, eh? After everything I've done for 'em as well. Broke my fucking heart they have, Viv.'

Vivian put her arms around her distraught sister and held her close to her chest. 'Your boys adore the ground you walk on, Queenie, and the only reason they would have kept this from you was to save you the hurt. I mean, if they went round and threatened Albie's little whore then they were obviously dealing with things in their own way. 'Ere, something's just occurred to me. What's the betting that Albie never got jumped on by a gang of youths? I'd put money on it that his injuries are down to your Vinny and Roy, you know.'

For the first time since she had found out the mindblowing news, Queenie managed a smile. She had smelt something fishy about Albie getting jumped from the beginning. 'I reckon you might be right, Viv, and if the boys did break Albie's ribs and legs, I shall thank 'em rather than telling them off. I don't want that tart having the baby though. No way do I want my kids to have to suffer that embarrassment.'

'Don't you worry. Vinny and Roy will make sure that kid goes down the khazi.'

Christopher was bowled over when he learned that Nancy's new friend Brenda just happened to be Vinny Butler's sister.

'Do you think one day your brother will let us see inside his club?' he asked, in a star-struck voice.

Thrilled that she had a new best friend and desperate to impress Nancy and her brother, Brenda nodded. 'I'll take you there now if you like. I pop in there all the time,' she boasted.

'I'd better go home for my tea now. Shall I meet you outside the café and walk to school with you in the morning?' Tommy asked Christopher.

'Yeah, see you tomorrow,' Christopher said to his new pal.

The club was only a couple of minutes away and praying that her brothers were inside so she wouldn't make herself look a fool, Brenda was relieved when Vinny answered the door.

'You OK, sweetheart?' he asked, noticing his sister had a grazed knee and dirty hands.

'I fell over playing hopscotch and I want to wash my hands and knee. Can my friends come in?'

Poking his head around the door, Vinny was surprised to see Nancy and Christopher standing there. He had no idea they even knew his little sister. 'Come on then. One glass of Coke and a bag of crisps each, then you'll have to go. I've got some business to sort out in a bit,' he said. The bent chief inspector was popping in to pick up his money for the alcohol licence and Vinny didn't want him to clock the kids inside the club in case he tried to sting him for even more dosh.

'What you doing here, trouble?' Roy said, as Brenda ran towards him and Michael.

'This is my new best friend, Nancy,' Brenda said proudly.

'Hello,' Nancy mumbled.

'Well, ain't you a pretty little thing,' Michael said, winking at her.

'Yep, she'll break some hearts one day, like they all do,' Vinny said, half-joking, half-serious, as he put the Coke and crisps on a table.

'You all right, boy?' Roy asked Christopher. The lad looked as if he was in a trance and was gazing around the club with his mouth wide open.

'That's my brother,' Nancy said, smiling at Michael. She found Roy and Vinny a bit scary, but had immediately taken to Michael because he had such a kind face.

'I really like your club,' Christopher said, looking at Vinny in awe.

'Cheers, boy,' Vinny chuckled.

'You been home from school yet, Bren? Is Mum and Auntie Viv OK?' Roy asked.

'Yeah, I've been home, but Mum was upset and she went to sit in Auntie Viv's house.'

Vinny was immediately alarmed. 'What do you mean, upset? What was wrong with her?'

'Dunno. She was sitting on Auntie Viv's sofa drinking brandy and she looked like she'd been crying.'

'Why didn't you bleedin' well tell me that when you knocked on the door?' Vinny asked, suddenly agitated.

'Don't have a go at her, Vin,' Roy urged. His brother's mouth could run away with him at times.

'Shall I pop round there and make sure everything's OK?' Michael offered. Since Vinny had had a go at him, he was trying to do his best to please.

Vinny and Roy glanced at one another. Both were thinking the same thing. Their mother was a tough old East End bird, she never cried, so she had either found out that Vinny had attacked their father, or she knew about his affair.

'I've gotta wait here for Geary, so you pop round home, Roy. You, Michael, can have the night off.'

'Do you want me to go home to Mum as well?' Brenda didn't understand what the hell was going on.

Vinny handed his sister a pound note. 'No. You take that, buy your friends some sweets and split the change equally between yous. Don't go home just yet, Bren.'

When Michael opened the door of the club, ruffled her hair and called her sweetheart, Nancy couldn't look him in the eyes. For the first time ever she had a crush on somebody, but unfortunately for Nancy, he was five years her senior.

CHAPTER SIX

'I'm really sorry, Mum. I was going to tell you in front of Dad at Michael's birthday lunch, but when I found out about the baby, I decided to sort it meself. Please forgive me,' Vinny said, staring at his expensive black leather shoes in shame. Vinny loved his mother more than anybody else in the world. If it wasn't for her sound advice, he wouldn't be the man he was today. 'Vinny, you do whatever it takes to make something of your life. It's better to be a somebody than a nobody, son, and if that means stealing and stamping out people along the way, then so be it. Don't ever knock or ill-treat your own kind though. You look after them,' his mum had told him on the day he'd left school.

Aware that her son looked distraught, Queenie put her arms around him and gave him a motherly hug. Vinny was genuinely sorry, she knew that, and she was also thrilled when he had admitted to her that it was him who had put his father in hospital. 'Let's put all this behind us now. Your father ain't worth the salt in our tears, boy. And thanks for giving him such a good going-over. You did me proud.'

Thrilled that his beloved mother was no longer angry with him, Vinny hugged her tightly to his chest.

Johnny Preston was parked up in his Triumph Herald approximately fifty yards from Queenie Butler's house. Johnny loved his new set of wheels. It was a white convertible and a real babe magnet, just like himself.

With his strawberry-blond hair, six-foot frame, and Adonis-like physique, Johnny Preston was a handsome bastard and he knew it.

'Cor, it's fucking taters sitting here. Run the engine, so we can warm ourselves up a bit,' Dave said to Johnny.

Johnny turned to his pal and shook his head in mock disbelief. Dave Phillips was his best mate. They had been as thick as thieves since the age of six and Dave was one of the toughest bastards that Johnny knew. Until it came to the weather, that was. As soon as the temperature fell below five degrees, Dave had a terrible habit of turning into a big girl's blouse.

'You're such a tart, Phillips,' Johnny said, starting the ignition. He turned up the volume of the radio. The Kinks were one of Johnny's favourite bands and as he sang along to 'Tired of Waiting for You', he thought how very apt the song was. The reason being, he was getting fucking sick of waiting for mummy's boy Vinny Butler to reappear from Queenie's house.

Vinny still being tied to his mother's apron strings was well-known amongst the criminal fraternity in London. As far as Johnny knew, nobody had ever said anything to Vinny's face, but Johnny was well aware that many people laughed at Vinny's almost incestuous relationship with her. He had even heard Mad Frankie Fraser joke about it once or twice.

It was because of his desperation to worm his way in with Mad Frankie and, in particular, Eddie Richardson, that Johnny had decided to confront Vinny Butler with only Dave as back-up. Their other pal Graeme was currently banged-up. You had to earn your kudos to be accepted by such people as the Richardsons and Mad Frankie and Johnny knew that to show such bravery as taking on the Butlers would win him a massive mark of respect. At the moment Mad Frankie and Eddie Richardson were keeping him at arm's length, but Johnny was determined to change his idol's opinion of him. Now twenty-seven, he had been forced to marry his wife, Deborah, several years ago after putting her in the family way and even though he still fucked anything with a pulse, he adored his two children, Joanna and Johnny Junior. He wanted to enrol them in the best schools and lavish them with untold wealth and he would do anything to make that happen, even if that did mean snuffing out Vinny and Roy Butler nigh-on single-handedly.

'Here he is now,' Dave said, his voice full of adrenaline. The plan was to give Vinny Butler the pasting of his life and warn him if he or Roy ever went near Judy again, they would both be shot to smithereens.

Johnny punched his steering wheel with frustration. 'Bollocks! The big fucking Mary-Ann is obviously going out on a family outing. What a waste of an afternoon.'

'Can't we just follow 'em and jump Vinny wherever he goes? His brothers ain't with him,' Dave suggested.

'Nah, I don't mind giving him a good hiding in front of his mother and aunt, but we can't touch him in front of that backward cousin,' Johnny replied sensibly.

'Why not?'

'Use your loaf, Dave. If we wanna move in the right circles we can't be involving little 'uns, especially simple ones. It ain't the done thing, mate.'

'What we gonna do now then?' Dave asked.

Johnny released the handbrake and put his foot on the accelerator. 'Call it a day and come back tomorrow. Don't worry, Davey Boy. Vinny Butler will get his comeuppance in the not-too-distant future. Nobody threatens my sister and gets away with it and I mean that with all my fucking heart.'

Albie Butler felt almost suicidal. Not only did he have two broken legs and three broken ribs, he was now homeless, and had a wife and a pregnant ex-girlfriend who both hated him with a passion.

'Hitler in a German tank, parlez vous. Hitler in a German tank, parlez vous. Hitler in a German tank, reading the *Beano* and having a wank. Inky pinky parlez vous,' sang old Mr Perry in the next bed.

Albie put his bruised head in his hands. Old Mr Perry had done nothing but sing war songs all day and if his legs hadn't been in traction, Albie would have leapt out of the bed and throttled him by his scrawny neck.

'Dad.'

Albie looked up and was thrilled to see Roy and Michael standing there. 'Oh, it's so good to see you, boys. That old goat in the next bed has been doing my bleedin' head in all day. You ain't bought your old dad a bottle of brandy by any chance?' Albie said, directing the question towards his youngest son. Unlike that sadistic bastard Vinny, Michael was a good kid and had visited him every day with an alcoholic gift. They say you shouldn't have a favourite son, but Michael had always been Albie's. They had a special bond between them, which Albie had never experienced with Roy or Vinny.

For the first time in his life, Michael looked at his father with hatred in his eyes. Learning his dad had betrayed his mum in such an awful manner had been like having a light switched on in his brain, and he now saw his father just as his brothers did. 'All we've bought you is your clothes from Mum's house. They're in two binliners and we gave them to the nurse. I never thought I would hear myself say this, but you are fucking scum, Dad, and I no longer consider myself to be your son.'

'Yee-haw,' old Mr Perry shouted with glee.

Roy looked at his brother in astonishment. Michael had always been the soft-as-shit pleasant one out of the three of them, yet within two days of working with him and Vinny, he seemed to have grown bollocks and turned from a boy into a man.

'And don't you ever contact us or our mum again,' Roy threatened, waving a finger in the direction of his father's shocked face.

'Don't go, boys. Please don't go,' Albie begged, near to tears.

When Roy and Michael ignored their father's plea and stomped out of the ward, old Mr Perry broke into song again. Vera Lynn's 'We'll Meet Again' was one of his all-time favourites.

Over at the café, Mary and Shirley were singing along to Sonny and Cher's 'I Got You Babe' as they buttered a loaf of bread between them. 'Christ, I totally forgot to ask you how the kids got on at school. No more tears from Nancy, I hope?' Shirley asked.

Mary chuckled. 'Nope, no more tears. Both of them absolutely loved their new schools and they've made friends already. Nancy has met a mate called Brenda and Christopher has palled up with a lad called Tommy.'

'Ah, bless 'em. I wonder if Nancy's mate is my friend Queenie's daughter. Her name is Brenda and she's about the same age as your Nancy.'

Realizing that Shirley was referring to the Butler family, Mary stopped buttering her bread and turned to her employee. 'I'll have to ask Nancy what her friend's surname is. What are they like, that Butler family? Queenie and her sister have been in here a couple of times and they seem nice enough. One of the sons came in as well. My Donald wasn't happy because he gave our Christopher some money. Donald doesn't like the children taking money off strangers, so he made Christopher give it back to him.'

'Queenie and Vivian are diamonds, Mary. Both got lovely houses that are spotlessly clean and their doorsteps are gleaming. Young Brenda's a good kid and so are the three boys. You don't mess with them though, if you know what I mean? Especially the eldest lad, Vinny. He has a bit of a reputation around here for being more than a handful, but he's different again with his mum. Worships the ground Queenie walks on, that boy does.'

A customer who wanted serving ended the conversation and as Mary wrote down the order, she said a silent prayer for Nancy's new friend not to be Brenda Butler. If she was and Donald found out, all hell was sure to break loose.

Under strict instructions from their father, Nancy and Christopher arrived home with their two new friends in tow.

'This is Brenda,' Nancy announced.

'And this is Tommy,' Christopher said, proudly.

The café was virtually empty and seeing as he and Mary now closed at four, Donald ordered the children to sit down at a table.

'I know both your mums are probably cooking for you, but we've some chips left over in the kitchen. Shall I put them on a plate so you can all share them? There's not that many so I doubt it will spoil your dinner,' Mary said.

'Yes please, and can I have a can of cola as well?' Brenda asked cheekily.

Donald took an instant dislike to Brenda. She had been far too brazen asking for a drink for his liking and he didn't want his Nancy copying that type of behaviour. He had brought her up to have impeccable manners.

'I really like your café, sir. Does that play music?' Tommy asked Donald, pointing at the jukebox.

Donald smiled before answering the boy. Tommy had already won him over by calling him sir.

'There you go,' Mary said, putting a plate of chips and four cans of cola on the table. She knew why Donald had insisted on meeting their children's friends. He was a very particular man and was bound to interrogate them to ensure they came from decent families.

'So, what does your dad do? Does he have a job?' Donald asked Tommy.

'Yeah, my dad grafts really hard, sir. He works down the docks.'

'And what about your mother? Does she work too?'

'No, sir. I have two younger brothers, so my mum stays at home to look after them.'

Mary was a bundle of nerves as Donald turned to Brenda. 'And what about you, Brenda? Does your dad go to work?'

'My dad don't live with us any more. My mum has chucked him out. He was always drunk, but my mum didn't chuck him out because of that. He got another woman pregnant. I'm not meant to know that, but I heard my mum and aunt talking about it in the kitchen last night.'

Absolutely appalled, Donald glanced at his wife.

Mary couldn't look at her husband. 'Oh well, I suppose you'd better hurry up and eat those chips in case your mums are wondering where you are. Me and Donald don't want to get ourselves into trouble for you two being late home,' Mary said, adding a false chuckle.

'I told my mum I was coming here,' Tommy said.

'Yeah, so did I,' Brenda added.

'So, do you have brothers and sisters, Brenda?' Donald asked.

'Yeah, I got three brothers, Vinny, Roy and Michael. Lenny is like a brother as well but he is really my cousin.'

Recognizing the name Vinny, Donald felt the hairs on the back of his neck stand up. 'And do your brothers work? Or are they still at school?' Donald pried.

'They have got their own business. They own the snooker club just around the corner. Michael used to be a mechanic but Vinny made him give his job up. Everybody knows my brothers. My mum reckons they're more famous than the Kray twins,' Brenda explained proudly.

Having already heard enough, Donald stood up and gestured for his wife to follow him into the kitchen. 'Did you know that our daughter's friend was part of that family of scoundrels?' he asked Mary accusingly.

'No, of course I didn't. I'm not a bloody mind-reader, Donald.'

'Well, I'm afraid the friendship will have to end. I will not have my Nancy involved with such people. You shall tell her tonight that she isn't to be friends with Brenda any more. Our Nancy will soon make other friends,' Donald stated.

'I can't stop them from being friends, Donald. They sit next to one another at bloody school. I really do think you are overreacting a bit. Brenda might be a little rough around the edges, but she seems a nice-enough child. Not all children have been lucky enough to have the upbringing that ours have.'

'I am not overreacting, Mary. I obviously just care about

73

my children's welfare a tad more than you do. Tomorrow, I want you to pay a visit to Nancy's headmaster and demand that she be moved into a different class.'

'I will do no such thing,' Mary said, her eyes blazing with anger.

'Well, if you won't, then I will,' Donald argued.

Mary was absolutely raging now. 'Are you determined to balls things up for us here, Donald? Our new business is a roaring success already. Our children are content and have new friends, yet you still can't be happy. For your information, Shirley was telling me about the Butler family only today. She said Brenda's mum is a lovely lady with a spotlessly clean house. She also spoke highly of the three boys. Obviously, as we already know, Shirley did say that they are a family not to be messed with, which is why you will not stop our Nancy from being friends with Brenda. For some reason, you seem intent on bringing trouble to our door and if you carry on doing so, and ruin our wonderful business that we have worked so hard for, I swear I will divorce you. Now, get off your high horse and leave me to decide what is and isn't best for our children, OK?'

Totally gobsmacked by the way his wife had just spoken to him, Donald decided that he was out of his depth with this particular argument. 'OK, we will do things your way, Mary. But, if that despicable family ever bring trouble to us or our children's lives, it will be me who files for divorce.'

CHAPTER SEVEN

Queenie spent the morning of her birthday putting up her Christmas tree and decorations. Vinnie had organised a small party for her at the club later, which had been Lenny's idea.

'What you doing now, Mum?' Brenda asked, when her mother climbed up the stepladder.

'Putting these paper chains across the ceiling to make it look a bit more festive.'

'Mum, you know your birthday party?'

Securing the paper chain with two drawing pins, Queenie stepped down from the ladder. 'Yes.'

'Would it be OK if I invited my friend Nancy?' Brenda asked hopefully.

Queenie smiled. 'Of course you can, angel. You'd best invite her little brother as well though. You can't invite one without the other.'

Over at the club, Vinny had been up since dawn getting things ready for his mum's birthday party. 'About fucking time you showed your face and I hope you've got rid of that slag,' Vinny said as his brother appeared looking dishevelled.

Roy sighed. He didn't often allow birds to stay upstairs in his bed. Once or twice a month, top whack. Yet every time he did so, Vinny would always have something to say about it. Deciding to stand up to his brother for once, Roy glared at him. 'The slag as you so politely called her went home a couple of hours ago. What is your problem, Vin? I'm a single eighteen-year-old fella, so why is it a crime for me to get me nuts in here and there?'

'No-one said it was a crime, Roy, but you knew how important it was to me that we made Mum's birthday special this year. After all the shit she has been through recently, don't you think she deserves to be treated like the Queen?'

'Of course I do.'

'Grab hold of the end of that banner. I want to put it on the wall facing the door,' Vinny said.

'Where's Michael?' Roy asked.

'You tell me. Went to some silly Mod party after we let him leave early last night. He's probably still under the covers with some slag as well.'

'What time is Mum's present arriving?' Roy was desperate to change the subject.

'Twelve on the dot and we need to be there to see her face when she sees it, which is why I needed you to get your arse out of bed early today.'

'Look, I'm sorry. But please, can we just forget about this now, Vin? We don't wanna spoil Mum's party, do we?'

'Yep, let's forget about it, but in future, Roy, business and family before pleasure, eh?'

Roy nodded. 'Of course.'

Johnny Preston was not a happy chappie. Vinny Butler ran the firm, the other brothers were nobodies compared to him, everybody knew that, yet catching Vinny on his own was proving to be a difficult task.

'Can't we just confront Vinny and Roy? We can take the pair of them on,' Dave Phillips suggested.

'Nope. I only deal with the organ grinder. No point involving the monkey. We'll get him on his own, Dave. Patience is a virtue,' Johnny replied as he drove past the club. 'I wonder what's going on in there? There's a bird turned up with balloons now. Perhaps it's his mummy's birthday and the incestuous freak is throwing her a party.'

'He reminds me of that geezer in the film *Psycho*, but I can't remember his name,' Dave added.

Johnny burst out laughing. 'Great call, me ole cocker. Vinny Butler, the East End's answer to Norman Bates.'

Mary was busy wiping down the tables when young Brenda wandered into the café. 'Hello, love. Nancy's upstairs with Christopher. Pop up and see her if you like.'

When Brenda ran up the stairs, Mary went into the kitchen to remind her husband of the conversation they'd had the other day.

'Don't worry. I won't say anything rude to the awful child,' Donald said cuttingly.

'Mum, Dad.' Nancy ran into the kitchen with Christopher and Brenda by her side.

Noticing that her daughter's eyes were shining with excitement, Mary smiled. 'What is it? Do you want to go out to play?'

'No. I've been invited to a party and so has Christopher. It's Brenda's mum's birthday.'

Donald frowned. If it was Queenie Butler's birthday party then her sons were bound to attend and there was no way his daughter and son were mixing with that motley crew. 'You and Christopher are far too young to be attending adult parties, Nancy. I'm sorry, but I will not allow you to go.'

'Oh, please, Dad,' Nancy begged, her lip trembling. She wanted to cry but didn't want to make a show of herself in front of Brenda.

Mary glared at her husband and then turned back to her distraught daughter. 'Where is the party, love? And what time is it? You're too young to be out late at night.'

'It's not at night, Mrs Walker. It's being held this afternoon in my brother's snooker club. My brother says it has to end by teatime because he has to open the club to his punters of an evening,' Brenda explained.

Donald sneered at Brenda's use of the word punters. She sounded like a docker or a navvy. Her speech was so unfeminine for a little girl.

'I think it's OK for Nancy and Christopher to go to the party, Donald, as long as they are back here by six, don't you? The snooker club is only around the corner, isn't it?' Mary said, giving her husband the evil eye.

'Yesss! I love parties,' Christopher shouted, clapping his hands with sheer delight.

Nancy was thrilled by her mum's remarks and both girls jumped up and down with glee.

With a face like a smacked arse, Donald glanced at his wife, then his children. 'Do whatever you bloody well like,' he spat.

Queenie and Vivian glanced at one another in amazement as the two delivery men brought a big wooden object inside.

'Aw, Queenie, ain't it grand? It's one of them posh radiograms,' Vivian whispered in her sister's ear.

'But we ain't got no records to play on it,' Queenie whispered back. Her only access to music was the radio she had in the kitchen.

After thanking the delivery men, Roy walked into the lounge with a cardboard box. 'Put one on, Vin,' he ordered his brother.

When the tones of Mrs Mills blasted out of the speakers, Queenie and Vivian looked at one another in delight.

'Oh, ain't it wonderful,' Vivian said, grinning at her sister.

'Bloody amazing,' Queenie replied. No longer did she have to put up with Albie and scrub his skid-marked pants until her hands bled so that when she put them on the washing line the neighbours wouldn't think they were a dirty family. Instead, she had a fabulous radiogram with Mrs Mills' LPs to entertain her and Vivian on these cold winter nights. Queenie stood up, put one arm around Vinny's neck and the other around Roy's. 'Thank you so much, boys. Not just for the radiogram, I mean for everything.'

Queenie Butler felt like the luckiest mum in the world when she walked into the club and saw the effort her wonderful sons had gone to on her behalf. There was a big banner wishing her a happy birthday, balloons, a buffet, a DJ, and most importantly friends and family members. 'Aw, this is wonderful, boys,' Queenie said, grinning at each of her three sons in turn.

Vinny sneered when she rested her gaze on Michael. Instead of being there to help him organize the bash, his youngest brother had only just turned up. 'Don't be thanking him, Mum. Unlike me and Roy, Michael did sod all to help.'

'Oh, don't have a go at him, Vinny. He's only a baby still,' Queenie said, stroking Michael's cheek fondly.

'No, he isn't a baby, Mum, Michael's a big boy now and for not turning up early like he was supposed to this morning, he will have his wages docked.'

Not wanting to get into a spat with his elder brother, Michael gave his mum a birthday hug. 'You look ever so nice today. That suit looks mint.'

Queenie grinned with pride. She and Vivian always liked to think of themselves as the best-dressed women in the East End and today Queenie was wearing her ultra-modern apple-green skirt suit.

'Hi, Michael. Sorry I'm a bit late,' said a pretty girl with long blonde hair.

'This is my girlfriend, Linda, Mum. You didn't mind me inviting her, did you? I really wanted yous two to meet.'

When Queenie clapped her hands with glee and started fawning over the girl, Vinny stomped off in a temper. How dare Michael take it upon himself to invite some tart to the party without even asking his permission first. Talk about take a liberty.

Back at the café, Mary was getting more annoyed by the second at her husband's childish behaviour. Donald had barely uttered a word to her since she had allowed the children to go to Brenda's mum's party and the silence was becoming unbearable. 'Two ham, egg and chips, Donald,' she said, walking into the kitchen.

Donald didn't answer. Instead he just took the ham out of the fridge.

'I am getting immensely sick of you acting like a ten-year-old, Donald. Even our children are more mature than you are. Nancy and Christopher have only gone to a little party, for Christ's sake. They will be back by teatime. It's boring and unhealthy for them to be cooped up in here with us all the time.'

'I don't mind them going to normal people's parties, but you know how I feel about that family, yet you still allowed them to go. That Brenda is a horrible child and I hate our Nancy being involved with her.'

Desperate to make things right again between them, Mary put her arms around his waist. 'I know what you mean, love, but we can't wrap the kids in cotton wool. They are old enough now to choose their own friends.'

Donald sighed worriedly. 'More's the pity, my dear. More's the pity.'

*

Queenie Butler had thoroughly enjoyed her birthday party. She and Vivian usually kept themselves to themselves, but Vinny had invited a few of the neighbours and apart from Sheila Jackson's husband, Kenny, who was drunk and becoming a fucking nuisance, it had been a lovely day.

'Shall we bring the cake out now?' asked Vivian.

Vinny didn't reply. He was too busy watching Kenny Jackson make a tit of himself. Vinny didn't like Kenny one little bit, and had he known Sheila would bring her husband along with her, he wouldn't have invited her in the first place. 'That prick is asking for trouble, Roy,' Vinny hissed.

'Why? What's he done?' Roy asked. Kenny was a local loudmouth who drank in the Blind Beggar. Roy had never liked him either.

'He keeps swearing in front of the kids. He's let a "cunt" fly three times now in front of Mum, and Nancy and Brenda are sitting next to her. Champ is there as well. It ain't right, Roy. I'm gonna have a little word in his shell-like.'

Knowing what his brother's temper was like, Roy urged Vinny not to say anything. 'You don't wanna spoil Mum's birthday, do you? Anyway, we'll be wrapping things up in a bit. It's gone five now. Who invited Kenny? It weren't me.'

'It's my fault. I invited Sheila, but 'cause that piss-pot is always in the Blind Beggar on Saturday afternoons, I didn't dream she'd bring him with her. I wanted to tell him to fuck off when he walked in, but bit me tongue.'

Desperate to stop Vinny from kicking off, Roy urged him to look at Lenny. Their cousin had just ran onto the dance-floor and was standing in the middle, wiggling his hips to the Hollies' 'Just One Look'.

About to watch his little cousin, Vinny heard another 'cunt' sail out of Kenny Jackson's gob and decided enough was enough. He flew out of his seat, walked over to where Jackson was sitting and tapped him on the shoulder. 'Tone your language down a bit, Ken. My little sister and her friend shouldn't have to hear such words. Neither should my mother and aunt for that matter either. You ain't in the Blind Beggar with your chums now, you know.'

Kenny Jackson looked at Vinny through glazed eyes. He didn't like the Butler boys, especially Vinny and Roy. It was fast becoming common knowledge that they were a cocky little pair of bastards who were getting far too big for their boots. Knowing how fast news travelled and how much respect he would gain by standing up to Vinny Butler, Kenny decided to do just that. 'You got some brass neck, you have. The grapevine is a funny old thing, kid, and everybody knows it was you who put your father in hospital because he was rumping some little dolly bird. Yet, you've got the front to tell me not to swear. Don't make me laugh.'

A few of the women and children screamed when Vinny lifted Kenny up by the scruff of his neck and head-butted him. 'You don't know who you're messing with, you cheeky fucker. And who you calling "kid"?' Vinny spat, as he bundled Kenny towards the exit.

Sheila wailed hysterically when she saw that her husband's face was covered in blood.

'Do something, Roy. Don't just sit there like a stuffed dummy,' Queenie yelled.

'Kenny Jackson asked for that, so don't you be having a go at your Vinny,' Vivian told her sister.

Young Nancy couldn't stop crying when she saw Roy and Michael follow Vinny outside. 'I'm frightened, Christopher. Can we go home now?'

'Don't be scared. No-one ever beats my brothers up because they are the hardest men around here,' Brenda said proudly to her friend.

As some yelling and shoving started between another two men on the table behind, Christopher grabbed his sister's hand. 'Come on. Let's go.'

Mary and Donald had closed for the day and were just doing their daily tidying-up routine when they heard the frantic banging on the door.

'Whatever's the matter?' Mary asked, when she noticed Nancy's tear-stained face and Christopher's ashen one.

'It's OK. You're home now. Just tell Daddy what has happened,' Donald said, glaring at Mary and hugging his daughter at the same time.

'There was a fight. The man looked like he was dead, didn't he, Christopher?' Nancy sobbed.

Christopher nodded. When he and Nancy left the party, Vinny had been outside beating seven bells out of Kenny Jackson. Roy and Michael were unsuccessfully trying to get Vinny away from the man, and when Christopher and Nancy had glanced at Kenny, he was bleeding profusely and looked like he was dead.

'Oh Donald. I'm so sorry. You were right and I was wrong,' Mary said, apologetically.

Donald liked to be proved right. 'I think you need to find a new best friend at school, darling. That Brenda and her family are far too rough for you to be around.'

'But I like Brenda. It's not her fault, is it?' Nancy said dismally.

Mary decided to back her husband to the hilt. 'Your dad's right, love. You can still be friends with Brenda at school, but I don't want you to see her outside.'

'But why not?' Nancy sobbed.

'Because I just bloody said so. The same goes for you, Christopher. I know you've been hanging around near that snooker club because Mad Freda saw you and told me. She only lives a few doors away from it, you see. You are not to go near there any more. I don't want either of you anywhere near them Butlers, OK?' Mary said sternly.

Thrilled that his beautiful wife's brain seemed to be in fine working order once more, Donald smiled at her. 'Thank you, my darling.'

CHAPTER EIGHT

Queenie put the topside of beef in the oven, then flopped down on the sofa next to Vivian. 'I wish we could find out how Kenny is. He couldn't have grassed Vinny up, else we'd have the police crawling all over us by now. Perhaps he is still out cold? Or, worse still, say he's croaked it,' Queenie said, her lips twitching anxiously.

Realizing her sister was going out of her mind with worry, Vivian got up and poured them both a glass of sherry. 'Of course Kenny ain't dead. The ambulance man said he was still breathing, didn't he?'

After Roy and Michael had managed to drag Vinny off Kenny Jackson, they had moved him away from the snooker club, dumped him in a nearby doorway, and rung an ambulance. Sheila had been told to say nothing and Queenie was sure that providing Kenny survived his ferocious beating, neither he nor Sheila would dare implicate her Vinny. Grasses were despised in London's East End, and treated worse than vermin.

'If Kenny dies and my Vinny goes to prison, it'll be the end of me, Viv. I'd die of a broken heart, I just know I would,' Queenie said dramatically.

'Oh for Christ's sake, stop talking bollocks and drink

your sherry, will ya? Vinny's got our dad's temper, that's his bloody problem. Anyway, Kenny Jackson took liberties and Vinny had every right to give him a good fawpenny one.'

'How dare you talk about my Vinny in the same light as that nasty old bastard,' Queenie spat. Their father was dead now, thank God, but before he had kicked the bucket, he'd led their poor mum a dog's life.

'I didn't mean it like that. Your Vinny is nothing like Dad. I just said he had a similar temper,' Vivian explained.

'No he has not! Have you forgotten how Dad used to beat Mum up? My Vinny would never lay a finger on a woman, Viv. He's a gentleman,' Queenie insisted.

Michael stomped in, ending the awkward exchange between the two sisters.

'What's up? Has something happened to do with Kenny Jackson? Vinny ain't been arrested, has he?' Queenie gabbled.

'No. I'm just pissed off because Linda has blown me out. Well, it weren't actually her. It was her dad that did the deed.'

'Why?' Queenie asked.

'Why do you think? Her dress got splashed in claret yesterday, didn't it? Her dad saw it when she got home and hit the roof. I tried to explain to him that what had happened had nothing to do with me, but he wasn't having none of it. He told me that under no circumstances would I be allowed to take Linda out again, then he shut the door in my face.'

'What a fucking liberty! Do you want me to speak to him? Or even better, send Roy or Vinny round to have a word?'

Michael shook his head. 'Nah, not worth it.'

'Oh well. Perhaps it's for the best, love. There's plenty

86

more fish in the sea and you need a girl who will understand your family, don't you? You're in business with your brothers now, so no point you being with someone too naïve who has up-their-arse parents. They won't fit in with us,' Queenie advised.

'And Vinny did say to you that you shouldn't have invited Linda yesterday, didn't he? Perhaps you should keep any future girlfriends away from the club. Business and pleasure should always be kept separate, Michael,' Vivian added.

'Don't be blaming me for inviting the girl. I didn't know my lunatic of a brother was gonna nigh-on kill a man in front of her very eyes, did I? As for the poxy business, I didn't want to be part of it and still don't. All I ever wanted was to be a mechanic,' Michael said, his eyes blazing angrily.

'Don't you dare call your brother a lunatic. And where do you think you're going?' Queenie shouted, when her son leapt out of his chair and put his parka back on.

'Out with Kev on me bike. It's the only time I get any peace and quiet,' Michael yelled, slamming the front door.

Vivian raised her eyebrows and smiled at her sister. 'Boys, eh? Who'd have 'em?'

Over at the café, young Christopher Walker was bored out of his brains and in desperate need of excitement. 'Please come out and play, Nancy? I really want to know if that man is dead or not, don't you? The police might be at the snooker club and if we walk past we might be able to see them and we can find out exactly what happened to him.'

Nancy immediately shook her head. She had been petrified yesterday when the fight had broken out at Brenda's mum's party, and the sight of that poor man lying on the pavement covered in blood would probably stick in her mind for life. 'No, Christopher! I am never ever going near that club again, and neither should you.'

Christopher put on his coat and ran down the stairs. There was no way his parents would let him play out on his own after what had happened yesterday, so he would have to pretend that he was popping round to see Tommy. Surely he could get away with telling one little white lie, couldn't he?

'You can visit Tommy, but I want you back by five. And don't you dare go near that club again, Christopher,' Donald warned his son.

Albie Butler was shocked to see the state of Kenny Jackson. Both men frequented the Blind Beggar pub, but rarely drank in the same company. 'Jesus wept! What happened to you, Ken?'

Ordering Sheila to leave them alone and come back in ten minutes, Kenny couldn't keep the sneer off his battered face as he turned back to Albie. His injuries included concussion, a fractured wrist, broken nose, and he felt and looked as though he had spent ten rounds in the ring with Henry Cooper. 'I had a fucking run-in with your psycho of a son, that's what,' Kenny wheezed.

Albie felt his pulse start to quicken. He had always been a bit wary of Kenny Jackson. He'd seen him do a bloke with a hammer in the Blind Beggar a few years back, and had always given him a wide berth since then. 'I'm sorry, Kenny, I really am.' Albie didn't have to ask which son had beaten the living daylights out of Kenny.

'You're sorry! Is that all you've got to say? That boy needs taking down a peg or two, Albie. Everybody knows it was your Vinny who put you in here. I mean, what type of boy does that to his own father, eh? The kid's a fucking animal to do this to me in front of my wife. Us men don't involve our women in such spats, you know that.'

Mortified that people knew that his own son was

88

responsible for his broken legs and ribs, Albie bowed his head in shame. 'I dunno what to say to you, Kenny. There is nothing I can do to help your predicament. The only thing I can suggest is you accept the beating and swallow your pride. Vinny has no respect for me. He has never listened to a word I say.'

Old Mr Perry smirked as he listened to the conversation going on a few feet away from him. He had been so bored cooped up in a hospital bed after his bowel cancer operation, but since Albie had arrived, the pure entertainment had lifted Mr Perry's spirits no end.

Christopher Walker felt the adrenaline pumping through his veins as he sat down on the step in the doorway opposite the snooker club. Popping a sherbert lemon into his mouth, the boy looked to his right. His mum had said that Mad Freda lived near the club and he wondered which house it was. About to turn back, Christopher noticed the white Triumph Herald convertible parked up. He could vaguely make out the silhouettes of what looked like two men sitting inside the car, and he wondered if they were friends of Vinny's or undercover policemen.

Taking his sweet out of his mouth to see how much longer he had to suck to reach the sherbet, Christopher thought back to the events of yesterday. When the fight had first broken out, he had been just as scared as his sister. But after he had got back to the safety of his parents' café, Christopher couldn't stop thinking about what he had seen. He had found the whole experience exhilarating, and he now couldn't wait until he was old enough to join the police force, so he could investigate people being beaten up and murdered.

Feeling his heart start to beat faster when the door of the club swung open, Christopher was disappointed to see

Roy come out alone. Christopher had never really spoken to Roy like he had Vinny, and even though he was dying to know if the man who had taken a beating had croaked it, he decided to hold his tongue until Vinny appeared.

A couple of minutes after Roy walked around the corner, Christopher heard a car door slam, glanced to his right, and saw the two men get out of the Triumph Herald. When they walked up to the door of the club, and rang the bell, Christopher ducked his head in the hope they wouldn't notice him. Vinny's car was parked outside the door of the club and as long as he stayed crouched down, Christopher guessed the men wouldn't be able to see him. Unfortunately for him though, he had already been spotted. The woman whom he and his parents referred to as Mad Freda had been glued to her window for the past fifteen minutes.

Vinny Butler was alone in the club when the doorbell rang. 'Who is it?' he shouted, his hand on the bolt, ready to open the door.

Having watched the club since seven a.m. that morning, Johnny Preston knew that he had finally got Vinny alone. He had seen Michael arrive and leave earlier, and Roy had left just a few minutes ago. 'It's Judy Preston's brother, Johnny. Can we have a quiet word, please?'

Vinny smirked and checked he had his knife in his pocket. He had been expecting a visit from Johnny Preston ever since paying Judy a visit, but he hadn't quite expected him to turn up on a Sunday afternoon. 'Too scared to come on your own, was you?' Vinny asked sarcastically, when he swung the door open and saw that Johnny had a pal with him.

Johnny immediately felt his hackles start to rise. 'Dave's my partner. He goes everywhere with me, a bit like your brother Roy does with you.'

Vinny stepped outside the club and slammed the metal door. He wasn't stupid. Johnny and his muggy sidekick might be tooled up for all he knew. 'Spit it out then? I ain't got all day,' he said.

Johnny Preston and Dave Phillips glanced at one another. Neither had ever been this close to Vinny Butler before and both were thinking the self-same thing. Vinny was exactly as the rumour mill described him. He looked like he had a bit of Italian in him. His eyes were deadly cold, and his attitude was as cocksure as they came.

Johnny suddenly felt extremely wary, but he'd come this far and there was no going back now. It was only the other evening that he and Dave had been bragging to Mad Frankie Fraser in a South London boozer that he was going to confront Vinny Butler so, like it or not, he now had to do so. 'You owe my sister an apology, Vinny. Who do you think you are, eh? Going round her gaff and threatening her in front of her young son? You're bang out of order and I ain't fucking putting up with it. Judy is keeping her baby and that is final,' Johnny said, sounding much more confident than he actually felt.

Vinny was very good at staring at people for long spells without blinking, and he had never met a man yet in his life who could hold his gaze. When Johnny dropped his eyes, Vinny grabbed him by the neck and smashed his head as hard as he could against the metal door. 'Your slag of a sister will get rid of that kid whether you like it or not. I'll kick it out of her personally, if I have to. Now go crawl back under your rock and tell that whore you're related to that I'll be round next week to check she's un-pregnanted her fucking self.'

When Dave punched Vinny in the side of the head, Christopher Walker stood up to get a better view.

'Silly move, you dumb cunt,' Christopher heard Vinny

say. He then saw Vinny repeatedly punch the man in the stomach, with what looked to be a knife.

When Johnny Preston saw his pal lying lifeless on the floor with blood pumping out of his abdomen, he knew it was time for a quick getaway. He ran like the clappers, leapt into his Triumph Herald and sped off as Vinny chased the car, screaming abuse at him.

Vinny could feel his heart beating ferociously as the car disappeared out of sight. It wasn't down to nerves, more annoyance that Preston had got away as he'd wanted to stab that bastard too.

Punching a nearby wall, Vinny quickly looked up and down the road. Thankfully, being a Sunday afternoon there wasn't a soul in sight, so Vinny stepped over Dave Phillips' dead body, picked up the knife he had dropped, jumped in his Jaguar, and was just about to drive off, when he saw young Christopher Walker sitting in the doorway opposite the club. Leaning across the passenger seat to unlock the door, Vinny ordered young Christopher to get in.

Christopher no longer had any adrenaline pumping through his veins as he did what Vinny asked. He had seen too much now, far too much, and he was petrified. When Vinny drove past his parent's café, Christopher started to sob. 'You're not gonna kill me as well, are you? I won't say nothing about what happened, Vinny. I swear I won't.'

With his head all over the place, Vinny pulled into a nearby sidestreet and stopped the car. He took a ten-pound note out of his pocket and handed it to Christopher. 'Take that and there is plenty more where that came from. You saw nothing, understand?'

'Yes. I understand,' the boy said, making a grab for the money and then the door handle.

Vinny leant across Christopher so he couldn't get out of the car. 'You need to dry them tears before you get home, boy, and when you do get home, you gotta act normal. Me and you will be best pals for life if you keep your trap shut about this, OK?'

'OK,' Christopher said, desperately trying to dry his eyes with the sleeve of his duffle coat.

Vinny tilted the child's chin up, and looked him in the eyes. 'This has to stay our little secret. You don't want anything bad to happen to your mum, dad, or sister, do you? Because if you say something, that's exactly what will happen.'

'No, I love my mum, dad and sister.'

'There's a good boy,' Vinny said, ruffling Christopher's hair.

When Vinny finally opened the car door for him, Christopher took off down the street like a rat up a drainpipe. To say he was terrified was putting it mildly.

Freda Smart knelt down next to the man and immediately knew he was dead. It wasn't just the blood that had seeped out of his stomach and decorated the pavement; it was seeing his shocked open-mouthed expression and his eyes rolled back lifelessly in his head.

After yesterday's events with Kenny Jackson, Freda had made a point of standing guard at her window today. Unfortunately for her, her house was on the same side of the road as the snooker club, so she hadn't had a clear view of exactly what had occurred. Even so, she was sure she'd seen and heard enough to put Vinny Butler in prison for life, where he belonged.

Seeing what she thought was the man's hand flinch, Freda screamed and ran towards Herbie Jacob's house. Freda couldn't afford such luxuries as a telephone, but old Herbie had one.

'Whatever's wrong, Freda? You look like you've just seen a ghost,' Herbie said, when he answered his front door.

'I have! There's a man dead on the pavement. Call the police, Herbie. I know who killed him.'

Word travelled fast in Whitechapel, and within minutes of the police turning up, a crowd of fifty or so onlookers had arrived at the scene.

'Was it you who reported the murder?' one of the police officers asked Herbie.

Freda immediately butted in. 'No. It was me. I know who killed him. I was looking out of my window, and I asked Herbie to ring you on my behalf.'

The police officer took Freda to one side. 'If you can tell us what you know now, that would be most helpful. Then, we will need you to come down to the station to make a formal statement for us at some point.'

'Vinny Butler killed the man. The man had a mate with him and I saw him chase the mate down the road. The mate got into a white car and drove off at top speed,' Freda gabbled.

'But, what about the actual murder? Did you see Mr Butler stab the victim with your own eyes?'

'No. My house is on the same side of the road as his club, so my view was blocked. I saw a boy I know standing opposite though. He saw everything and then Vinny made him get inside his car with him. I hope he ain't killed that poor child as well, like he did Jack's son, Peter,' Freda cried.

'If you could just give us the name of the boy involved, we can get our team onto it to make sure he is OK,' the officer said kindly.

'His parents have just opened the café along the road there. It was their son that saw everything. He'd been sitting in the doorway opposite the club for a while beforehand. His name is Christopher. Christopher Walker.'

CHAPTER NINE

Mary Walker clocked her son's pale complexion as soon as he returned home. 'What's up with you? Not been near that club again, have you?'

Seeing his father look at him with suspicion in his eyes, Christopher bowed his head. 'I don't feel well. I got belly-ache,' he said, rubbing his stomach in the hope that it would make his lie seem more believable.

'Go upstairs and have a lie-down then, boy. Dinner will be ready in about an hour or so,' Mary told him.

Donald grinned as he finished going over the figures, then in a jovial mood, put his favourite record on the jukebox. Since employing Shirley to help them out, his and Mary's takings had gone up even more. Their wonderful café was on its way to making them a bloody fortune, and Donald couldn't believe their luck. Things were going even better than he had predicted.

Hearing a knock at the door, Mary switched the jukebox off at the mains. 'You answer that, Donald, and if it's someone complaining about the music being too loud, best you apologize. I told you not to turn the volume up, didn't I?'

Donald answered the door and was rather taken aback

when he came face to face with a policeman. 'Come in, officer,' he said, guessing that the visit was probably to do with the incident his children had witnessed at the snooker club the previous day.

'Would you like a cup of tea?' Mary asked, politely.

'No, thank you. Is your son, Christopher, at home by any chance?' the officer asked Donald.

'Yes, he is upstairs. I take it this is about yesterday's awful turnout? I hope that poor man is OK. My Christopher thought he was dead, but you know how kids exaggerate,' Donald said, knowingly.

'Actually, it's about the incident that happened today. We have reason to believe that your son was at the scene of the crime and is a key witness to a man's murder.'

Donald shook his head in a pedantic manner. 'No, officer, you have got it all wrong. The incident at the party which my son attended was yesterday, wasn't it, Mary?' he said, looking at his wife for back-up.

'Yes, it was round at the snooker hall yesterday afternoon. My daughter attended the party as well. She is upstairs too, so would you like to speak to both of our children?' Mary asked, feeling anxious. She wasn't that keen on the police involving Nancy and Christopher, but the law was the law.

The officer cleared his throat loudly. 'I'm afraid we have our wires crossed here somewhat. There was a murder not two hours ago outside the snooker club that you referred to, and according to an eye-witness your son saw exactly what happened and then got into the suspect's car. I know nothing about any other incident that may or may not have happened yesterday.'

Donald was livid when he realized his son must have disobeyed his orders. He flung open the door that led to the living quarters. 'Christopher, get down here now,' he yelled.

Feeling rather faint, Mary flopped onto one of the chairs. No wonder the boy had looked so white and near to tears when he'd arrived home.

Christopher was almost paralysed through fear when he came face to face with the police officer.

Donald couldn't help but glare at his son as he sat down next to Mary. Christopher had guilt written all over his deathly-white face.

'Were you sitting in the doorway opposite the snooker club earlier, Christopher?' asked the policeman.

'Yeah I was, but not for long. I went to knock for my mate Tommy, but he wasn't in, so I sat on the step on my way back to eat my sweets.'

'You must tell the truth, boy,' Donald ordered, pointing his finger dangerously close to his son's face.

'A man was murdered outside the snooker club earlier, Christopher, and the police know you were there when it happened. We have a witness who recognized you. Can you tell us exactly what you saw?'

Christopher racked his brain for the best way to get himself out of the mess he was in. If he had been spotted at the scene, he would have to admit to seeing something, but there was no way he was grassing Vinny up. He was way too scared for his own safety and he didn't want anything bad to happen to his mum, dad, or sister. 'I did hear some shouting, then I heard someone running away, but I didn't see what happened because there was a car parked in front of where I was sitting.'

The officer sighed. He was sure little Christopher was lying. 'Did you get into anybody's car?'

'No. My mum and dad have told me never to get in a stranger's car. I walked home on my own.'

'Please don't be frightened to tell me the truth, Christopher. The man who has committed this murder will be locked up for many years to come, so it will not be possible for him to hurt you.'

'I did see a man run away, and I think he was the killer, but I didn't see the murder,' Christopher wept.

Donald squeezed Mary's hand. Everything had been going so well for them since moving to Whitechapel. So why did this drama have to bloody well happen?

The officer stood up. Obviously Vinny Butler had already nobbled the child, and it would take one of his superiors to get the truth out of him. He personally had been ordered to go gently on Christopher, which was why he had been sent to the café alone.

'So, what happens now? Will you need to interview Christopher again?' Donald asked, as he opened the door and followed the policeman outside.

'Yes, he will almost definitely have to come down to the station to give a formal statement. In the meantime, perhaps you could have a little chat with him. I have a feeling that Christopher knows more than he is letting on.'

'Do you mind if I ask who your suspect is?' Donald enquired. He had already guessed that it was something to do with the Butlers, but was interested to know exactly who was involved.

'I'm afraid I can't speculate at the moment, Mr Walker. Us police officers have to abide by our innocent until proven guilty rule, and until somebody is actually charged, it would be very unprofessional of me to give out any names. I will speak to my superior and will be in touch again soon, OK?'

Donald nodded, shut the door and leant against it. Christopher was crying and Mary was cuddling the deceitful child. Unable to stop himself, Donald ran towards his son and clouted him as hard as he could around the ear.

'Stop it, Donald! He's upset enough as it is,' Mary exclaimed.

Grabbing his son roughly by the arm, Donald took his shoe off and swiped it against Christopher's backside. 'How dare you defy my orders and hang around that bloody club? Now, get up those stairs and have a re-think about what you actually saw. As upstanding citizens of the community it is our duty to catch criminals, not harbour them. Also, just think of how beneficial it will be to your own career if you do decide to join the police force and they are aware that you helped catch a murderer at such a young age, eh?'

When Christopher ran upstairs sobbing, Mary put her head in her hands. 'Why did this have to happen to us, Donald? Why?'

Holding his distraught wife in his arms, Donald shook his head sadly. For once, he really did not have an answer.

As usual on a Sunday afternoon, Queenie cooked a roast for all the family.

'Whatever's wrong? Has Kenny kicked the bucket?' she asked worriedly, when Vinny walked in. Just one look at her eldest son's face told her that something terrible had happened.

'Vinny,' Lenny yelled, running out of the lounge and throwing his arms around his big cousin's waist.

Vinny took a ten-bob note out of his pocket and handed it to Lenny. 'I want you and Brenda to go to the shops and buy yourselves some sweets, Champ.'

'What's up?' Roy asked, shutting the lounge door.

'Where's Michael?' Vinny replied, ignoring his brother's question.

'Out on his moped.'

Vinny explained everything that had happened outside the club, then put his head in his hands. He didn't feel any remorse whatsoever over what he had done, but he didn't want his mother thinking she had given birth to a cold-blooded killer. 'I didn't mean to kill the geezer, but it was two against one, Mum. I had to stick up for myself, didn't I? They could have been tooled up or anything for all I knew.'

Both Queenie and Vivian put comforting arms around Vinny's slumped shoulders. 'You did what you had to do, boy. Nothing more, nothing less,' Vivian told him.

'Yep. Vivvy's right. They turned up looking for a row and unfortunately for them, they got one. I know it's sad that you accidently killed the man, but there's no point crying over spilt milk. What's done is done, boy. Now apart from that young lad, was there anybody else about?'

'No. It all happened so quickly, and apart from the kid, the street was desolate. Thank Christ our club is in a quiet sidestreet, eh, Roy?' Vinny said, staring at his brother.

Roy nodded, but said nothing. Vinny had always been a volatile bastard with a foul temper even when they were kids. Just lately though, Roy could sense his brother's unpredictability and violent nature getting worse, which worried him greatly. In the past couple of weeks alone, he had put their own father in hospital, smashed the living daylights out of Kenny Jackson, and now he had stabbed some poor sod to death.

Guessing what Roy was thinking, Vinny glared at him. 'Say something then, if it's only bollocks. What was I meant to do, eh? Stand there like a lemon and let them do me over? You weren't there to back me up, was ya?'

Queenie butted in before Roy could retaliate. 'Arguing between us isn't gonna solve this, is it? What we need is a watertight alibi in case the police start sniffing round. You were here with me, Vivian, Roy and the kids, OK, Vinny? I'll word Brenda and Lenny up and worst ways, you give me fifty quid and I'll give it to Old Ivy next door to say she saw you arrive early as well.'

'Thanks, Mum,' Vinny said, his voice full of relief. Old Ivy had given him an alibi once or twice in the past in exchange for cash, and Vinny knew she could be trusted.

'Well, that's that then. You both got here at one o'clock. Now, all you've got to hope is that child keeps his mouth shut, Vinny. Did you threaten him to do so?'

Vinny nodded his head. He liked children and felt more guilty about threatening Christopher Walker than committing the murder.

'What exactly did you say to him?' Vivian asked.

'Not much. I just made sure he knew that if he opened his trap something bad would happen to his family. I gave him a tenner an' all.'

Queenie squeezed her son's hand. 'Do you want me and Vivian to have a word with him as well? We can catch him on his way to or from school.'

'No, leave it for now, Mum. The boy looked petrified enough, so let's just see what happens, eh? It will only be my word against his if he says anything. Johnny Preston definitely ain't gonna grass me, so I think it's best we just ride the storm. I mean if you, Viv, Roy, Ivy and the kids all swear blind I was here, what can the Old Bill do?'

When the doorbell rang, Vivian sprang up and spied through the net curtain. 'It's the police.'

Queenie shoved Roy out the back door. 'You need to clue Brenda and Lenny up. Go find 'em, quick.'

When Roy bolted out the back, Queenie took a deep breath and wiped her clammy hands on her apron. She then opened the front door and smiled. 'Good afternoon, officers. What can I do for you?'

'Oh my God! I hope that isn't the police again,' Mary exclaimed, when she heard a pummelling against the front door of the café.

'You stay here. I'll sort it,' Donald insisted, running down the stairs.

'Hello, I'm Detective Inspector Stevens. I understand one of my colleagues popped in to see you earlier?'

'Yes, that is correct. Would you like to come in?' Donald asked, apprehensively.

'No. I would actually like you and your son to come along to the police station with me. We have organized an identification parade, and it would be most helpful if your son could pick out the man he saw arguing with the victim.'

'I'm very sorry, but Christopher is only eight years old and I think it is wholly inappropriate that he be involved in something as nerve-racking as an identification parade. I have just had a very long chat with Christopher myself and I can assure you that he has told you everything he knows. My son has been brought up with morals and he would never lie about something as serious as this.'

DI Stevens nodded understandingly. 'I do see what you mean, but this identification parade will not take very long and I can assure you our suspects will not see or even know that your son is there, sir.'

Donald sighed. He had always classed himself as a pillar of the community, so how could he say no? 'Wait there while I speak to Christopher.'

Vinny Butler followed the seven other men into the empty room. He hadn't been arrested, his alibi was watertight, and when the police had asked him to participate in an identification parade, he had readily agreed. He had to act as though he was innocent, and it would be a sign of guilt if he refused.

Wondering who was behind the blacked-out window, Vinny felt his heart rate quadruple. Asking himself if there had been another witness he hadn't spotted, Vinny made a mental note to dispose of the knife and the clothes he had been wearing the following morning. After dropping off Christopher earlier, he had hidden them as best as he could, but the clothes needed burning as they were splashed with blood, and the knife needed to be got rid of properly. Roy would have to sort both out for him, in case he himself was being watched.

Vinny glanced at the other men in the line-up. They were all roughly his age, but none was as good-looking or oozed class like he did. When the officer barked orders for all eight men to stand up straight and stare at the blackened window, Vinny, being Vinny, stood tall and more confidently than any other.

Christopher chewed his lip nervously when he was told to study the men one by one. His dad was sitting in the room with him, which was making him feel even more anxious. 'Nope, it's definitely none of them who I saw,' he mumbled, after a couple of minutes.

'Take your time, Christopher. We have reason to believe that the perpetrator of this terrible crime is amongst these men. You sit here and have a long hard look, while I have a little chat with your dad outside.'

Donald followed the officer out of the room.

'My colleague said something about your children attending a party at a snooker club yesterday that is owned by Vinny and Roy Butler. Are you two families friends?'

'Oh, dear God, no! We have only moved into the area recently and my wife and I have barely spoken to the Butler family. My daughter has just started a new school and is in the same class as young Brenda. That is the only reason why she and Christopher got invited to the party.'

'And what was this incident your son was involved in yesterday? My colleague mentioned that somebody was attacked at the party?' DI Stevens asked. He was well aware of Kenny Jackson being admitted to the London Hospital, but his wife had insisted he had fallen over drunk, which both she and he knew was a big fat lie.

'No, as far as I'm aware nobody was attacked, officer. My children ran home scared because they saw a man lying on the floor bleeding nearby the building as they left,' Donald lied. His Christopher was in too deep as it was, and he wasn't in the right frame of mind for even more questioning.

'Does your son know Vinny Butler well, Mr Walker?'

'No, of course he doesn't,' Donald spat.

Furious that he was getting nowhere fast, D.I. Stevens strode back into the room and left Donald standing outside. Whitechapel was becoming a hotbed for gangland families and murders these days and it was his duty to stamp out such scum.

'Have you recognized anybody now, Christopher?' he asked, with a hint of sarcasm creeping into his voice.

'No, sir. It was none of those men that I saw near the club.'

'Take a look again at number one, Christopher. Are you damn sure it wasn't him?'

Number one was Vinny and when Christopher stared at him again, it felt as though Vinny was staring straight back at him. Thinking what scary eyes Vinny had, Christopher remembered the threat to harm his parents and sister and frantically shook his head. 'It definitely wasn't him, sir. If anything, the man I saw looked more like number four.'

CHAPTER TEN

As Christmas beckoned, not for the first time in his life, Vinny truly believed he had got away with murder.

'Morning, Vin. Mental last night, weren't it? I bet you wish we weren't shutting tonight now, don't you?' Roy said, putting two mugs of tea on the coffee table. The boys had properly moved into the club earlier this week, and now the upstairs had been re-decorated, it looked much more homely than before.

Vinny shook his head. Friday was usually their busiest night of the week, but it had been his decision to close the club because it was Christmas Eve. 'Nope. I ain't got no regrets. We could do with a break ourselves. I'm meeting Geary at lunchtime. How much do you think I should bung him on top of what we pay for this place?' Vinny asked his brother.

George Geary had been keeping them up to date with developments on the murder of Dave Phillips. Obviously, Vinny hadn't admitted anything, but it was very comforting to know that the only witness who had come forward was Mad Freda. It was also through Geary that Vinny knew that it had been Christopher Walker behind the blacked-out window at the identification parade, and Vinny had thought it fucking hilarious that the kid had picked out bloke number four rather than him. Vinny had sensibly kept well away from the café, and hadn't seen Christopher since.

'Wait and see what info Geary has got for us. If he tells you Jack shit again, just give him fifty on top as a Christmas drink. If he has found out where the Prestons are though, you'd better give one an' half at least,' Roy advised.

Vinny nodded. It had been just over a week since Roy had paid Judy Preston a visit to check if she'd had the abortion. There had been no answer, then a neighbour had come out to inform him that Judy had moved out ten days earlier. Vinny had been absolutely furious and, unable to get involved himself just in case Geary had got it wrong and he was being followed, he had sent Michael to visit his arsehole of a father in hospital just to find out where Judy's mother lived. He had then sent Roy round there only to find out that Mummy had done a runner too. So, Vinny had asked Geary if he could find out their where- abouts. He had also heard through the grapevine from a couple of his South London punters that Johnny Preston had disappeared off the face of the bloody earth, so Vinny wanted Geary to check out that story as well. Seeing as Johnny had run and left his best pal to die in a pool of blood like the coward he was, Vinny was sure that he wouldn't go mouthing off about the murder. Geary hadn't yet put two and two together, Vinny was sure of that. If he had, the chief inspector would have been on his case for more money like he usually was when he had something on him, and even if he did see the light, Vinny had his answer ready for him.

Roy jumped as the doorbell rang. 'Who the fuck's that this time of the morning?'

'It might be Mum, so answer it, Roy.'

Roy did the honours, then ran back up the stairs. 'It's

that Karen bird that used to work here. She wants to see you and says it's urgent.'

Vinny sighed. Karen was the stripper he had slept with a couple of times. She had become a bit obsessed with him after their last night of passion, and had spouted her mouth off to all the other strippers, so Vinny had promptly sacked her. 'Tell her I ain't here,' Vinny ordered his brother.

'I've already told her you are here. I ain't going back down there, Vin. You shagged her, so she's your problem,' Roy chuckled.

With only a towel around his waist to cover his nakedness, Vinny ran down the stairs and flung open the big metal door. 'If you've come to ask for your job back, the answer is no. I told you what would happen if you started blabbing about what had happened between us, didn't I?'

Ignoring the callous tone in Vinny's voice, Karen brushed past him and stepped inside the club.

'What do you think you're fucking doing?' Vinny spat.

Karen looked Vinny in the eyes and smirked. 'I'm having a chat with the father of my unborn baby.'

'You what?'

'You heard. I'm pregnant, and it's yours. Congratulations, Vinny.'

Absolutely starving after driving up to Carnaby Street and back, Michael and Kevin bumped their mopeds onto the pavement and parked them outside Mary and Donald's café.

'Wow, this looks well ace compared to when Old Jack had it. You never told me they had a jukebox,' Kevin said, highly impressed.

'I ain't been in here since it re-opened, but my mum has and she said the food's really nice,' Michael informed his pal.

Unaware that Michael was a Butler, Mary took his and

107

Kevin's order. 'Two cheeseburgers and chips, love,' she said to Donald.

'How are the kids? Have you checked on them again?' Donald asked, putting the burgers into the frying pan.

'Nancy's OK, still absorbed in her Enid Blyton book, but Christopher is in bed, Donald. He didn't eat any lunch again either, and he's started to worry the bloody life out of me.'

Donald turned away from the cooker and hugged his wife to his chest. Ever since the two incidents involving the Butler family, both of their children had changed dramatically. Nancy was still friendly with Brenda at school, but even though she seemed happy enough in herself, all she ever seemed to want to do these days was lose herself in books.

Christopher, on the other hand, was not happy in himself. He had lost a hell of a lot of weight in the past couple of weeks, looked pale, was extremely withdrawn, and it was an effort to get him to school in the mornings. Christopher had always been an adventurous boy who loved the outdoors, but not any more. Whatever he had seen outside that club, and the interrogation by the police afterwards, had obviously knocked the stuffing out of the poor child.

'I think perhaps in the new year we should consider selling this café and moving to a different area, Mary. It's too dangerous around here to bring up our children. There are far too many unsavoury characters.'

Mary looked at her husband in horror. Their business was barely a month old, but it was booming, and she had settled well in East London. 'Don't be daft, Donald. I'll speak to Christopher, he'll be fine. As for Nancy, I'm glad she's got into her books rather than raking the streets. You wait until tomorrow when they open all their nice presents.

We have never been able to afford to give them much before, have we? Once Santa has been, they'll perk up no end. You mark my words.'

Not sharing his wife's optimism, Donald turned around to flip his burgers.

Because of recent events, George Geary didn't want to pick up his monthly bung from the club any longer. He was too frightened of being spotted there, so insisted that Vinny meet him at the entrance of a park a few miles away.

Vinny sat in the chief inspector's car and listened to what he had to say, while nodding politely. Geary had a habit of trying to dress things up to make it look like he had found out lots more information than he had, so he could suck more money out of his victim. 'So, what you're trying to say, George, is you have no idea where any of the Prestons are? Including Johnny, right?'

'Well yes, but that doesn't mean that I haven't got a few leads on the go,' Geary said, licking his lips in anticipation of what sort of Christmas bonus he might be getting.

'And what about that poor bloke who was murdered? Does your mob still think I had something to do with it? Just because it happened near my club?'

'Well, I would be lying if I said they didn't still see you as a suspect, Vinny, but to be honest they are concentrating more at the moment on finding the bloke who was with Dave Phillips at the time of the attack.'

'Perhaps yous boys in blue have been barking up the wrong tree all along then, George? Don't you think it's strange that whoever was with the deceased did a runner? Perhaps that's your murderer?' Vinny suggested, handing over a wad of notes.

When Geary began counting the money, Vinny smirked. 'There's a fifty on top of your usual as a Christmas drink,

George. You find out where those Prestons are for me and there'll be an even bigger drink in it for you.'

George Geary was not amused. He had put his neck on the line sniffing around for snippets of information to throw Vinny's way, yet all he was being given for his trouble was a measly fifty quid. He wasn't stupid. He had spoken to a few of his colleagues over in South London.

When Vinny tried to shake his hand, George snatched it away. 'Don't take me for a fool, Butler. Fifty sovs! Is that it? Do you not think I know that Dave Phillips and Johnny Preston were partners in crime, eh? What do you take me for?'

Vinny chuckled. 'A bent chief inspector.'

'Don't fuck with me, Vinny, because I can have you banged-up for murder at the drop of a hat,' George said, pointing a fat finger in Vinny's face.

Realizing that his joke had been a bad one, Vinny apologized immediately. He also dug his hand back into his pocket and handed Geary another hundred pounds. 'Look, I don't want to fall out with you, George, but I swear I know nothing about the murder of Dave Phillips, OK?'

'So, why do you want me to find Johnny Preston then?'

Vinny sighed, put on the most innocent expression he could muster, and stared George Geary straight in the eyes. 'Because my father has impregnated Preston's sister, Judy, and she has done a fucking runner. Would you not want to know where your future brother or sister would be living?'

Geary put the hundred pounds in his pocket, then held his right hand out to Vinny. 'I'm sorry, boy. I'll do my best to find them for you, OK? I'd best go now before my wife wonders where I've got to. Merry Christmas.'

Vinny got out of the chief inspector's car and walked back to his own. Karen's bombshell earlier had left him in

110

a bit of a daze, and he really didn't know if he was coming or bloody going.

Thrilled that the jukebox had some songs on it by their favourite band, the Who, Michael and Kevin put on 'I Can't Explain', 'Anyway, Anyhow, Anywhere', and 'My Generation'.

'Excuse me. Do you think you can turn it up a bit?' Michael asked Mary.

'I'll turn it up a touch, but I can't have it too loud because it's not fair on the other customers,' Mary replied, walking over to the jukebox.

'Bleedin' racket is giving me a headache. Don't be turning it up no louder just because the murderer's brother has asked you to,' Mad Freda shouted out.

'Who you calling a murderer? Michael's brothers are good lads,' Kevin said, sticking up for his best pal.

'Who rattled your cage? You little black bastard,' Freda spat back.

Michael grabbed Kevin by the sleeve of his parka. 'Come on, mate, let's go. Everyone knows that Freda is off her head, so there's no point arguing with a bigoted nutjob. It's like talking to a brick wall.'

Albie Butler was not in the best of moods. The doctors had told him he could be discharged before Christmas if he had somebody who could care for him until the plaster was taken off his legs. Trouble was, he couldn't find anyone who could do so. Even his own brother had refused his pleas for help. Bert had made the excuse that his wife was ill.

Knowing that Queenie was his last chance of getting out of the hellhole of a hospital before Christmas, Albie decided to swallow his pride and call her.

'What do you fucking want?' Queenie hissed down the receiver.

'I need a favour, love. The doctors said I can leave hospital if I've got somewhere to stay and a bit of help. Now, I know it's over between us, but it won't be for long, Queenie. As soon as I'm up and about again, I'll find meself a little bedsit or something. Please help me, even if it's only for old time's sake?'

Furious by the cheek of the untrustworthy waste of space, Queenie gave her deceitful husband what for. 'For all I care you can go and sleep under the arches with the rest of the fucking tramps. I will never allow you to darken my doorstep again, you dirty old toad. You're dead as far as me and my sons are concerned. Even little Brenda don't ask about you no more. I hope you rot in that hospital, and I pray you get bedbugs and sores as well. I'm hanging up now. Happy Christmas, you old cuntbag.'

When the line went dead and the nurse wheeled the phone away, Albie couldn't stop the tears running down his cheeks. He didn't want to spend his Christmas in bloody hospital. Now his family had disowned him, he had no visitors at all, and couldn't even get somebody to sneak him in a bottle of brandy.

Old Mr Perry opened one eye. He had been pretending to be asleep, but he had heard Albie ask Queenie if he could move back in with her. It was now time for one of his little singsongs. 'Daisy, Daisy, give me your answer, do. I'm half crazy all for the love of you.'

Unable to take any more of Mr Perry, or life in general, Albie put his hands together and said a little prayer. 'Just let me croak it, God. Please, just let me fucking die, so I can get some bastard peace.'

Absolutely seething over what they'd just heard, Queenie and Vivian marched into the café like two bulls in a china shop.

'See you, you fucking old cow. I have just about had enough of you slandering my family. Who do you think you are, eh? My boys are good boys. And how dare you call Kevin a black bastard, you bigoted old hag,' Queenie yelled, her face dangerously close to Freda's.

Pushing her dinner plate away, Freda stood up. She was a stout woman with more than a bit of meat on her, whereas Queenie and Vivian were skinny as rakes. 'I ain't frightened of you, you pair of old dragons. Ruined my beloved Whitechapel, you and that scum you raised have.'

When Queenie and Vivian both lunged at Freda, Mary screamed in fright.

'What the hell is going on?' Donald asked, running out of the kitchen with a tea towel in his hand.

'Oh my God, Donald. Do something,' Mary shrieked hysterically, when a cup and saucer got smashed in the fracas.

Sturdy or not, Freda was no match for Queenie and Vivian, and was already lying on the floor with her legs open, showing her bloomers.

Being Christmas Eve afternoon, the café was empty now, so Donald had no alternative other than to break up the three brawling women himself.

Nancy and Christopher had both heard the commotion and, petrified, they ran down the stairs. 'What's happening, Mummy?' Nancy screamed, when she saw Vivian hit her father with her umbrella.

'Get out,' Donald shouted, as he grabbed Vivian's wrists to stop her from hitting him again.

Thinking that his father might get stabbed and die like the man outside the snooker club, Christopher put his hands over his eyes. 'Leave my dad alone,' he screamed.

When Freda suddenly leapt up and grabbed Queenie around the throat, Mary was rather relieved to see Vinny

Butler barge through the café door. 'Mum, Auntie Viv, get in the car now,' he barked.

'And don't bloody well come back. You are officially barred from my premises,' Donald spat, as the two women stopped fighting and dusted themselves down.

'Watch it, mate. That's my mother and aunt you are talking to,' Vinny hissed. He had been stuck in traffic outside and had only glanced inside the café to see if he could see little Christopher, when he had spotted his aunt attacking Donald with her umbrella.

'Come on, Queenie. The food was shit in here anyway,' Vivian said, grabbing her sister by the arm.

'Yep. You're right. That last sandwich we had in here was fucking rotten,' Queenie lied.

Seeing Christopher standing behind the counter with his mother and sister, Vinny took a twenty-pound note out of his pocket, screwed it up, and chucked it on the floor at Donald's feet. 'That's to pay for any damage and whatever's left, give it to your kids as a Christmas present,' he said, generously.

'Silence money, that is. I know that Christopher witnessed you murder that man, 'cause I bloody saw him standing there,' Freda yelled.

Absolutely terrified of Vinny, and unable to cope with the lie he had told, Christopher burst into tears and ran up the stairs.

'Get out, all of you. Get out now,' Donald bellowed.

Heads held high, Queenie and Vivian strutted out of the door as proud as peacocks.

'And I don't want your dirty money,' Donald said, picking up the twenty-pound note and chucking it back at Vinny.

Vinny did not like Donald one little bit. In his eyes he was nothing more than a jumped-up pompous prick. If it hadn't been for the fact that Christopher had lied on his behalf, Vinny would have upped him there and then. 'The money's yours, if you don't want it, give it to your kids,' he ordered.

'Am I barred too?' Freda asked Donald.

'Yes. Get out,' Donald yelled.

Terrified that Donald and Vinny were now going to start fighting, Mary took Nancy upstairs. 'I don't like it here, Mummy. Can we please move back to Stoke Newington?' the girl sobbed.

Realizing that they now had no spectators, Vinny gave Donald his special stare. 'I'd watch your back if I was you, mate. No-one speaks to my mother and aunt like shit and gets away with it, and I mean fucking no-one.'

When Vinny walked out and slammed the door, Donald quickly locked it, then crouched down with his head in his hands. They had only been in Whitechapel for a short while and already their lives were in ruins. There was no way back after today's events. Whether Mary liked it or not, Donald was determined to put his foot down now. The quicker he got his family away from this godforsaken area, the better.

CHAPTER ELEVEN

Queenie Butler absolutely loved Christmas. The festive season was all about family, and there was nothing she enjoyed more than having all her brood around her. She opened the oven door to check on the sausage rolls and mince pies. Most women that she knew did the bulk of their cooking on Christmas Eve, so all they had to concentrate on the following day was cooking their vegetables. Not Queenie though. She had been up since six pottering about in the kitchen as she wanted everything to be nice and fresh. Only the best for her family.

Queenie grinned as Vivian let herself in and Lenny bounded up to her. 'Has Santa been yet, Auntie Queenie? Mummy said he was delivering my presents to your house this year because he knew I would be here.'

'Yes, Santa's been, but he told me to tell you that you're not allowed to open your presents until Vinny and Roy arrive,' Queenie said, giving her wonderful nephew a loving hug.

'Vinny not here yet? I hope he still ain't got the hump with us,' Vivian said, referring to the altercation in the café the previous day.

Vinny had been none too pleased when he had driven

116

his mum and aunt home. 'Why did you have to go in there of all places and kick off? You know their little boy lied for me in the identification parade. Think before you act in future, for Christ's sake,' Vinny had bellowed.

Queenie sent Lenny upstairs to tell Brenda and Michael to get their skates on, then turned to her sister. 'Vinny'll be fine, Viv. Loves the bones of me and you, you know he does. I'm sure he had something else on his mind yesterday and that's why he went on the turn. Them people in the café won't kick up no fuss. Didn't you see the petrified look on that Donald's face when you started whacking him with your brolly?'

Vivian couldn't control the fit of giggles that followed. 'And what about when you punched him in the side of the head? That overbearing wife of his started squealing like a pig.'

Laughing hysterically, Queenie held her crotch with one hand to prevent herself wetting her knickers, clinging onto her sister's arm with the other. 'What are we like, eh Viv?'

'Salts of the earth, Queenie. Salts of the earth, girl,' Vivian roared.

Less than a mile down the road, the festive spirit in the Walker household was anything but jovial.

'Well?' Donald asked, when Christopher pulled the wrapping paper off the plastic policeman's helmet.

Unable to stop himself, Christopher burst into uncontrollable tears. How could he ever wear that hat and join the police force now after he had told such an awful lie?

'Whatever's the matter, love?' Mary asked, holding her sobbing son in her arms.

Christopher could hide the truth no longer. 'I lied to the police. Vinny did kill that man. I saw him do it.'

Outraged by his son's confession, Donald let out a few

expletives, then clouted the boy around his ear. 'How could you lie to the police, Christopher? Your mother and I brought you up to be honest. Disgusted with you, I am. Bloody appalled!'

When Nancy began to cry as well, Mary ordered her husband to calm himself. 'Hitting Christopher is not the answer here, Donald. You need to take him down to the police station to sort this mess out once and for all.'

'Why did you lie to us all, boy? Why?' Donald bellowed, his face red with temper.

'Vinny threatened to hurt you, Mum and Nancy if I told the truth. Please don't tell the police, Dad. Vinny scares me so much,' Christopher begged.

Donald paced up and down the room in a total frenzy.

'It's OK. It's not your fault,' Mary soothed, putting a comforting arm around her son.

'Please can we go back to Stoke Newington, Mum? Me and Christopher hate living here,' Nancy pleaded.

'Let's see what happens after your dad has spoken to the police, love,' Mary croaked, in a voice that sounded nothing like her own.

Donald turned to his wife. 'I am not going to the police. Our lives will be hell if Christopher now admits to what he saw. He will be tarnished as a liar for the rest of his life, and we will forever be looking over our shoulders for repercussions from the Butler family.'

'Well, what do you suggest we do then, Donald? A man has died. We can't just let his killer roam the streets,' Mary pointed out.

'Oh, yes we can. We have to for our own safety. I will not have my children's lives put in danger, Mary. We must pack up our belongings and leave this café immediately. We can then put the property on the market, and start afresh in a much nicer area.'

'But we can't just do a moonlight flit, Donald. I love this café. You know I do.'

'And I love my children and you, Mary, which is why we have to leave.'

'I'm so sorry I lied to you, Dad,' Christopher cried. He felt so guilty. Everything was his fault.

Donald crouched down and stared his son in the eyes. 'You did what you thought was right to protect your family, son, and I'm sorry that I hit you. What you told us today, I want you to now forget about. Can you do that for me?'

Relieved that he wasn't about to be carted off to the police station, Christopher managed a weak smile. 'Yes, Dad.'

Donald stood up. 'And that goes for all of us. What Christopher admitted to today, I never want to hear mentioned again. Do we all agree on that?'

When her mother nodded her head, Nancy did the same.

'Right, that's settled then. Now, let's start packing. The quicker we get out of this hellhole, the better.'

Donald fitted as many of his family's belongings into the boot of the car as he could, then darted back into the café. Being Christmas Day, the street was empty, and that had pleased him immensely.

'Where are we going to live then, Dad?' Christopher asked chirpily. The thought of never having to see Vinny Butler again was already a weight off his young shoulders.

'We are going to stay with your Auntie Phyllis in Ilford for a couple of days, and once the Christmas period is over, I will find us a place of our own to live.'

When Donald ordered the children to get in the car, Mary looked at her husband in despair.

'I know you're upset, my darling, but we will open another café one day, I promise you that,' Donald said, sadly.

Unable to stop herself, Mary turned around to take one last look at her broken dream. She then burst into a sea of tears.

Vivian wiped the last of the dishes with the tea towel, then patted her bloated stomach. 'Bleedin' handsome that turkey, weren't it? Melted in me mouth, it did. You cooked that to a tee.'

Ignoring the compliment, Queenie whispered in her sister's ear. 'Something is wrong with my Vinny today. He ain't himself, you know, and he left all his Christmas pudding. He always eats his pudding, Vivvy.'

'Perhaps he was full up, Queenie. It was a big dinner you cooked. Vinny seems all right to me. He's been laughing and joking with the kids all day,' Vivian whispered back.

Queenie shook her head. Nobody knew her Vinny like she did and something was troubling him. 'Come on, let's go and put some music on in the lounge.'

The sing-a-long was still going strong two hours later. Michael had bought his mum a Gracie Fields album for Christmas and Queenie and Vivian were even doing the hand movements as they sang 'Wish Me Luck As You Wave Me Goodbye' for the fourth time at the top of their voices.

'Can we please have some rock and roll on now, Mum?' Lenny asked impatiently, tugging on Vivian's arm.

'No. I want to play the Beatles,' Brenda whinged.

'Let Lenny put his rock and roll on first, Bren, then you can put your Beatles on straight after,' Queenie ordered.

When the sound of Buddy Holly filled the lounge, Queenie proudly studied her boys. All three were incredibly handsome and looked so smart today. Vinny and Roy were always suited and booted, but even Michael was dressed up in his blue tonic suit and as he discussed a bit of business regarding the club with Roy, Queenie thought how grown-up he suddenly seemed.

Aware that Vinny wasn't really listening to his brothers' conversation, Queenie watched him light up his cigar. He looked like he had the weight of the world on his shoulders as he took his first puff and she wondered if it was to do with the man he had accidently stabbed to death.

Even though as a mother Queenie knew you should love all your children equally, she had always had a special bond with her Vinny. He was her first-born, so surely the way she felt about him was understandable?

'You OK, Mum?' Vinny asked, clocking his mother staring at him.

Queenie jumped out of the armchair and gestured to her eldest.

Vinny followed his mum upstairs and sat awkwardly on the edge of her bed. 'You're not missing Dad, are you?' he asked her.

'You having a bleedin' laugh, or what? Best Christmas I've ever had without that drunken old drop-out sitting in the chair scratching his cobblers.'

Vinny chuckled.

'What's up, boy? You ain't yourself today. Are you still annoyed with me and Vivvy for kicking up a stink in that café?'

'Don't be daft. I could never have the hump with you and Auntie Viv for long.'

'Well, what is it then? Is it that man who died? You can't blame yourself for that, Vinny. It was two against one, and you never meant to kill him. It was an accident, son.'

Vinny took a deep breath. He had to tell somebody his little secret, and there was nobody in the world better to confide in than his beloved mother. 'I've got a girl pregnant, and she wants to keep the baby,' he blurted out.

Queenie was momentarily stunned. Since that little slag Yvonne Summers had broken Vinny's heart many years ago, she had never even known him to court again. 'Who is she, boy? Why didn't you tell me you had a girlfriend?'

Vinny put his head in his hands and propped his elbows on his knees. 'She ain't my girlfriend, Mum. She is a pretty girl who works at the club who I've had a couple of flings with.'

'Well, why didn't you put a thingy on the end of it?' Queenie asked, accusingly.

'I did, well, apart from the once. What am I gonna do, Mum? I've offered her big bucks to get rid of the kid, but she knocked the dosh back.'

Unable to stop herself, Queenie slapped her pride and joy around the face to bring him to his senses. 'You will not kill my grandchild, Vinny. I will not allow that to happen.'

'But, I don't even like the girl, Mum. I ain't getting lumbered with her for the rest of my life.'

'Who is she? Is she a decent girl?

Feeling more embarrassed than ever before, Vinny shook his head. 'No, she's a stripper.'

Instead of scolding him for being stupid as her son expected her to, Queenie squeezed both of his hands and looked him in the eyes. 'Buy the child off her, boy. Offer her what she wants to give birth to it, then I'll bring it up for you.'

Vinny was astounded by his mother's strange suggestion. 'I can't do that, Mum. I'm only twenty and I don't want no ties.'

'It won't be your tie, it'll be mine. You listen to me, Vinny, and you listen good and proper. You need something in your life to calm that temper of yours down. Being a father will save you from going to prison, I guarantee that.

God works in mysterious ways, and this will prove to be your saviour, I just know it will. Look how good you are with kids. Lenny worships the ground you walk on, so imagine having a little Champ running around who is actually your own. You can't murder your own child, boy. That baby will be my first grandchild and I would never forgive you if you took that away from me.'

Not wanting to admit to his mum that he had thought about bumping off Karen and the baby by drowning them in the Thames, Vinny suddenly felt a surge of guilt and had tears in his eyes.

'Don't get upset, boy. Everything will be all right, your mum will make sure of that,' Queenie said, cradling him to her chest.

Vinny quickly pulled himself together. His mother was never wrong. Whatever advice she had ever given him in the past had always been proven as sound, so why should he doubt her wisdom this time round?

'Well? What you gonna do?' Queenie asked.

Vinny smiled at her. 'I will sort out a deal with Karen and then we will bring up my baby together, Mum.'

CHAPTER TWELVE

Summer 1971

Nancy Walker felt a surge of excitement as she took in the electric atmosphere of the funfair. The waft of fried onions hung heavily in the air, music was being played at full blast, and the sound of laughter was prominent wherever you walked. Nancy's dad had never allowed her go to the fair with just a friend before. He said the rides were run by gypsies and they preyed on innocent young girls like herself. It had been her mum who had come up trumps for her in the end. She had argued that now Nancy was sixteen and in full-time employment, she was old enough to make her own decisions.

'I just love the smell of fairgrounds, don't you?' Nancy said to her best friend, Rhonda Gibbs. Nancy had met Rhonda soon after her family had moved to Ilford from Whitechapel. They had been in the same class at school, and were rarely seen out and about without one another now. They even had jobs working side by side in their local Woolworth's store.

'Yep. I love the smell too. Shall we get some candyfloss? Or a toffee apple?' Rhonda suggested.

Nancy giggled. 'We have come over here to see if we can

find the men of our dreams, Rhon. Candyfloss and toffee apples are hardly man magnets. If we are munching on them, we are gonna look like kids.'

'But you've already found the man of your dreams. You've got Roger,' Rhonda joked.

Nancy punched her pal playfully on the arm. Roger Robins was the son of her parents' friends, Margaret and Derrick. At twenty-one, Roger worked for a branch of Barclays Bank in London. On numerous occasions, he had invited Nancy to go dancing or to the pictures, but much to her parents' dismay, Nancy had politely declined.

With her size-eight figure, ample breasts, and long blonde hair, Nancy wanted a bit more out of life than boring Roger. The pop star Marc Bolan was Nancy's perfect vision of a man. Marc was wild, cool and handsome, everything that Roger wasn't. Nancy liked excitement and she would rather entertain a bad boy any day of the week than date some complete and utter bore.

'Wow! He's nice,' Rhonda exclaimed.

'Which one?'

'He's got shoulder-length dark hair and is standing by the coconut shy with a group of lads.'

Nancy surreptitiously glanced around. 'All of them have shoulder-length dark hair. What's he wearing?'

'A cream flowery-patterned shirt and brown flared trousers.'

Fashion had changed immensely since the sixties when drainpipe trousers and button-collared shirts had been all the rage for young men. The Mod era had also now come to an end and the hippy look had taken over as the new trend. Spotting the guy who Rhonda had referred to, Nancy screwed her face up. 'Nah. His nose is too big for his face, Rhon. You know I have a thing about little button noses.'

Hearing the current song by Middle of the Road being

blasted out of the speakers on a nearby ride, both girls linked arms. Giggling, because they were aware that the group of boys were now watching them, Nancy and Rhonda began wiggling their hips and singing the words to 'Chirpy Chirpy Cheep Cheep'.

Vinny and Queenie Butler smiled proudly at one another as Little Vinny put on his boxing gloves and started to spar with his Uncle Roy. Roy was kneeling on the carpet and when his nephew caught him on the chin, Roy fell backwards to pretend he had been knocked out cold.

'He's a real natural, ain't he, Mum? I knew he would be,' Vinny gushed.

'He's a little bruiser. A proper Butler boy, just like his daddy was at his age,' Queenie chuckled.

Buying his son off Karen had been one of the best decisions that Vinny had ever made. It had cost him three grand, but had been worth every penny. Being a stripper, Karen wouldn't exactly have been his first choice of woman to bear his child, but she was a stunning bird, and with his own dark smouldering looks, his son was always destined to be a handsome kid.

Karen hadn't wanted to part with her baby at first. She'd had delusions of Vinny marrying her and the three of them becoming one big happy family. It took the wad of cash, plus a few threats, to finally make Karen see sense and flee the area. Vinny had never heard from her since and had no wish to. His son had all the family he needed. He had told Little Vinny that his mother was dead, and if Karen ever caused him any trouble, he knew he could quite easily turn his little white lie into the truth.

'Answer the door then, Nan,' Little Vinny ordered, pummelling his nan on the arm with his boxing gloves to get her to move off the sofa.

'Don't hit your nan. You must never punch girls or women with them gloves, boy,' Roy said sharply.

'Chill out, bruv,' Vinny ordered, glaring at Roy as his mum stood up.

'I am chilled out and stop getting on my case all the time. Ever since you've been knocking about with the poxy Turk, all you seem to do is give it the large,' Roy said, referring to Vinny's pal, Ahmed. Truth be known, Roy was a bit miffed about his brother's close friendship with the man. Once upon a time, it had been just the two of them. Back then it was him who Vinny had been as thick as thieves with, not some bloody foreigner.

Vinny had always vowed when they were younger that they would never let an outsider into their lives. He reckoned that you could only really trust family, yet over the past ten months or so, Ahmed was hanging around with Vinny more and more. This worried Roy greatly, as he'd heard through the rumour mill that Ahmed was a drug kingpin. He'd even once asked Vinny if the word on the street was true, but his brother had just laughed in his face. He had sworn to him that Ahmed was a legal businessman, but Roy still wasn't sure if he believed Vinny. Ahmed was a wrong 'un, Roy could see it in his cold dark eyes.

Threatening her boys if they argued any more they would have her to deal with, Queenie ran into the hallway to hand over her football bets to the Pools man. She was then relieved for once to see her sons and grandson making a move. It was Little Vinny's fifth birthday tomorrow, and seeing as it had been her idea to throw him his very first proper party, she intended to make it as special as possible. 'That's it, get out of my way so I can crack on,' Queenie said, kissing both her sons, then cuddling her grandson.

'Well, I'll keep little 'un all day and bring him back about seven before I open the club,' Vinny informed her.

'Where you taking him?' Queenie asked.

'The fair at Barking Park.'

Mary Walker served old Mr Sams his two weekly packs of Old Holborn, then ordered Donald to take over at the till while she stocked the shelves. Mary sometimes still dreamt about her fabulous café with its smart red and white décor and fashionable jukebox, but she had learned to deal with what had happened.

Doing a Christmas Day flit to Ilford had proved to be a good move. Donald and Mary's café in Whitechapel had sold for more than they had expected, which had enabled them to buy a newsagent's instead. Their shop was situated on the corner of a road near Ilford town centre, and over the years they had made it into far more than just a newsagent's. It was more like a general store now which sold virtually everything. From toilet paper to ham, from greetings cards to daily delivered bread and cakes, there wasn't much Mary and Donald didn't sell and they were very proud of the service they provided to the public.

'Hi, Mum. Do you need me to help with that? Have you and Dad been busy today?' Christopher asked, as he walked into the shop.

Mary smiled. Christopher looked so smart in his Boy Scout uniform, and he was such a sensible lad. He had turned fourteen a couple of months ago, and was a real credit to her and Donald. Christopher was still determined to follow his dream and become a policeman, and Donald was in full favour of his son's choice of career. Mary wasn't though. After the terrible experience they'd endured in Whitechapel, Mary was frightened of Christopher dealing with the likes of the Vinny Butlers of this world, day in day out, and was concerned for her son's safety.

'Are you in a daze, Mum? I asked you if you wanted any help and you haven't answered me yet.'

'Sorry, son. You can help me stack that tinned stuff, if you like,' Mary said.

Christopher picked up the tray of corned beef. 'Where's Nancy?' he asked.

'She's gone to the fair with Rhonda.'

'What! You shouldn't have allowed her to go there, Mum,' Christopher said, dropping the corned beef with a thud, just to show his displeasure. Unlike him, with his rather plain looks, Nancy was absolutely stunning and this worried the life out of her brother.

'Oh, don't you start as well, Christopher. I've had enough with your dad harping on about what Nancy should and shouldn't be allowed to do. She's sixteen, and she can't be wrapped in cotton wool forever. Your sister is sensible enough to look after herself, so for goodness' sake stop fretting.'

Christopher stacked the rest of the shelves in silence. His false statement to the police about Dave Phillips' murder had never been mentioned again since he had admitted his lie. But, even though his family seemed to have forgotten all about it, Christopher never had. What had happened between himself and Vinny Butler had changed him completely. He was no longer the carefree lad he had once been. He was serious, a worrier, and there was no way he would be able to rest now until his sister arrived home safe and sound from that fair.

Queenie took her fairy cakes out of the oven and showed them to Vivian.

'Oh, they look perfect, Queen. Now let's see if my jellies are set so I can put some Angel Delight and hundreds and thousands on top of them.'

129

Queenie smiled. Her Brenda was sixteen now and Viv's Lenny fifteen, but thankfully they could remember all the things that little 'uns liked.

'Can I have one of them cakes?' Lenny asked, appearing at the kitchen door.

'No, you bleedin' well can't. You had a big lunch and these are for the party tomorrow,' Vivian said sternly.

'Oh, one won't hurt him, Viv. Go on, take that and go and watch the telly,' Queenie ordered, handing her nephew a plate.

Vivian tutted in pretend annoyance. Even as a young child, her Lenny could wind anybody and everybody around his little finger, and he had become even more of an expert in the art of manipulating people since he'd gone to a special school. Lenny could read and write fairly well now, but even though he was tall and resembled Michael, he was slightly overweight, and his facial expressions clearly gave away that he had been born with disabilities.

Thinking about her own brood, Queenie iced her grandson's birthday cake in total silence. Vinny and Roy had sold their snooker club just over a year ago now and had bought a bigger club along the Commercial Road. They held jazz nights and all sorts in there. They even had a proper licence for their roulette table. Queenie felt like Her Majesty the Queen whenever she had an evening out there. Her boys were treated like royalty and so was she. To say she was proud of how well her sons had done in life was an understatement. She was absolutely fucking ecstatic about it.

Queenie had never seen Albie again since that day she had found out about his affair. She'd had one or two drunken phone calls from him a few years back, but Vinny had her number changed and she'd heard nothing since. Bits of gossip popped up through the grapevine from time to time, and the last Queenie had heard was Albie was living in Becontree Heath with some drunken old trout called Pauline. Queenie was quite pleased that Albie had moved in with a woman roughly his own age, as it meant she wouldn't be able to bear his kids. Queenie did often wonder what had happened to Judy Preston though. Vinny had tried his hardest to track her down over the years to see if she had kept Albie's baby, but Judy and her family had disappeared off the face of the earth.

'I'm off out now, Mum,' Brenda said, snapping Queenie out of her trance.

'Where you off to dressed like that? Look like a bloody hussy in that outfit you do, don't she, Viv?'

Vivian poked her head around the kitchen door. 'It's a bit revealing, Bren.'

'You got your boobies and your bum hanging out,' Lenny added, joining in with the fun.

Brenda tutted, pulled her flowery vest-top up to cover her breasts and wiggled her hotpants down a bit. 'You are such an old fogey, Mum. And you, Auntie Viv. All the girls are wearing clothes like these. It's the fashion.'

'You won't be saying that if you fall arse over tit in those monstrosities on your cloppers,' Vivian chuckled, pointing at Brenda's bright red plastic platform-heeled boots.

'See you later,' Brenda scowled, running her fingers through her short brown hair. Unlike all her friends who had long hair, Brenda had recently had hers chopped off. She liked to stand out in a crowd, not be a clone, and the short feathered cut she had opted for suited her elfin-like face perfectly. She was also incredibly slim and the only thing that Brenda wished she could change about herself was her flat chest. Her boobies looked more like two fried eggs than actual formed breasts.

'You ain't going nowhere until you tell me where you're

going dressed like that, young lady,' Queenie shouted, chasing her daughter up the path.

'I'm going to the fair, OK?' Brenda replied.

'You can't go there dressed like that! Vinny has taken Little Vinny over there and I'm sure Michael said him and Kevin were going to the fair too. Put something more respectable on. You don't want your brothers to think you are over there hawking your mutton, do you now?'

Brenda turned around in fury. She was sick of being told what she should wear and what she should do. Her brothers had always been allowed to run riot. 'Balls to what my brothers think, Mum, and balls to you and Auntie Viv too.'

When Brenda slammed the gate and tottered off down the road, Queenie and Vivian looked at one another in unadulterated shock. Neither woman was used to being sworn at by their own flesh and blood.

Roy's mouth was as dry as a bone as he strolled along Roman Road market holding his girlfriend Colleen's hand. It had been at this very market where Roy had first met her. He had been shopping for a new overcoat, and had decided to grab a bit of lunch in Kelly's pie and mash shop. Colleen had walked in just as Roy had started to eat, and his appetite had disappeared in a flash. In her wedge-heeled sandals, tight-fitting denim shorts, and red chiffon top, her beauty left Roy gobsmacked. She wore her blonde hair straight and long and had the most fully-formed luscious lips that he had ever seen. Unable to take his eyes off her, it wasn't long before Colleen caught him staring and treated him to a dazzling smile. Roy had noticed she had no ring on her finger, and he knew he would never forgive himself if he let her walk out of his life without even finding out her name, or where she was from.

Colleen had told him she was eighteen, a trainee nurse,

and had recently moved to Bow from Cork in Ireland. Her gentle Irish lilt made her even more attractive to Roy and he had been elated when he had asked Colleen out and she had agreed. Their first date had taken place in a West End restaurant. They had got on like a house on fire and their relationship quickly became serious. Roy had had quite a few girlfriends in the past, but apart from one whom he had courted for six months, none was particularly important, but today, Roy had brought Colleen back to Roman Road market for a very special reason.

'Do we have to have pie and mash? I'm not that hungry. I'd rather just have a sandwich, I think,' Colleen said.

'I'm starving, Col. Let me have me pie and mash, eh? You haven't got to have none. I'll get you a sandwich after I've eaten, if you like?'

'Oh, go on then. You might as well just get me pie and mash too. Don't put that horrible liquor on mine though.'

When Roy entered the shop, he was disappointed to see the table Colleen was sitting at the day he had first met her was taken.

'Aren't you going to order, then?' Colleen asked, as Roy hovered near the table.

'These people are nearly finished,' Roy said, noting that the old couple sitting there had already eaten their meals and were now drinking their mugs of tea.

'But there's two empty tables over there,' Colleen said.

'They're going now. We'll sit here,' Roy insisted, even though the old couple still hadn't moved.

'I'm not standing here like a wally, Roy. Give me the money and I'll order our food. I take it you want double pie and mash?'

Roy nodded and was relieved when seconds later the old couple stood up to leave. He waited for the waitress to wipe the table, then flopped nervously onto a chair.

'There we are,' Colleen said, placing the tray on the table.

Roy took a mouthful of pie and immediately felt sick. He had been lying to her, he felt far too anxious to eat and knew the quicker he got this over with the better.

'Bejesus. Whatever are you doing, Roy Butler?' Colleen asked, when her boyfriend dropped to one knee.

'It's virtually a year to the day that I first met you at this very table in this pie and mash shop. I love you so much, Colleen O'Connell, and I know you are the woman I want to spend the rest of my life with. I have already spoken to your father and asked for his blessing, so will you marry me?'

Colleen burst into tears as she stared at the diamond ring Roy held in a black box in his shaking hands. 'Of course I will marry you, you daft bugger.'

When Roy placed the ring on her finger, everybody in the shop, including the staff, gave a loud cheer.

Vinny Butler helped his son onto the ride then, deep in thought, watched him go round and round on the metal horse. Since the Krays had been banged-up in 1969 for the murders of Jack McVitie and George Cornell, Vinny had really made his mark on the East End. The Mitchells were still a force to be reckoned with, but they were based in Canning Town, and were currently too busy feuding with a travelling family called the O'Haras to be bothered about what he and his brothers were doing.

Vinny was overjoyed with the success of his new club. His old gaff had become so popular he'd been turning people away from nine o'clock onwards, and he had known he would quadruple his takings if he could find a much bigger place. He had suggested naming the new venue after his mum, but Roy said they would be made laughing stocks because to name it Queen's or Queenie's would make it sound like a club for bum-bandits.

Michael had come on in leaps and bounds over the years and was now a valuable asset to the business. Once Vinny had drummed into his little brother that driving around on a silly scooter with a soppy oversized parka on was not a cool or adult look, Michael had grown up overnight. Roy was a different matter. Ever since he had fallen hook, line and sinker for the Irish tart he was dating, he expected to take nights off at will to wine and dine her. Vinny had always put work before pleasure and to say he was displeased with Roy's carefree attitude this past year was putting it mildly. Things hadn't come to a head just yet, but Vinny knew he was very near to blowing his top with his brother. He'd only tried to keep a lid on it because he knew if they fell out, not only would it affect their business, it would also greatly upset their mother.

'Well? Did you enjoy that?' Vinny asked, when his son jumped off the ride and ran towards him.

'Nah. It was shit, Dad. Can I go on the Dodgems?'

Chuckling, Vinny lifted his son up in the air above his own head. 'There's Auntie Brenda over there,' Little Vinny said.

'Where?'

'Over there with them boys.'

Vinny put his son down and looked to where he had been pointing. Brenda was standing scantily dressed with her friend Susan Shipton. They were blatantly flirting with a crowd of long-haired lads and when Vinny saw one put his hand on Brenda's backside, he saw red and marched over. 'Oi, what do you think you're doing touching her like that?' he asked, pushing the culprit so hard, he fell backwards and landed on his backside.

'We're only having a laugh, mate. We ain't taking no liberties,' one of the lads said to Vinny.

'Don't you "mate" me, you cheeky fucker,' Vinny said, roughly grabbing hold of his sister by the arm.

'Leave me alone. I am entitled to a life, you know. We ain't done nothing wrong. Tell him, Sue,' Brenda screamed, trying to wriggle out of Vinny's grasp.

Susan Shipton said nothing. She was well aware of Vinny's temper and if she opened her mouth it would only make matters worse.

Marching Brenda away from the group of lads, Vinny pushed her against the side of a nearby hula-hoop stall. 'How dare you embarrass the family name by coming out dressed like that? You look like a slag, Bren, a cheap fucking whore, and I will not put up with it.'

'But all the girls are dressing like me. I'm not a slag, Vinny. It's the fashion,' Brenda wept.

'I don't care what the fashion is, Bren. You are my sister and I will not be laughed at because you are roaming around town dressing and acting like some hooker. I have my reputation to consider, understand? Now, get yourself straight home. I will be checking with Mum to make sure you obeyed my orders.'

'I hate you,' Brenda screamed, running away.

The song being played on the waltzer as she bolted past was Three Dog Night's 'Mama Told Me Not to Come', and if there was one song Brenda did not want to hear at that very moment, it was that.

Unaware that the girl who had just run past her crying was her old schoolfriend Brenda Butler, Nancy whooped with delight as the waltzer started up.

'Don't spin us too fast,' Rhonda said to the man who was standing directly behind them.

The man winked, and then of course spun the girls around until they screamed like babies, begging him to stop.

'Oh, I feel dizzy. I think I'm going to be sick,' Nancy joked, clutching her friend's arm as they staggered off the ride.

'Don't look now, but there's a bloke staring at us. Actually, I think it's you he's looking at. He is wearing a dark suit and he's very handsome,' Rhonda said, giggling.

Nancy looked around and immediately locked eyes with the lad. He looked a bit older than her and Rhonda, and there was something slightly familiar about him. When he smiled at her, Nancy felt her insides knot together. He didn't look anything like Marc Bolan. He had more of a sixties look. He wore his hair swept forward like the Beatles used to wear in their heyday. Nevertheless, he was incredibly stunning and Nancy could not take her eyes off him.

'Oh my God! He's coming over to you, Nance,' Rhonda exclaimed.

How her knees never buckled under her when the handsome lad approached her, Nancy would never know. He was even more beautiful up close than from a distance. His hair was jet black, his eyes were a piercing green, and his perfect straight teeth were as white as driven snow. He was even better-looking than Marc bloody Bolan.

'Is your name Nancy?' the lad asked politely.

Nancy couldn't trust herself to speak, such was the effect this stranger was having on her, so she nodded instead. How the hell did he know her name?

The lad held out his right hand. 'You used to knock about with my little sister, Brenda, for a short spell many moons ago, and I never forget a pretty face.'

Nancy clapped her hand over her mouth as recognition engulfed her. 'Michael. Michael Butler,' she mumbled.

Michael smiled and flicked his hair out of his eyes in a seductive manner. 'You remembered me then?'

At the tender age of eleven, Michael Butler had been her first major crush, so how could Nancy ever have forgotten him?

CHAPTER THIRTEEN

'You all right, love?' Queenie shouted, as she heard her daughter stomp down the stairs.

'No. I'm anything but all right which is why I've decided to go out, and seeing as I am sixteen, there is nothing you can do to stop me,' Brenda replied. She had been fuming when she'd arrived home yesterday from the fair. She had expected some sympathy off her mother, but instead her mum had stuck up for Vinny. Talk about old habits dying hard.

'If you walk out of this house, young lady, don't you bother coming back. You know it's Little Vinny's birthday party,' Queenie yelled.

Yesterday had been a wake-up call for Brenda and she could kick herself for not standing up to Vinny at the fair. All her brothers were overprotective of her, they had been ever since they had found out she had a boyfriend at thirteen, but Vinny was by far the worst. Glaring at both her mother and her aunt, Brenda put her hands on her hips. 'Fine! I'll go and pack my case now.'

'Will all my friends be there yet?' Little Vinny asked his father as they drove towards Queenie's house. He had already received some great presents. His dad had bought him a bike, a Hornby train set, and an Airfix Spitfire, and his Uncle Michael had given him some Stickle Bricks and a Meccano set.

'No. Your party don't start till one and it's only twelve,' Vinny explained, glancing at Michael. His brother was sitting in the passenger seat staring out of the window like a zombie. 'What the fuck's up with you? You were acting really weird last night.'

Michael shook his head as if to try to wake himself up. Over the years he had dated more girls than Vinny and Roy put together, but not one had ever had the effect on him that Nancy Walker seemed to be having. His mum and aunt often joked he should be called Alfie, after the playboy in the Michael Caine film, such was his thirst for pretty girls, but since meeting Nancy yesterday, Michael could think of little else. 'Sorry I've been a bit distant, but I can't stop thinking about someone I bumped into. Do you remember the girl whose parents ran Old Jack's café for a while before it was turned into a butcher's shop?'

'Yeah, course I do. It was her little brother who lied to the Old Bill for me,' Vinny chuckled.

'Well, that's the girl I met at the fair yesterday. Her name's Nancy and she has to be the most beautiful creature I've ever seen.'

Vinny looked at his brother in pure disgust. 'Fuck me, you are making me want to vomit. Don't be getting involved with her. Her father was a right sanctimonious bastard, and I don't fancy opening up a can of worms over the Phillips you-know-what. You ain't arranged to take her out, have ya? I thought you were still shafting that Denise bird?'

'What's you-know-what mean, Dad?' Little Vinny asked curiously.

'Not now, son. I'm talking to your Uncle Michael.'

'Me and Denise have done nothing but argue for the past month, Vin. She keeps talking about marriage and babies and I'm gonna have to end it with her. I'm just not that into her.'

'So, have you asked this Nancy out?' Vinny asked, as he parked the car outside his mother's house.

'Well, not exactly. But, I did invite her and her mate to come to the club on Friday night,' Michael replied, rather sheepishly.

'You did what? That Nancy was roughly the same age as our Brenda. We run a nightclub, not a fucking playgroup, Michael. Anyway, as I've already told you, I don't want you having nothing to do with that family. Talk about open up old wounds.'

Michael said nothing. Nancy had told him that she worked in Woolworth's in Ilford, so he would pop in there and speak to her. Vinny might be able to stop Nancy from coming to the club, but he couldn't stop him from taking her out somewhere else. Michael didn't usually dare disobey Vinny's orders, but there was something so special about Nancy that for once ignoring his brother's instructions seemed like a risk worth taking.

Over in Ilford, Donald turned the open sign to 'closed' on his shop door and breathed a sigh of relief. Sunday was the only day he and Mary closed early, and now Nancy was working full-time in Woolworth's, Sunday afternoons were the only quality time they got to spend together as a family. Today, Donald had invited his and Mary's friends, Derrick and Margaret Robins, over for a traditional roast dinner. Young Roger would be accompanying his parents and Donald hoped that today would be the day when his stubborn daughter would finally see sense.

Nancy's favourite TV programme was *Top of the Pops*

and Donald had quietly suggested weeks ago to Roger that he should apply for tickets. Going to watch some of her favourite pop stars appear live was much more Nancy's cup of tea than going dancing or to the pictures, and Roger receiving the tickets this week had worked out very well because Nancy's all-time idol was currently at number one in the charts, which meant he would definitely be performing on the show. Donald grinned as he took the stairs two by two. There was no way Nancy would refuse a date with Roger if it meant her being able to see Marc Bolan up close, so his plan had worked out perfectly. Donald patted himself mentally on the back. He was such a clever man at times. He really was.

Little Vinny's party wasn't going quite to plan. 'Where are all my other mates, Dad? Why ain't they come yet?' the boy asked, a sad expression on his face.

Absolutely gutted that his pride and joy was upset on his birthday, Vinny hugged his son tightly to his chest. 'Your guess is as good as mine, boy,' he said, seething inside. He had no idea why only fifteen of Little Vinny's friends had turned up, but when he saw the fathers of the other fifteen who had failed to show, Vinny would make the bastards pay.

Another two people currently discussing why only half of Little Vinny's mates had turned up were Queenie and Vivian. 'I reckon there's been a bug going around his school or something,' Queenie said, trying to make some sense out of the awkward situation. It would never have occurred to her that people might not want their children mixing with her notorious family, as she only saw her brood as perfect.

'Lenny, come over here now. You're too old to play musical chairs. You'll squash all the children,' Vivian shouted out.

Realizing that Lenny looked near to tears, Vinny walked over to him and put a comforting arm around his shoulders. 'I've got a special job for you, Champ. I want you to be the DJ and stop the music. Can you do that for me?'

'Yeah, course I can,' Lenny replied, his eyes lighting up with excitement. His life's ambition was to become a DJ, such was his love for music.

'Your Vinny is just so good with Lenny, ain't he, Queen? He has far more tolerance with him than I seem to have lately. Don't get me wrong, I love him to bits, but he do drive me mad at times,' Vivian confessed.

'So, where's Roy and Brenda?' Michael asked, plonking himself on a chair next to his mum.

'Roy rang up this morning, said he'll be here by two, and Brenda stormed out with her suitcase earlier. Leaving home again, she reckons.'

Vivian chuckled. 'Do you remember the last time Bren packed her case and left? She was back by bleedin' teatime.'

Queenie raised her eyebrows in acknowledgment. 'So, how did you get on at the fair yesterday? Was you there when Vinny and Bren started arguing?' Queenie asked Michael. Then, noticing the blush on her youngest son's cheeks and the twinkle in his eye, she changed tack. 'Alfie strikes again! Come on then, who is she?'

About to tell his mum about meeting up with Nancy, Michael was interrupted by a scream and a thud.

'Oh my gawd! You all right, love? What happened?' Queenie asked, rushing to the aid of the child who had fallen and cut his head open on the hearth that surrounded her fireplace.

'It was Vinny. He pushed Jacob over so he could sit on the chair first,' a little blonde girl informed Queenie.

'No, I didn't. You're a lying grass,' Little Vinny replied, glaring at the girl.

Worried that her grandson was about to lunge at his little guest, Queenie grabbed him by his arms so he was facing her. 'Now, tell Nanny the truth. Did you push that boy over?'

'No, I did not.'

'Yes you did,' the injured little boy said, holding his bloodied head in his hands.

Michael and Vinny glanced at one another. Both were aware that apart from some of the children playing musical chairs, they were the only two people in the room who had clocked what had happened. Even when the injured child started crying for his mother, both Michael and Vinny kept schtum. They were Butlers through and through and snitching on their own was totally out of the question.

Realizing that his difficult daughter was obviously bored, Donald decided the time was right to spring the surprise on her. 'Mary, go and get the Pomagne out of the fridge, so I can open it.'

Mary knew that the Pomagne had been bought to signal Roger's surprise, and she had a feeling her daughter wasn't going to be as elated with the *Top of the Pops* tickets as Donald insisted she would be.

'What are we celebrating?' Nancy asked, when her father handed her a glass.

'Roger has a wonderful surprise for you, don't you, Roger?' Donald replied, with a stupid grin on his face.

Nancy's eyes lit up when she saw what the tickets were for and the date on the front. 'Oh my God! T-Rex! Marc Bolan!' she screamed, as she threw her arms around Roger's neck.

Donald was elated by his daughter's response and display of affection towards Roger, and he treated Mary to one of his I-told-you-so smiles. The smile was soon wiped off

Donald's face though, when his daughter announced that she was going to take her friend Rhonda with her.

Mary, Margaret and Derrick all flinched as they realized that Nancy had got the wrong end of the stick.

Clocking the embarrassed look on his father's face, Christopher decided to take the bull by the horns. 'Roger is going to accompany you to the *Top of the Pops* studio, Nancy. He has got the tickets for you to go with him.'

Appalled by the very thought of Roger accompanying her anywhere, Nancy knew she had to stand her ground. She was truly poxed off with her father's cumbersome matchmaking skills, and now she had met Michael, was damned if she was going to put up with it one minute longer.

'Where do you think you are going, young lady?' Donald yelled, when Nancy ran from the table and grabbed her jacket.

'Out! I am quite capable of finding myself a husband, thank you, so in future, just keep your noses out of my bloody business.'

Red-faced with embarrassment as Nancy slammed the door, Donald turned to Roger and his parents. 'I am so sorry for my daughter's rudeness. I really don't know what's come over her.'

Vinny was fuming. Not only had his brother Roy turned up at the party two hours later than promised, he also had his Irish tart in tow.

Watching his mother and aunt fawn all over Colleen, showering her with compliments like they always bloody seemed to, Vinny ordered Roy out into the back garden.

'Look, I'm sorry about not turning up for work last night, but I'll make it up to you, I promise,' Roy said, holding his hands face upwards.

'We run a fucking prestigious nightclub, Roy. Not a chip shop,' Vinny replied cuttingly.

'Yes, I know that. Look, why don't you take the next couple of nights off, Vin, and let me and Michael hold the reins. It's ages since you did that, and we all need a break at times. Perhaps we should start a rota?'

'So, why did you take last night off, Roy? You know Saturday is our busiest night,' Vinny spat.

Even though he knew his brother wouldn't be happy with his reply, Roy couldn't wipe the grin off his face. 'Because I got engaged.'

Vinny looked at Roy as though he had completely lost the plot. 'You did what?'

'I asked Colleen to marry me yesterday, and she said yes.'

Vinny crouched down and put his head in his hands. Roy had changed so much since he had met Colleen that Vinny knew if Roy married her, he would all but lose his brother for good. Vinny was jealous – not of Roy's actual relationship, but of the hold that Colleen had over his brother. The reason being, that hold used to belong to him. Even as kids, Roy would always dance to his tune, but since he'd met that Irish slag, he had stopped bloody dancing. Yvonne Summers had once had a hold over him, and Vinny would hate Roy ever to suffer the heartbreak he'd been through. Colleen was just a gold-digger.

'You OK, bruv?' Roy asked, worriedly.

Vinny stood up with a smile on his face that didn't quite reach his eyes. He was well aware that Roy was none too keen on his friendship with Ahmed. 'You treat him more like a brother than you do me these days, and I don't trust the bastard as far as I can throw him,' Roy had said in a hissy fit only last week. Well, from now on Vinny would make sure Ahmed spent even more time at the club than he already did. Two could play at Roy's game.

CHAPTER FOURTEEN

Nancy was just about to take her tea break when Rhonda dashed towards her waving her arms like a lunatic. 'What's up with you?' Nancy asked, bemused.

'It's that Michael! He's just walked in the shop!' Rhonda exclaimed, unable to contain her obvious excitement.

'What shop?' Nancy asked, dumbly.

'This shop, you div! He's up by the till. I said I was coming to find you.'

'I can't talk to him now. What am I meant to say? What do you think he wants?' Nancy asked, her heart beating wildly in her chest.

'He wants you, you daft mare. And you will speak to him. Come on,' Rhonda said, linking arms with her pal and dragging her towards the till.

Michael smiled as Nancy walked towards him. 'No need to be so nervous. I don't bite,' he joked.

'What do you want?' Nancy asked, staring at her sandals. She was far too nervous to look Michael in the eyes.

'I wanted to know if you would be kind enough to accompany me to the pictures tonight?'

'Yeah, course she will, won't you, Nance?' Rhonda said,

nudging her friend who was currently standing there like a stuffed dummy.

'Er, all right then. I'll meet you at Ilford station at seven, if that's OK?' Nancy mumbled.

Michael grinned. Nancy had been quite shy when he had met her at the fair the other day and seemed even more reserved in her work environment. He hated loud girls, and found Nancy's obvious awkwardness rather endearing. 'Sounds perfect. See you at seven then, darling.'

When Michael strolled out of the shop, Rhonda jumped up and down excitedly. 'He really likes you, Nance, I can see it in his eyes. I bet you end up marrying him.'

Vinny smiled as his son fed the ducks the last of the loaf of bread. 'Shall we have a sandwich ourselves now, boy? Bloody starving, I am.'

'So am I, Dad. Where shall we park our arses?' Little Vinny said, putting his hands in his trouser pockets as he walked next to his father.

Vinny chuckled. His son seemed to have a memory like an elephant and remembered every saying going. Parking one's arse was one of Vivian's favourites. 'Right, let's sit here, shall we?'

When his son flopped down on the grass next to him, Vinny handed him a ham sandwich, then decided to get the little talk out of the way before he ate himself. 'Now, I don't want you to think I'm telling you off, boy, because I'm not. Just think of it more as a bit of fatherly advice. I know you was excited yesterday because it was your birthday, but you really can't go through life punching, kicking and pushing people like you do.'

'But you told me to stick up for myself when I started

school. You said if anyone hit me, I was to hit them back,' Little Vinny reminded his father.

'If somebody hits you, you should hit them back, boy. But, you shouldn't hit people for no reason. Look at yesterday for instance, when you pushed that little boy and cut his head open. If you behave like that at school, you won't have many friends, and you'll get in trouble with the teachers.'

Used to his father worshipping the ground he walked on, Little Vinny's lip began to wobble. 'I didn't push Jacob. He fell over and cut his head,' he insisted.

'Do not lie to me, boy. I saw you push him, so did your Uncle Michael.'

'No, I never.'

Furious at being lied to, Big Vinny grabbed his son roughly by the arm, put him across his knees and gave him a good clump on the backside. 'Don't you ever fucking lie to me again, do you hear me?'

Thrilled by Roy's engagement, Queenie and Vivian had been busy discussing his forthcoming wedding. Queenie liked Colleen. She was good for her Roy and as a couple they were extremely well-suited.

'Where's Brenda? Is she talking to you yet?' Vivian asked. Brenda and her suitcase had turned up on the doorstep at twelve o'clock last night and Queenie had given her daughter a bloody good wallop for worrying the life out of her by coming home so late.

'Nope. Still in her room, the obnoxious little mare. Who the bleedin' hell is this?' Queenie looked out of the window to see who was knocking on her door. 'Oh Jesus, it's the police. I hope one of the boys haven't been nicked,' she said, panicking.

'I'll answer the door,' Lenny shouted, running down the stairs.

'No you won't, nose ointment. You let Auntie Queenie do it,' Vivian ordered her son.

'What's up?' Queenie asked, when she opened the door. There were two officers standing there looking rather sombre.

'Is Vivian Harris here, Mrs Butler? I'm afraid we have some rather bad news for her.'

'Whatever's wrong?' Vivian asked, running into the hallway followed by Lenny.

'I'm afraid it's your ex-husband, Mrs Harris. Unfortunately, Mr Harris was involved in an incident outside the Brewery Tap public house in Barking late last night. He suffered a stab wound to the chest and even though the ambulance got there extremely quickly, I'm afraid he couldn't be saved.'

'Is my dad dead?' Lenny asked, bursting into tears.

Vivian clouted her son around the head. 'Shut up. We didn't even like the old bastard.'

When the two officers glanced at one another, Vivian smiled at them. 'Well, thank you for popping round to tell me. You can go now.'

After dropping his son off, Vinny headed to the club. He and his brothers had got the upstairs looking like a palace now and all three of them lived there together. 'Where's Michael?' Vinny asked Roy coldly. He still hadn't forgiven his brother for springing such a surprise on him yesterday.

'You ain't still got the hump because I've got engaged, have you? Just because I plan to get married, doesn't mean that I won't still be dedicated to the club.'

Vinny gave a sarcastic half-laugh. 'Dedicated to the club! Don't make me chuckle. Colleen had you under her thumb even before you stuck a ring on her finger. You'll have to ask her permission to have a shit now you've popped the question.'

'Don't talk bollocks, Vin. Colleen ain't like that. She's a good girl who understands how important our business is to us. Surely it must have occurred to you that one day I would want to settle down and in time have children? It's what most men do, so can't you just be fucking happy for me for once?'

Vinny unwillingly shook his brother's hand. 'Congratulations. Now, where's Michael?'

'Gone out. All ponced up he was in his best suit. Reeked of aftershave an' all. Gotta be another new bird on the scene if you ask me.'

Vinny snarled. 'Well, it better not be who I think it is, because if Michael has disobeyed my orders, there will be big fucking trouble.'

Queenie had just put the dumplings in her rabbit stew when the doorbell rang. Vivian had taken Lenny back to her own house, Brenda had gone out, so Queenie ordered her grandson to open the door for her.

'Who are you?' Little Vinny asked the tall, glamorous dark-haired lady.

'Who is it?' Queenie shouted out.

The woman crouched down so she was at eye-level with Little Vinny. Unable to stop herself, she stroked his rosy cheeks.

'Get off me,' Vinny said, pushing her hand away.

Queenie ran to the front door, ordered her grandson into the lounge, then glared at the woman. 'Who the fuck are you?' she asked.

'Look, I don't want no trouble, but it's breaking my heart not being able to see him,' the woman replied.

'Not being able to see who?' Queenie asked, expecting the woman to say one of her son's names.

'My son. I'm Vinny's mother.'

*

Nancy felt sick with anxiety when she spotted Michael leaning against the station wall smoking a cigarette. He had a smart dark-grey suit on and looked so stunningly gorgeous, she felt like turning around and running back to the safety of her home.

Michael grinned as he spotted his date. She looked amazing in her lime green halter-neck catsuit. 'You look really beautiful, Nancy,' he told her meaningfully, before he kissed her politely on the cheek.

'Thank you,' Nancy replied coyly.

'Look, I was thinking, and please feel free to say no if you don't want to, but seeing as this is our first date, I thought it might be nice if we went for a meal instead of the pictures? I thought we could chat in a restaurant and get to know one another a bit better. What do you say?'

'OK. But can we go to a different area? My parents are local shopkeepers and I can do without being interrogated by their customers.'

'Course we can! Let's jump in my car and see where it takes us, shall we?'

Amazed that Michael owned a car, Nancy smiled. 'Yes, I'd like that.'

After receiving the phone call from his mother, Vinny shot round to her house like a bat out of hell. He couldn't believe after all these years that Karen had the nerve to show her face. He'd paid her good money to stay out of his son's life, so how dare she turn up like a bad penny?

Vinny had ordered his mother to send Little Vinny upstairs to his bedroom, then invite Karen in and keep her there. When he let himself in with his own key, he was dismayed to see Karen sitting on the sofa next to Little Vinny who was happily showing her all his birthday presents. 'Take Vinny upstairs now, Mum. I need to talk to Karen alone,' Vinny barked.

'You said my mum was dead. You're a liar too, Dad,' Little Vinny said accusingly.

'Just get upstairs, boy,' Vinny demanded. 'I'll explain everything later.'

'No,' Little Vinny replied. He was ever so confused. He had always wanted to have a mum like all the other kids at school had, and this mum who had turned up today seemed quite nice.

'Get up them fucking stairs now,' Vinny bellowed, grabbing his son's right arm and yanking him off the sofa. He hated being disobeyed at the best of times.

'Don't do that! You'll hurt him,' Karen said, appalled.

'Come upstairs with Nanny,' Queenie urged, trying to pick up her grandson.

Little Vinny wriggled out of his nan's grasp. 'I wanna see my mum,' he sobbed.

Seething with Karen for upsetting his little boy so much, Vinny decided to let his son know exactly what she was really like. He crouched down, grabbed Vinny by the hand and pointed towards Karen. 'That woman there isn't good enough to be a mother to you, boy, and do you want to know why?'

Little Vinny nodded.

'Because she sold you to your daddy. That's how much she wanted you.'

Karen was crying now. 'It wasn't like that, son. I had to go away. But, I'm not going away any more, I promise you that much.'

When Little Vinny ran up the stairs and Queenie followed him, Karen suddenly felt nervous. It had taken a lot of guts and planning to come back to Whitechapel, and she couldn't bottle it now. If she was to have regular contact with her son, then she needed to stand up for herself. It was the only way forward.

'You got some front turning up here. What you after? More dosh?' Vinny asked, shutting the lounge door.

'No, I don't want your money. All I want is to have contact with my son, Vinny. I don't want to take him away from you. I just want to see him on a regular basis. He is absolutely adorable, just like I knew he would be and as his mother I have a right to see him grow up.'

'You lost all your rights as a mother when you took my fucking money and bolted. Now, you have two choices. You can either walk away now and live, or continue this bollocks and die. The choice is yours, so what is it to be, Karen? And don't think I won't kill you, because I will.'

'I know you will, which is why I have already sought legal advice and been to the police, Vinny. They have everything logged on record and if I go missing, or my mutilated body is found, you will go down for the murder. I have made damn sure of that.'

The mention of the police being involved put the fear of God into Vinny. His main source of information on the inside had retired from his position as chief inspector last year, and even though he still gave Geary a backhander for any odds and sods he needed, now he was all legal he had no reason to have the Old Bill on his payroll any more.

'So, can I see our son from time to time?' Karen asked. She had noticed the look of fear on Vinny's face when she had mentioned the police, and was pleased that she sounded so confident, because her insides actually felt like jelly.

Vinny flopped onto the armchair opposite Karen. He knew he had been lucky to get away with topping Dave Phillips and there was no way he could chance getting rid of Karen himself if the bitch had already spoken to the police. The thought of doing life in prison and not seeing his son grow up was unbearable, so instead of strangling Karen and watching the life seep out of her like he wanted to, Vinny forced a smile. 'I suppose it's only right with you being his mother that you see him. It has to be on my terms though, and I don't want him going out on his own with you until he gets to know you better.'

Thrilled that Vinny had actually seen sense, Karen nodded her head. 'I understand that, but I would love my mum to meet him. Perhaps I could bring her round to your mum's house?'

Much to his displeasure, Vinny forced himself to smile again. 'Look, why don't I book a nice restaurant and your mum can meet him over lunch?'

Karen was suddenly suspicious. Vinny was being a bit too nice for her liking. 'OK. What day shall we arrange it for?' she asked. There was nothing Vinny could do to harm her in such a public place.

'How about Wednesday? I'll give you the phone number of my club, bell me tomorrow afternoon and I'll have somewhere nice booked. I'll talk to Little Vinny tomorrow and explain everything properly to him. Sorry for the way I reacted earlier, I was out of order. Just the shock of you turning up out the blue, I suppose.'

'That's OK. I'm sorry for turning up like that as well. I never wanted to give our son up in the first place though, you do know that? I was just so scared of you, Vinny. That's why I took the money and ran. I've sorted myself out now though. I gave up the stripping and I now work as a barmaid in a pub in Dagenham. I could be a good mum to Little Vinny now, I know I could.'

Vinny nodded as if to agree with her. 'Look, I've gotta shoot now. I've got a meeting with a guy at the club at eight. Do you need a lift anywhere?'

'No, I'm fine, thanks. I'll walk to the station, it's only round the corner.'

Escorting Karen to the front door, Vinny handed her his

phone number on a piece of paper and told her to ring him after two tomorrow.

'Thanks for everything, Vinny, and I'll see you on Wednesday,' Karen said, as she walked down the path.

Vinny closed the door and sighed deeply as he leant against it. Plan A had been to brazenly murder Karen, and seeing as it was far too dangerous to do that now, he needed to quickly think of a Plan B.

Once she had got over her initial nervousness, Nancy had thoroughly enjoyed her date with Michael. He had taken her to a steakhouse in Stratford and even though she had been far too excited to eat very much, Nancy had felt very grown-up and had even had a couple of Cinzanos and lemonade.

Nancy had never had a proper boyfriend in the past. She had been on a few first dates with different lads, but had never enjoyed herself enough to bother with a second one. Being with Michael was different. Not only was he the most handsome lad that she had ever seen, he was also funny, interesting and an absolute gentleman. The five-year age gap didn't bother Nancy one little bit. She would much rather date a man than a boy. Especially one who drove a red Mustang convertible like Michael did. Nancy had nearly wet herself with excitement when she had clapped eyes on his car.

'Do I go straight on at these lights?' Michael asked, snapping Nancy out of her deliriously happy daydream.

'Yes, then first right and you can drop me on the corner. I live in the next road along and I don't want my nosy parents to know my business. They keep trying to fix me up with their friend's awful son, Roger.'

Michael chuckled, followed Nancy's directions, then pulled over near a couple of garages. He'd had a wonderful evening, so much so, he had decided to pay Denise a visit tomorrow to break up with her for good. Obviously, he hadn't mentioned to Nancy that he currently had a girlfriend. What was the point if he was going to end the relationship?

Michael turned down the volume on the radio to drown out the sound of Dawn singing 'Knock Three Times' and turned to face Nancy. He had never been as desperate to kiss a girl in his life. 'I really had a good time tonight. Can I see you again, Nancy?'

Nancy stared into Michael's kind green eyes and smiled. If her parents found out she was dating one of the Butler boys she knew they would go ballistic, but as long as she and Michael kept well away from the Ilford area, it was highly unlikely her parents would find out. 'Yes. I don't want my mum and dad to find out though, Michael, so we can't ever go out around here. My parents are very protective of me and Dad is such an old stick-in-the-mud. Apart from boring Roger who I told you about earlier, he would find fault with anybody I dated.'

'Don't worry about your parents. They won't find out about us. What day can I see you again?' Michael asked. It had occurred to him in the restaurant earlier who Nancy reminded him of. With her luscious lips and long mop of blonde hair, she looked uncannily like a young Bridgette Bardot.

'I can see you on Wednesday, if you like? That's my day off this week.'

'OK. Let's go out for the day then, shall we? Leave it with me and I'll think of something special. Is ten too early for me to pick you up? I can meet you where my car was parked earlier, instead of at the station.'

'Ten is fine. I'd better go now, Michael. I have to get up for work early.'

'Can I kiss you first?' Michael asked, amazed by his own

words. He usually just went in for the kill, rather than be polite about it.

'Yes,' Nancy whispered, her nerves coming back to haunt her once again.

When Michael leant towards her and their lips entwined for the very first time, Nancy forgot all about her anxiety and responded eagerly. Michael's kiss was perfect, just like he was.

CHAPTER FIFTEEN

When Brenda Butler was violently sick for the second morning running, alarm bells began ringing in her head. Her mum had gone to visit her nan's grave with her Auntie Viv, which would thankfully avert another interrogation like she'd had to endure yesterday morning.

Brenda washed her face, then stared at her reflection in the bathroom mirror. Her relationship with Dean Smart had been one of secrecy and passion until he had dumped her just over six weeks ago. 'Look, Bren, you're a lovely girl, and I really like you, but I am sick of sneaking around like a couple of silly schoolkids. Your brothers will go mental if they find out about us, and my family will probably disown me. I think we should stop seeing one another before any real damage is done,' Dean had told her bluntly.

Seeing as Dean was the lad who had taken her virginity, Brenda was heartbroken. Her heartbreak soon turned to anger, though, when she was informed by a few of her friends that less than a week after dumping her, Dean was parading his new girlfriend around town.

Hell hath no fury like a woman scorned and Brenda had considered telling her brothers what had happened just to pay Dean back for betraying her so cruelly. But in the end she had chosen to keep schtum. Vinny had had many a run-in with Dean's dad, Terry, and Brenda knew if Vinny found out that she had slept with Terry's son, he would probably throttle her.

Feeling the bile in her throat begin to rise again, Brenda put her head back over the toilet and retched. It was sod's law she was pregnant with Dean's baby. That would be just her fucking luck.

Over at Bow Cemetery, Vivian was about to blow a fuse. 'Don't you dare! You're far too old to be doing that now. Christ, if anyone sees you, you'll be nicked for indecent exposure. You're a big boy now, Lenny, and big boys have big dingle-dangles.'

Ignoring his mother, Lenny turned his back on her and his Auntie Queenie and pissed all over Old Man Taylor's unkempt grave.

'I shall give him such a fucking doughboy when I get him home. Played me up something rotten since we found out about Bill's death, he has. In fact, just lately, I think that poxy school is doing him more harm than good. I think I'm gonna have to pull Lenny out of there for the sake of his own sanity.'

'Now he's fifteen, surely it would be better for him if he had a little job?' Queenie suggested.

'Doing what though?' Vivian asked wearily. Her Lenny was hardly Einstein, poor little sod.

Queenie smirked. 'I'm sure the boys will find him a job at the club. You just leave it to me.'

Michael was open-mouthed when Nancy climbed into his car. She was wearing chunky wedge-heeled sandals, a faded denim waistcoat, mauve hotpants, and her legs were the longest Michael had ever seen.

Noticing Michael looked rather taken aback by her outfit, Nancy suddenly wished she had worn something else. 'I've got a wrap-over skirt in my bag. I only wore this because I was so hot,' she explained awkwardly.

'You look fine. In fact, you look better than fine. You look incredible.'

'Thanks. You look nice too,' Nancy replied. Michael was dressed casually today.

'Right, shall we be on our way then?'

'Yep. Where we going?' Nancy asked, feeling her stomach churn with excitement. Michael had the roof down on his Mustang, and Nancy couldn't wait to hit the road and feel the breeze fly through her hair.

'Hainault Forest. I've got a picnic in the boot fit for a princess and that's what you are, darling.'

Vinny politely kissed Karen's mum on the cheek, then introduced his son to her. 'This is your Nanny Maureen. Go give her a hug, boy.'

When his son hugged his nan then wanted to sit on his mother's lap, Vinny urged him to do so. He had already thought of a way of getting Karen out of his and his son's lives for good, but firstly he had to gain her trust.

'Do you want to open your presents, Vinny? This one is from me and that one is from your nan,' Karen said, pointing to two wrapped-up boxes.

Vinny plastered a false grin on his face while watching his son open his presents. Karen actually seemed quite good with Little Vinny, but sharing was not in Vinny's nature. The boy was his property, he had raised him and that's the way it would stay.

Brenda Butler ordered her pal to meet her in a café in Aldgate rather than their usual one in Whitechapel.

'Whatever's wrong? Why did you make me schlep all the way up here?' Susan Shipton asked.

Brenda was near to tears as she explained all about her morning sickness. 'And I can't fit into my white jeans any more. I must be pregnant, I know I am. What am I gonna do, Sue?'

'Well, you're gonna have to get a test done for a start. I'll come to the doctor's with you.'

'I can't go to my doctor in case he tells my mum or brothers. Can't you take a water sample to your doctor's and pretend it's yours?' Brenda asked hopefully.

'No, I bloody can't! My mum would kill me if she thought I was up the spout, Bren. Why don't you go to that dodgy doctor where Gillian Trott went? He does pregnancy tests if you pay him. In fact, he sells you tablets and all sorts if you pay him. He even arranged Gillian's abortion for her. A pal of his did it.'

'Where's his surgery?' Brenda asked.

'It ain't a proper surgery. It's a room in his house where he sees his patients. He is a real doctor though, I think. Gillian will know his address. Shall we go and find a phonebox after we've finished our drinks? I know her number off by heart.'

Gulping the rest of her tea down in one, Brenda stood up. 'Come on, let's ring her now.'

With Michael and Vinny both out, Roy decided to make up for taking the other night off by tackling the paperwork alone. Within seconds of sitting down to start his tedious task, he was disturbed by the doorbell ringing. 'Who is it?' he shouted when he looked through the spyhole and couldn't see anybody standing there.

'It's me, boy. It's your dad.'

Recognizing his father's voice, Roy yanked open the door. 'Fucking hell, Dad. What you doing here?'

'That's a nice greeting. Can I come in? I need to sit down for a bit.' Albie's breathing was clearly laboured.

'Do you want a drink?' Roy asked, as he led his father inside.

'I could murder a brandy, boy. Can you make it a large one?'

Roy was in a daze as he poured out two large brandies. His dad was only fifty-one, but looked more like an old-age pensioner. Gone was the thick mop of dark hair and the twinkle in his eye. His barnet had thinned and was now swept over his head to hide any bald patches. As for his eyes, they had completely lost their sparkle.

Roy sat opposite his father. The last time he had seen his dad had been about six years ago, and him turning up out the blue was a shock to say the least.

'Nice club, boy. Much bigger than the last one, ain't it? Where are your brothers?' Albie asked.

'Out. Look, Dad, what do you want? Vinny has only gone for lunch and he could be back any time. He ain't gonna be too happy to find you sitting here, is he?'

'How's your mum? Still a handful?' Albie chuckled, avoiding answering Roy's question.

'Mum's fine. We're all fine. Just cut the crap and tell me why you're here, will you? Do you need money? Is that it?'

Knocking his brandy back, Albie shook his head sadly. 'I've got the cancer, boy. I'm a very ill man.'

Michael grinned as he unpacked the picnic. He had asked his mum to do him proud and she hadn't let him down. A whole roast chicken, pork pies, a knuckle of ham, tomatoes, six crusty buttered rolls, a big lump of cheese. She had even packed hard-boiled eggs, brown pickle, and a jar of her home-made pickled onions. Michael laid all the food out, then popped open a bottle of champagne.

Nancy propped herself up on her elbow. Michael had laid a big blanket on the grass and had brought a portable radio with him as well. It was very romantic.

Michael handed Nancy a glass of champagne and grinned. He had finished with Denise the previous day. It hadn't been easy. At first she had burst into tears and begged him not to leave her. Then, five minutes later, she had flown at him and called him every name under the sun. Still, it was all over now, and he was free to do what he wanted. 'Haven't you ever been to Hainault before?' he asked Nancy.

'No. I didn't even know there was a forest here. It is incredibly pretty.'

'And so are you,' Michael said, gazing intently into Nancy's eyes.

Nancy looked away. Her feelings for Michael frightened her a bit.

'Well, eat something then. There's a paper plate there. I told my mum I had met a special young lady and she helped me with the picnic,' Michael said, winking at Nancy.

'How is your mum? I remember her and your aunt coming into my parents' café. And I remember your little cousin who loved our jukebox.'

Michael chuckled. 'My little cousin ain't so little now. Lenny's fifteen and is nearly as tall as me. My mum's a diamond, Nance, so is my Auntie Viv. So are my brothers deep down. They've got their faults, but who hasn't?'

'Oh, my family have lots of faults. Especially my dad who still treats me as though I'm about ten. My brother drives me mad sometimes as well. He is turning more into my dad as every day passes. I do still love 'em though.'

'Of course you do. Your family is your family, babe, and you only inherit one.'

'So, what is Brenda like now, Michael? I can't really remember what she looked like, but I do remember really liking her. Has she got a job and a boyfriend?' Nancy enquired.

'Bren's a good girl, but she's a bit headstrong. She doesn't like work very much either. She's had three different jobs since leaving school and didn't last at any of them for more than a week. To my knowledge, she hasn't got a boyfriend at the moment. I suppose, being the only girl, me and my brothers are a bit strict with her, so she probably wouldn't tell us if she was courting. In fact, she was over the fair last Saturday, the day we met there. So was Vinny. He spotted Brenda arsing about with some lads and they had a bit of a fall-out.'

The mention of Vinny brought Nancy back to reality. It was his fault that her family had fled Whitechapel in the middle of the night, so how were her parents ever going to accept her dating Vinny's brother? As much as she liked Michael, Nancy momentarily wondered if she should back out of the relationship before she got in too deep.

Noticing the vacant expression on Nancy's face, Michael decided he had to broach the subject that they had both so far avoided. 'Look, Nance, I know what happened was heavy duty, but Vinny has mellowed now. He was young then, we all were, and shit happens, don't it? I like you so much, I really, really do, so please don't let the past spoil whatever future we might have. I know if we carry on seeing one another, one day our families will have to find out, but let's worry about that at the time, eh? Always remember, I ain't Vinny, I'm Michael Butler.'

Nancy edged towards Michael and laid her head against his chest. He was right. Nothing that had happened was their fault, so why should they stop seeing one another?

When Nanny Maureen excused herself to go to the toilet, Vinny leant across the table and gave Karen's hand a friendly squeeze. 'Didn't it go well? Little 'un really enjoyed himself,' he said, gesturing towards their son who had overeaten and was now fast asleep on the chair.

Karen smiled. Vinny had been the perfect gentleman today, and the restaurant he had brought them to was top-class. 'It's been wonderful, Vinny, it really has. I can't tell you how many nights I have laid awake imaging what our son was like, and to now finally be part of his life truly means the world to me.'

'You know what, I was thinking earlier. Seeing as you are a barmaid now, why don't you come and work at the club for me? You could see so much more of Little Vinny then, couldn't you?'

'Oh, I don't know. I do days in the pub where I work now. If I come and work for you, it's nights, isn't it? It will cost me a fortune to get home to Dagenham in a cab as well.'

Vinny raised his eyebrows and chuckled. 'Course it won't. That's one of the benefits of being my child's mother. I'll pay all your fares and I'll double whatever wages you are currently being paid. To be honest, I'm on the look-out for a manageress, so if things work out and you fit the bill, then I don't see why the job can't be yours.'

'Manageress! Oh my God! What type of club do you have now? It's not all seedy old men and strippers, is it?'

'No, of course not. We don't have strippers at all now. It's proper classy. We have jazz nights and lots of live music. It's members only, and although they are allowed to sign guests in for a fee, there is no riffraff. You will love it, Karen, trust me. Far better for you than working in some shitty boozer in Dagenham.'

'But, I won't get to see much more of Little Vinny, will I? Surely you don't have him at the club of a night?'

Vinny chuckled. 'Yeah, he pulls pints. No, what I was

thinking was, say you start work at seven, well you can come up this way earlier and spend a couple of hours with Little Vinny before you begin. You'd get to see him most days then, wouldn't you? Now he has met you, he is going to need to see you regularly.'

Karen couldn't believe how much Vinny had changed over the years. He used to be a nasty bastard once upon a time, with a vile temper, and even though he had been horrible to her when she had turned up at his mum's house, Karen now guessed that his behaviour that day was down to shock. At twenty-six, Vinny had matured into a real man, and being a dad had obviously brought out the best in him, Karen thought.

'Well?' Vinny asked, impatiently. He wanted an answer before Nanny Maureen returned from the toilet and started sticking her oar in.

'How could I say no when it means seeing my wonderful son every day. Of course I'll come and work for you, Vinny, and thank you so much for being understanding about everything. You're a good guy deep down, you really are.'

Vinny grinned. 'You're very welcome, Karen.'

CHAPTER SIXTEEN

Johnny Preston opened the door of his van and grimaced as the stench of dead animals hit his nostrils. Working in a slaughterhouse was an awful fucking job and the only saving grace for Johnny was he was able to nick a load of meat which he would then sell on to a few butchers he knew on the cheap.

The hot July weather was making the dead animals smell even worse than usual, and when Johnny climbed into the van and a lifeless pig fell on top of him and sent him sprawling, he knew enough was enough.

'What you doing?' Johnny's pal Keith asked him.

Johnny took off his overalls and slung them in the back of the van. 'I'm doing something I should have done years ago. I'm moving back to London.'

'But, I thought you couldn't set foot in London? You said that heavy mob would kill you if you ever went back.'

Johnny grinned. 'Not if I kill them first.'

As Johnny strolled up the road, Keith chased after him. 'Don't do anything stupid, mate. Think of your kids. You don't wanna end up six feet under like you said Dave did, do you?'

Johnny turned to his mate and gave him a manly hug.

Keith was the only real friend he had made since moving out to Tiptree in Essex, and he was the only one Johnny had ever trusted to tell about his past. 'You look after yourself, Keith, and don't worry about me, I'll be fine. I need to get revenge for my pal's death. An eye for an eye an' all that. Only I can make sure Vinny Butler gets his comeuppance.'

Knowing how his elder brother was prone to flying off the handle, Roy had decided to wait until the club was shut and he was alone with Vinny before he mentioned their dad's reappearance.

'You're quiet. Has the lovely Colleen kicked you into touch already?' Vinny asked.

'No, course she ain't. Look, we need to talk. I had a visit yesterday from Dad, and before you start shouting and swearing, or jumping down my throat, he's ill, Vinny, really ill.'

'Oh diddums. Poor Daddy. My heart bleeds for him. So, what did the old cunt want? Money? You better not have given him any of our hard-earned dosh, Roy, else there will be trouble.'

Roy stared into his brother's eyes in the hope of seeing a glint of emotion. He didn't. All he saw was coldness. 'You really are one callous bastard at times, Vin. Dad didn't ask for money actually. He's got cancer and he wants to try and make things right with us and Mum before he dies.'

Vinny flopped onto the armchair. 'Does he look ill? He weren't spinning you one of his yarns, was he? You know what a conniving old bastard he can be.'

'Nah, he looked really ill. In fact, he could barely breathe when he arrived. He's lost weight and most of his hair. You wouldn't recognize him, Vin. Looks about seventy, he does.'

Vinny ran his fingers through his jet-black hair. If he

didn't have enough on his plate with Karen turning up out of the blue, he now had his father to contend with as well. 'Have you told anyone else yet? Does Mum know?'

'I haven't told a soul. I thought perhaps me and you could pop around Mum's and tell her together? Do you think she'll be upset? Or not bothered?'

Vinny shrugged. 'I dunno. All I know is I'm a big believer of things happening in threes. First Karen turning up, then Dad. I wonder which unsavoury cunt will be the next to darken our doorstep?'

Brenda Butler felt nauseous with fear as she approached the house in Bromley-by-Bow for the second time that day. The pregnancy test had cost her three pounds and the doctor had been quite cold towards her. He had just snatched the money and water sample out of her hands and told her to come back three hours later for the result.

'Dr Ali has a patient with him at the moment, so take a seat,' the woman who answered the door said.

Brenda and Susan sat down. It definitely wasn't a proper doctor's surgery. It was just like a bare lounge with a few old plastic chairs in it.

'I hope we haven't got to wait long. I just want to know one way or the other,' Brenda whispered to her friend.

'So, what you going to do if you are pregnant? Will you let Dr Ali arrange an abortion for you?' Susan whispered back.

'I don't know. I haven't got any money. I don't know what I will do, but I suppose telling my mum would be a better option than telling my brothers. I wasn't sick this morning, so I am just hoping I had a bug.'

'Dr Ali will see you now,' the woman shouted out.

Clutching her friend's arm for moral support, Brenda walked into the room.

'I have your results here and I can confirm you are indeed pregnant, Miss Butler. Now, would you like me to make an appointment with my friend Dr Khan for you? He will perform your abortion very cheap. He will charge you fifty pounds.'

Brenda felt her legs buckle beneath her and if she hadn't been holding Susan's arm she was sure she would have collapsed on the floor.

'Well, do you want me to book the appointment with Dr Khan?' Dr Ali asked impatiently. He dealt with trashy English girls like Brenda all day long and had no time for them whatsoever. If they'd thought of the consequences before dropping their knickers, then these stupid girls wouldn't have got themselves pregnant in the first place.

'No, she doesn't want an appointment with Dr Khan. Come on, Bren, we're going,' Susan said, leading her friend towards the door.

When they got out of the makeshift surgery and the warm air hit her, Brenda leant tearfully against a nearby wall. 'What am I gonna do? My mum is gonna kill me,' she wailed.

Susan would have loved to have been able to reassure Brenda that everything would be fine and her family would be supportive, but she couldn't lie. So instead she said nothing.

Walking on air because his relationship with Nancy seemed to be going so well, Michael was brought back down to earth with a thud when he learned that his father was seriously ill. Unlike his brothers, who had refused to discuss his dad over the past five and a half years, Michael had often thought about him, and wondered what he was up to. 'So, where is he living? Is he still in Barking with that bird?' Michael asked.

Roy shook his head. 'He's living back in Whitechapel by all accounts. He didn't say where, but said he needed to be near the London Hospital for all his appointments and stuff.

He also said that he wanted to spend his final days back in the place he grew up in and loved. He said it reminded him of us and Mum,' Roy explained.

Vinny chuckled sarcastically. 'Fuck me, shall we get the violins out? You never said any of this earlier, Roy. Good old Dad can certainly still come up with a great sob story, can't he?'

Michael glared at his eldest brother. He had always been closer to his father than Vinny and Roy, and unlike Vinny, he also had a heart. 'If Dad is as ill as Roy reckons, then we have to be there for him. I know he wasn't the perfect father and the way he treated Mum was bang out of order, but he certainly ain't the devil. He was just a drunk and a womanizer, and if truth be known I've really missed him.'

Vinny shook his head in mock disbelief. 'You're a sucker for punishment, Michael, you always was when it came to Dad. Changing the subject, who is this new bird of yours? It had better not be the tart whose parents used to run that café. You haven't disobeyed my orders, have you, Michael?' Vinny asked, his voice full of accusation and anger.

Michael wanted to blurt out the truth, but he had sworn to Nancy only yesterday to keep their relationship a secret for the time being and he couldn't break his promise to her. 'No, of course not. My new girlfriend comes from Hainault and her name is Lydia,' he lied.

'Right, what I suggest we do is the three of us go and speak to Mum together. However she reacts, without us influencing her in any way, shape, or form is what we end up doing, OK?' Vinny said. He then turned back to Michael. 'As for you, if I find out you are lying to me, and this Lydia bird is just a figment of your imagination, there'll be trouble, Michael, and I mean that with all my heart.'

171

Mary Walker hugged her son and wished him a lovely time. Christopher had just been promoted in his scout group and now proudly wore a stripe on his shirt. Today, he was off on a camping trip.

Donald put an arm around Mary's shoulders as they both waved to Christopher. 'What a fine child we have created there, my love. A pillar of society is Christopher. What a shame our Nancy doesn't have the same values.'

'Oh, don't keep picking on Nancy, Donald. She might be a little more headstrong than Christopher, but so are most girls of her age. She is just finding her feet in life, that's all,' Mary insisted.

'And do most girls of Nancy's age tell blatant lies to their parents? You know as well as I do, Mary, that our daughter has some boyfriend on the go. So, why the big secrecy about him? He must either be a lot older than her, or he is some hellraiser from a damn awful family.'

Mary turned to face her husband. Donald did have a tendency to let his mind run away with him at times. 'Look, I am sure Nancy will tell us about him when she is good and ready. I bet the reason she is too frightened to say anything is because of your awkward matchmaking skills with that bloody Roger.'

'What do you mean by bloody Roger? He is a fine young man, as well you know. That lad will make a fantastic husband and father one day.'

'Yes, but our Nancy doesn't seem to think so, does she, Donald? And do you know what? I don't blame her for standing her ground one little bit. I wouldn't fancy Roger if I was in Nancy's shoes either. Have you looked at our daughter lately? She is a stunning young woman with a vibrant personality, so why should she settle for an average-looking, boring lad like Roger?'

Donald tutted, shook his head in despair, then went out the back to do some stocktaking. He didn't understand a woman's way of thinking. Never had and never would.

In the heart of Essex, Johnny Preston was in a pub that he didn't usually frequent, deep in thought. It was over five and a half years now since he had left the hustle and bustle of London for the tranquillity of life in Tiptree and he had hated virtually every second of it.

At first, it had been bearable. His family were safe. Nobody knew who they were from Adam, and that was all that mattered. Then, he'd had a massive fall-out with his sister over a bloke she had met on holiday at Butlins. The argument had turned nasty and Johnny had ended up hospitalizing his sister's new beau. His mother had been furious, and when his sister had decided to move to Suffolk to be near her new man, his mum had opted to move there as well. Johnny was a man to hold a grudge, and had never spoken to his mother or sister since the day they had left Tiptree. He had bent over backwards to take care of them, and in his eyes they had thrown his kindness back in his face.

Seeing a blonde bird who was standing at the bar smile at him, Johnny gave her figure the once-over then smiled back at her. He still had his good looks and had succumbed to many a one-night stand since moving to Tiptree.

Trying to struggle with temptation, Johnny sank his pint and went to the toilet. It was all his wife's fault that he couldn't keep his penis in his pants. Deborah was a good wife, a great mother, but had let herself get so fat that physically she made Johnny feel sick.

'Hello, handsome. I haven't seen you in here before,' the woman said, approaching Johnny as he walked back to his seat.

Johnny grinned, then began a conversation while studying

the woman closely. She was certainly no oil painting up close, but she was better than what he had on offer back home. Johnny glanced at his watch. He'd had far too much to drink to head back to London tonight now anyway. The best thing he could do to take his mind off stuff was drown his sorrows, have one last fling, and then tomorrow he could plan his revenge.

Needing some space to clear his jumbled-up thoughts, Vinny told his brothers he had some personal business to attend to, and would meet them at their mum's house that afternoon. Usually, Vinny would inform his brothers of any foul play he intended to be involved with, but for once he had decided to keep his cards close to his chest. What he had planned for Karen was a bit below the belt even by his standards, and apart from his pal Ahmed, whom Vinny trusted implicitly, the fewer people that knew about it, the better.

Driving along the Whitechapel Road, Vinny spotted his mother walking along laden with carrier bags. He pulled over and opened his driver's-side window. 'Mum, jump in. I'm on my way to yours.'

Queenie dumped her bags on Vinny's back seat, and grinned as she saw some of the passers-by staring at her son's new car. All her boys now had flashy top-of-the-range motors and that made Queenie extremely proud. 'I'm glad I've caught you alone, Vinny. I need you to do me a couple of big favours.'

'What?'

'One, I want you to throw our Roy a surprise engagement family get-together, and secondly I need you to give our Lenny a job at the club. Vivvy's been worried sick about him recently. She reckons he is picking up bad habits off them kids he mixes with at that school. He needs something to stimulate his mind properly, boy. Been performing something rotten since he found out his father's been murdered.

Keeps cocking his leg up in the air and pissing like a dog, he does.'

Vinny turned right and pulled up outside his old club. 'Looks a shithole now, don't it, Mum? I've heard it might close down soon. Such a shame. Good little club that was when I owned it. Yeah, I'll organize something for Roy. Just leave it with me.'

'And what about Lenny?'

Vinny turned to his mum and smiled. 'How about I employ Champ as our little handy-man? He can do a bit of everything then. He can collect the bottles and glasses, help with changing the barrels and stocking the bar up. He can even do a bit of DJ-ing if it makes him happy.'

Queenie hugged her son. 'Oh, that's brilliant, Vin. Vivvy will be made up. You're a good boy, you are. Heart of gold, you've got.'

'Talking of which, I'm giving Karen a job behind the bar. She wants to see more of Little Vinny, so I said she can pop round to yours for an hour or so to see him before she starts work. Is that OK? I don't want her taking him out alone, and I won't worry so much if you're there to keep an eye out.'

Queenie's usually thin lips curled into a frightening snarl. 'I ain't happy about that tart coming round my house or being part of Little Vinny's life. He's changed since he met her. Right soppy little bastard he's becoming. We'll lose him to her if we ain't careful, boy, you mark my words. If you want my advice, you need to nip it in the bud.'

Vinny couldn't help but smirk. He would do more than just nip it in the bud.

Brenda was dismayed to walk into her house and find virtually all her family present, bar her mother and eldest brother. She had planned her speech in her mind, but there was no way she was disclosing her big secret in front of them all.

'What's up with you? You look like you've lost a pound and found a penny,' Vivian chuckled.

'Where's Mum?' Brenda asked, looking thoroughly miserable. She wasn't in the mood for jokes, no matter how funny they were.

'Here she is now. Vinny's with her as well,' Roy said, looking out of the window.

The mention of her big brother was enough to make Brenda want to escape the family gathering. 'I'm gonna go for a lie-down. Tell Mum I've still got that bug and I don't want no dinner,' she lied, darting up the stairs.

'Well, this is a nice surprise. All my boys visiting me together without warning,' Queenie grinned.

'We need to talk to you about something, Mum. Or, has Vinny already spoken to you about it?' Roy asked suspiciously.

'Yes, he has. Now, shall you tell Lenny the good news? Or shall I?'

Michael and Roy looked at one another in bewilderment. What the hell was their mother going on about?

Vinny sat down on the sofa next to his cousin, winking at his brothers, as if to warn them to keep their mouths shut. 'Me, Roy and Michael have been thinking, Champ. You're a big boy now and it's about time you joined the family firm. You will have to leave school obviously, but it will be good for you to work and earn your own money, won't it?'

'But, I don't wanna leave school. I will miss all my friends.'

'No, you won't. This is your last year at school anyway. You'll be working with me, Champ, and I thought your job could involve a bit of DJ-ing. How's that grab ya?'

Like magic, Lenny's eyes suddenly shone with excitement. 'What, I can be the DJ in your club? And can I play whatever music I want?'

'Well, not every night, but sometimes you can,' Vinny laughed, ruffling his cousin's thick mop of dark hair.

When the boy began leaping up and down as though he had just won the football pools, Vivian and Queenie shared a satisfied smile.

Roy and Michael stared at one another while the rest of the family celebrated Lenny's new job. Neither was happy with Vinny making decisions behind their backs, and both thought that the club was a far too dangerous place for somebody of Lenny's mentality. Roy was the first to find his voice. 'Right, can we discuss what we came here to discuss now?' he asked, glaring at Vinny.

'Mum, sit down a minute,' Vinny ordered.

'What's the matter?' Queenie asked, clocking the sudden serious expressions on all three of her boys' faces.

Knowing what a bastard Vinny could sometimes be, Roy decided to spill the beans himself. 'It's Dad, Mum. He came to see me at the club yesterday. He's ill. In fact, he's dying I think, and he wants to make things right with all of us before he croaks it.'

'You don't have to see him though, Mum. Don't feel pressurized if you don't want to,' Vinny added.

'Fucking old bastard. Deserves to rot in hell after what he did to you,' Vivian spat.

About to agree with her sister, Queenie looked at the hopeful expressions on Roy and Michael's faces. She had no feelings for Albie whatsoever, so whether he was dying or not, seeing him wouldn't upset her at all.

'I want to see Uncle Albie. If I don't he might die like my dad did and then I will never see him again,' Lenny said.

'Shut up, you, and eat your fucking sweets,' Vivian barked.

Queenie looked at Vinny. They had a sixth sense between them and she could tell by his eyes he was urging her to say no. 'Look, boys, this has been a bit of a bombshell dropped on me, so can I sleep on it and decide tomorrow?'

'Course you can, Mum,' Vinny replied.

Queenie stood up. 'Right, I dunno about yous lot, but I'm bleedin' starving. Now, who wants some liver and bacon?'

CHAPTER SEVENTEEN

After a sleepless night in which she must have finally dozed off for an hour or two, Brenda woke up feeling nauseous then dashed to the toilet to be violently sick. When she opened the bathroom door planning to crawl back to bed, she was confronted with her mum leaning against the wall outside, her face like thunder.

'I think me and you need to have a little chat, young lady, don't you?' Queenie said, folding her arms in a stern manner.

Brenda nodded sheepishly, then promptly burst into tears.

'No point bastard-well crying after the horse has bolted, Bren, and don't lie to me 'cause I know all the signs. Now, who is the fucking father?' Queenie spat.

'If I tell you, will you promise me you won't tell my brothers? It wasn't a fling, Mum. I'm not a slag. He was my boyfriend,' Brenda wept.

Queenie was struggling to hold her temper, but knew she had to get the important information out of Brenda before she let fly at her. 'Just tell me who he is, love, then we'll sort it out from there.'

Relieved that her mother seemed to be taking the news so well, Brenda decided to come clean. 'It's Dean. Dean

Smart. I haven't told him yet. He dumped me for another girl last month,' she admitted.

At the mention of the surname Smart, Queenie felt her pulse-rate shoot through the roof. Unable to stop herself, she let her hands do the talking with repetitive slaps. 'You stupid little fucker! How could you even think of getting involved with a Smart when you know how much this family hates that revolting mob? You ain't a true Butler, girl. We are loyal to the core, but not you, you take after that shitbag of a father of yours. Now, get in your bedroom, before I kick you from arsehole to breakfast time.'

Feeling incredibly sorry for herself, Brenda let out a loud wail and did exactly as she was told.

Because he worked nights and there was no way he could invite Nancy to his club now, Michael had devised a rota where he got to spend a few hours with her every day. Firstly, he would meet her at work and spend her lunch break with her. Then, he would pick her up when she had finished, so he managed to grab a couple of hours with her before he started work.

Because it was stifling hot, instead of going to the café like they usually did, Michael had made a packed lunch so they could sit in the sun and eat it.

'Are you OK? You're not your usual chatterbox self,' Nancy remarked, holding Michael's arm and giving it a reassuring squeeze.

Michael put down his sandwich and kissed his girlfriend on the lips. 'I'm OK, babe. Just got one or two things on my mind.'

'What? You're not having second thoughts about us, are you?'

'Don't be daft. I'm not worried about us, babe. It's my dad.'

Nancy listened intently while Michael explained about his dad turning up at the club, his illness, and the fall-out between Albie and the rest of the family. 'You have to forgive your dad, Michael, and visit him. Why don't you go and see your mum on your own, tell her how you are really feeling. I'm sure she will listen to you,' Nancy advised.

Amazed by his girlfriend's maturity and thoughtfulness, Michael put both arms around her and held her tightly to his chest. Nancy was the girl for him, he was sure of it.

When their mum rang up the club and summoned them to get to her house as soon as possible, Vinny and Roy guessed she had come to a decision about whether she was going to allow their father back into their lives, or not.

'I'm glad you made your mind up quickly, Mum. It's this afternoon I told him to ring back,' Roy said, walking into the lounge.

Queenie looked confused. 'What the bleedin' hell you going on about?'

'Me dad,' Roy replied.

'Oh, I ain't even had time to think about that old goat yet. We've got far more on our plates than him to worry about at the moment, ain't we, Viv? Lenny, take Little Vinny out to play,' Queenie ordered.

When her sulky nephew had stomped out of the house dragging her grandson behind him, Queenie ordered her sons to sit down on the sofa. 'It's your sister. She's got herself in the family way,' she explained bluntly.

'She's fucking what? Where is she? I'll kill her,' Vinny said, leaping up like a jack-in-the-box.

'No, you won't. You leave her to me. I need yous boys to deal with the little bastard who has sewn his seed in her. Can you do that for me?'

'Who is he, Mum? We'll sort it,' Roy said.

'Well, you ain't gonna like this but she is up the spout by Mad Freda's grandson, Dean. She ain't even with him now, but reckons she was in a relationship with him. He don't know she's in the club. Dumped our Bren last month in favour of another girl, apparently.'

'Did he really? Well, me and Vin will have to pay him a little visit, won't we, bruv?' Roy said.

Vinny was deep in thought. Terry Smart hated him with a passion, so did his old bat of a mother. Neither would be happy if he visited young Dean and forced him to make an honest woman out of his sister. That would be the payback of all paybacks.

'I hope you give him a bloody good hiding, boys. She can't have the baby. Not by a Smart,' Vivian declared.

'Well, I ain't having my grandchild aborted,' Queenie argued, glaring at her sister.

'Bren can't keep a Smart baby, can she, Vin?' Roy urged, wishing his brother would have a bit more input into the conversation. Apart from proposing to Colleen, Roy had always been indecisive when making big decisions.

Vinny smiled. He had heard good things about young Dean Smart. The lad might only be eighteen, but he had recently got away with a robbery at a post office at Stratford, so for someone so young, Dean was obviously no man's fool. Brenda wasn't the brightest bird on earth and she could do a lot worse than Dean. Pissing off Terry and Freda in the process was just an added bonus. It was a case of every cloud having a silver lining. 'I'll go and speak to young Dean. He'll stand by our Bren and make an honest woman of her, I'll make sure of it.'

Roy was furious. 'You can't marry her off to a Smart.'

Vinny stared at his mother and aunt. There seemed to be no further objections from either of them, so he continued. 'Oh, yes I can. Our Bren will not darken the name of this family. If she's old enough to hawk her mutton and get herself in the family way, then she's old enough to be married. Brenda has made her own bed, and now she can fucking well lie on it.'

Unaware of the drama unfolding less than five minutes away, Albie was currently enjoying a pint in his old local, the Blind Beggar. The pub hadn't changed that much since his last visit, and even though there were quite a lot of new faces dotted about, there were still a few of the old regulars too.

'Christ almighty! Albie Butler, I thought that was you. Blimey, it's been years since I've seen you around this neck of the woods. How you doing?' Big Stan asked, plonking himself on the seat next to Albie.

Albie put down his *Sporting Life*. Big Stan only lived five doors away from Queenie, so Albie had no alternative but to tell him about his cancer.

'Crikey, that's awful, mate. Can they cure it, like?' Big Stan asked.

Feeling a tad guilty at Stan's obvious concern, Albie shook his head. Part of him wished that he hadn't made up such an awful lie, but now he had told Roy, there was no going back. It had been pure desperation that had forced Albie to invent such a fib in the first place. Pauline had kicked him out, his money was running out fast, so what was a man to do? Also, there wasn't a day that had gone by since leaving Whitechapel where Albie hadn't thought of his children. He had missed Michael the most, as he was the one he had been the closest to. He also missed Brenda, being the only girl.

The only people in his family that Albie still harboured a grudge against were Queenie and that old bat of a sister of hers. Between them, they had slowly pushed him out of the family circle. Then, by bringing the boys up in the way they had, they had created a monstrosity.

'So, where is the cancer, Albie? Has it spread all over, like?' Big Stan asked, snapping Albie out of his daydream.

'Don't know yet. It's in me stomach somewhere and I've got to have more tests done next week,' Albie replied.

'Such a shame, mate. I thought you looked ill when I saw you. Didn't even recognize you at first.'

Thinking what a cheerful bastard Stan was, and wishing he would sod off so he could work out the horses for his accumulator, Albie picked up his empty pint glass. 'I would offer to buy you a drink, mate, but money's a bit tight at the moment, if you know what I mean? I've been that ill, I haven't grafted for ages.'

'You sit yourself back down, Albie. The drinks are on me, mate. 'Ere, put that in your pocket as well,' Stan said, chucking a screwed-up five-pound note on the table.

When Big Stan went up the bar to get the drinks, Albie couldn't help but smirk. Being on death's door certainly had its advantages.

Queenie was mopping the kitchen floor when Michael let himself into her house. All her boys still had their own keys, and came and went as they pleased.

'Hello, son. You spoke to your brothers yet? Have they told you the news?'

When he shook his head, Queenie made a brew, sat Michael down, then explained all about Brenda's pregnancy, and what the family had decided to do about it.

Michael listened attentively, then surprised Queenie by agreeing with Vinny's idea.

'Well, Roy and Vivvy don't agree. They both think we shouldn't have a Smart in the family. Viv even suggested she had an abortion. I won't allow that, Michael. Whether

184

that child is a Smart or not, it's still my grandchild.'

'I'll go with Vinny to speak to Dean Smart. Mum, can I ask you for a favour?'

'Of course. What is it, Michael?'

'I want you to speak to my dad, and permit me to do the same. You don't have to truly forgive him in your heart, just be polite if you can. He's a prick, I know that, but whatever he is, he's still part of me, my brothers and Bren. If he weren't dying, I wouldn't ask you to do this for me.'

Thinking how mature her Michael had become all of a sudden, Queenie gave him a motherly hug. She would do anything to make her boys happy, absolutely anything. 'All right, we'll both see the old bastard together and I promise I will be as polite as I can, OK?'

Michael smiled broadly. 'Thanks, Mum. You're a real star.'

Dean Smart and his pals drank in the Black Horse in the Mile End Road, and when Vinny and Michael Butler walked in, the pub immediately fell so silent you could have heard a pin drop.

Dean wasn't a scaredy-cat by any stretch of the imagination, but seeing the menacing look on Vinny and Michael's faces, he could have kicked himself for ever getting involved with Brenda Butler.

It was Michael that finally ended the awkward silence. 'We need a quiet word with you,' he said, gesticulating towards the door.

Feeling more nervous than he ever had during the robberies he had pulled off, Dean followed the Butler brothers outside the pub. 'Look, if this is about Brenda, we finished on good terms. I do have another girlfriend now, but I swear I weren't seeing her when I was seeing Bren,' Dean gabbled.

'No! I think you meant to say that you used to have another girlfriend,' Michael said, pushing Dean against a nearby wall.

'Look, I'm sorry about dating your sister, but I really did like her. I only ended it because I was frightened of your family and my family finding out. I didn't want it to cause World War Three. I would have stayed with Bren other than that, I swear I would,' Dean stated.

'Well, that's nice to hear, isn't it, Michael?' Vinny said, grinning at his brother.

'Yep, sure is,' Michael replied in an equally jovial tone. He was thoroughly enjoying watching Dean Smart squirm. Served the little bastard right for taking such liberties.

'What you doing? I swear I won't go near Brenda again. On my nan's life I won't,' Dean croaked, when Vinny grabbed him around the neck and began squeezing his windpipe.

Unable to stop himself from giving Dean the knee of all knees in the bollocks, Vinny said what he had come here to say. 'You will go near my sister again, boy. Dipping your wick without protection has now mapped your life out for you, unfortunately. I will arrange the wedding a.s.a.p., and you will be a good husband to my sister and an even better father to your unborn child. Now, do we understand one another?'

Learning that he was about to become not only a father but also a husband was all too much for young Dean to take in and when Vinny let go of his throat, he slid down the wall and slumped onto the pavement.

'Well, answer my brother, then,' Michael ordered, giving Dean a sharp kick in the ribs.

Dean knew when he was beaten. His dad was a wannabe gangster, but had never achieved much in his life, and seeing as he was the only boy in the family, he had no proper back-up. When Vinny grabbed him by the hair and dragged him to his feet again, Dean held his palms upright as if to surrender his fate. 'I understand, OK?'

Smirking, Vinny ruffled the boy's long hair. 'Sensible lad you are, Dean. Now, let's have a proper family discussion about the wedding tomorrow, eh? Meet us round my mother's house about twoish.'

Wanting to cry, Dean took a deep breath and instead nodded miserably.

'And try and put a smile on your face before you arrive. Our Brenda won't wanna see you with a face like your cat's just been run over by a bus,' Michael added.

Vinny chuckled. Michael had excelled himself in his eyes today, and he was dead proud of his little brother's wit and attitude. Vinny unlocked the car door, then took one last look at Dean's shell-shocked face. 'Oh, and Dean, I need you to do one more thing for me.'

'What?'

'Get that fucking hair cut before you meet your future mother-in-law. You wanna make a good impression, don't you now?'

CHAPTER EIGHTEEN

Brenda was lying in bed feeling dreadfully sorry for herself when her mother traipsed in with a tray. On it was a boiled egg, toast, and a steaming mug of tea. 'Now, get this down your neck. I'm not having no grandchild of mine being born malnourished.'

Brenda sat up. 'I'm not even sure I'm keeping the baby yet, Mum. I don't think I'm old enough to cope with a kid.'

'If you're old enough to drop your drawers and get yourself up the duff in the first place, then you're old enough to be a good mother. And don't you dare even think about getting rid of that child. The family have made a decision. You're having it, and that's that.'

'You haven't told my brothers, have you?' Brenda asked, alarmed. She knew they'd been at the house yesterday because she had heard all three of their voices, but she had surmised they were there discussing her father.

'Well, of course I've told them. You'll be as fat as a bull soon. Hardly something we can disguise, is it? You daft apeth.'

When her daughter leapt out of bed and began to get dressed, Queenie asked her what she was doing.

'Going to see Dean. It's mine and his baby, and it should be us deciding if we want to keep it, or not.'

'Sit your arse back down, you silly little mare. Vinny and Michael have already spoken to Dean and told him about the baby. He's coming round here at two, so best you have a wash and smarten yourself up a bit before he arrives.'

In shock, Brenda almost fell back onto the bed. 'Why is Dean coming here?'

'To sort out the wedding of course. You, young lady, are getting married.'

Dean Smart felt like a man on death row who was walking in the direction of the gallows as he trudged dejectedly towards the Butler household. Apart from Brenda, Dean knew none of the family particularly well. Thanks to their notorious reputation, he obviously knew who each of them was, but last night was the first time he had ever really had a conversation with Vinny, or Michael.

On reaching the pathway that led to the front door, Dean felt physically sick. He had sort of liked Brenda, but not enough to bloody well marry her.

When the bell rang, Queenie ordered Lenny to answer the door for her. Vinny hadn't arrived yet, but the rest of the family were all present.

Brenda couldn't remember ever feeling more nervous. The palms of her hands were sweaty, her heart was beating rapidly, she hated the outfit that her mother had forced her to wear, and she couldn't bring herself to make eye contact with Dean.

Neither Queenie and Vivian had ever been one to suffer soppy, childish behaviour. 'Don't sit there like a bleedin' lemon then, Bren. Say hello to the boy,' Queenie barked.

'She obviously weren't that shy with him before,' Vivian mumbled.

'Hello, Dean. How are you? Thanks for coming round,' Brenda gabbled, staring at her hands.

'Jesus Christ! Do excuse my daughter for acting like silly-girl-got-none. Now, what would you like to drink? Cup of tea? Or a beer?' Queenie asked, smiling at Dean. She and Vivian had had a little chat about the boy's arrival this morning, and both had agreed if Vinny and Michael thought Dean was good enough to marry Brenda and become part of the Butler clan, then they should make an effort to be nice to him.

'Er, is it OK if I have a beer, please?' Dean asked. He had noticed Roy drinking one, and hoped it might calm his nerves a bit.

'Have what you like, mate. You've already had me sister,' Roy said, glaring at Dean.

'Now, don't start performing, Roy. I want this to be a pleasant get-together. Where's Colleen by the way? I haven't seen her since you got engaged.'

'At work. I don't like bringing her here anyway. Vinny obviously doesn't like her, and we all know what Vinny says goes, don't we, Mum?' Roy spat. He was furious that Vinny and Michael had paid Dean a visit and decided his sister's fate without involving him. It had made him feel like an outcast yet again. He'd felt like that a lot lately, especially when Ahmed was at the club.

When his aunt handed Dean a beer, Lenny grinned at him. 'So, when you shagged my cousin, did you plan to get her pregnant?'

Vivian wanted to laugh and congratulate her son on asking such an awkward question, but instead she pretended to be annoyed. 'You'll be going upstairs to wash your mouth out in a minute, young man. Now leave poor Dean alone.'

Queenie and Vivian then began asking him question after question, and Dean was almost relieved when Vinny turned up with his little boy in tow.

'So, have you told your family about the baby yet, Dean? Bet your nan weren't too pleased,' Queenie chuckled.

'Bet his old man weren't either,' Vinny said, smirking at his brothers. Terry Smart was a trappy nobody who had got a bit too lippy a year or so back. He had been spouting his mouth off in the Grave Maurice about how the Butlers were no match for some of the other London firms, so Vinny had decided to teach him a lesson with a hammer. Vinny had concentrated just on Terry's mouth in a bid to teach him to keep it shut in future. It seemed to have worked. Terry couldn't eat and drank only through a straw for a month after the attack, and had never bad-mouthed the Butlers since.

'To be honest, I haven't had a chance yet,' Dean admitted, sheepishly.

'Why don't you let me tell them for you? I can see you're dreading it, boy,' Vinny offered. It wouldn't just make his day breaking the news of the baby and the forthcoming marriage to Dean's dad and grandma. It would make his fucking year.

Remembering the state of his father's face after his altercation with Vinny Butler, Dean immediately shook his head. 'No. If I'm gonna be a father, then I should tell them myself. I'm a man now, not a boy.'

'Well, in that case, best you ask my sister to marry you properly then. I take it you haven't done so yet?' Vinny asked.

Debating whether to leg it out of the front door and jump on the first train to a different part of the country, Dean just ended up shaking his head instead.

Thoroughly enjoying watching Dean squirm, Michael joined in with the fun. 'Chop, chop then. What you waiting for, Deano?'

Knowing he had no choice but to propose properly, Dean got down on one knee in front of Brenda and held her trembling hands. 'Will you do me the honour of becoming my wife, Bren?'

Brenda looked into Dean's eyes and could see quite clearly by his horrified expression that he was only asking her to marry him because he was too frightened to stand up to her brothers. Still, she didn't care. Dean was her first real love and once they had their own house and a baby, he would be tied to her forever. 'What about your new girlfriend?' Brenda asked. She was determined to play a bit hard to get even though she was gagging to say yes.

'She's history. I never wanted to split up with you in the first place, Bren, you know that. I only ended it because I thought it would cause murders if our families found out,' Dean lied.

'So, what did she say when you finished with her, then?' Brenda asked, suspiciously.

'For Christ's sake, Bren. The boy will have cramp kneeling down like that if you don't bloody well answer his question soon,' Queenie said.

With all eyes on her, Brenda grinned broadly. 'Yes, Dean. I will be your wife.'

An hour later, Dean Smart stood outside the house he shared with his grandma and father. His mum had died while giving birth to him, and so Dean had been raised an only child.

He let himself into his home with a heavy heart. His nan despised the Butlers so Christ knows what she would make of him impregnating Brenda.

'That you, boy? Do you want a corned-beef sandwich? I'm just making your dad one,' Freda said.

Thankful that his nan and dad were both at home so he could kill two birds with one stone, Dean asked her to sit down in the lounge.

'You ain't got yourself bleedin' nicked, have you?' Freda asked accusingly.

'Spit it out, then. What you done?' Terry Smart asked.

Freda sat on the armchair. She knew neither her son nor grandson were what could be described as life's role models, but they both had a good heart, and weren't bloody thugs or murderers like members of a certain family she could mention.

Dean clasped his quivering hands together, then took a deep breath. 'Please don't hate me, but I've got a girl pregnant and I've agreed to marry her.'

Freda felt her heart leap with joy. Dean might only be young, but getting hitched and being responsible for a child of his own was exactly what he needed in her opinion. If that didn't keep him on the straight and narrow, then nothing would.

Terry Smart grinned. His pal had just become a granddad for the very first time, and Terry couldn't wait to brag about the soon-to-be newcomer to his family too. 'You'll be a great dad, Deano. Don't be asking me to change any nappies though, will ya? I've got my street cred to consider.'

'So, what did Sandra's parents say, boy? I hope you asked her dad for permission to take her hand in marriage before you proposed?' Freda asked. She had met Sandra a couple of times now, and even though Freda was a little disappointed she had given herself to her grandson so early in their relationship, she still liked the girl immensely.

'It's not Sandra that I've got pregnant. It's Brenda Butler,' Dean mumbled, staring at his shoes.

Freda burst out laughing and nudged her son. 'He's a wind-up, ain't he, Tel?'

Terry Smart chuckled, but then clocking the shameful look in his son's eyes, his laughter dried up. 'You are kidding us, right?'

When Dean shook his head regretfully, Terry leapt up and went absolutely berserk. 'You stupid little cunt,' he screamed, while punching his son numerous times in the side of his head.

'Leave him! You'll do him damage,' Freda hollered, leaping on her son's back.

'Do him damage! I'll fucking kill him,' Terry yelled. How could his son do this to him when he knew how badly Vinny had beaten him? He had lost most of his teeth for fuck's sake, and now had to rely on false ones to chew his food.

Freda ran into the kitchen, grabbed her rolling pin and hit Terry over the head with it. 'Go down the pub and calm yourself down. I will sort this mess out,' she shouted.

Terry grabbed his jacket. 'You'd better fucking sort it, Muvver, because over my dead body is he gonna marry into that cunting family.'

When the front door slammed, Freda sat down on the sofa next to her grandson. Unusually for Dean, he was crying, but Freda could not find it in her heart to comfort him. 'You stupid, stupid boy. Whatever possessed you to poke your Hampton in Brenda Butler, eh? To say I'm disappointed in you is an understatement, Dean, but I'm gonna use the money I've got saved in me old biscuit tin to sort this mess out for you, OK? Now dry them bloody eyes. No point crying over spilt milk, is there?'

Furious with himself for acting like a big girl's blouse, Dean Smart wiped his eyes furiously with the cuff of his shirt. 'I have no option other than to marry Brenda, Nan. Her brothers will annihilate me if I don't. And what you going on about money for? That ain't gonna change nothing, is it?'

'Oh, yes it will! Nearly fifty pounds I've saved over the years. I shall take it round to Queenie's house right now, and insist that little tart of a daughter of hers gets an abortion.'

When his nan darted into the kitchen and ran back waving

a tin, Dean leapt up and snatched it off her. 'Don't be so stupid. Don't you think the Butlers could afford an abortion, if they wanted Brenda to have one? They don't agree with all that, which is why I have to marry the girl.'

'Marry her, my arse,' Freda spat, grabbing back the tin. Seconds later, she stomped out of the front door.

Unaware that her future son-in-law was currently chasing his gran down the road begging her not to cause any trouble, Queenie was busy discussing the day's events with Vivian. After Dean had left, the subject had turned to Albie.

'I still can't believe we have to suffer that old bastard for dinner. Can't we put some arsenic in his?' Vivian suggested.

Queenie chuckled. It had been her idea that Albie come round to hers for dinner tomorrow. There was no way that she would humiliate herself by being seen out in public with the womanizing old drunk. 'I wonder what the boys will dress him up as? Be funny if they make him look like one of them Orthodox Jews. That will give the neighbours something to talk about, won't it?'

Vivian burst out laughing. It had been Queenie's plan to bring her husband to the house in disguise. She hadn't wanted any of the neighbours to clock him.

'I'm only doing this for the boys, you know. My Michael is especially upset that his dad is dying, but I couldn't give a shit to be honest. Would have divorced him years ago and changed my name back to Wade, but I didn't want the kids to feel like bastards,' Queenie explained.

'But they are bastards. The whole of the East End knows that,' Vivian joked.

Holding her crotch to prevent herself from piddling her knickers, Queenie was about to top up Vivian's glass when the doorbell rang. 'Who the bleedin' hell's this? Look out the window, Viv. I need a wee.'

'Oh, my giddy aunt! It's only Mad Freda,' Vivian exclaimed.

Forgetting about her desire to use the toilet, Queenie ran to the door like a thoroughbred racehorse. 'Come to offer your congratulations, have you?'

'Yep, I bet she has, Queenie. Must be thrilled our families are about to be joined in matrimony,' Vivian added, putting a supportive arm around her sister's shoulder.

Freda opened her tin, took the notes out and handed them to Queenie. 'There's enough there for the abortion. Take it, it's all yours.'

Queenie chuckled. 'But, we don't believe in killing babies, do we, Vivvy?'

'Nope,' Vivian replied. The look on Mad Freda's screwed up face was absolutely priceless.

'Well, best you start believing, because there is no way my grandson is getting involved with your shitbag family. May God be my judge, I would kill for that boy, if I was forced to.'

Queenie grinned at Vivian, then ripped the notes that Freda had given her into little pieces and threw them into the air. 'Well, best you go get your gun, you mad old bat. Your Dean is a Butler now, whether you like it or not.'

Laughing when Freda crawled along the garden path trying to retrieve the money while showing her bloomers, Queenie then slammed the front door.

CHAPTER NINETEEN

Johnny Preston grinned when he stared at his reflection in the mirror. He hardly recognized himself with short, dark hair, so he doubted anybody else would.

'Right, stick this on now,' Graeme Bradley urged, handing his pal the false moustache.

'I don't like this thing. I'd much rather have grown a bit of a beard,' Johnny complained.

Graeme chuckled. He and Johnny went back years, and people used to refer to them and Dave Phillips as the three musketeers. An eight-year prison sentence for attempted murder had then narrowed it down to the two musketeers, and Graeme had been gutted when he had learned of Dave's death while serving time in Pentonville.

'You do look a bit like Hitler, but you're just gonna have to like it or lump it, I'm afraid. I've already told you, you can't have dark hair and a blond beard. You'll look a freak, and bring unwanted attention to yourself.'

Graeme had dyed Johnny's eyebrows as well, and thinking how he looked like one of the Marx brothers, Johnny ordered his pal to trim them for him. The plan they had hatched was for Johnny to park up on a motorbike near Vinny's club, shoot Vinny at point-blank range, then meet Graeme who would be waiting nearby with a van. The bike would then be loaded in the back of the van, and disposed of as quickly as possible.

Johnny did not need his disguise for the actual hit because he would be wearing a crashhelmet. His new appearance was just so he wasn't a prisoner in Graeme's home, and could pop to the shops, café, or wherever he wanted. Graeme said, as far as he was aware, there wasn't anybody in Dagenham that knew who Johnny was, but you could never be too careful. He had also told Johnny to avoid the local pubs at all costs in case the regulars started asking awkward questions.

'Does that look better?' Graeme asked, handing his pal a mirror.

'Yep, much better. Right, we ready to go and pick this bike up, then?'

Graeme reached for his keys. 'Come on, Hitler, let's go.'

Queenie and Vivian hadn't long been back from visiting their mother's grave when Vinny let himself in. 'Just checking you're both OK? That mad old cow, Freda, hasn't given you any more grief, has she? I shall have a fucking word with Dean later. He needs to man up and learn how to keep his nutty nan under control.'

'Don't you be having a go at that boy. Look at the flowers he bought me as a way of an apology. Our Bren's got herself a good 'un there. Gone out engagement-ring shopping, they have. You've only just missed them.'

Vinny grinned. Young Dean was certainly making an effort and that's what he liked to see. If Dean carried on excelling himself in the same way then Vinny might even employ him as part of the firm. Paying him a decent wage would also ensure Brenda and the baby were well looked after. 'Where's me little terror?' Vinny asked.

'Gone round the shops with Lenny to get me some pearl barley. I'm cooking lamb stew, your father's favourite,' Queenie said.

Vinny chuckled. 'I've got some rat poison at the club. I should have bought it round so you can add an extra bit of spice to Dad's.'

'Would have probably killed him. He is a fucking rat,' Vivian added, with a grin on her face.

'Mum, has Michael said anything to you about this new bird of his? Don't say I mentioned anything, but he's been disappearing at odd times of the day and it all seems a bit secretive for my liking.'

'No, he ain't. He's definitely loved up though, I know that much. Maybe our Alfie's found the one,' Queenie chuckled.

He and Michael had been getting on quite well recently, but Vinny still had a hunch that his brother was lying to him about the identity of his bird. The only way to find out was to follow him one day. 'Oh and Mum, while I think of it, I've organized a joint engagement party for our Roy and Brenda. Monday week at the club. I thought Lenny could do his first disco for us that night,' Vinny said, grinning at his aunt.

Vivian clapped her hands together with excitement. 'Oh, wait till I tell him. He'll be made up, Vinny.'

'Lenny might be made up, but I doubt Roy and Colleen will, son. Not only is it bloody short notice, but I think they will want their own big moment. They did get engaged first.'

Vinny did his best to look serious. He knew that Roy and Colleen would be pissed off sharing an engagement party with Dean and Brenda, which had been the idea in the first place. 'Don't be daft, Mum. It ain't like they're sharing it with strangers. Brenda and Dean are family, and sharing is what families like ours do.'

Michael Butler laughed when Nancy told him the story about Roger's visit to the *Top of the Pops* studio. 'Honestly Michael, he really thought he was making me jealous when he said Marc Bolan kept looking at him when he was singing. He really is a such a twerp.'

Michael put his arm around his girlfriend and, even though they were sitting on a park bench in broad daylight, kissed her passionately. When he had first met Nancy she had been quite shy with him, but she had now come out of her shell a lot. Her stories always made him laugh and his feelings for her were becoming stronger as every day passed. 'I wish we could spend more time with each other, Nance. I know we always spend the whole of Wednesdays together, but an hour or two here and there the rest of the time just don't seem enough, does it?'

Nancy sighed and laid her head on Michael's shoulder. 'I know. I feel the same, but with me working days and you nights, it's so bloody awkward.'

Michael racked his brain for a minute then came up with a suggestion. 'Look, please don't take this the wrong way, but can't you pretend that you are staying around a mate's next Tuesday night? I can easily get that night off and I can book us into a nice hotel in London. No hanky-panky, unless you want to, I promise. It will just be so nice to spend the whole night together even if we just kiss and cuddle, then we can spend all day Wednesday up the West End. I'll take you shopping, then we can go for a nice meal. What do you reckon?'

Nancy grinned broadly. Her parents were bound to give her a Spanish Inquisition as she rarely stayed out all night, but she could handle them. Also, her brother had just spent two nights away camping and seeing as she would soon be seventeen, they had no right to dictate to her what she could and couldn't do. 'As long as you keep those wandering hands of yours to yourself, Michael Butler, I reckon we just might have a deal.'

Queenie was delighted when Brenda burst through the door and excitedly showed her the ring on her finger. Her daughter had never been the cheeriest of girls, and Queenie couldn't help but think how happy and radiant she looked for a change. 'Vivvy, come and have a look at this. Oh Bren, it's beautiful. Where did you get it?' Queenie asked Dean.

'At a jeweller's shop in Bethnal Green, Mrs Butler.'

'You're virtually family now, so we'll have no more of that Mrs Butler, you call me Queenie, boy. What happened to your eye by the way? Walk into a door? Or your dad's fist, did ya?'

'Yeah, something like that,' Dean replied.

'Oh, it's stunning, Bren. What a lucky girl you are to have a handsome ring like that. My stone was no bigger than the head of a pin on the ring that Bill bought me. And it was a bastard fake,' Vivian said bitterly.

Lenny hated being left out of anything that the adults were talking about. 'How much did that cost then?' he asked.

'You don't ask people how much things cost, Lenny. It's rude,' Vivian scolded her son.

'Are you gonna stay for a bit of dinner, Dean? Vinny, Roy and Michael will be here soon,' Queenie said.

'No, but thanks anyway. I need to sort things out with me dad and stuff.'

'Well, if he clumps you again, you tell my Vinny. He'll sort any differences out for you,' Queenie told her future son-in-law.

Feeling totally out of his depth with such an overpowering family, Dean pecked Brenda on the cheek, told her he would pop around to see her the following day, then darted out the front door.

Both Queenie and Vivian were glued to the window as Roy ushered Albie up the path. He had a great big brown hat on and a long tan raincoat.

'Oh, for fuck's sake. He looks like Clint Eastwood in *A Fist Full of Dollars*,' Queenie laughed.

'He looks like a fucking flasher more like. I hope he ain't got his meat and two veg hanging out under that mac,' Vivian chuckled.

'Yuck! That ain't worth seeing, trust me on that one. Right, try and keep a straight face 'cause if you laugh, then so will I,' Queenie ordered her sister.

'Hello Uncle Albie. Auntie Queenie reckons you look like Clint Eastwood now,' Lenny said, hugging his long-lost uncle.

'You can't say nothing in front of him. Ears like Dumbo he's got,' Vivian mumbled.

'Hello, Lenny. Ain't you got big, eh? And look at you, Brenda. My, my, you were only a little girl last time I saw you, and now you're a proper young lady. How are you, darling?' Albie asked his daughter fondly.

'Up the spout! And how are you, dear Daddy?' Brenda replied, glaring at her father.

About to giggle at her daughter's warped sense of humour, Albie turned to his wife, so somehow Queenie managed to contain herself.

'Hello, Queenie. Thanks for inviting me round for dinner. It truly means the world to me to see you all again.'

Queenie stared at her estranged husband and couldn't help but be shocked. He had aged so much, and his face was wrinkled and gaunt-looking. 'Take your coat and hat off, Albie. What do you want to drink? Tea? A beer? Or brandy?'

'I wouldn't say no to a brandy, Queenie, and is that your legendary lamb stew I can smell cooking?'

'It sure is. I remembered how much you liked it. Right, come and help me pour the drinks, Vivvy,' Queenie ordered her sister.

'What you being so nice to him for?' Vivian spat, as soon as they were out of earshot.

'I'm not. I only asked if he wanted a fucking drink and answered his question about the stew. Oh, thank Christ for that, here's Vinny and Michael. They can talk to the old bastard now,' Queenie whispered.

Albie stood up nervously. 'Hello, lads. How are you? And who is this? I needn't ask that actually because you look so much like your daddy did at your age,' Albie said, his voice full of emotion at seeing his grandson for the very first time.

When Little Vinny hid behind his father's legs and shouted, 'Go away, creepy old man,' Albie got a bit tearful. His daughter was up the duff by Christ knows who, his first grandchild hated him on sight, Vinny could barely look him in the eye, and it was obvious that Vivian still despised him as she hadn't even said hello.

Michael sat down next to his father and hugged him. 'Don't cry, Dad. You've got all your family around you again now, and we're all here to support you, aren't we?' He glared at his siblings.

When each of his children said an unenthusiastic 'Yes', Albie glanced up and happened to catch Queenie and Vivian smirking nastily at one another. In that split second, he knew he wasn't to blame for anything he had done in the past. His drinking had only escalated when Queenie and Vivian had taken over the upbringing of his children, and made it clear he wasn't wanted around the house any more. His affairs had only begun when he'd realized that Queenie had just used him as a breeding machine and once she'd had all the children she wanted, she'd made it obvious that he repelled her. Even now, he had been forced to tell such a dreadful lie and pretend he was dying as he knew his children would never have agreed to speak or meet up with him if they hadn't first had approval from their mother. Everybody thought that Vinny ruled the roost, but he didn't. Queenie would always be top dog.

Aware of Albie staring at her as though he had lost his marbles, Queenie smiled to break the awkward moment. 'You OK, Albie? Do you want another brandy?'

Albie looked at Vivian and then back to Queenie. Both were evil vicious women who had ruined his life and his children's. Determined not to ruin the only chance he might ever get to be close to his kids again, Albie took a deep breath, smiled falsely, and held out his glass. 'I'm fine thank you, Queenie. And yes, I would love another brandy, please.'

'Hello, love. How was your day at work? I've saved you some toad in the hole. Shall I warm it up for you now?' Mary asked her daughter.

'No, I'll have it later, and work was fine, thanks. Erm, you don't mind if I sleep over my friend's house next Tuesday evening, do you? It's her eighteenth birthday and her parents are organizing a little get-together for her.'

'And what friend is this, may I ask?' Donald enquired, casting his beady eyes on his daughter.

'Katie. She hasn't been working at Woolies long. But she is so lovely, and we get on really well,' Nancy lied.

'I've never heard you mention a Katie before,' Christopher remarked accusingly.

'Well, seeing as this past year or so you've turned into an irritable little shit, why would I tell you anything about my life?' Nancy demanded, her eyes blazing with anger.

Mary immediately tried to defuse the situation. 'Now, can we talk sensibly for once, please? Let's not all start arguing.'

Donald glared at Nancy. 'You are getting far too big for your boots just lately, young lady. You do not swear at your brother like that, so apologize to Christopher at once. And you can make more of an effort to be polite to poor Roger in future as well. So rude to him you were again yesterday evening, I barely knew where to look. Right, the answer to your question, you can go to your friend Katie's birthday gathering, but you're not staying at her house all night. I want you home here by midnight at the latest.'

Since Michael had suggested them spending the night together in a hotel room, Nancy had thought of little else. She had been in a delirious trance at work all afternoon, and her friend Rhonda had been just as excited about Michael's idea as she was. There was no way she would allow her father to spoil her big date. Michael would see her as some silly child if she had to be home by midnight. 'I am nearly seventeen years old, Dad, not seven, and if I want to stay over at a friend's house, then I shall.'

Hating being defied, Donald jumped from his chair and wagged a stern finger in his daughter's face. 'I know full well that you aren't planning on staying at a friend's house, Nancy. You have a young fancy-man and I will not permit you to indulge in debauchery of any kind. Do you hear me?'

'You calling me a slag?' Nancy screamed.

'For goodness' sake, you two. I've been run off my feet all day in the shop and I now need to relax. A slanging match is the last thing I bloody well need. Now, you go and warm that dinner up, Nancy, and you sit back down and watch the TV, Donald,' Mary ordered.

When Nancy stomped out into the kitchen, Donald's face was red with temper. 'My daughter will not become a whore,

Mary. I will not allow it. She stays at home next Tuesday night, and that's final.'

Albie sat in silence as Roy drove him back to his bedsit. It had been great to see his family again, but it had also been awkward, upsetting and had dredged up many bad memories. Albie was no drunk when he had first met Queenie. He had been a vibrant, handsome young man who was full of laughter, self-confidence and could have taken his pick of any woman he wanted. It had been Queenie who had chased him. Oh yes, she had trapped him all right, and had then discarded him like a dirty piece of old rag when he'd served his purpose. Even their Brenda's conception had been a complete fluke. Queenie had allowed him one fumble for the first time in nearly a year, and Brenda had been the outcome of it.

'You OK, Dad?' Roy asked.

'Yep, as good as can be expected, boy. I enjoyed your mum's stew. The only decent meal I've had in months, that was.'

'Well, I'm sure you'll be invited round for another meal. Look, I know things were a bit stifled tonight, but it will get better given time, you know. And don't take no notice of Little Vinny's rudeness. He's like that with most people he meets and needs a good right-hander if you ask me. Vinny and Mum have spoilt him something rotten.'

Albie nodded understandingly. The grandchild had given him a terrible time. 'So, when will I see yous all again?' he asked, when Roy brought the car to a halt.

Feeling dreadfully sorry for his disconsolate-looking father, Roy pulled a wad of money out of his pocket. 'Here, that should see you all right for a while.' He peeled off fifty quid.

'Thanks, Roy,' Albie said gratefully.

'Dad, if I ask you something, will you give me an honest answer?'

'Yes, son.'

'What happened to that Judy Preston? Did she keep your kid?' Roy asked. It had been Vinny who had persuaded him to raise the question.

'I have no idea. Never seen, spoken, or heard a word from or about Judy since I was in hospital that time when your brother broke my legs.'

Satisfied that his father was telling the truth, Roy nodded. 'Go on, you get off and I'll see you again real soon. Look after yourself, Dad.'

'When will I see you?' Albie asked for the second time.

Roy winked. 'You leave it with me and Michael and we'll sort something out. I know where to find you. I'll either come here, or pop in the Blind Beggar.'

'Well, don't leave it too long in case I'm brown bread,' Albie muttered morosely, as he shut the car door.

When Roy drove away, Albie took the five ten-pound notes out of his pocket and grinned. Tonight might not have been perfect, but he now had his beer money for the foreseeable future, so it was definitely a step in the right direction. It was the years of heavy drinking that had made Albie lose weight and look so ill. As for his hair thinning rapidly, that happened to most blokes over fifty, didn't it? The breathlessness was down to his chain smoking, and all Albie had to do now was continue his little lie until he had won his children over. He would then pretend his cancer was in remission and they would all live happily ever after.

CHAPTER TWENTY

Johnny Preston watched the comings and goings at the club with interest. He and Graeme wanted to get a rough idea of Vinny's movements before they finalized their plan, which was why they were parked up in a red Transit van with false number plates. Johnny had made the mistake of being ill-prepared the last time he had stalked Vinny and was determined not to make the same mistake twice.

'Rumour has it that our mate Vinny has a lucrative little sideline in the drug business now, you know. Him and some Turkish geezer are meant to be the two Mr Bigs behind most of the substances being punted around London. Don't know how true it is, or if his brothers know about it, but I heard it from a good source,' Graeme informed his friend.

'It wouldn't surprise me. Who told you?' Johnny asked.

'Ronny Mitchell told Gerry when he was pissed in the Flag. You know how Gerry can't keep a secret, don't ya? Told me the following day, he did.'

Johnny smirked and then slid down in his seat. 'Get your head down, Grae, he's just pulled up again. That's the divvy cousin with him this time, ain't it?'

'I wouldn't know what the divvy cousin looks like now.

Big lump, whoever it is. He's got a bird with him as well, and a kid.'

Johnny peeped over the dashboard. 'That has to be his kid. I dunno who the tart is though. I was always under the impression he was shafting his own mother.'

Graeme chuckled. 'He's gone inside now. Do you want to wait for a bit longer to see if he leaves? Or, shall we go and grab some lunch?'

'I don't think we should hang about here any more in the day. We need to start watching his movements of a night. Obviously Friday and Saturdays are a no-go because he probably don't leave the club. Not only that, it will be heaving with punters and far too risky anyway. I reckon we should keep watch every night from tonight onwards, and the first moment that presents itself, I will shoot the cunt straight through the skull.'

When Vinny had finished showing her the ropes, Karen grinned enthusiastically. The club's décor was truly spectacular. The chairs and sofas were bright red leather, the ceiling a maze of spotlights. There was even a VIP section which was as opulent as anything Karen had ever seen. It was certainly a far cry away from the dirty, drab-looking pub she had recently been working in in Dagenham.

'What do you think of this?' Vinny asked, flicking a switch.

Karen gasped and clapped her hands together excitedly. The spotlights had different coloured bulbs inside them and rotated in the ceiling to form the most incredible pattern on the dancefloor. 'Wow! That is fabulous, Vinny. In fact, I think the whole club looks amazing. You and your brothers must be so proud of owning a place like this! It reminds me of one of those clubs in an American film.'

Vinny grinned. He had based the décor of his club on

one that he had seen in an American gangster movie. He had even added to the effect by placing portraits of legendary mafia members, famous American film stars, and jazz musicians around the walls. 'I'm glad you like it, Kaz. Means a lot to me, that does.'

Karen didn't want to feel the way she did about Vinny, but spending time with him as part of a family had made all her old feelings resurface. She had seen a much softer side to him as a dad, and as a person, and knew she was falling in love with him all over again.

Aware that Karen was looking at him with a drippy lovesick expression, Vinny was relieved by Lenny's re-appearance.

'I've swept out the front like you asked me too. Will you show me the disco equipment now? I need to get some practice.'

'Yep. Follow me, Champ.'

Creatures of habit, both Queenie and Vivian were scrubbing their doorsteps when Michael pulled up in the car.

'Auntie Viv. I've got a bit of news about Bill's murder for you,' Michael said.

Vivian dropped her scrubbing brush in the bucket and followed Michael inside Queenie's house. 'Don't tell me the old fucker woke up at the mortuary,' she joked.

Michael chuckled. 'No, but they have charged someone with his murder and are ready to release his body now. His funeral is to be held at the City of London Crematorium at 2 p.m. next Wednesday. I thought I'd better tell you because Champ has been banging on about going to it. Reckons he wants to say a proper goodbye to his dad.'

Vivian pursed her thin lips. 'Well, he can want on, I'm afraid. Over my dead body will I allow my Lenny to attend that bastard's funeral. Glad he is being cremated though.

As the old saying goes, you bury treasure and burn rubbish.'

Unable to concentrate on work, Nancy had been like a cat on a hot tin roof all day. Her father hadn't spoken to her since their argument at the weekend, and Nancy now knew that the only way she would be able to stay out with Michael was by pretending she was coming home straight from work on Tuesday.

'So, what you wearing? Show me,' Rhonda Gibbs said, grabbing her pal's arm as they took their tea break together.

Nancy led her friend out the back. She knew to avoid suspicion she would have to bring her belongings into work in dribs and drabs. 'I hope it isn't creased. I'm wearing this tomorrow night. What do you think?'

When Nancy pulled the chiffon black and white polka-dot catsuit out of a carrier bag, Rhonda gasped. 'Oh Nance. It's beautiful. Do you think you will end up sleeping with him?'

'No, I won't! I don't want him to think I'm some slag. I wish you and Kevin could have hit it off. I wouldn't be so nervous if all four of us were going to the hotel.'

Rhonda smiled, but said nothing. She had kissed Michael's best friend on the night they had met at the fairground, but she hadn't wanted to take the relationship any further. Kevin was sweet, but Rhonda knew that her dad would have murdered her if he found out she was dating a mixed-race lad. 'You won't be nervous when you get there. Have a couple of Cinzano and lemonades. That will take the edge off a bit. I'm dreading your mum or dad ringing my house, Nance. I hope I don't put my foot in it.'

'Course you won't! Just say what I told you to say. I have gone to Katie's birthday bash and will be home Wednesday teatime, OK? They can't call you a liar as well,

Rhon. Anyway, I am only lying to them because my dad is so bloody unreasonable. I'm sick of him treating me like a child and I'm not putting up with it any more.'

'But say your dad kicks you out or something?'

Nancy shook her head confidently. 'No way could he ever kick me out. My mum would never allow it.'

Unaware that he had a spectator, Michael was eating fish and chips and sharing a bottle of cider in the park with Nancy.

Vinny studied the two lovesick fools through his binoculars. The bird was stunning, looked like a model, but tarts like that were trouble. Yvonne Summers had been a beauty, and look how that slag had treated him. Vinny could barely remember what Nancy looked like as a child, so had no idea whether this was her or not. What he did know was that she worked at Woolworth's, and his soppy brother looked absolutely smitten with her.

When Michael began kissing her passionately, Vinny immediately felt queasy and put down his binoculars. He hated kissing. Mouth-to-mouth contact was far too personal for his liking.

Vinny left it a few minutes, picked his binoculars up again, and was pleased to see Michael and the bird were walking back towards his car. Hopefully time to find out where the bitch lived now. Then, if she was Nancy Walker, he would have to work out what to do next.

'Eat something then, boy. I know you're worried about your father, but he's probably just gone on one of his benders like he always does when the going gets tough. You know what he's like.'

Dean put down his knife and fork and puffed out his cheeks in exasperation. His dad hadn't been seen since the day Dean had told him about his relationship with Brenda, and Dean was desperate to speak to him to try and smooth things out a bit. Obviously, his father wasn't going to be happy about the situation whatever he said, but if his nan could see a light at the end of the tunnel, then why couldn't his old man do the same? Surprisingly, Freda had managed to get her head around her grandson's predicament. Obviously, she was still appalled that the Smarts and Butlers would soon be joined in matrimony, but she was willing to overlook who the mother of her first great-grandchild was, because she was determined to be a good nan herself. At least the child's surname would be Smart and that alone was a consolation. 'I'm gonna have to go and find him, Nan. He's clearly still got the right hump, and this needs to be sorted out.'

'Don't be going confronting him in a pub, Deano. Wait till he comes home and sobers up, eh?'

'But, he's always bastard-well pissed lately, Nan, and he ain't been coming home. I know you're worried about him too, and seeing as this is all my fault, it's my duty to make things right.'

Freda grabbed hold of her grandson's arm. 'Let me go and find him. He's probably in the Grave Maurice, or the Prince Regent in Salmon Lane.'

Dean gently removed his nan's hand. 'No. This is my mess and I am quite capable of sorting it out myself.'

Even though she was close to all three of her boys, Queenie Butler now saw far less of Roy than the other two. Since he had met Colleen, any spare time Roy had he liked to spend with her, so it had been a nice surprise when he turned up on his own today. 'Want some spotted dick with syrup, boy? I've only just steamed it.'

'No thanks, Mum. I'd love a cup of tea though. Where's Vinny and Brenda? Champ's still at the club with Michael. Doing OK he is, you know.'

Queenie chuckled. 'I knew he'd be an asset to yous boys. Vivvy's knackered, Roy, gone indoors for a lie-down she has, and Brenda has popped out with Susan. Never seen your sister so happy before. Perhaps having a sprog and getting hitched is all she ever wanted in life.'

'Well, I hope it works out between her and Dean for all our sakes. Actually, it was my wedding that I came here to talk to you about. Neither me nor Colleen want to rush into things, but I would like to organize a surprise engagement party for her in the near future and wondered if you would help me? I was thinking of arranging it on the weekend that Colleen's birthday falls at the end of August. I want to get all her family over from Ireland for it, and I was hoping you would do all the ringing around for me. You know how crap I am on the old rag and bone.'

Queenie's heart lurched. If Roy was planning a big event where he was going to surprise Colleen by inviting all her family, then he wasn't going to be too thrilled with Vinny's bright idea of holding a joint engagement party as early as next week.

Vinny Butler was a very private man; therefore when he did participate in the occasional sexual encounter, he told nobody, and would rather pay for it than have any emotional involvement whatsoever.

Soho was Vinny's preferred destination. He had found a tasteful, discreet whorehouse there, with a quiet little bar nearby.

'Another large Scotch, sir?' the barmaid asked.

Vinny nodded. He had earlier followed Michael's girl-friend back to what looked like a newsagent's or general store, but the shop had been closed and the girl had then used a side door. Vinny had managed to get a closer look at her as she had entered the building, and he had a strong feeling that she was in fact Nancy Walker. The shop must belong to her parents, and he would find out for sure tomorrow when he paid another visit to see who was running it. He would recognize that pretentious bastard Donald in an instant.

'Would you like another?' the barmaid asked again a couple of minutes later.

Slamming the glass on the bar, Vinny shook his head. He was stressed out, angry, and the quicker he released his pent-up frustration on whatever slag took his fancy, the better.

Dean Smart felt the atmosphere in the Grave Maurice change as soon as he walked in. His father was standing with the usual half a dozen cronies he drank with, and when a few of them spotted his presence, there was a deathly silence. 'Dad, can I have a word with you in private, please?' Dean asked, politely.

Terry Smart was extremely drunk. He was also very aware that the pals he was currently standing with were the same mates he had been drinking with the day Vinny Butler had strolled in the pub, dragged him outside, then smashed his boat race to smithereens. Desperate to save face, Terry picked up his pint glass, and lunged at his only son. 'You Judas little cunt. You're no son of mine.'

Lucy Brown was quite new to the wonderful world of prostitution, so when Vinny Butler began to shag her violently up the arse, she wondered if she had stumbled into the wrong profession. 'Can you please slow down? You're hurting me,' she gasped. Lucy had experienced anal sex with one or two of her previous clients, but Vinny's penis was over double the width of theirs.

'Just deal with it, you slag. I am fucking paying you for

this pleasure,' Vinny panted, as he grasped the back of Lucy's neck and shoved her face against the pillow to shut her up. Vinny loved inflicting pain on people, especially women, and as he rammed himself even harder into Lucy's backside, her muffled cries of agony only added to his pleasure.

CHAPTER TWENTY-ONE

Brenda was gobsmacked when she opened the front door and saw the state of her handsome fiancé. 'Oh my God, Dean! What happened to you?' she exclaimed.

'My dad glassed me. Me and him are finished now, Bren, for good.'

Queenie ran down the hallway and ushered her future son-in-law into the lounge. 'Right, that's it. I want you to go home and pack your stuff and you can move in here with Bren,' Queenie insisted, when Dean finished explaining.

'I will be fine staying at my nan's house. Honest, I will. But, thanks for the offer anyway, Queenie.'

Queenie shook her head vehemently. 'No, you bloody well won't. I'm not having the father of my Bren's baby living with a thug like Terry Smart. Go and get your bits and bobs now. You're moving in here, and that's final.'

Vinny Butler waited until the people walked away from the shop with their groceries, then casually approached it himself. As luck would have it, there was an Articles for Sale board in the shop window, so Vinny pretended to be engrossed in that while he tried to get a better look inside. Recognizing Donald Walker, Vinny felt an element of fury surge though his veins. How dare Michael disobey him in such a way? And how could he put their relationship in such jeopardy over some stupid tart?

Walking away, Vinny kicked a nearby wall in pure frustration. Michael might be about to open the biggest can of worms ever and he needed to put a stop to their tainted affair as soon as he possibly could.

Freda Smart was distraught as her grandson walked up the path with his suitcase in his hand. Twenty-two stitches the poor little sod had, and Freda would give her Terry what for when he finally showed his drunken face.

'Don't cry, Nan. You're making me upset. I promise I will ring you every day and we can meet whenever. I just don't wanna come back here any more because of Dad.'

Freda nodded miserably. She had been more of a mother than a nan to Dean, and now he was leaving her. When he waved one last time before he traipsed off down the road, Freda knew she had lost him for good. Once that vulgar Butler mob got their evil claws in him, Dean's life would be all but bloody over.

Vinny was still livid when he popped into his mother's house.

'You won't believe what our Michael has gone and done, Mum. He's heading for a good fucking hiding, I'm telling ya.' Aware that Lenny and his son were both ear-wigging, he handed his cousin a crisp pound note. 'Take Little Vinny round the shops, Champ, and get yourselves some of them Jamboree Bags, eh? I need to talk to your Auntie Queenie about a few things.'

When Lenny and his son had left the house, Vinny explained to his mum about Michael's secret relationship.

'Well, it ain't ideal, but I don't think you should worry

too much, Vinny. That unfortunate incident with Dave Phillips happened years ago, and if that Nancy's brother was ever going to retract his original statement and blab, he'd have done it long before now. You know what our Michael is like for chopping and changing his birds. Give it a month, it will have fizzled out with Nancy and he'll be onto his next victim,' Queenie chuckled.

'Well, I really ain't happy about it, Mum. That family fled the area because of what happened and I just don't want them to be reminded of it. If the brother finds out that Nancy is involved with Michael, I bet he fucking tells her and his parents the truth. The police re-opening the murder case is grief I really don't need.'

''Ere, before I forget, I've been meaning to tell you, Roy is organizing a surprise engagement party for Colleen and secretly inviting all her family over from Ireland. You're gonna have to make your one just for Brenda and Dean. Roy will be furious if it's a joint do, I know he will.'

'The party is just a small family celebration, and if Roy wants to organize another big bash later in the year, then he can. There ain't even fifty people going, Mum. It's just us and a few friends, that's it.'

'OK, but if Roy isn't happy, don't say I didn't warn you. As for Michael, you gonna confront him with your findings?'

'No, I've got a better idea than that.'

'What?'

Vinny grinned. 'I'm gonna pay his ex-bird a visit to get her to pretend she is pregnant and it's Michael's. If that don't make Nancy Walker run a mile, then nothing will. It will also teach Michael a lesson for dipping his wick so often. Don't worry, it's just a bit of fun, Mum. As soon as Nancy has scarpered, Michael will see sense anyway.'

Queenie raised her eyebrows. Her Vinny was as sharp as a razor, only he could think that one up. 'You need to sort that Terry Smart out an' all, boy. He's gone and glassed Dean now. It doesn't look good on us as a family if he isn't dealt with. We don't want people to think they can take liberties with us and get away with it, do we?'

'We can't be seen to be doing anything too rash, but Terry will be dealt with good and proper this time. Smart by name that prick is, but obviously not by nature,' Vinny replied.

Knowing that dealt with good and proper meant dead, Queenie smiled at her son. She had never liked that Terry Smart anyway.

Johnny Preston was not in the best of moods. The engine of the van he and Graeme had purchased had blown up this morning, so they were now back to square one. Part of Johnny just wanted to risk shooting Vinny, then driving back to Dagenham on the bike, but he had to think of his kids' welfare if he got a life sentence. He knew that he stood far more chance of getting away with his crime if he put the bike in the back of the van and made his escape that way, so as Graeme had insisted earlier, they just needed to be patient.

'Right, I'm gonna pop out and see my daughter for a couple of hours,' Graeme informed his pal.

Johnny nodded miserably. He wanted to get the job over with, then get back to his kids. He decided to call home. 'Hello darling. What you been up to? I hope you're looking after your mum for me while I'm away?' Johnny asked his daughter.

'You've got some front. I know your dirty little secret,' Joanna hissed, her voice full of anger.

Johnny immediately felt his pulse start to race. 'What?'

'I'm talking about having sex with women behind my mum's back.'

'I wouldn't do that to your mum, Jo. If someone has told you that, they are telling you lies.'

'No, they aren't. That lady whose house you stayed around last week is my mate Georgia's mum. I haven't told Mum, it will break her heart, but I really hate you, and I never want to speak to you again.'

When his daughter slammed the phone down on him, Johnny put his messed-up head in his hands. Sod the bloody van. The quicker he killed Vinny Butler and got back to Tiptree to sort out this terrible mess, the better.

Nancy Walker had never stayed in a hotel room in her life before, and she was amazed by how plush it was compared to her poky little bedroom. Soft beige deep-pile carpet, satin bedding, even the lampshades looked like they had cost a fortune. 'Wow, isn't it ace, Michael?'

'Only the best for you, my darling,' Michael said, truthfully. He usually shagged in the back of his car, or at the club. He had never spent this kind of money on any girl in the past.

Michael looked gorgeous in his dark suit, white shirt and black tie, and when he began kissing her passionately, Nancy felt the first stirrings of unrest. Michael made her feel alive and the thought of spending the whole night in bed with him was exciting, yet frightening at the same time.

Denise Thompson was amazed to see Vinny Butler's posh motor parked near her house. She was even more amazed when he leapt out and asked to have a quiet word with her. Surely, he hadn't got wind of her news? She had only found out herself yesterday and, apart from her best friend, had told nobody.

'How are you, Denise? Are you still working at the

telephone exchange?' Vinny asked, being ultra polite, when Denise got into the car.

'I'm fine thank you, and yeah, I'm still at the telephone exchange. What do you want? Has Michael sent you?' Denise's face was a picture of hope.

'No, not exactly. I've come to see you of my own accord, as I have a little proposition for you.'

'What?'

'Well, firstly you have to promise me that this conversation will never be repeated, Denise. You're a nice girl, which is why I would like you to get back with my brother, and you wouldn't cross me, would you?'

With his jet-black hair, menacing eyes, and fearsome reputation, Vinny Butler was the last man Denise would ever cross. 'No, I won't say a word, I promise.'

Vinny smirked. He had never particularly liked Denise. She was tarty, tawdry, and he knew of at least three other men she had slept with before she had dated his brother. Nevertheless, anyone was better than Nancy Walker, hence his little visit. 'I don't know if you are aware, but Michael has a new girlfriend, Denise?'

'Well, sort of. I've heard that he was seeing someone, but no-one's really seen him about with her. What's she like?'

'Not a nice person by all accounts, which is why I'd like you to do me a little favour. It will be in your best interests too, especially if you want Michael back.'

'What do I have to do?' Denise asked.

'Next Monday, I am holding a family party at my club. Michael will be there without his bird. I want you to turn up and tell him and the rest of my family that you are up the spout. A few weeks down the line, you can just pretend you've had a miscarriage, can't you? I'll pay you for your trouble of course. How does a hundred pounds sound?' Vinny enquired.

Denise couldn't help but smirk. She had only found out yesterday that she was actually pregnant with Michael's baby, so being paid to tell him was just a bonus. Vinny could hardly ask for his money back afterwards, could he? And from what he'd just said, he would probably be thrilled by her real news anyway.

'Well?' Vinny asked, impatient.

'OK, I'll do it. But, can you pay me the money up front?'

Vinny took his wallet out and chucked five tenners on Denise's lap. 'Half now, and half when you've done it, OK? Oh, and turn up about ten.'

'OK,' Denise said, scrambling out of the car.

Vinny grinned as he restarted his ignition. 'Bye-bye, Nancy Walker,' he mumbled.

After eating her first ever Chinese meal and thoroughly enjoying it, it was Nancy who suggested they pop into a club on the way back to the hotel.

Watching his girlfriend sway her body seductively to Curtis Mayfield's 'Move On Up', Michael noticed how he wasn't the only guy unable to take his eyes off her. Nancy's beauty shone out like a beacon and she looked incredible in her halter-neck catsuit. 'Shall I get us another drink, babe? Or, shall we make tracks?' Michael asked.

Grabbing her boyfriend around the neck, Nancy treated him to a big sloppy kiss. So what if he was a Butler? Nancy knew if she lived until she was a hundred, she would never meet another guy who made her feel the way that Michael did. 'Let's go and snuggle up in that big bed, shall we?' she whispered, the alcohol playing a big part in her bravery.

Grinning like his Premium Bond numbers had just come up, Michael grabbed Nancy's hand and whisked her out of the club before she had a change of mind.

*

223

Vinny smirked as he scanned his brother's address book and found the phone number of Colleen's parents. He and Roy had had words earlier over Ahmed being at the club more often, but Vinny didn't give a shit what his brother thought any more. Roy should have stayed loyal to him and the business instead of putting birds at the top of his priority list. 'Hello, is that Mrs O'Connell?' Vinny asked politely.

The telephone conversation continued for a good few minutes, and when the O'Connells finally agreed to attend their daughter's engagement party, even though it was at very short notice, Vinny couldn't help but smirk. Colleen's family hadn't had the pleasure of meeting the Butlers yet, and he would make damn sure they never fucking forgot them in a hurry. If his plan worked, not only would Michael be single again, but so would Roy.

Donald Walker was totally incensed. He had warned his wife that he thought his daughter was going to ignore his orders and stay out all night, but Mary had insisted otherwise. 'Ring that Rhonda, now,' Donald ordered, his voice booming even louder than usual.

'I don't want to wake the girl's parents up, Donald. It's gone eleven, for goodness' sake.'

'I don't care if it's three in the bloody morning. I have every right to know where my daughter is.'

'Dad's right, Mum. Nancy could be lying in a ditch somewhere for all we know,' Christopher added solemnly.

Mary snatched at the phone. Fortunately, it was Rhonda who answered and not her parents. Mary hated people ringing people late at night. She deemed it unthoughtful and rude.

'Well?' Donald asked, hands on hips as his wife ended the phone call.

'Rhonda said Nancy told her that she is going to their

friend Katie's birthday party and will be home tomorrow teatime.'

A police officer in the making, Christopher was the first to reply. 'Their friend! Why hasn't Rhonda gone to this make-believe party as well then? Nancy is pulling the wool over your eyes, Mum. Ever since she went to that fairground she has been acting strangely. I told you not to let her go there, didn't I?'

'And I told you that she shouldn't be allowed to attend such events too. If our daughter is currently shacked up with some rebel in a seedy hotel room somewhere, I will personally hold you responsible, Mary,' Donald added.

Mary sighed wearily. She needed Nancy disobeying her father's orders like she needed a bloody hole in the head. She now believed that her daughter was probably with some lad, but she wasn't about to admit that to Donald and Christopher. They could light a fire without a match or petrol, those two. 'If our Nancy said she is going to her friend's party, then that's where she is. I trust our daughter and there is no way she would lower herself by going to hotel rooms with some bloke, Donald.'

'Well, I hope you are right, Mary, because if I find out that girl is lying to us, I will not allow her to darken our doorstep any more. She will not bring shame on this family. I am too proud a man.'

Nancy Walker sighed as Michael Butler made some funny noises and rolled off her for the second time that evening. Losing her virginity had had its high and low points. Having Michael on top of her and being so intimate with him had been the high point, but she hadn't really felt much in a physical way apart from some pain. Rhonda had been telling her on their lunchbreak today that if she did do the deed she was bound to have one of them orgasms that everyone was talking about, but even though Nancy didn't know exactly what they were, she was sure she hadn't had one.

'Are you OK, Nance? I didn't hurt you too much, did I? Did you enjoy it?' Michael asked. Nancy had earlier admitted that she was a virgin, so he had done his best to be as gentle as he could.

'Of course I enjoyed it. I just love being with you.'

Michael grinned, and propped himself up against the pillow with his elbow. 'Do you know what? That is the first time either of us has ever mentioned that daunting L-word. Do you love me, Nancy? I love you, I am proper sure of that.'

When Nancy nodded shyly, Michael held her in his arms and sighed deeply. He had always been a player ever since he had lost his virginity at thirteen years old, but no girl had ever made him feel the way that Nancy did. Even though he wasn't positive that he could always remain faithful to her, he was sure she was the girl he wanted to spend the rest of his life with.

'What's up? You look very serious all of a sudden,' Nancy said, laying her head on Michael's chest.

'You're gonna have to tell your parents about us soon, and I'm gonna have to tell my family. It's the only way forward, Nance.'

Nancy felt fear engulf her stomach. 'Oh, I can't do that. Say my dad chucks me out?'

Kissing his girlfriend on her forehead, Michael said the words he thought he would never hear himself say. 'If your dad chucks you out then we'll move in together, Nance. In fact, we can even go better than that. We can get married.'

CHAPTER TWENTY-TWO

Albie Butler hadn't expected his family to go into meltdown over him supposedly staring death in the face, but he had thought Roy and Michael would have shown a bit more concern. Nearly two weeks it was now since Albie had been invited to dinner at Queenie's house, and he had not heard hide nor hair from any of his family since.

Counting out the loose change in his pocket, Albie shuffled despondently towards the bar. He only had enough money left for a couple of drinks, and once that had gone he would have to suffer starvation and dehydration until he got his unemployment benefit handout on Thursday.

'The usual, Albie?' the barmaid asked.

'No, just a pint today, love. Times are hard at present, so no more chasers for a while. Big Stan not been in today?' Albie asked, hoping the man was about. Ever since he had told him that he had cancer, Stan bought him a drink or two virtually every day.

'No, not seen him today. 'Ere, ain't that your son just walked in, Albie?'

Albie looked around and was shocked to see Vinny walk towards him. Roy or Michael, he might have expected to pop in and buy him a pint, but not his eldest.

'Get me dad a chaser. I'll have a large Scotch on the rocks, and have a drink yourself,' Vinny ordered the barmaid.

'Thanks, son. It's a nice surprise to see you, I must say. Was you local? Or, did you make a special trip to see your old dad?'

Ordering his father to sit down at a table, Vinny sat opposite him and smirked. 'No, I was local. Popped over the hospital to see a pal of mine, who just happens to be a doctor there. Was worried about your illness, you see. But, you ain't got one, have you, Dad? I knew when you stuffed two big bowls of Mum's lamb stew down your gullet there was fuck all wrong with you, and surprise, surprise, the hospital you are supposedly having regular treatment at has never even heard of you. What a devious, wicked old fucker you are, eh?'

Knowing he'd been caught like a kipper, Albie Butler hung his head in shame. 'I'm sorry, Vinny. I just missed yous kids so much, I said it out of pure desperation. I knew none of yous would have agreed to see me unless you thought I was dying. Have you told your brothers and your mother yet? They will hate me more than ever now, I know they will.'

'Nope, and I might even keep your despicable lie a secret if you do something for me in return.'

'What? I'll do anything, boy, anything you want, providing you don't tell anyone what I did. I will never be able to show my face round 'ere again if you do.'

'Well, this is the deal. Tonight, I am holding a joint surprise engagement party at the club for Roy and Brenda. Unbeknown to Roy, I've invited his fiancée's family over from Ireland. I want you to have a quiet word in the mother and father's shell-like. Tell them that Roy is a ladies' man. Say that he's never been faithful to any bird in his life, and you have good reason to believe that he's already cheated on Colleen, blah, blah, blah. You know what to say, being a serial womanizer yourself, eh, Dad?'

Albie didn't like the sound of his task at all. Roy wasn't a bad lad, and it was obvious that Vinny wanted to ruin his brother's relationship for his own selfish means. 'Can I ask why you don't want Roy to marry this Colleen?' Albie asked his son.

'After what you've done, you don't really have the right to ask me anything, Dad, but I will tell you anyway. I don't hate Colleen, but Roy has changed so much since he met her. He has little interest in the club, our family, or bettering his life like he once did. If he gets hitched and starts banging out sprogs, then things will just get worse. Apart from a bit of help from Michael, I will have to run the business nigh-on single-handedly, and I ain't willing to do that.'

Albie sighed wearily. He hated the thought of ruining his son's happiness, but what choice did he have? 'The thing I don't understand, Vinny, is when Roy and the rest of the family find out what I've done, they will hate me anyway. I don't stand to gain much, do I?'

'You gain them never knowing what a wicked old con man you are. I mean, what type of father tells his four children he is dying when he isn't? As you said earlier, your life is over in the East End if that one ever gets out.'

'OK, I'll do it,' Albie said, thoroughly miserable.

'Good! I also want you to tell Colleen's mum and dad the story of you being hospitalized that time with all your broken bones. Tell 'em it was Roy who beat you up though, not me. Anything you can think of which will make the family want Colleen to end her engagement to Roy, you tell 'em. Then in return, in a few weeks' time, I will tell the family that I went to the hospital with you and your cancer is now in remission, OK? I will also try and smooth over what happens tonight for you. Your excuse for your outburst will be that you have more tests at the hospital tomorrow, and you were so worried about being told you only had weeks to live, you got plastered and didn't know what you were saying. With a bit of luck Colleen's family won't make a fuss at the party, and will speak to their daughter on the quiet, so what you said might not ever come to light anyway.'

'What time do you want me to get there?' Albie mumbled.

'Seven o'clock, and take that to have a drink or two before you arrive,' Vinny ordered, throwing a twenty-pound note at his father. Then, without a backward glance, Vinny strolled casually out of the pub.

When Nancy got home from work she immediately knew that something was wrong. The mood indoors had been very frosty ever since she hadn't come home one night last week, but today she could have cut the atmosphere with a knife.

'Sit down, Nancy,' Donald growled.

Her mum and Christopher were sitting opposite each other in the centre of the dinner table, her dad at the head, so Nancy sat down on the chair opposite him. 'Have I done something wrong?' she asked anxiously. Since making love to Michael, Nancy had wanted to shout their relationship from the rooftops, but somehow she couldn't find the right time or words to tell her parents. Michael hadn't told his family yet either, but that was only because Nancy had insisted she wanted to tell hers first.

Donald cleared his throat. 'Your little secret is out in the open now, Nancy. You and your fancy-man were spotted canoodling in a flash American car. Now, who the bloody hell are you courting?'

'Just tell us the truth, love. We won't be angry with you, but if you're serious about this lad, we will want to meet

230

him,' Mary said, squeezing her daughter's hand to reassure her everything would be OK.

Christopher, his arms folded, was glaring at her. He had an evil glint in his eyes and reminded Nancy of a python waiting to strike. It was at that point that she knew it was now or never. 'OK, I will tell you, but please try not to be too angry with me. Michael is the loveliest, kindest lad I have ever met, and what happened in the past had nothing to do with him.'

'What do you mean, what happened in the past? Do we know this Michael?' Donald asked impatiently.

'Just tell us who he is then, love?' Mary urged her daughter. Nancy was now crying and Mary hated seeing her so upset.

'It's Michael Butler,' Nancy wept.

Feeling like he had just been shot through the heart, Donald was too stunned to even speak. The name Butler was enough to put the fear of God into him, on its own.

'That isn't one of Queenie's sons, is it?' Mary asked her daughter, in total disbelief.

When Nancy nodded miserably, Christopher banged his fists on the table. 'How could you be so stupid to have got involved with that awful crime-ridden family? You know they ruined our lives, so how could you be so bloody selfish? You are no sister of mine any more, Nancy Walker. In fact, you truly repulse me.'

Usually, Mary would always stick up for her daughter, but today Nancy had gone one step too far even for her liking. 'You have to finish with Michael immediately, Nancy. You cannot get too involved with that mob.'

Knowing that there was no point in lying any more, Nancy shook her head. 'I can't, Mum. I love Michael and he loves me.'

Like a phoenix rising from the ashes, Donald leapt out

of his chair. 'You have two choices, Nancy. You either end your relationship or you pack your bags and leave our home immediately. Now, what is it to be?'

Seeing all three family members looking at her with a mixture of disgust and disappointment on their faces, Nancy knew she only had one choice.

'Where're you going?' Mary cried, as Nancy stood up.

'To pack my stuff. I'm moving out.'

Not wanting there to be any trouble in front of Colleen's relations, Queenie decided to have a quiet word with Roy to tell him what Vinny had planned.

Roy breathed a sigh of relief that his future in-laws had been invited. It wouldn't have been fair if it was just his family there, and perhaps now that he had been spared the aggravation of organizing his own party, he might take Colleen away for a weekend somewhere nice instead.

After Roy left, Queenie and Vivian spent the whole day cooking and preparing food. Vinny had wanted to hire professional caterers, but Queenie and Vivian had been outraged by his suggestion. 'If you think I'm allowing my family to eat a load of old shit that's been prepared by a bunch of strangers who have the cleanliness morals of a polecat, then you've got another think coming,' Queenie told her son.

'And you've got all them migrants coming over here now. Lots of them work in catering and they're dirty bastards. Most of the countries they come from ain't even got proper khazis. They shit in a hole in the ground, so you don't think they will wash their hands before they make the sandwiches, do ya?' Vivian added.

Vinny had just left them to it after that, and as Queenie stood with her hands on her hips studying their handiwork, she turned to her sister and smiled. 'Well, that's it. All done we are, I think.'

'I still ain't sure we'll have enough grub, Queen. Vinny said earlier there could be anything up to seventy or eighty people there now, and we ain't got enough for that amount. My Lenny eats enough for fucking five people alone.'

'Stop worrying. We'll have plenty, trust me. Vinny's ordered a load of seafood as well. Right, I think I'll ring Michael and get him to come and pick this lot up, then me and you can get ourselves looking all glam. I still can't believe I'm celebrating not one, but two of my babies getting engaged. It only seems like yesterday that I was wiping the pair of 'em's shitty arses.'

Sitting approximately thirty yards from the nightclub on a Kawasaki motorcycle, Johnny Preston watched the comings and goings with interest. He was behind a lorry, so nobody could really see him, and even if anyone did, the road was a main one, and there were always cars, bikes, vans and lorries parked near the club.

Worried about his daughter opening her mouth and the shit hitting the fan back home, Johnny couldn't wait for Graeme's pal to get back from holiday and exchange their clapped-out van, so had decided to go it alone. Graeme was still going to help him dispose of the bike and gun, but other than that he was totally on his jacksie.

Johnny felt his heart start to beat faster as he saw Queenie Butler and her sister get out of a bright red Mustang. He'd had a feeling earlier that there was some private family event at the club tonight and he had obviously guessed right. Feeling sweat dripping down his face, Johnny didn't know if it was the heat under his crashhelmet causing it, nerves, or a mixture of both. What he did know was that Mummy's boy, Vinny Butler, would most definitely see his mother into a car later, or he might even take her home himself. To shoot Vinny in front of Queenie would be the crème de la crème of all murders. If Johnny could pull that off, not only would it avenge Dave's death, it would also put him on the gangland folklore map for many years to come.

Vivian beamed with pride when she spotted her Lenny standing on the stage behind a DJ console. He even had earphones on and looked ever so professional. 'Look at him. Reminds me of that Tony Blackburn, don't he you?' Vivvy said, nudging her sister.

'Aw, bless him. I notice he's playing Elvis. You have told him he's got to play alternative stuff other than just rock and roll, haven't you, Michael?' Queenie asked.

'Yep. Champ knows what he's doing. Now come and sit down. This table has the best view in the club which is why Vinny wanted you and Auntie Vivvy to sit here.'

Queenie sat down and as she glanced around to see who else had been invited, she very nearly fell off the chair in shock. 'What's your fucking father doing here?' she hissed at Michael.

'I don't know to be honest. I didn't even know he was coming until he bowled in about half an hour ago. I think Vinny must have invited him.'

Vivian pursed her lips to show her disapproval. 'He spent most of Roy and Brenda's childhood gallivanting with other women, or propping up the bar in some grotty pub, yet he has the cheek to show up at their engagement party like the doting father. What a fucking liberty.'

When Queenie clocked Vinny, she leapt out of her chair and marched towards him.

'Look, I know what you're angry about, but I just thought seeing as Dad is dying it was the right thing to do. My father is the last person I would want at my club, but for once I decided to put Roy and Brenda's feelings before my own. It is their engagement party, and the way I saw it was if Dad is found bloody dead in that bedsit of his next week or sometime soon, they might never have forgiven me for not inviting him.'

Queenie stared into her son's eyes. She knew her eldest better than he knew himself at times. 'Don't take me for a fool, Vinny. I know you're up to no good. It had better not be something to do with Roy and Colleen, because if it is I won't be happy at all.'

'What do you take me for, eh? I try and make a bit of an effort and throw a nice party at all my own expense and this is the thanks I get. Well, cheers, Mum. Thanks a lot. I even got in touch with Colleen's work pals and invited them.'

'OK, I'm sorry,' Queenie said, aware of how hurt Vinny looked.

'Dad. Uncle Michael says Brenda and Dean are outside,' Little Vinny said, tugging his father by the sleeve of his suit jacket.

'Tell Champ to turn the music off, Mum, and get ready for the big entrance. He knows what he's got to do. I'm gonna keep Bren and Dean outside until Roy and Colleen arrive. I want them to all walk in together.'

After Queenie gave Lenny the heads-up, she sat back down opposite Vivian.

'I hope you had a go at Vinny for inviting Albie. What on earth was he thinking of, eh?' Vivian asked.

Queenie shrugged. 'Oh, for fuck's sake. Albie has spotted us and is coming over.'

Vivian glared at her ex-brother-in-law as he plonked himself on a seat next to her. 'Jesus, you smell like a fucking brewery and the party ain't even started yet. How many you had?'

Dreading doing what Vinny had ordered him to do, Albie had been merry on arrival. Vinny had then served him up a few large brandies. 'I'm a dying man, Vivian. Is a man staring death in the face not allowed to have a few drinks?' Albie slurred.

'Well, hurry up and croak it then,' Vivian muttered.

'The bleedin' state of you, Albie. You haven't even had a shave and the collar of that shirt is filthy. Looks crusty, it does. Don't you dare introduce yourself to Colleen's parents. They'll think their daughter is marrying into *The Beverly Hillbillies*,' Queenie remarked.

'I've already met Colleen's parents. Very nice people. They're standing up by the bar.'

About to scold Albie for embarrassing the family name, Queenie was stopped by Lenny's voice booming out over the microphone. 'Surprise! Congratulations Roy, Colleen, Brenda and Dean. This party is for you and so is this record.' He then proceeded to play the Dixie Cups' 'Chapel of Love'.

'Always reminds me of our wedding day this does, Queenie. One of the happiest days of my life, that was,' Albie said wistfully.

'Oh, shut up, you silly old bastard. This record didn't come out until the bleedin' sixties. We'd been married donkey's years by then,' Queenie spat.

'I ain't sitting here listening to this old bollocks. Come on, Queenie, let's go and say hello to all the guests,' Vivian said.

Queenie stood up. 'And don't you dare do anything to ruin the evening, Albie. I know what an arsehole you are in drink.'

When Queenie and Vivian walked away from the table, Albie felt like crying. He would have liked to have attended the party in a nice suit, celebrated the joyous occasion with his children, behaved himself and done them proud. Yet here he was, resembling a tramp, three sheets to the wind, all because his eldest son was an evil bastard and was using him as a pawn in his latest game. Albie put his head in his hands. A brave man would walk away now rather than ruin his own son's engagement. But Albie was a weak man, who would do anything to save his own bacon, and that had been his biggest downfall.

Mary Walker was begging her husband to calm down and think sensibly. 'If we let Nancy go, Donald, she will be married and pregnant in no time, then we will lose her forever. We have to stop her from making the biggest mistake of her life. Perhaps if we allow her to see Michael, their relationship will fizzle out in a matter of months. But, if we force her to leave, and she moves in with them Butlers, we might as well have handed our own daughter over to a hungry pack of wolves.'

Donald was devastated, but extremely angry at the same time. For years he had worked his bollocks off to provide his children with the best possible start, and Nancy had just thrown everything he had ever tried to do, including teaching her good morals, back in his face.

Mary let out a traumatized sob when Nancy bounded out of her bedroom with a suitcase in her hand. 'Please don't go, darling. You will regret this for the rest of your life if you end up a part of that family. You'll be pregnant and trapped before you know it.'

Wanting to hug her wonderful mum more than anything else in the world, Nancy knew that she couldn't. If she did, she might not ever leave, and she loved Michael too much to give him up. If she did stay, it would be like living in a prison cell and her overbearing father and brother would watch her every move to make sure she never set eyes on the love of her life again. 'I'm sorry, Mum, but I have to leave. I'll be in touch soon, I promise.'

'Oh, no you won't. If you walk out that door and choose

those Butlers over us, we want no more to do with you, do we, Dad?' Christopher stated.

'Your brother is correct, Nancy. For your mother's sake, I will give you one last opportunity to apologize to your family and stop all this nonsense once and for all. Because if you don't, I swear on the Bible you will vacate our lives forever.'

Not wanting her obnoxious father to see her falter, Nancy picked up her case, stormed out of the door, and did not cry until she had reached the pavement outside the shop.

'Donald, do something. Please, go and bring her back,' Mary sobbed.

Donald held his hysterical wife in his arms and did his best to comfort her. 'None of this is our fault, Mary, so let's not blame ourselves that Nancy has turned out to be a bad apple. We have given that girl everything, and for her to throw it back in our faces like she has is thoroughly appalling. It will be difficult, but from this moment on, Nancy doesn't exist any more in this household. My old mum used to say, "If you lie down with dogs you catch fleas." Well Nancy will be infested with those fleas for life now, and as much as it breaks my heart, we have to say goodbye and good riddance to her.'

Johnny Preston was well aware of his hands physically shaking when he replaced the receiver on its cradle in the phonebox. He had just rung Graeme to update him on what was happening and how he felt it in his bones that tonight was the night.

Spotting an off licence, Johnny headed towards it. His nerves were jangling and a half-bottle of Scotch should help to calm him down. Trying to shoot Vinny with trembling hands was a no-go. He would probably gun down somebody else by mistake.

Ten minutes later, Johnny was parked in a secluded alleyway off the Mile End Road. He took the bottle of Scotch from the inside of his jacket, unscrewed the lid, and drank half of it in one gulp. Immediately feeling more calm and confident about the task in hand, Johnny decided to stop at another off licence on the way back to the club to purchase another bottle in case he needed it later. With a few Scotches inside him, Johnny felt as though he could conquer the world, and that's exactly what he needed to pull this one off successfully.

Glancing at his watch, Johnny re-started the bike's engine. Hopefully, in the next few hours, Vinny Butler would exist only in memory.

Back at the party, Colleen's parents, Rosa and Eugene, were in total shock as they listened to what Albie Butler had to say about their future son-in-law. 'Go find Colleen, Eugene. Bejesus, I can barely believe what I've just been told. No way is she marrying into this family now,' Rosa said to her husband.

'So, you're telling us that Roy broke both your legs, plus some ribs, and put you in hospital for over a month?' Eugene asked Albie. Before he took Rosa's advice and forced Colleen to cancel her engagement, he needed to get his facts straight. Roy had seemed such a decent chap.

'Yep. He has a violent temper, does my Roy. You should warn your Colleen never to upset him. He will definitely get violent with her if she does,' Albie continued. The horrified expressions on Colleen's parents' faces were enough to make him feel dreadful, but then when he saw Vinny grinning at him from a distance, Albie knew that for once he would rather face the music himself than ruin Roy's life. Albie tore his eyes away from his eldest son and stared at his tatty shoes. 'Ignore everything I just said. It isn't true. It was Vinny that put me in hospital, not his brother. My Roy is a good boy and he will make your Colleen very happy,' Albie said, walking away from an open-mouthed Rosa and Eugene.

Knowing that he would rather admit his awful lie to Queenie himself and explain why he had said it in the first place, rather than let Vinny expose his secret, Albie went in search of his estranged wife. He hadn't walked more than ten steps when Vinny collared him though. 'That was a quick conversation. You better have told Rosa and Eugene everything I asked you to, otherwise you're in shit street.'

'I did start to tell them, boy, but then I saw you watching me and it put me off. I will have another bash again later,' Albie replied, playing for time. He already knew what he was going to do. He was going to speak to his family one by one, and explain why he had pretended to be at death's door. He would also warn Roy about Vinny's cunning plan. He just hoped that Roy would show some gratitude in return by bunging him some money so he could leave the area. He wouldn't be able to live locally after disobeying Vinny's orders, that was for sure.

Vinny sneered. 'If you let me down, I swear I will jump on that stage, grab the mike, and tell everybody what a despicable lying old cunt you are. Oh, and then I will have to kill you, Dad. Now, do we understand each other?'

Albie nodded sadly. He knew without a doubt that Vinny wasn't bluffing. His first-born was toxic. In fact, he was more than that, Vinny was rotten right down to the core.

CHAPTER TWENTY-THREE

Surprised by what a fantastic little DJ Lenny was turning out to be, Vivian grabbed her sister's hand as she heard the opening chords to Joe Loss and his Orchestra's 'March of the Mods'.

'Michael, Kevin, come on. You used to both be Mods,' Queenie said, gesturing for her son and his friend to join her and Vivvy on the dancefloor.

'Leave it out, Mum. This ain't a proper Mod tune,' Michael informed her.

'So, what did you think of Colleen's family?' Vivian asked Queenie, when they had finished their little dance routine.

'Seemed pleasant enough. Couldn't really understand what they were saying though, could you?'

Vivian shook her head. 'Not a lover of the Irish, me. Don't trust the bastards.'

Queenie chuckled. Vivian didn't like or trust anyone who came from north of Watford.

'Oh, for fuck's sake. What does he want now?' Vivian said, when she and Queenie walked back to their table to find Albie hovering nearby.

'Can't I have a dance and drink in peace without you bloody pestering me now?' Queenie asked.

'I need to speak to you alone, Queenie. It's really important that I do.'

'Well, she don't fucking wanna talk to you, do you, Queenie? Now go away and leave us alone, Albie,' Vivian ordered.

When Albie slunk away like a scolded puppy, Queenie bit her lip to stop herself having a go at her sister. If Albie had something of importance to tell her, then she wanted to bloody well hear it. As much as Queenie loved Vivian, she was quite capable of fighting her own battles, and sometimes she wished that her sister would butt out and let her do the talking.

Michael and Kevin were having a right good laugh. Vinny had invited half a dozen of Roy's old school pals to the party. One of them had bought his sister with him and Kevin had just been winding her up by telling her because his father was black, he had been blessed with a gigantic-sized penis that white men could only dream of owning.

'Michael, sorry to interrupt your conversation, but there's a girl outside asking for you. She's very upset and has a suitcase with her,' said Paul, who worked on the door.

Hoping it wasn't one of his many ex-birds turning up on his doorstep, Michael darted out to reception and was amazed to see Nancy standing there. He hadn't even realized she knew the actual address of the club. 'What's wrong, babe? Has your mum and dad found out?' he asked, when Nancy threw herself into his arms.

'Yeah. Somebody saw me in your car, so I told them the truth. They said I had to choose them or you, so I chose you and left home,' Nancy wept.

Aware that Paul and the other doorman Pete were both watching with interest, Michael ordered them to put Nancy's case somewhere safe, then led his girlfriend outside.

'You are OK with me turning up here, aren't you? You don't seem very pleased to see me,' Nancy mumbled.

'We'll talk in the motor,' Michael said, putting his arm around her and steering her towards where his car was parked. His mind was all over the place. He loved Nancy, he was sure of that, but now she had turned up with her suitcase in her hand, he felt slightly trapped already. What was he meant to say to his family? None of them even knew he was bloody dating her. And what the hell were Vinny and his mother going to say when they realized who she was?

'You're not going to make me go back home, are you?' Nancy asked, when she got in the passenger side of the car.

Michael tilted Nancy's chin towards him. 'Of course I'm not going to make you go back home. It's just a bit awkward this has happened tonight, that's all. I so wished I'd have already told my family about you. Gonna be a bit of a shock for them when I march in the club, and introduce you in a minute, isn't it?'

'I can't meet your family tonight, Michael. I'm not even dressed for a party. You'll have to tell them about me tomorrow, then I'll meet them the day after or something.'

'Babe, I am in the middle of a double family engagement party. I can hardly not go back to the club, can I now? Plus, where do you think we are going to sleep tonight? I live upstairs at the bloody club, remember?'

Knowing that Vinny and Roy also lived at the club, Nancy was horrified. 'But I thought we would sleep at a hotel?'

On the verge of losing his temper, Michael took a deep breath. 'Just dry your eyes, Nancy, clean your face up a bit, and we'll get this over with. There's no time like the present and you'll be fine once you've had a couple of drinks.'

Knowing she had little say in the matter, Nancy took the handkerchief off Michael, got her compact mirror out of her

243

handbag, and began to wipe away the smudged mascara. She was dreading seeing Michael's family again, especially Vinny, but now she had left home, what choice did she have? She and Michael were a couple now. They were going to be living together. So, the quicker she got the awkwardness with his family out of the way, then bonded with them, the better.

When Karen took her break from behind the bar, Vinny grimaced as his son threw himself at his mother and smothered her in kisses. Little Vinny had never been the most touchy-feely child, but with Karen he acted differently. Even his behaviour had improved since he had met her, and the thing that pissed Vinny off the most was that Karen actually seemed like a bloody good mum.

'We need to start the fucking ball rolling,' Vinny hissed in his pal's ear.

Twenty-nine years old, Ahmed Zane was originally from Istanbul. Young Turkish lads were taught at an early age how to charm the birds from the trees, it was how they survived, and with his perfect physique and chiselled features, Ahmed had been more blessed than most. At the tender age of nineteen, Ahmed had met a rich English woman fifteen years his senior. He had married her within weeks of meeting her, moved to England, stayed with her for two years, then took off with half of her money. He was eligible to stay in the country for life now because he had been kind enough to provide her with his child.

Ahmed and Vinny had met approximately three years ago. Both hard-nosed businessmen, they had clicked immediately, and were now best buddies and partners in crime. Vinny was used to having a sidekick. He and Roy had been inseperable growing up and for many years afterwards, but that had all changed when Colleen had come on the scene.

Their closeness had now dwindled and in the past year, Ahmed had all but taken Roy's place in Vinny's life.

With Vinny's financial backing, Ahmed was now considered to be the drug lord of London. Once upon a time, Vinny had got his thrills through violence, but he had promised his mum when Little Vinny was born that he'd do his utmost to curb his awful temper.

Flooding the streets of London with heroin was a different kind of buzz to beating somebody to a pulp, but it still gave Vinny a natural high. So did the fact that it was all top secret. Nobody bar Ahmed knew that Vinny was involved, and the money he was raking in gave Vinny the biggest adrenaline rush of all. That beautiful brown powder had made both him and Ahmed incredibly rich almost overnight.

'Daddy, Mummy says she is gonna take me to the zoo soon. Will you come too? I want to see the reptiles. Can we bring the snakes home with us?' Little Vinny asked, snapping his father out of his trance.

Karen raised her eyebrows. Her son had an obsession with snakes, and she hated the bloody things. 'I don't think we can bring the snakes home with us, can we, Daddy?' she asked, grinning at Vinny.

Playing along with the happy family façade, Vinny chuckled. 'Yeah, I'll come to the zoo as well.'

'I'm gonna tell Nanny,' Little Vinny said, skipping away happily.

'Karen, I'd like you to meet my pal, Ahmed. I've been telling him what a good mum you are to Little Vinny and how we have managed to forget the past and build a happy relationship once again, and Ahmed has just come up with a fabulous idea.'

Karen allowed Ahmed to kiss her on both cheeks, then smiled when he complimented her on her beauty. 'So, what is this idea then?'

'Well, it seems daft you travelling up here from Dagenham most days, doesn't it? Ahmed rents out properties, and he has a beauty not far from here in Beckton. I've seen it. It's a luxurious three-bedroom flat, and I am willing to pay the rent on it, Karen. It will enable me, you, and our son to spend some quality time alone as a family. What do you think?'

Staring into Vinny's piercing green eyes, Karen's heart leapt. Even though he had been the perfect gentleman up until now, she was sure that he wanted to make another go of it with her. Little Vinny had brought them closer together than they had ever been in the past, and the chance to become a proper family was far too much for Karen to turn down. Her council flat in Dagenham was on the twenty-first floor of a tower block, so what the hell did she have to lose? 'That sounds fab. When can I view it?'

Ahmed smiled at Karen's enthusiasm. 'I can show you tomorrow, then you can move in the following day, if you want? I am only renting this flat at a cheap price because Vinny is a pal of mine, and I know how much he thinks of you,' he replied in a broken cockney accent.

Karen was ecstatic. 'Thank you, Ahmed, and thank you, Vinny. I'd best get back to work now.'

When Karen darted back behind the bar, Vinny shook Ahmed's hand. 'Well played, pal.'

Ahmed chuckled. 'English women are just so dumb.'

Queenie was amazed when Michael plonked a stunning-looking girl in the chair opposite her, then introduced her as his girlfriend who would be moving in with him. Queenie had lost count of the amount of girlfriends Michael had ploughed through, but none had ever tempted him to give up his bachelor lifestyle before.

'Oh, Queen. Ain't she a pretty thing? The face of an angel,' Vivian gushed.

Queenie looked around the club, her heart beating rapidly. If Vinny was to spot Nancy, there would be murders and she would hate things to kick off in front of Colleen's family. Roy would go apeshit if that were to happen. Knowing she had to play along and pretend that Vinny hadn't spoken to her about the girl, Queenie forced a smile. 'An absolute princess. So, where do you come from, darling? Are you local?'

Nancy squeezed her boyfriend's hand to urge him to answer the question for her. She didn't have a clue what she was meant to say.

'Mum, Auntie Viv, there is something I need to tell you. Do you remember that couple who took over the café that used to belong to Old Jack? They weren't there for long. Their names were Donald and Mary.'

'Yep, I remember 'em. They had a little boy who witnessed the murder outside your old club,' Vivian remarked.

Michael took a deep breath. 'Well, Nancy is their daughter. Her parents have just found out about our relationship and chucked Nancy out. I need you to help me square things with Vinny, Mum. Nancy and I are very much in love and I want you to back me up. I think it's probably best that we don't tell him Nancy's true identity until tomorrow though. I would hate to spoil Bren and Roy's party. You know how hot-headed Vinny can be after a few Scotches, and I'd rather talk to him when he's sober.'

Queenie's nerves were suddenly shot to pieces. Vinny already knew what Nancy looked like, but Queenie could hardly tell Michael that his brother had been stalking him. Then there was Brenda. She and Nancy had once been friends, so surely Bren would recognize the girl as well?

'Can I say something, Mrs Butler?' Nancy asked timidly.

'Call me Queenie, love, and yes, of course you can.'

'I just wanted you to know how serious I am about your

son. My parents didn't exactly chuck me out. They offered me a choice. It was either them or Michael, and I chose Michael. He is the kindest, funniest, loveliest person that I have ever met and there was just no way I could give him up. I love him so much.'

Queenie felt her heart lurch in her chest when she saw the way Michael and Nancy looked at one another. They were clearly in love, and there was no way Queenie would allow Vinny to ruin his youngest brother's happiness now by forcing Denise Thompson to make up wicked lies. That would be so very wrong.

Johnny Preston felt as cool as a cucumber. No longer was he shaking. He was absolutely brimming with confidence now. He had also moved away from the main road and was tucked nicely in between two cars that were parked nearer the club's entrance. Annoyed with himself for having drunk his Scotch so quickly, Johnny glanced at his watch. He definitely had another hour or two to kill before the party in the club wrapped up. Desperate not to lose his bravado, Johnny decided to pop to another off licence. Surely it was better to be slightly merry than a bag of bloody nerves? Turning on the ignition, Johnny pulled away from the kerb right in front of a Rover 2000 that had to screech to a halt to avoid hitting him.

'You absolute idiot! Did you not check your mirror? How I didn't kill you I'll never know,' the driver yelled, leaping out of the car.

Realizing he was attracting unwanted attention from gawping passers-by, Johnny revved the bike's engine and sped away.

Vinny had had his beady eyes on his father all evening, and was just about to march across to him and order him to tell Colleen's parents what he had instructed him to, when Paul the doorman walked over to him. 'There's a girl in reception, boss. Says her name is Denise and she asked for you.'

Vinny grinned. He had always prided himself at having eyes in the back of his head. In his line of business, you needed to, and he had been well chuffed when he had seen Michael sneak Nancy Walker in earlier. If Denise hadn't been popping in to break the news of her pregnancy, Vinny would have probably smacked Michael in the mouth and turfed his slag of a bird out immediately. 'Go and have a chat with Karen while the bar is quiet, Ahmed. I have a bit of business to attend to,' Vinny said, winking at his pal.

Ahmed grinned when his friend sauntered away. Vinny had told him earlier that Denise Thompson would be turning up to drop the baby bombshell. There were very few secrets between him and Vinny. They were more like brothers than friends, and seeing as Ahmed had already made Kenny Jackson disappear off the face of the earth on Vinny's say-so, and was soon to work his evil magic on both Karen and Terry Smart, they already had a massive bond to keep them united for the rest of their colourful lives.

Up on the stage, Lenny was having a ball, and for the first time in his life, he truly felt like king of the castle. 'And this song is going out especially for my mum and Auntie Queenie because I know that they both like it,' he said confidently over the mike.

The song was Mary Hopkin's 'Those Were the Days', and when his mum and aunt dashed onto the dancefloor, Michael was open-mouthed to see Denise Thompson marching his way with Vinny by her side. 'I'm sorry, bruv, but she skipped past the doorman. Reckons she has something important to tell you,' Vinny said.

Michael stood up. 'Shall we talk outside? The music in here is very loud, Denise.'

'No. Here's fine. I thought you should know that I'm pregnant, Michael, and the baby's yours,' Denise blurted out, in the exact way that Vinny had instructed her to.

Hardly able to believe her ears, Nancy let out a racking sob, put her hand over her mouth to stop herself from retching, and ran from the club.

Having spotted the drama from the dancefloor, Queenie dashed towards Michael and dragged him away from his ex-girlfriend. 'It's all lies, son. You go and find Nancy and go straight back to mine. You can both sleep in Little Vinny's bedroom. Go on. Don't leave that lovely girl outside the club on her own,' Queenie ordered.

Michael was perplexed. 'But, how do you know Denise is lying?'

'I just do. Now fucking go,' Queenie shrieked.

Johnny Preston put his hand on his gun in anticipation of Vinny appearing as he watched the scene outside the club with interest. There was a girl crying, another one screaming abuse, and that old bat of an aunt had just come into view as well. The bloke present was Michael, Johnny surmised. He hadn't seen the youngest Butler boy for many years, but it certainly wasn't Roy or Vinny.

When he saw a police car slow down nearby, Johnny cursed his luck and immediately turned the ignition. He would have to go for a little ride, then come back once this silly argument had calmed down, as there was no way he was going to get caught with a gun in his possession. Feeling a bit edgy for the first time since he'd nearly got knocked off his bike earlier, Johnny decided to head to another off licence to help calm his nerves once more.

*

Back inside the club, Vinny was on a roll and had just approached his father to hand him an ultimatum. 'There's two hundred quid in there,' Vinny said, stuffing an envelope into the pocket of Albie's threadbare jacket. 'Now, you've got ten minutes to do what I told you to, otherwise I shall leap on that stage, grab the mike and tell everybody what a nasty, lying, deceitful old cuntbag you are.'

Usually, Albie would do anything for fifty quid, let alone two hundred, but he had been watching his Roy tonight and he and Colleen seemed so ideally in love and well-suited that for once Albie was willing to put loyalty above money, or his own pride. 'I can't do it, Vinny, so do your very worst, boy,' he mumbled, almost apologetically.

To say Vinny was furious by his father's decision was an understatement. 'You think I'm bluffing, you old bastard, don't ya? Well, watch this, Daddy dearest.'

When his eldest son strutted towards the stage like a lion hunting its prey, Albie darted towards Roy. 'I need to talk to you, son. It's urgent,' he begged.

Excusing himself from Colleen, Roy led his father aside. There was something about the look on the older man's face that told Roy this was serious and when Albie began to gabble about Vinny's plan to spoil his relationship, Roy shook his head in disbelief. 'I know Vinny has never been that happy for me and Colleen, but he wouldn't do something as bad as that to me, Dad. He's my brother, for fuck's sake. You have had a good drink. You sure you ain't got muddled up?'

'I swear to you, boy. Look at this. Vinny just gave it to me,' Albie said, showing Roy the envelope with the money inside. 'Ask Colleen's parents if you don't believe me. Your brother blackmailed me. He found out that I didn't have cancer and said if I didn't tell them that you were a womanizer, who had cheated on their daughter, and that you had broken my legs and put me in hospital, he was going to tell everyone I lied about my illness. I started to tell Colleen's parents earlier, but I couldn't go through with it. I panicked, but I swear I only lied about having cancer as I wanted to see my family again. I know none of yous kids would have agreed to see me unless you thought I was dying.'

Roy already had the hump with his brother because of Ahmed being at the party, so when he heard Vinny's booming voice interrupt Edison Lighthouse's 'Love Grows Where My Rosemary Goes', Roy ordered his father to stay where he was and walked back into the club area.

'Sorry to interrupt Champ's wonderful disco and your dancing, ladies and gentlemen, but I would just like to say a few words. Firstly, I would like to congratulate Roy for finally finding a woman who will put up with him.'

When everybody laughed, Vinny did the same, while scanning the club for his mother and father, but unfortunately he could see neither, so just carried on with his speech. 'Secondly, I would like to congratulate Brenda and Dean on their engagement, and also a big well done for getting my sister in the family way, Deano. She ain't an easy bird to live with, I can vouch for that, so trust me you're gonna need all the luck you can get.'

When everybody laughed again, Vinny was relieved when he spotted his mother and Vivian standing together by the entrance. 'And finally, I would like to inform my mum, brothers, sister, and all our friends that our dad is nothing more than a despicable old liar. I have checked out his story, and Albie Butler doesn't have cancer at all.'

Amazed that his father had predicted exactly what would happen, Roy knew Albie was telling the truth for once and dashed towards Colleen's parents. 'Rosa, Eugene, I need to ask you something important. Did my father start telling you an awful story about me earlier, then backtrack on it?'

Eugene looked at his wife, then glared at Vinny. This was turning out to be some engagement party all right. 'Yes, your dad did tell us some pretty harrowing things, but he then said he was making them up, and that it was something to do with your brother Vinny. However, I think you and I need to have a little chat tomorrow, Roy. There are certain things I am very concerned about.'

'What's going on, Roy?' Colleen shrieked, when Roy darted towards the stage like a madman.

After sending Denise packing with a flea in her ear, Queenie was now faced with crisis number two. 'Where is the old bastard? I'll kill him,' she seethed, looking around for Albie.

'Told you not to trust him, didn't I? Ate like a fucking horse when he turned up at yours and drank like a bleedin' fish. Cancer, my arse,' Vivian spat, staring at the stage. Were her eyes deceiving her, or were Vinny and Roy having a massive barney?

'Aw, my gawd! It's all going off. I'll get Vinny and Roy outside, and you tell your Lenny to play some more music and just act like nothing's happened. Whatever will that girl's parents think?' Queenie panted, dragging her sister towards the stage.

When Lenny put on Bill Haley's 'Shake, Rattle and Roll' it seemed quite appropriate as Roy and Vinny were now rolling around the dancefloor trying to smash one another's face in. Furious that her sons had embarrassed her in such a way, especially in front of Colleen's family, Queenie leapt on top of them and punched both very firmly in the side of their heads. 'Take this outside, before I maim the pair of you,' she yelled. It was extremely difficult to make herself heard over Bill Haley.

Never one to disobey his mother, Vinny was the first to leap up. 'This ain't my fault. It's his. He's pissed and he's delusional,' Vinny said, pointing at Roy.

'Can I just say something?' Ahmed asked.

'No you bastard-well can't! This is family business,' Queenie roared.

'You are one evil cunt, Vinny, and you've gone too far this time,' Roy spat, trying to lunge at his brother again.

'Get outside now, the pair of ya,' Queenie ordered for the second time. It was Vinny who seemed the more drunk to her. He was the one with the glazed expression in his eyes, not Roy.

When Lenny played the Hollies' 'He Ain't Heavy, He's My Brother' and dedicated it to his two cousins who liked to mess about but loved one another really, Queenie cringed with humiliation as she followed Roy and Vinny outside the club. She had told Vivian to tell Lenny to try and keep things normal, not make a shark out of a goldfish. 'Right, do yous pair want to tell me what the bleedin' hell is going on?' Queenie yelled, as she witnessed her two boys throwing punches at one another yet again.

'Roy, stop it,' Colleen screamed. Knowing that something was seriously wrong, she had followed her fiancé outside too.

No more than twenty yards away, Johnny Preston cursed his luck. He had only been slightly inebriated earlier when he'd almost got hit by that car, but now as he was trying to focus, he seemed to be suffering from double vision. He could see two of Queenie and two of Vinny and Roy. Knowing it was now or never, Johnny closed one eye to help him focus more clearly. He then pointed the gun at Vinny. 'Die, you bastard,' he mumbled, as he bravely put his finger on the trigger.

A loud bang, Vinny dropping to the ground, and a deathly

scream was the last that Johnny saw and heard before racing away from the scene of the crime. Finally, he had got revenge for the death of his best pal and it didn't just feel good, it felt fucking terrific.

CHAPTER TWENTY-FOUR

'Ring an ambulance. Ring a fucking ambulance,' Vinny shouted at his doormen.

With her smart cream suit covered with splashes of Roy's blood, Queenie knelt down next to him. 'Don't you dare die on me. Don't you dare, Roy Butler,' she sobbed. There was a gaping hole in the side of her son's head, and he was as still as a statue.

Realizing that her fiancé had been shot, Colleen was bordering on hysterical. 'Don't touch him. Leave him alone. You're not meant to move him,' she screamed.

Vinny began kicking and punching a nearby wall. 'I will fucking kill whoever has done this. I'll torture the fucking cunt with my bare hands.'

When a tearful Albie pushed his way through the crowd to kneel down next to Roy, Queenie began hitting him. 'This is all your fault, you lying old bastard. Get away from him. Get away from all of us,' she screamed, her face contorted with pain and anger.

Lenny was screaming blue murder, so Vivian led him back inside the club and asked Michael's mate Kevin to look after him for her.

Colleen's family were in complete shock and were doing

their best to calm down their heartbroken daughter.

'Is he alive? Is my baby still alive?' Queenie wept, when the ambulance crew pushed their way through the onlookers to attend to Roy.

Realizing how serious Roy's injuries were, the ambulance men answered no questions and instead set to work on trying to save Roy's life and get him to hospital as quickly as possible.

'Brenda, you and Dean take Lenny and Little Vinny home and wait there with them. Tell Michael what has happened, and tell him to get his arse straight up the London. I'll stay with your mum,' Vivian ordered her niece.

Ahmed was trying to calm Vinny down when the police turned up and started asking questions. 'Do not say anything you might regret, my friend.'

Vinny's head was all over the place. He just knew that the bullet had been meant for him, and was trying to work out who was behind the shooting. If he had to take a wild guess, he would say there was a good chance it was something to do with Kenny Jackson's son, Bobby. Vinny had had many run-ins with Kenny over the years, including the one at his mother's birthday party when Vinny had put him in hospital. Kenny had got too cocky for his own good a year or so back, and courtesy of Ahmed, had ended up in a cement mixer. Not one bone or tooth of Kenny Jackson had ever been traced, but there had been a lot of speculation over his disappearance and even though he had a rock-solid alibi on the day that Kenny went missing, the finger of suspicion had still been pointed Vinny's way. He had even been questioned by the Old Bill. Bobby Jackson was a mouthy little shit just like his father had been, and it wouldn't surprise Vinny one bit if it was him who had pulled that trigger.

'Look, lads, no disrespect, but I ain't in the mood to even think straight, let alone answer any questions right now. My brother has just had his brains blasted out, if you failed to notice, and my priority is to get to the hospital to be with my family. Ain't any of yous cunts got a heart?' Vinny spat at the young PC.

Ahmed glared at the police, put an arm around Vinny's shoulder and led him away. 'Come on, let's go. Pete and Paul will stay at the club until we get back. We need to go to the hospital.'

Old Sidney Palmer had just picked his wife up from her regular Monday-night jaunt at the bingo hall when he had driven past the Butlers' nightclub and heard a loud bang that sounded like a gunshot. He had seen the motorbike race away, and being the good citizen that he was, Sidney had decided to give chase in his Ford Cortina.

Dorothy Palmer had begged her husband to stop at a phonebox, ring the police, and give them the registration number, but Sidney being a stubborn old mule had ignored her wishes, carried on chasing the bloody bike, and now the rider had just hit the car in front, flown off his bike, and was lying in a crumpled heap in the middle of the A13. 'If we're up on a murder charge I will brain you, you senile old bastard,' Dorothy hissed. When a dazed Johnny tried to get up and run, he collapsed immediately. Cursing his luck, he took the gun out of his jacket and threw it across to the opposite carriageway.

When the police arrived a few minutes later, Dorothy got out and stood with Sidney while he explained to them what he had heard, seen, and how he had followed the suspect. When the police called Sidney a hero, and said his bravery would more than likely be rewarded, Dorothy held her husband's arm with pride. Perhaps he wasn't such a senile old bastard after all.

Unable to sit still, Vinny paced up and down the hospital corridor. Roy had been rushed into theatre for an emergency operation to remove the bullet from his skull, and the doctors were yet to tell them any real news of his condition.

Seeing his devastated mum lay her weary head on Vivian's shoulder, Vinny bit his lip to stop himself from crying. His mother was such a strong woman, as hard as nails, and to see her so upset tugged at his heart-strings.

'There yous are. What's happening? Any news yet?' Michael asked, dashing straight over to his mum.

'Oh Michael. It was awful. You should have seen him. I thought he was brown bread, I really did, but the ambulance men said he still had a pulse,' Queenie explained, hugging her youngest son.

'How's my Lenny, Michael? Hysterical, he was. Never seen him like that before. Has he calmed down a bit now?' Vivian asked.

'He's still upset and very tearful, but Brenda and Dean will take good care of him,' Michael replied.

'What about Little Vinny? Is he OK? I just thank God he was asleep in the club when it happened. I would have hated him to witness it first hand,' Queenie said.

'Little Vinny weren't with Bren and Dean. They only had Champ with them,' Michael informed his mother.

Vinny felt his blood pressure rapidly start to rise. 'What do you mean, he weren't with them? I thought you told Bren to look after him, Auntie Viv?'

'I did. Bren and Dean was gonna take him home with my Lenny. I wouldn't worry too much. Karen was still at the club. Perhaps he wanted to stay with her?' Vivian replied.

Unable to stop himself, Vinny punched the wall with pure frustration. 'Ahmed, shoot down the club and find me my son. I want him brought back here, OK?'

With a curt nod, Ahmed dashed down the hospital corridor.

*

Back at Queenie's house the initial awkwardness between Brenda and Nancy had just started to thaw. 'So, how long you been seeing Michael then? Where did you meet him?' Brenda asked, inquisitively.

'I've not been seeing him long. We bumped into one another over at Barking fair last month. Your Dean seems like a nice guy, Bren. Yous two been together long?'

Glad that Nancy was there as it took the edge off waiting for news about poor Roy, Brenda spoke frankly about her relationship with Dean, her plans for her wedding day, their unborn child, and her hopes and dreams for the future. 'So, what about you? Do you still live with your parents? And do they know you and Michael are together?' Brenda asked.

About to explain that she had just left home and would be moving in with Michael, Nancy was stopped from doing so by Dean's reappearance. 'Lenny reckons he's going up the hospital, Bren. I've tried to talk him out of it, but he got a bit bolshy and sort of told me to mind me own business.'

'Well, you're gonna have to stop him,' Brenda ordered.

'Bren, he's a big old lump and nearly as tall as me. I ain't even properly related to him, so what am I mean to do? You're his cousin, you bloody well stop him.'

Hearing the front door slam, Brenda leapt out of the armchair and opened the lounge window. 'Lenny, get back in 'ere now,' she yelled.

'No. I ain't some kid no more, and if I want to go to the hospital to see how Roy is, there is nothing you can do to stop me. I want to be with my mum and Auntie Queenie, not sitting here doing nothing.'

Realizing that her cousin had a point, Brenda told him to wait a minute, then turned to Dean and Nancy. 'Come on. Let's all go up the hospital.'

'Me and Nancy will be better off staying here, Bren. You go with Lenny. It ain't right for us to go. We're not even family.'

There was no way that Brenda was leaving Dean alone with somebody as beautiful as Nancy, so she stood her ground. 'You are family, you div. We're having a baby together and getting married, remember? You're gonna have to come too, Nancy. Unless you want to go home. My mum barely knows you and I can't leave you alone in her house, she'll kill me.'

With no home to go to, Nancy nodded miserably. Queenie had insisted earlier that Michael's ex-girlfriend was lying about being pregnant, but Nancy still didn't know that for sure. Say she was at the hospital too? Also, Vinny was bound to be there, and just being within a fifty-yard radius of him gave Nancy the heebies.

'Yous two coming, or what?' Brenda asked, impatiently.

Knowing she had two choices, none and sod all, Nancy followed Brenda and Dean out of the house.

When Ahmed returned with both Karen and his son, Vinny wasn't happy. According to a nurse he had just spoken to, Roy was still being operated on and he needed Karen around him at a time like this like a boil on his arse. 'Why didn't you send him home with Brenda like I asked? Is it too much for you to respect my wishes, even though my brother is on death's door?'

Karen was rather taken aback. 'Our son was confused and upset, Vinny. He couldn't understand what was going on. He wanted to stay with me, and seeing as we've been getting along well and I am his mother, I didn't see it as a problem. I wasn't going to take him home to Dagenham with me. I was worried about you and Roy, so was going to stay at the club with Little Vinny until you got back.'

Colleen had been in a hysterical state after arriving earlier at the hospital, and was currently being treated for shock. Seeing her parents walking back towards him, Vinny led

Karen around another corridor. 'Look, I'm sorry, OK? I'm just stressed and off my head with worry.'

Little Vinny followed his parents, and desperate to get his dad's attention, leapt up and down while holding his arm.

'Stop it! What's a matter?' Vinny shouted at his son.

'Is Uncle Roy dead?' Little Vinny asked.

'No, he's being operated on.'

'But, might he die?'

Vinny bent down and shook his son violently. 'Stop asking such fucking morbid questions. Do you want your uncle to die, do ya?'

'Stop it, Vinny, you'll hurt him. He's only five. He doesn't know what he's saying,' Karen pleaded.

When his son burst into tears, Vinny stood up, put his head in his hands and leant against the wall. 'You had the right idea originally, Karen. Just take him back to the club and wait there until I get back. I should imagine I'll be stuck here all night, so you can both sleep in my double bed. Tell Pete and Paul I said it was OK.'

Putting Vinny's foul mood and temper down to the family crisis he was currently experiencing, Karen kissed him politely on the cheek and dragged her son down the corridor.

When Nancy arrived at the hospital, Michael immediately clocked how glum she looked and, desperate to speak to her alone, led her away from the rest of his family. He stopped at the nearest drinks machine. 'Here you go,' he said, handing her a plastic cup filled with weak-looking tea.

'I'm so sorry there is no good news about your brother yet, and I hate to bother you with trivial things at an awful time like this, but I remembered on the way here that I left my case at the club earlier. I have to pick it up at some point tonight, as I won't be able to go to work tomorrow otherwise.'

Realizing that Nancy was near to tears and guessing the reason why, Michael put his cup on the floor, did the same with hers, and then held her tightly to his chest. 'I spoke to my mum about Denise turning up like she did. She definitely isn't pregnant. My mum wouldn't say how she knows, she isn't a grass, but I think we can safely say that Vinny already knew about you and I and set the situation up. Roy might have been involved as well, and I will find out the truth, but obviously now is not the right time for me to be kicking off about it.'

'So, your mum is absolutely one hundred per cent positive that Denise is making the whole thing up?'

'Cross my heart, and don't worry about work. We're gonna be getting our own place soon and your job will be to cook and clean indoors then. It's only poxy Woolworth's. I don't really want you working there anyway. It looks bad on me.'

Nancy was immediately startled. She liked her job in Woolworth's, had made some good friends there, and she adored working alongside Rhonda. They had such a laugh in Woolies, and sitting at home bored stiff didn't bear thinking of. 'Look, Michael, once we get married and start a family, I will obviously give up work to bring up our children, but until then I want to continue working. I know it's not the best job in the world, but I actually really enjoy it.'

Knowing that it was the wrong time to argue this point, Michael kissed Nancy on the forehead. 'OK, but I insist you take tomorrow off. We're bound to be stuck up here all night and you can't go to work with no sleep. Now drink your tea, and let's get back to the others and see if there is any news on Roy yet.'

After going outside to get a bit of fresh air to try to clear his fucked-up head, Vinny was amazed when his mum and aunt informed him that Colleen had now been sedated and given a bed in the hospital herself for the night. Vinny couldn't help but smirk. 'Fuck me. She's gonna make a great nurse her, ain't she?' he quipped.

For once, Queenie was in no mood for Vinny's little jokes. Even though he hadn't admitted it when she had asked him earlier, Queenie was no fool and she knew that the bullet that was currently being removed from Roy's shattered skull had actually hit the wrong son. 'Don't be so sodding heartless, Vinny. How did you expect the girl to react? Her engagement party was meant to be one of the best days of her life. Colleen didn't expect it to end not knowing if her future husband was going to live or die, did she?'

'Mum, the doctor's coming now,' Lenny said, rushing down the corridor.

Vivian and Queenie both leapt out of their seats. Brenda laid her head on Dean's shoulder and for the first time in her life, silently prayed.

'Is he OK? Please tell me the operation was a success?' Queenie gabbled, beside herself once again.

'He is alive, ain't he?' Vivian asked, noting the serious expression in the doctor's eyes.

'Yes, Roy is still alive. Shall we have a chat in one of the family rooms, Mrs Butler?'

Clinging to her sister's arm, Queenie shook her head. 'Whatever you've got to say, just say it here. We're all family.'

Urging Queenie to sit down, Dr Howard sat on a chair next to her. 'Overall, the operation performed on your son was a success.'

'Thank you, God. Thank you so, so much,' Queenie whispered, clasping her hands together and staring at the ceiling.

'However, even though we are sure we have removed most of the fragments of the bullet, there has been some bleeding to the brain, which might well cause other complications.'

Vivian chewed at her fingernails. 'What sort of complications?'

'My brother is gonna be OK, right?' Vinny asked.

Dr Howard took a deep breath. 'To be honest, it is a miracle that your brother is still with us. We will be able to tell you more about what the future holds if and when Roy regains consciousness.'

Feeling the colour drain from his face, Michael clutched Nancy's hand for support. 'What do you mean, if and when he regains consciousness? You must know if Roy is gonna wake up or not?'

If there was one thing that Queenie hated it was being kept in the dark. 'Look 'ere, Doctor. That is my son lying in there and, good or bad, I want to know the truth about his condition. We're a strong family and you don't have to dress things up for the likes of us.'

'The truth is, Mrs Butler, brain injuries of this kind are very hard to predict the outcome of. Obviously, there is a chance that your son might never regain consciousness, but we are extremely hopeful that he will.'

'I don't want my cousin to die. I love him,' Lenny wept.

Vivian cuddled her distraught son. 'Roy needs you to be brave, son. He ain't gonna die, not with his genes.'

'My poor boy. When he wakes up, he will still be able to walk and talk properly, won't he, Doctor?' Queenie asked.

'I really can't answer that question, Mrs Butler. We will not know the full extent of Roy's injuries until he wakes up.'

Vinny began pacing up and down the corridor. 'Apart from my brother actually dying, I wanna know the worst scenario, Doctor. As a family, we need to be prepared for what might lie ahead of us.'

Dr Howard sighed. He was used to giving out bad news to people, but never found it an easy task dealing with families such as the Butlers. Hardcore East Enders were always pessimists rather than optimists, and seemed to crave to hear the worst.

'OK. I will explain this as thoroughly as I can to you all. Obviously, there is a small chance that Roy might wake up and be exactly as he was before, but this is highly unlikely. The probability is, Roy's memory will be affected and he will have to learn some basics all over again. By basics, I mean, walking, talking, dressing himself, eating, even using his arms possibly. That is the usual scenario with injuries such as Roy has sustained, but you never know what to fully expect until the patient is fully conscious, and Roy could turn out to be one of the lucky ones. If he isn't, then we have specialists that he will work with to help rehabilitate him back into society once more.'

Realizing there was a strong chance that his brother might wake up to be what he had always called a vegetable was far too much for Vinny to take in, and he started to head-butt a nearby wall.

When Queenie and Vivian both leapt up to try and calm him down, realizing they were having no joy, Michael quickly took matters into his own hands. He put his arm around his brother's shoulders and spoke softly to him. 'You're upsetting everyone, mate. Roy's gonna be OK. We both know he's as strong as an ox. Let's go outside and get some fresh air, eh? I dunno about you but I could really do with a smoke.'

When Vinny allowed Michael to lead him down the corridor, Queenie put her head in her hands. What she had gone through tonight was every mother's worst nightmare, and she knew in her heart of hearts that her strapping, handsome middle son would never be the same again. Mother's intuition was a strong thing, and Queenie had been born with a bucketful of the stuff.

CHAPTER TWENTY-FIVE

The days that followed Roy's shooting were probably the worst of Queenie's life. She had suffered much hardship over the years, especially as a child when living with her brute of a father, but not even seeing her mother beaten to a pulp compared to sitting at her son's beside day after day willing him to pull through.

Roy was still in a coma and Queenie felt completely helpless. As a doting mother, she had always done her utmost to be there for her children in a crisis but for once, apart from pray, there was little she could do. Her son's life was in the hands of the gods, and not knowing if he was ever going to wake up was giving Queenie sleepless nights. Even worse was the thought of Roy waking up permanently brain-damaged. Queenie knew in her soul that she would rather Roy never wake up at all than be a completely different person to the one that he was before.

Queenie was snapped out of her depressing thoughts by the return of Colleen. Her parents had just gone back to Ireland, where they had two other young children to care for, and had begged Colleen to do the same. Colleen had flatly refused and, once she had recovered from the initial shock of the shooting, had spent day and night at her fiancé's bedside.

'Hospitals always make you feel so grubby, don't they? I never noticed it so much working in one, but I do as a visitor. I take it the doctor hasn't been in today yet?'

Queenie shook her head sadly, watching as Colleen sat down next to Roy and lovingly clasped his lifeless hand in her own. Colleen had been a real little diamond these past few days, but Queenie was worried about her health and state of mind. She had a sickness bug that just wouldn't budge. She wasn't eating at all, and spent all her time chatting happily to Roy as though he could actually hear her. 'Have you thought about when you are going to go back to work yet, love?'

Colleen looked at her future mother-in-law in horror. 'I'll think about that when Roy wakes up. I need to be here with him, Queenie. He's my life.'

'I understand that, darling, but he could be in a coma for a while yet. My Roy would hate to see you mess all your nurse's training up. He was so proud you were doing so well with it.'

'I can't concentrate on my exams at a time like this, Queenie. It's impossible.'

Queenie nodded. She could understand where the girl was coming from. 'You must sort out that bug and start eating more though, darling. Not gonna look good in your wedding dress if you are all skin and bones, are you?'

Appreciating Queenie's optimism, Colleen smiled. 'I'll book a doctor's appointment as soon as I get a chance, OK?'

'There's a good girl.'

Over in Ilford, Donald had spotted the MAN SHOT OUTSIDE NIGHTCLUB headline earlier in the day, but had been far too busy to read the article. However, as his eyes now scanned down the page and he spotted the name Roy Butler, he felt his heart begin to beat wildly. Not wanting to worry Mary, Donald ran upstairs with the paper in his hand and waved it in Christopher's face. 'Read this, son. It's definitely the same Butlers, and the shooting happened the same evening your sister left home. Can you to go down to Woolworth's and try to talk some sense into that stupid girl? Surely, she now must realize what a mess she has got herself into.'

Christopher read the article through to the end, then stood up. 'OK, Dad. I'll go and speak to Nancy right now.'

When Karen saw her new flat for the very first time, she literally clapped her hands with glee. It was spacious, modern, fully furnished and even had its own little garden.

'Well? What do you think, Karen?' Ahmed asked politely.

Karen grinned at Vinny, then turned to Ahmed. 'Oh, I love it. Is the TV, oven, sofa and fridge all included?'

Ahmed nodded.

Unable to wipe the smile off her face, Karen asked to see the garden properly. The sun was shining as Ahmed lifted the blind and unlocked the door and when Karen strolled outside, she could just imagine hanging her washing out and sunbathing. After being stuck in a tower block for the past four years, it really was a heavenly feeling.

'So, it's OK then?' Vinny asked.

Karen grinned. 'Yeah, it's great. I'm going to look at the bathroom and main bedroom properly now.'

'Get in there and explain,' Vinny hissed, when Karen opened the wardrobe door and asked who all the clothes belonged to.

'My previous tenant. There has been a problem with them picking up their belongings, so you cannot move in until Monday now,' Ahmed told Karen.

'That's fine. I need to sort out my own stuff at the flat anyway. I won't need to bring much with me now, seeing how this is already furnished. It will just mainly be personal belongings and all my clothes and shoes.'

'Well, I'll help you sort that out, babe. Now, shall we go grab a bit of lunch? I need to eat before I go back up the hospital,' Vinny suggested.

Thinking how wonderfully kind Vinny had been to her recently, Karen held his arm and squeezed it.

When Vinny glanced back as he walked towards the car, Ahmed winked at him. Even though there were personal belongings scattered all over the flat, the not-so-bright Karen had fallen hook, line, and sinker into their web of deceit.

Terrified of being spotted, Albie Butler hung around outside the London Hospital in the long tan raincoat and big brown hat his sons had made him wear to visit Queenie. Rumours spread like wildfire in Whitechapel, and Albie knew without a doubt that his little white lie would now be common knowledge. His evil son had put the boot in good and proper once again, which is why Albie had had no choice than to leave the East End on the same night Roy had been shot. He hadn't wanted to, of course. He had been desperate to go to the hospital with the rest of his family, but Vinny had pulled him to one side and all but told him that if he came near any of the family ever again he would end up in a coffin.

Albie crouched down against a nearby wall. He had been ringing the hospital daily, but even though he had sworn he was Roy's dad they had still refused to update him on his son's condition. The only thing they would tell him was that Roy was still alive.

When Albie had quickly packed his few belongings and left Whitechapel, he had luckily still had the two hundred quid that Vinny had stuffed in his jacket pocket as a bribe. Not knowing where to go, Albie had returned cap in hand to Becontree Heath and as luck would have it, Pauline had snatched a hundred quid out of his hand, proclaimed she had missed him, and welcomed him back into her home with open arms.

Albie put his hand inside the pocket of his raincoat and checked that the letters were still there. He had spent all yesterday evening writing them in the Matapan pub, and although he had never been a man of words, for once he felt he had done himself proud. For all Queenie's faults, she deserved to know the truth, not only about how she had made him feel over the years, but also that her eldest son was out of control. He had to warn her if only for Roy and Colleen's sake. As much as Albie hated to admit it, his sperm had produced a wrong 'un, and he would wait at the hospital for as long as it took. Michael was the only one he could truly trust, which is why he had written him a separate letter. His family were entitled to know what they were dealing with, and Albie was determined that they read the truth from him. Whether or not they believed it was another matter.

Nancy was incredibly anxious as she walked over to her brother. Rhonda had told her he was standing by the till, and apart from her father, Christopher was the last person she wanted to see. 'What's up?' she asked, as casually as she could. She then gestured for her brother to follow her outside the shop.

'I would rather say what I have to say here, thank you, Nancy. I feel your colleagues might be able to help me make you see sense,' Christopher stated, hands on hips.

Clocking both her colleagues' and the customers' awkward glances, Nancy grabbed Christopher by the arm and tried to lead him outside the shop. 'Don't you dare show me up. We'll speak outside,' she hissed.

'Oh, no we won't,' Christopher said in a loud voice while waving the *East London Advertiser* in the air and pointing at the front page. 'You see these people on the front page, everybody? The gangsters who were shot at? Well, this is the family my stupid sister has left our own family home for and moved in with. My mother is devastated, my father is distraught, and all I want is my sister back.'

Feeling herself blush the colour of crimson, Nancy first looked at Rhonda, then her manager Steven, and then the queuing customers. 'I am so sorry about all this, everybody,' she said apologetically.

'And so you should be, Nancy. Mum, Dad and I have been out of our minds with worry. So, are you coming home with me after work? Or not? I am willing to wait for you if you wish.'

Nancy had never ever felt so humiliated in her whole life. 'No, Christopher. I am not coming home with you. Now, please get out of my shop and leave me alone. And if you come back here again and jeopardize my job, I swear I will tell Michael about it, OK?'

Unable to believe his ears, Christopher sneered at Nancy, his face a picture of disgust. It was too late to save his sister. She was already a Butler.

After dropping Karen home, Vinny headed to the club. Out of respect for his brother, Vinny hadn't opened up since the shooting.

Checking that everything was just as it should be, Vinny was about to leave the premises when he heard the shrill ring of the phone, and so he dashed behind the bar to answer it.

'That you, Vinny?'

Even though he hadn't heard the voice for a long time, Vinny recognized it immediately. George Geary was the now retired chief inspector Vinny had had in his pocket for many years. 'You all right, George? What's up?'

'Just heard a bit of inside info, boy, which I thought you might be interested in. Obviously, I will expect a drink in return. Fifty quid, shall we say?'

'Go on,' Vinny replied.

'My old mob are just about to charge a man with the attempted murder of your brother. They caught him the same night it happened, but wasn't allowed to question him immediately, because he'd been involved in a road accident.'

'Who is it, George?' Vinny asked, his heart beating like a drum.

'Johnny Preston.'

Shocked to the core, Vinny told George to pick up his dosh the following day and slammed the phone back on its cradle. He then smashed his fist against the bar. Johnny Preston would pay for what he had done in the very worst way possible. What that was yet, Vinny did not know. But, what he did know was that by the time he had finished with him, Johnny cunting Preston would wish he had never been born.

CHAPTER TWENTY-SIX

The following morning, Queenie and Vivian arrived at the hospital at eight a.m. and soon realized that even though she had promised to go home and get some sleep, Colleen had stayed at Roy's beside again all night.

Queenie sat down next to her future daughter-in-law and squeezed her hand. 'Look, sweetheart, I know how much you love Roy, we all do, but sitting here nigh-on twenty-four hours a day isn't the answer. You need to eat, kip, and start looking after yourself. You heard what the doctor said yesterday: they have no idea when Roy will wake up, so you must get a grip, darling. Every human being needs food and sleep. We can't survive without it.'

'Queenie's right, Colleen. You look ill, and your Roy ain't gonna want to wake up to a skeleton, is he?' Vivian added.

'You OK, love?' Queenie asked, as Colleen stood up and stared blankly at her and Vivian.

'No, I feel a bit ...' Colleen mumbled, and then collapsed before finishing her sentence.

Unaware that the police were currently at the hospital talking to his mother, Michael was on his way there. Since Roy had been shot, apart from the first night, Michael had barely seen or spoken to his eldest brother. Unlike the rest of the family who had visited Roy on a daily basis, Vinny had stayed well away, his excuse being that it broke his heart to see his brother in a coma, and it was pointless being there until he actually woke up.

'Michael, why do they call this area the Waste?' Lenny asked.

Michael couldn't help but smile. Ever since the lad had started work at the club, he seemed to ask questions all day long. Last week, Michael had spent the whole day trying to explain why elephants had trunks to his young cousin.

'Michael, why are you living at Auntie Queenie's now? Why ain't you living with Vinny no more? Have yous two fallen out?' Lenny asked, without even waiting for the first answer.

Putting a protective arm around Lenny, Michael led him safely across the road. 'No, course me and Vin haven't fallen out. He's been staying with his Turkish mate in Camden, and I've been stopping at your Auntie Queenie's house because Nancy has now moved in with me.'

'Do you love Nancy? Are you going to marry her?' Lenny asked bluntly.

'Yes, I love Nancy, Champ, and one day if she is lucky, I might just marry her,' Michael said, with a wink.

Lenny chuckled, but Michael missed his inquisitive cousin's next question, as he had just spotted his father standing by a wall, waving frantically at him.

Over in Dagenham, Karen had spent the past hour deciding what she was going to take to her lovely new home. Vinny had sworn her to secrecy about her new gaff. He had insisted he wanted her to surprise her mum and friends by organizing a little flat-warming for them.

Desperate to tell somebody about her stroke of good luck all the same, Karen debated whether to inform her next-door neighbour, Debbie. Guilt stopped her from doing so, as she knew her mother would never forgive her if it came out that she wasn't the first to hear the good news. Karen couldn't afford an indoor phone, so she picked up her purse and headed off towards the nearest phonebox.

Not wanting Lenny to spot his father, Michael had taken him inside the hospital, then pretended he had left his wallet at home. 'Go and sit with your mum and Auntie Queenie. I won't be long, Champ,' he said.

Dashing back down the corridors, Michael ran out of the entrance and around the side of the building, where by a flick of the head he had gestured to his father to wait.

'Hello, son. I'm so glad you came back. I didn't know whether you were telling me to sod off, or meaning for me to wait here,' Albie said.

'You've got some brass neck coming here, Dad, after what you did. How could you pretend you were dying?'

'I did it because I knew it was the only way I would get to see or talk to yous. I'm really sorry. It was a stupid thing to do.'

'You can fucking say that again! Now, what do you want?' Michael asked.

'Well, obviously I want to know how Roy is? I've been ringing the hospital, but they won't tell me anything. Worried sick, I've been.'

'Roy's in a coma. He's very lucky to even be alive, so the doc reckoned.'

'Do the doctors think he will make a full recovery?'

Michael shrugged. 'Nobody knows until he actually wakes up. There was bleeding to the brain which might result in permanent damage. We just have to keep our fingers crossed.

The quack we saw yesterday said that most patients in comas wake up within a month.'

Albie's eyes welled up. 'Why couldn't it be Vinny lying in a coma instead of poor Roy? There's something I need to tell you, Michael, and I want you to listen carefully to me.'

'What?'

When Albie began to explain about Vinny's evil plan to split up Roy and Colleen, Michael's face went white and he leant his back against the brick wall for support. Part of him wanted to believe that his father was spinning another of his yarns, but in his heart Michael knew that Albie wasn't lying. The pieces of the jigsaw seemed to fit too well. 'So, what did you actually say to Colleen's parents?'

'Well, I started to tell them what Vinny had asked me to, but then I backtracked. Roy and Colleen look so happy, I just couldn't go through with it, boy. Then Vinny came and threatened me, said if I didn't do what he'd asked, he was going to jump up on stage and tell everyone I had lied about my cancer. Vinny ain't right in the head, Michael. He has real problems and I'm worried he will start on you next. He won't like you being with that Nancy. He doesn't want to lose you and Roy, therefore will stop at nothing to get his own way. He wants to be in total control.'

Michael put his head in his hands and sank to his haunches.

Albie crouched down next to Michael, took a small bottle of brandy out of his raincoat pocket and swallowed a large gulp. He then handed the bottle to his son, who did the same. 'You ain't got to tell your mum, boy. I've written everything down in a letter for her to save you the task.'

'Where is it?'

Albie handed him two envelopes. 'The bigger envelope is the letter I wrote for you. Now I've told you all this, I think

Vinny will try and finish me off. If I disappear or die, hand your one over to the police. Can I trust you to do that for me, son?'

'Oh, don't say shit like that. Vinny might not be your greatest fan right now, but you're still his dad. He wouldn't harm you.'

Albie took another swig of his brandy and screwed the top back on the bottle. 'Do you remember that time I was in hospital with two broken legs and broken ribs?'

'Yeah, course I do. You were mugged and it was while you were in hospital that Mum found out about that Judy Preston bird, weren't it?'

'Yeah. Your mother came to visit me and bumped into Judy. The thing is, I never got those injuries through being jumped. There was no mugging. Vinny beat me up.'

'No! You're lying, Dad.'

'I swear I ain't, boy. Roy knows. He turned up just after Vinny had nearly killed me. Your mum and Auntie Viv know too. Ask them if you don't believe me. You and your sister were quite young at the time, so the truth was hidden from you.'

'I weren't that young. That all happened around my sixteenth birthday. I remember it clearly as when I found about about you and that tart, I went for a long ride on my moped to clear my head.'

'Well, I don't know why you wasn't told. Perhaps it was because I was always closer to you than your brothers. You and Brenda were always the apple of my eye. Your sister wouldn't even talk to me at her engagement party, you know. I tried to wish her good luck, but she all but told me to eff off.'

'So, where are you living? I know you're not at the bedsit as I popped round the other day and the bloke downstairs said you'd moved out,' Michael asked, changing the subject.

'I had to, didn't I? That's why your brother leapt on the stage and outed my lie. He knew I would never be able to stay in Whitechapel after that. You know what people are like around here. I'd have every bastard gunning for me and rightly so, I suppose. I've had to move back in with Pauline for the time being, but I can't stay there for much longer. Once you give your mother that letter, I need to get away. I have to go somewhere where Vinny won't find me.'

'Dad, you know we were talking about that Judy Preston? Did she have your kid? Or, do you truthfully not know?'

'On my life I don't know, son. I swear I ain't ever seen or heard a word from her since that day she visited me in hospital.'

Satisfied that Albie was telling the truth, Michael smiled at him. His father wasn't a bad person. He might be a pisshead and do and say stupid things at times, but his heart was certainly in the right place, which is more than what Michael could say in Vinny's defence right now. 'So, where you gonna go? Do you need money?'

'Yeah, I could do with some readies, boy. I was thinking of going to stay with Bert down in Ipswich. Ivy died last year and he's rattling about in a house on his own down there now.'

'Who are Bert and Ivy?' Michael asked.

'Your uncle and aunt. Bert's my elder brother. You have seen him, but not since you were a kid. Your mother never had any time for my family. She reckoned they all had a screw loose.'

Michael put his hand in his pocket and handed his dad three ten-pound notes. 'Take that for now so you've got some beer money. Then tomorrow, I will drive down to Pauline's gaff and give you some money to go away with. I won't give Mum the letter until after you've gone, OK?'

Albie nodded his head gratefully and pocketed the thirty

quid. 'Do me a favour, boy. I don't want Pauline to know I'm leaving, so can you meet me at a pub with the dosh?'

'Which one and what time?'

'Meet me at the Royal Oak in Green Lane tomorrow at twoish. Pauline's barred from there. I've only got a dustbin liner full of clothes, and I'll pretend to her that I'm going to the launderette. How will I get to Ipswich by train, Michael? Do you know what station takes me there?'

For the first time in ages, Michael felt dreadfully sorry for his father. Having to leave London and never return because you were frightened of being murdered by one of your own kids was horrendous. 'I'll tell you what, Dad. Why don't you let me drive you to Ipswich? I'll get Nancy to take a day off work and she can come for the ride too. It will be nice to see Uncle Bert again, and also I'd like to know where you are living so I can pop down and see you from time to time.'

Choked up because one of his family was being so kind to him for a change, Albie let out an uncharacteristic sob and put his arms around his youngest son. 'You're a good boy, Michael. The best. Please watch your back with Vinny, won't you?'

Wiping the tears away from his own eyes with the cuff of his shirt, Michael cleared his throat. 'Right, I'd better get inside and see how Roy is now. See you tomorrow at two.'

'Oh, that reminds me. Inside your letter, there is also a short letter for Roy and Brenda too. Make sure you give or read them to 'em one day. But, only when you feel the time is right, of course.'

Nodding, Michael walked away.

Disappointed by her mother's reaction to her good news, Karen decided to give her neighbour Debbie a knock.

'Aw, Kaz, I ain't 'arf gonna miss you, but I am pleased

281

for you at the same time,' Debbie said, when her friend finished explaining the situation.

'I wish I could say the same about my mum. I thought she would be thrilled for me, but I just rang her and she said I was a silly girl for rushing into things.'

Debbie chuckled. 'She sounds just like my mum.'

'You must come round when I move in. There's enough room for you and the kids to sleep over,' Karen said, referring to Debbie's sons.

'Oh, I'd love to. Anything to get me away from this shithole for a day or two. Honest, Kaz, I am so thrilled for you. Vinny is incredibly handsome. In fact, on both occasions I've met him, he has literally charmed the knickers off me.'

Laughing at her mate's way with words, Karen put her hand inside the carrier bag she had brought with her. 'I got this, although I dunno what it tastes like. It's fizzy wine. I thought we could open it to celebrate my news.'

Debbie ran into the kitchen and came back with two cups. 'Sorry I ain't got no glasses. The kids broke the few I had.'

'It doesn't matter,' Karen said, pouring the drinks out.

Grabbing a pen and paper, Debbie handed it to her pal. 'What's that for?'

'To write your new address down, you div.'

'Oh, that's another thing my mother had a go at me about. I was so excited when I went to view the property, I didn't look at any road signs. It's in Beckton, I know that, but I'll have to ask Vinny for the exact address tomorrow. I'll give it to you then.'

Debbie held her cup aloft. 'To new beginnings, eh?'

Karen smiled broadly. 'And health and happiness.'

When the police left the hospital, Queenie took Michael to one side so she could have a word in private with him.

The officers had popped in to inform her that they had charged a man called Johnny Preston with the attempted murder of Roy, and he would be appearing in court to be remanded in custody the following morning. 'Is he to do with that little tart Judy, Michael? Don't lie to me. I deserve to know the truth, and his name rings a bell,' Queenie said.

'Yeah, Johnny's her brother.'

Queenie was furious. 'This is all your bastard of a father's fault. If he hadn't have suffered from wandering cock syndrome my Roy would still be as fit as a fiddle, not lying in a fucking coma in hospital.'

After the emotional conversation he and his father had just shared, Michael couldn't help but stick up for him. 'This ain't Dad's fault, Mum. This is revenge for Vinny killing that Dave Phillips. Preston was there when Phillips got stabbed.'

'Yeah, and why did that happen? To do with your father humping Preston's sister, if I remember rightly.'

'Preston only came to the club because Vinny went round his sister's gaff and threatened her. He just wanted to have it out with Vinny, but Vinny being Vinny had to go one step further and murder his fucking mate. There's no way Preston meant to shoot Roy. It would have been Vinny he wanted dead, so if you want someone to blame, then blame your own son.'

Queenie was furious that Michael had sided with his father rather than his brother. 'You should be ashamed of yourself, you. Been a wonderful brother to you, Vinny has. Who do you think put food on the table when you and Brenda were young, eh? Well, it weren't that useless drunken old man of yours, that's for sure.'

Very nearly blurting out what Vinny had planned to do to Roy at his own engagement party, Michael shut up as he saw Brenda and Dean walking down the corridor with his nephew.

'Where's Vinny, Mum? Is he here? Really annoyed with him, I am. He promised me faithfully when he dumped Little Vinny on me and Dean yesterday that he would pick him up first thing this morning and we ain't seen hide nor hair of him. Dean's taking his nan out for lunch and I'm going shopping with Susan, so you're gonna have to look after him. He ain't my bloody responsibility.'

'Is Roy dead yet, Nanny?' Little Vinny asked innocently.

'No, he is sleeping, and how many times have I told you not to ask that question, eh? What's the matter with you? Do you want your Uncle Roy to croak it, do you?'

Realizing that his mother was stressed out and in a foul mood, Michael picked Little Vinny up. 'I'll look after him. I'm taking Nancy out for a bite to eat after she finishes work, so he can come with us, can't you, boy?'

Watching her grandson and son share a hug, Queenie quickly forgave both. Michael had a heart of gold, and Little Vinny was far too young to understand what a coma was, or the seriousness of his uncle's condition.

'Right, me and Dean are gonna go now,' Brenda said.

'Oh, no you are not, young lady. You go and see your brother for five or ten minutes first. You didn't visit him all day yesterday.'

'That's only because I was stuck indoors babysitting. I was gonna come up here last night. How's Colleen today? Has she eaten or slept yet?'

'Colleen ain't well. She collapsed earlier next to Roy's bed. The doctors are doing some tests on her, apparently. It's probably just stress, or lack of sleep and food, but they haven't come back and told us anything yet. Viv asked a nurse to find out what was going on about an hour ago, but she never came back either.'

'Right, I'm gonna make tracks, Mum. Give your nan and aunt a kiss, Vinny.'

Queenie hugged her grandchild, then turned to Michael. 'Do us a favour, love. Before you go for your meal, see if you can find your brother. It ain't like him not to pick the little 'un up, is it? I hope he's all right and nothing bad's happened to him. My heart can't withstand any more drama.'

'To be honest, Mum, since Roy got shot, Vinny has hit the bottle a bit. I spoke to him for about a minute yesterday when he dropped the little 'un off, and he said he was going to some club up the West End with Ahmed. I will see if I can find him, but if I can't, he's probably just on a bender somewhere.'

'Well, best you encourage him to open the club up again, Michael. I've got enough on my plate without worrying about Vinny going off the rails as well.'

Michael couldn't help but smirk. Did his mother honestly think that Vinny had ever been on the fucking rails?

Mary Walker felt sick with anxiety as she approached the entrance of Woolworth's. Christopher had been full of it yesterday evening, saying how rude Nancy had been to him, and how she wasn't worth bothering with any more because she was already one of them. Well, Mary didn't believe that for a second. Her daughter would never be a Butler other than in perhaps name one day, and Mary just prayed that things didn't even get that far. Donald had insisted last night that he was now completely washing his hands of Nancy for good, and Mary had been so angry listening to husband and son speak about the girl as though she had committed the crime of the century. She was a smitten teenager for goodness' sake, and her only crime was to fall head over heels in love.

'Hello, Mrs Walker. Are you looking for Nancy? She has just gone out the back,' Rhonda informed Mary.

'That's why I came in at this time, love. Didn't want to disturb her while she was working. To be honest, I was hoping she might spend her lunch break with me. I miss her terribly at home.'

'Oh, I'm sure she will. Michael isn't meeting her for lunch today. Here she is now.'

'I hope you haven't come here because of what happened yesterday with Christopher, 'cause if you have Rhonda will tell you he was bang out of order making a scene in the middle of the shop, weren't he, Rhon?'

Mary smiled. 'Do you think I live in cloud-cuckoo-land, love? I know exactly what your brother is like. My fault for marrying your father I suppose. Now, seeing as I've missed you so much, will you make your old mum happy by allowing her to buy you a sandwich somewhere? It would make my day if you said yes.'

Realizing that her wonderful mum still loved her as much as she always had, Nancy grinned from ear to ear. 'You try stopping me.'

Vinny Butler thought he was having a surreal experience when he dreamt that some bird was giving him a blowjob, but when he opened his eyes he was appalled to find that the encounter was actually real. Apart from treating his mother, aunt, and sister with respect, Vinny had never regained the art of being diplomatic towards women since Yvonne Summers had broken his heart, so instead of telling the tart to stop sucking his penis, Vinny punched her gently in the side of the head.

Astounded, the girl looked up. 'What's the matter? Are you not enjoying it?'

Vinny stared at the girl. She only looked about eighteen,

had long blonde hair, decent breasts, amazing hips, and a bit of a Janis Joplin look about her. However, Vinny couldn't wait to get shot of her, so he leapt out of bed, grabbed his trousers that were lying on the floor in a crumpled heap, put his hand in the pocket and threw forty quid at the girl.

'What's that for? I ain't a prostitute if that's what you think. You invited me here.'

'Well, now I'm uninviting you. Just get dressed, take the money, and fuck off.'

The girl hurriedly put her clothes on. Furious with the way she had been treated, she screwed up the two twenty-pound notes and threw them at Vinny. 'Stick your money up your arse, you bastard. And, please do not add me as a notch on your bedpost. You couldn't even get it up, you loser.'

No bloke liked their manliness to be knocked and the words he had just heard were like a red rag to a bull for Vinny. Stark bollock naked, he grabbed the girl by the neck and slammed her stupid head against the door of his wardrobe.

'Stop it! Look, I'm sorry. Please, can you just let me go home now?' the girl begged tearfully. She wasn't a slag, had never even had a one-night stand before, but last night she had taken a stupid LSD tab, and because all her friends were into the free love scene, had decided to go back to Vinny's empty club with him. How she regretted that now. Trust her to pick a lunatic.

Aware that the girl seemed absolutely petrified, Vinny released his grasp on her hair. 'Look, I'm sorry. I just ain't thinking straight at the moment. Go on, go home.'

The girl didn't need telling twice. She ran for her life.

Nancy held her mother's arm and led her to the tiny park where she and Michael usually went. 'So, I take it you haven't told Dad that you were coming to see me?' she asked, as they sat down on the bench.

'No. You know what he's like, Nance. So set in his bloody ways. I told him I wanted to have a mooch around the shops before Christopher went back to school next week. I had to see you, love. I read about that shooting and it worried the life out of me.'

Nancy sighed. 'Me and Michael wasn't there when it happened. We had already left the club.'

'Well, thank God for that.'

'It's still been awful though. Roy is in a coma, and the doctor said that he might wake up with brain damage.'

Mary squeezed her daughter's hand. 'Nance, I know you love Michael, but do you really want to be connected to a family like that? Say they try to shoot Michael next and you're there with him? I would die of a broken heart if anything ever happened to you.'

'Nothing bad will happen to me, Mum, so please try not to worry. Michael will protect me. He loves me and I love him.'

'So, where are you living?' Mary asked.

'At Queenie's at the moment. Michael did live above the club, but I told him there is no way I am living with Vinny. We will get our own place soon, but things have been so hectic with Roy being ill that we haven't had a chance to look yet.'

'Is Queenie nice to you, love?'

'Yeah, she is, Mum. Both her and Vivvy have been really kind to me. The house is a bit cramped because Brenda is living there with her boyfriend. She's pregnant you know.'

The word pregnant made Mary's stomach churn. She didn't want Nancy to get herself into that situation. 'I want you to promise me you'll be careful, love. I would hate to see you get pregnant before you've even got a ring on your finger. That would really give your dad and brother something to kick off about.'

Nancy looked at her mother in bewilderment. 'I'm not planning on getting up the duff, if that's what you think?'

'I know you're not, love. But as your mum, I felt it my duty to warn you of the pitfalls of being in such a serious relationship at your age. If you do end up marrying Michael, I want it to be because you want to, not because you have to. Many young girls your age get caught in a trap, and believe me if you ever give birth out of wedlock to a child who is a Butler, then you will be trapped for life.'

Back at the hospital, Queenie, Vivian and Lenny were all still sat around Roy's bedside. Lenny had sworn earlier that when his mum and aunt were out the room that he had seen Roy's right foot move, but even though Queenie and Vivian had been staring at Roy's feet for the past hour, they couldn't see any sign of life.

About to launch into an anecdote, Queenie was stopped by the return of the young nurse who had gone off hours ago to find out how Colleen was. 'Where is she? Is she OK?' Queenie asked, anxiously.

'Colleen is fine. She is resting at the moment, but we have decided to keep her in overnight just to keep an eye on her.'

'Why? What's a matter with her?' Vivian asked sharply.

The nurse smiled. 'You'll have to ask Colleen that yourself.'

Queenie leapt out of her seat and pointed her finger in the young nurse's face. 'Don't be playing games with me, darling, 'cause I'll wipe that smile off your face in a minute. My sister just asked you a question. Now fucking answer her.'

The nurse took a step back. 'Colleen's pregnant, but don't say I told you so in case you get me into trouble.'

Overjoyed by the unexpected news, Queenie hugged the terrified young nurse. 'We won't say a word, will we, Vivvy? Thank you so much for telling us, sweetheart.'

'It's a miracle, Queen. It really is,' Vivian said, wiping a tear of joy from her eye.

Queenie couldn't agree more. 'It's a gift from him upstairs, it has to be.'

'Who's him upstairs then?' Lenny asked, perplexed.

Vivian tutted. 'God, you silly bastard.'

CHAPTER TWENTY-SEVEN

The following morning Michael got up early and once again pleaded with Nancy to take the day off work so she could accompany him to Ipswich with his father.

'No, Michael. I can't just take time off like that. It isn't fair on the other girls.'

'But, we could have stayed in a hotel or bed and breakfast. I mean, how nice would it be to have a night on our own together? We haven't even had sex since you moved in here, because you think everybody will hear us.'

Nancy sighed. It was so difficult to snuggle up to Michael every night and not be intimate, but she was an old-fashioned girl at heart. Michael's sister had the bedroom next door to them and his mother was the other side. The thought of anybody hearing them make love seemed deeply wrong to Nancy, which is why she had insisted that Michael sleep with his back towards her.

'Please do this for me, babe. I really want you to get to know my dad better as well,' Michael said, with a sorrowful expression.

Torn between her job and her loyalties towards her boyfriend, Nancy made her decision. 'OK, Michael, I will come to Ipswich with you. But, after today I can't take any more time off in case I get the sack, all right?'

Pleased that he had got his own way, Michael grinned and hugged Nancy tightly to his chest. 'Thanks, darling. You're a star.'

When his dad turned up at the hospital, Little Vinny galloped towards him. 'Where you been, Daddy?'

Queenie glared at her eldest son. 'Yeah, where have you been? Call yourself a good father. You don't know the meaning, boy. And what about your brother? You ain't even visited him for days. Colleen's pregnant and we haven't even been able to tell you because you've been on the missing list.'

'Pregnant! That's amazing! Michael never said when he popped in the club.'

'That's because we didn't find out until after Michael had left the hospital yesterday. Unlike yourself, that boy has been up here every day supporting us and Roy.'

Ordering Lenny to take his son outside, Vinny turned to his mum and aunt. 'I haven't been up here because I felt so fucking guilty if you want the absolute truth. I know deep down that my brother took a bullet that was meant for me which is why I went on a bit of a bender. But I've got my act together again now and there'll be no more pissing it up, I'm gonna re-open the club, and I promise you faithfully whatever happens to Roy from now on, I will be there for him and for you.'

Queenie smiled. 'That's my boy.'

After picking Albie Butler up from the Royal Oak pub, the journey to Ipswich took over three hours as Michael insisted on stopping for a bite to eat on the way. Out of politeness, Nancy sat in the back of the car. Her dad had always insisted that men should sit in the front.

Flicking through the latest copy of *Jackie* magazine, Nancy hummed along to her current favourite chart song, Diana Ross's 'I'm Still Waiting', which reminded her a bit of her relationship with Michael because it was about a couple who had first met at a young age.

'You all right in the back there, babe? We're in Ipswich now. What do you think of it?'

Nancy put down her magazine and stared out of the car window. The hippy look was all the rage where she lived, but she couldn't see anybody in Ipswich sporting a cool hairstyle, or wearing flares. 'It's nice, but in a different way.'

Michael chuckled.

'So, what do you think of my choice of woman, Dad? Do you reckon that she will one day make me a good wife?'

Sensing Nancy's embarrassment, Albie turned around in his seat. 'Don't you be taking no notice of him, sweetheart. Has the gift of the gab like his old dad, he does. If you want my honest opinion, I think you are far too good for him.'

Nancy giggled. Even though it was plain that Michael's father looked a bit dishevelled and was a heavy drinker, she couldn't help but like him.

Denise Thompson felt like an idiot as she sat opposite her doctor and explained why she needed a letter as proof of her pregnancy.

'What are you trying to tell me? Are you not in a relationship with the father of your child, then?' Dr Patak asked in a bemused tone.

'No, he has a new girlfriend now. But, he does have good morals, and I know as soon as I can prove to him that I am pregnant, he will be there for me and my child. I want you to address the letter to him and put your surgery number on it, so he can ring you if he doesn't believe the story. I will deliver the letter to him personally.'

Dr Patak sighed. Writing letters to disbelieving boyfriends was really not part of his work as a GP. 'You will have to pay for the letter,' he informed Denise.

'How much?'

'Two pounds. Is that OK?'

'Well, I suppose it will have to be. Can you write it now for me?' Denise asked, impatiently.

'No. I have a surgery full of unwell patients who need my time. Pop back tomorrow when surgery has finished and I will have it ready for you then.'

When Vinny took her to one side and told her he was arranging a surprise gathering at the club for Vivian's birthday, Queenie was immediately against the idea. 'Don't be daft. We can't have a party while poor Roy is in a coma and I never want to set foot in that club again.'

'I didn't say a party, Mum. It will be more of a family gathering. We can't spend our whole lives in this hospital. It isn't healthy for any of us.'

'It's a nice thought, Vinny, but I am not going back to that club. I just can't.'

'Well, how about I organize a little something at yours then? You haven't got to do sod all. The staff at the club can do all the catering. Colleen will sit with Roy while you and Auntie Viv have a break. It will do you both good, Mum. Please say yes. It will do me good to have something to focus on as well.'

Queenie reluctantly agreed. When Vinny put it like that, how could she say no?

In Ipswich, Michael had just spent the past hour catching up with the uncle he didn't remember. Bert was nothing like Albie. He wasn't a big drinker, seemed quite normal in fact, and Michael hoped that Bert might prove to be a good influence on his father. 'Right, Nancy and I had best be making a move now. Uncle Bert's given me his phone number, Dad, and I will ring you in a few days to see how you're settling in. Don't lose that money I gave you, and don't forget to change your details over with the DHSS.'

'I'll do it tomorrow. Thanks for the money, Michael. You're a good lad.'

Michael had given his dad an envelope which contained five hundred pounds, and when he tried to give Bert the same to put towards his dad's upkeep and the bills, he was surprised when his uncle refused to take it. 'Please don't insult me, Michael. I'm not short of a few bob and since my Ivy died, I've hated living alone. Having my brother stopping with me is a pleasure, and I certainly don't want paying for it.'

Wondering if Bert would still be saying that in a month's time after his father had staggered home pissed on a daily basis, Michael shook his uncle's hand.

'Don't forget the letter, Michael. Can you let me know what your mother says about it?' Albie asked.

'Yes, but I'm not sure when I will give it to Mum yet. I don't want to do it at the hospital, so will have to wait for the right moment.'

Albie nodded. 'I'll just leave it in your capable hands, boy.'

Pleased that he was now in his mother's good books again, Vinny took his son back to the club with him. Money was no object to Vinny these days. His dealings with Ahmed had seen to that. The club was a lucrative enough business on its own, but importing heroin into the capital had made him richer than his wildest dreams. However, he needed to re-open soon. He had promised his mum and it was what Roy would have wanted, too.

'Can I speak to Mum on the phone? I miss her, Dad,' Little Vinny whinged.

His son's words cut deep into Vinny's heart. Not once had Little Vinny ever said he missed him and he had brought the ungrateful little bastard up. About to tear him off a strip, and remind the boy where his loyalties should lie, Vinny was saved from losing his rag by the shrill ring of the phone.

'All right, mate. It's Paul. How's Roy?'

'Still the same. I'll be opening up again soon. I'm still paying you full whack, though. You won't be out of pocket,' Vinny told his doorman.

'It weren't that I was ringing for. I just thought you should know that my younger brother Scott was in the Grave Maurice last night. That Terry Smart was in there. Pissed up, he was, and spouting his gob off something chronic about you, apparently. He was even joking about Roy waking up as a spastic. I just thought you should know the score, mate.'

Absolutely fuming, Vinny thanked his loyal employee, then immediately rang Ahmed. 'Mate, you know that little plan we was speaking about the other evening and we agreed to wait a while?'

'Yes.'

'Well, I've changed my mind. We need to set the ball rolling now,' Vinny hissed.

'Leave it with me and I will sort it for you.'

'Cheers, mate. The sooner the better, eh?'

'Count it as done.'

Michael and Nancy were in a hotel in Suffolk. It was nowhere near as opulent as the previous one they'd stayed in but it was comfortable and clean. Having already made love to Nancy once, Michael was about to do so again when Nancy started questioning him about them getting married. Quickly losing his erection, Michael propped himself up on the pillow with his elbow. 'I love you, Nance, you know that, but we don't want to rush into things, do we? Getting hitched is a massive step, and it ain't like you're up the duff or anything, is it? If you was, then I suppose we would have to get wed.'

'But, you was the one who first mentioned it, Michael. When we spoke about my parents chucking me out, you said don't worry, we can get married.'

Desperate to avoid their first lover's tiff, Michael stroked Nancy's beautiful face. 'And I meant it, babe, but what's the rush? I can't think straight with my brother being in a coma, let alone plan a poxy wedding.'

'I'm sorry. It's just that I'm sure my mum would be happier if we got married rather than lived in sin. As for my uptight dad and brother, well, they would have to accept our relationship if they realized we were that serious about one another. Obviously, we won't discuss it in detail while Roy is ill, but we can start arranging it when he is better. I'm sure your mum and Auntie Viv would be thrilled as well, Michael. They both said to me the other day that they love a wedding and think I'll make a lovely bride. I am positive they were hinting.'

Suddenly feeling like a wild bird who was now in captivity, Michael leapt out of the bed. He was only twenty-one for Christ's sake and even though he adored Nancy, he was far too young to commit himself to her for the rest of his life. Say he got bored with her like he had all the others?

Watching Michael's reaction to the thought of their marriage was a wake-up call for Nancy. She might be young, but she wasn't stupid, and some of the little quips she had heard from Michael's family made it obvious to her that Michael had had many girlfriends. Desperate not to lose the lad she loved so much, Nancy made her decision there and then. That pill she had recently asked her doctor to prescribe her, she would stop taking immediately. If trapping Michael was the only way to get him down the aisle, then trap him she would.

Many miles away in Wormwood Scrubs prison, Johnny Preston was sat alone in a cell. Thanks to nerves, then his stupidity at trying to calm them by getting drunk, he was now looking at a long sentence. If Roy died, he might even get life. Feeling absolutely dreadful, Johnny put his head in his hands. Deborah had asked for a divorce earlier thanks to Joanna grassing him up and now he'd lost everything: his reputation, his freedom and his family.

CHAPTER TWENTY-EIGHT

Vivian Harris was absolutely knackered thanks to a rotten night's sleep. She had dreamt that her Lenny had died, and after she had awoken from her nightmare had been too traumatized to doze off again.

As usual on a Sunday morning, Queenie and Vivian had gone to visit their mother's grave. From there they had gone straight to the hospital, which was always a tiring experience as well as stressful and upsetting. 'Bleedin' shattered, I am today. You don't mind if I don't come in yours now, do ya? I'll pop in tonight after I've had a snooze,' Vivian said, yawning.

Feeling drained herself, Queenie sighed. A houseful of people was the last thing she wanted or needed and she just knew Vivian was going to feel the same. But, what could she do now that Vinny had gone to the trouble of arranging it all? 'Vivvy, you ain't gonna fancy this any more than I do, but you're gonna have to come straight in mine. The boys have got something planned for your birthday.'

Vivian stopped in her tracks outside the Blind Beggar pub. 'Like what? It had better not be a surprise party, Queen. I hate surprises at the best of times. I also hate fucking

299

birthdays. Who wants to celebrate being another year nearer to your bastard grave, eh?'

'I know what you're saying, Viv, but we're gonna have to show willing. Vinny wanted to arrange it at the club but I said no, which is why he's doing it at mine now. It will only be family and a couple of the boys' mates. It's nothing major.'

Vivian felt so tired and ratty, she couldn't help but sound ungrateful. 'It had better fucking not be, Queen. Because if it is, I'm walking out.'

With the bond between herself and the father of her child growing stronger every day, Karen had made a special effort to look nice today. Bell-bottomed halter-neck catsuits were all the rage at the moment, and the white one that Karen had treated herself to showed off her figure and dark skin to a tee.

'Wow! You look fab. I love that outfit. Where did you get it?' Nancy asked, when Karen walked into the lounge after getting changed upstairs. Nancy was wearing a catsuit too, but hers was denim.

'Roman Road. I love shopping there. You get some real unusual bits,' Karen replied, searching for Vinny with her eyes to clock his reaction to her new outfit. Unfortunately for Karen, there wasn't one. Vinny gave her a half-smile and then turned his back on her to speak to his sister's boyfriend.

Nancy had only met Karen briefly once before, and when Michael excused himself to go and have a chat with his pal Kevin, the girls seemed to hit it off instantly. Both were big fans of Marc Bolan and obsessed with fashion, but most importantly, they were both involved with men from the same notorious family. As usual, Lenny had taken on the role of being DJ for the day, and when he played Rod

Stewart's current chart hit 'Maggie May', Karen and Nancy both chuckled as Little Vinny appeared in front of them wiggling his tiny hips. 'Aw, he is so gorgeous, isn't he?' Nancy gushed.

'Not always. He can be a little sod at times, but can't they all? Have you and Michael discussed having children yet? I'd like another one, but I don't want them to have different fathers, and Vinny and I aren't really together at the moment.'

'We haven't been together that long, so no, Michael and I haven't really discussed kids yet,' Nancy replied. She could hardly tell Karen that she had thrown her birth control pill down the sink this morning because she was planning on tricking him into marrying her.

'Well, I think you've picked a good 'un. Michael is a lovely bloke, and if he has any sense it won't be long before he pops the question. A girl as stunning as you could get any man she wanted.'

'Thank you and I think you're stunning too. So, are you and Vinny not, you know?' Nancy asked. Vinny scared the life out of her with his blunt manner and evil eyes and Nancy was amazed that a girl as pretty as Karen had ever given him the time of day.

'We aren't sleeping together if that's what you mean, but we are heading towards it, I think. We often go out for meals and spend time together as a family now, and Vinny has just rented me a lovely flat in Beckton. I'm moving in tomorrow, and I'm hoping once I do, mine and Vinny's relationship might move onto the next level. There were a lot of bridges to build because of stuff that happened in the past, but we are getting there. I know we are.'

About to pry some more, Nancy was stopped by Brenda walking over to her.

'Don't ever repeat anything we speak about to Michael

or anybody else, will you? Hardly anyone knows about my flat yet. Vinny wants me to surprise everyone when I move in,' Karen whispered.

Nancy squeezed her new pal's hand. 'Don't be daft.'

Vivian was not amused when she followed Queenie inside the house and saw not only three people she didn't know, but also most of their neighbours. 'Nothing major! I don't even know or like half these cunts,' Vivian spat in her sister's ear.

Seeing his beloved mother appear, Lenny turned down the sultry tones of Elvis and picked up his microphone. 'Happy birthday, Mum. I love you. Do you like your surprise? We did all this for you, and we've bought you a big cake.'

Forcing a smile, Vivian walked over to her son and hugged him close to her chest. 'Of course I like my surprise, boy. It's lovely,' she lied.

Denise Thompson felt as jumpy as a cat on a hot tin roof as she trudged along the Whitechapel Road with her mother beside her. She had wanted her best friend to go with her to confront Michael with the doctor's letter, but her mum had insisted that it was her duty to accompany her. 'I am the baby's grandma and if that Queenie kicks off I shall give her a piece of my bleedin' mind. How dare that boy get you in the family way, then call you a bloody liar? I'll give him liar if he starts all that with me, let me tell you,' Madge Thompson had told her daughter.

At the top of Michael's road, Denise suddenly came over nauseous. She had heard through the grapevine that he was now living at Queenie's with his new tart, and the thought of them playing happy families was all too much for her. She was also frightened that Vinny might be at the house like he usually was on a Sunday afternoon. Surely, he would go apeshit when he found out that she had taken his money even though she was actually pregnant?

'What's the matter with you, girl? Come on, keep walking. I didn't bring you up to be a coward, did I?'

'I can't, Mum. I've done something really stupid, and I can't face Vinny.'

Madge felt her heart begin to beat wildy. 'Stupid! What do you mean, stupid? You better not have been hawking your mutton at Vinny an' all, young lady, 'cause if that baby you're carrying is his, then I'm disowning you.'

Denise burst into tears. 'How could you say such a thing, Mum? I loved Michael and would never have betrayed him in such a way.'

'Well, what you done then?' Madge asked anxiously.

When Denise explained she had accepted money off Vinny to tell Michael she was pregnant, Madge shook her head in exasperation. Everybody who lived locally knew that Vinny Butler was a sandwich short of a picnic, and took no prisoners when people upset him. Unable to control her annoyance, Madge slapped her stupid daughter around the face. 'Right, I'll tell you how we're gonna play this. You never, ever admit to anyone what you have just told me. If and when Vinny asks about his money, you say that you didn't know you were pregnant when you took it off him and you spent it ages ago, OK? To be honest, if Vinny went to those lengths to split Michael up with that Nancy tart, then I should imagine he will be thrilled you really are up the duff. If he isn't and threatens you in any way, then I'll deal with it. I'm sure he won't want his mother to know about his resorting to blackmail to ruin his brother's relationship. Now come on, dry them eyes and let's get this over with.'

When Karen had first re-entered her son and grandson's lives, Queenie had all but hated the girl on sight. However, the more she saw of Karen and the way she was with Little Vinny the more Queenie had grown to like her.

Queenie had thoroughly expected Karen to barge her way into their lives and try to take over, but the girl had done no such thing. Karen had behaved impeccably towards all of the family, and there was a definite improvement in Little Vinny. Her grandson was no longer as tempestuous or violent as he had once been; having his mum around him seemed to have worked wonders. Queenie walked over to where Vinny was standing. 'I need to speak to you for a minute, boy,' she said, nodding politely at Ahmed. She had never really taken to Ahmed.

Vinny followed his mother up the stairs. 'What's up?' he asked, as he sat on the edge of her bed.

'Nothing really, love. I just wanted to have a chat with you about Karen.'

'What about her? I haven't forgotten about nipping things in the bud. Things are in hand, Mum.'

'Well, this is what I wanted to talk to you about. I've changed my mind about her. Not only do I think she is a good little mum, I also think Little Vinny's behaviour has improved dramatically since she's been part of his life. I never thought I would hear myself say it, but I quite like the girl. She is ever so polite to me and Vivvy, and she hasn't tried to take over in any way, has she?'

Absolutely livid, Vinny did his best not to show it. His plans were already in place and as much as he loved his mother, if she thought that he was going to change his mind at this late stage, then she had another think coming. 'Listen, Mum. Karen's an ex-stripper, and on top of that she's a fucking druggie. I am not having my son exposed to that. As his father it's my duty to protect him.'

'A druggie! She don't look like she's on anything to me. What does she take then?' Queenie asked, horrified. She

had always been very anti-drugs, and had once nearly throttled her Michael when he was going through his Mod stage.
She had found a packet of blue pills in his trouser pocket,
and had threatened him with all sorts.

'Karen don't take anything in the day, which is why
whenever you see her she acts normal. But, of a night, it's
a different story. I've seen her with her eyes rolling around
in her head. Off her nut, she's been. That ain't no mother,
is it? Would you ever act like that?'

'No, I bloody well wouldn't. I'm shocked, Vinny, I really
am. I honestly had begun to think she was a really nice girl.
Why ever did you give her a job then if you knew she was
a druggie?' Queenie asked, perplexed.

Vinny had always been a good liar, even as a young lad.
'Because she's the mother of my child. Like you, Mum,
when she first turned up on the doorstep, I wanted rid of
her. But then, I saw how good she was with Little Vinny
too and thought I should give her a chance. She's let me
down big style. I'm really disappointed in her.'

Queenie was stunned. Karen looked so glamorous and
healthy. But Queenie was interrupted from asking anything
further by Vivian bursting through her bedroom door.
'Whatever's the matter?' Queenie asked her sister.

'You had better come downstairs. That Denise has just
turned up with her mouthy mother. She has a letter from
the doctor saying she's got a bun in the oven. Nancy's ever
so upset. You need to sort it.'

When his mother dashed out of the room, Vinny couldn't
help but smile. Denise Thompson had more than earned his
money.

'You bastard. You lying bastard. You swore to me that it
wasn't true,' Nancy sobbed, pummelling her fists against
Michael's chest.

'It ain't true. Ask me mum if you don't believe me,' Michael insisted.

'Let's sort this out in the back garden, shall we? Lenny, turn the music back up,' Queenie ordered her nephew. She wished the neighbours hadn't been invited. Most were nosy bastards and they would have a field day with this little drama. It was bound to be the talk of the street for the next few days at least. 'Right, what the hell is going on?' Queenie asked, after she'd shut the back door.

Barging her daughter out of the way, Madge waved the letter in Queenie's face. 'This is what's going on. Read it, go on, read it. Your son has put my daughter in the family way, and that is the proof. My daughter might be a lot of things, but a liar she isn't.'

Seeing his distressed girlfriend being comforted by Karen, Michael stormed back inside the house and grabbed Vinny roughly by the arm. 'I know all this is your doing, so best you get in that garden and fucking sort it out. Pay a doctor to write a fake letter, did ya?' Michael spat.

'I have no idea what you are talking about,' Vinny replied, his face a picture of innocence, as he followed his brother outside.

Queenie read the letter twice, then handed it to Vivian. It looked official enough, and she knew Dr Patak personally. He was once her deceased Aunt Edna's doctor.

When Karen led Nancy upstairs to try to calm her down, Denise was about to speak up for herself when she saw Vinny swagger into the garden behind Michael. Putting her head down to avoid eye contact with either man, Denise shut her mouth and stared at her feet.

'I know this is his doing, Mum, and so do you, so you might as well just admit it,' Michael yelled, pointing at Vinny.

'He's talking out of his arse, Mum. I ain't said sod all to

you, have I? Why would I care if Denise was pregnant or not?'

Desperate to keep the peace, Queenie waved the letter in the air. 'I will pay Dr Patak a visit tomorrow and find out the truth. Now, can we stop all this arguing and accusation for today? This is meant to be a birthday party, not a bastard soap opera.'

Madge knew she and Denise were being dismissed, and she was determined to have the final say. 'So, what happens when you find out tomorrow that my daughter is telling the truth? I take it your son is going to fully support Denise and their child?'

'As you well know, Madge, I have decent morals and have brought my sons up to be the same way. If what you are saying turns out to be true, then yes, of course Michael will be there to support Denise and his child. Won't you, Michael?' Queenie said, giving her son a sharp kick on the ankle.

Michael turned to his mother and despairingly nodded his head.

Upstairs, Karen was doing her best to comfort Nancy. 'Things will sort themselves out, they always do. Chances are, that girl is lying just to split you and Michael up and even if she isn't, it's you he loves and wants to be with, isn't it?'

'I don't want him if she has his baby. I want me and Michael to have children together. It won't be the same if he already has one. What am I gonna do if Denise is pregnant, Karen? I'll have to move back home.'

Before Karen could tell her new-found friend not to do anything rash, the bedroom door opened and Michael walked in. 'Best I leave yous two to it. See you downstairs, Nancy,' Karen said, making a quick exit.

When Michael tried to put his arms around her, Nancy flinched, then pushed him away.

'Babe, it is you I love.'

'Go away. Just leave me alone, Michael. I don't want you anywhere near me ever again.'

Downstairs in the kitchen, Ahmed had just discreetly dropped two LSD tabs into a glass of champagne. 'Do you want to give it to her? Or shall I?' he asked Vinny.

'Neither. Champ, 'ere a minute,' Vinny shouted, as his cousin walked past him. Lenny had taken a break from his DJ-ing duties to use the toilet.

'What's up, Vinny? You do like my music, don't you?'

Vinny ruffled his cousin's thick mop of hair. 'You're doing an absolute brilliant job. I've poured a glass of beer for you, but if your mum asks it's shandy, OK? And can you give that glass of champagne to Karen for me? She is standing right by your box of records.'

'Yep, I'll give it to Karen, and thank you, Vinny. I promise I will tell Mum that mine is a shandy,' Lenny said, trotting away happily.

'Well?' Vinny asked his pal.

Ahmed grinned. 'He has given it to her, and she is sipping it. Let the fun begin.'

A short distance away from the party, Colleen was sitting by her fiancé's bedside, stroking his hand and chatting away to him like she always did when they were alone. Speaking to Roy normally, like he could actually hear her, was the only way Colleen could cope with what had happened, and today she had been telling him that the doctor had told her she was approximately three months pregnant. 'So, I was thinking, Roy. Obviously, if it is a boy he will be named after you, but I quite like Jennifer for a girl, what do you think? Then again, I bet my mum and dad want me to chose a more Irish-sounding name.'

When she felt Roy's hand move slightly, Colleen leapt out of her chair. She hadn't imagined it. She was sure she hadn't. Staring at Roy's face, Colleen screamed when she saw his eyes start to flicker. 'Nurse, nurse. Come quick,' she yelled.

Vivian was amazed when Lenny played Johnny Kidd & the Pirates' 'Shaking All Over' and Karen started doing a strange dance, which included throwing her arms in the air, in the middle of the lounge carpet. Queenie was busy trying to get rid of the neighbours, therefore had her back turned. When Karen put her arms seductively around Lenny's neck, Viv ran over to her sister and prodded her in the arm. 'Is she pissed, or what? Do me a favour and get her away from my Lenny. I don't want to make a big scene in front of Vinny.'

When Queenie looked around, she was startled. Karen was behaving just as Vinny had described earlier. Her eyes were glassy. She looked on a different planet, and as she let go of Lenny and picked Little Vinny up to swing him around in the air, Queenie was worried for her grandson's safety.

Vinny and Ahmed had been watching Karen for the past ten minutes, and had found the change in her hilarious, but when Queenie walked towards them they both pretended to be engrossed in their own conversation. 'You all right, Mum? Want another drink?' Vinny asked.

'No, I'm not all right. You seen the state of Karen? She's acting really weird. She better not have been taking that shit you told me about in my house, Vinny, because if she has, get fucking rid of her now,' Queenie hissed.

Vinny looked around, then pretended to be shocked. 'Oh for fuck's sake. See, told you what she was like, didn't I?

Believe me now, do ya? I'll take her home in a bit. Little Vinny can come with me for the ride.'

'You ain't taking Little Vinny with you if she's off her head. Leave him here. Me and Vivvy will look after him. He looks upset to me. I think he's trying to get away from her.'

'Well, she won't be working for me and seeing him for much longer, so best he knows the truth about her, Mum. At least if he sees her acting strange, then it's easier for me to explain why she is no longer part of our lives.'

'How you gonna get rid of her? Druggie or not, you can't do anything bad to her, Vinny.'

'As if I would, Mum. When I say get rid of her, I mean send her away to one of those special clinics to sort out her drug abuse. I have already spoken to my doctor about it, and he is looking into it for me.'

'Oh my gawd, Vinny! What's she doing now? Everyone's staring at her, look. You'd better get her out of here now. She's embarrassing herself and my good name.'

Watching Karen crawl along the carpet while mumbling something about big spiders, Vinny desperately tried to keep a straight face. The audience around her was getting bigger by the second. 'I'll just finish my drink, then Ahmed can help me put her in the car,' Vinny said. He wanted to ensure that everybody had seen Karen in her current state. It was all part of his plan.

Snatching the glass out of her son's hand, Queenie threw the contents down the sink. 'When I say I want her out of my house now. I mean fucking now.'

Less than half an hour after Karen had left the house another drama occurred.

Big Stan had always hated One Eyed Harry ever since the drunken old bum had run over his beloved dog Shep, and when Harry made a derogatory comment about his wife's weight and food intake, Big Stan saw red and demanded an apology.

'I'm not saying sorry. Why should I? I'm only being honest and saying what everybody else is thinking. Never seen such a greedy fat beast in all my life. Six plates of grub I've seen her eat. I'm surprised she ain't fucking burst,' Harry said, in his usual blunt manner.

Big Stan draw back his right fist and hit One Eyed Harry so hard that he went flying backwards into Queenie's beloved glass ornament cabinet.

'Aw, my giddy aunt! He's smashed me cabinet and all me fucking china,' Queenie screamed.

Big Stan was mortified. 'I'm so sorry, Queenie. I'll try and pay for any damage I've caused. It was an accident, honest it was.'

Absolutely seething, Queenie picked up her china fruit bowl and began clouting Big Stan around the head with it. 'You couldn't afford to reimburse me for one of them ornaments let alone all of them, you great big lummox. Now, get out my house and take that gluttonous wife of yours with ya.'

When Big Stan and his wife left, Queenie snatched the mike off Lenny. 'Right, that's it. The party is over. Apart from family, you can all drink your drinks and fuck off home. The quicker you leave the better. Thank you all for coming.'

'Fucking birthdays, I hate 'em. Let's sit out in the garden and drink our sherry, eh? We can clear the mess up later,' Vivian suggested, handing her sister a cigarette.

'Good idea. I'll tell you something, Vivvy, that is the last time I ever have a party here. Not only has my lovely home been smashed up, but what a fucking show-up with that Karen, eh? Kicking and screaming like a loony she was when

Vinny tried to get her in the car. Nosy Hilda clocked everything. I'm gonna have such a go at Vinny for inviting all the bleedin' neighbours. He knows we don't really mix with them, and we like to keep our business private. What was he thinking, eh?'

'Don't ask me. The party was a shambles from start to finish. The only thing I liked was me cake, and some bastard knocked that on the floor. Such a shame about all your lovely china though.'

Sipping her sherry, Queenie suddenly saw the funny side and began to laugh. 'Only last week I looked at that china cabinet and thought how dated it seemed. My Vinny can buy me one of them posh sideboards now. What a day eh, Viv? And what with Denise turning up with her pregnancy letter. What must people think of us? Talk about free entertainment.'

Vivian raised her eyebrows. 'As for my Lenny showing me up again. Pissed in your rose bush he did because there was a queue for the toilet. Flopped his todger out right in front of poor old Ivy. She was out here having a fag.'

Queenie held her aching sides. 'Do you know what, Viv, I've come to the conclusion that none of our kids are normal. Most families have one black sheep, but between me and you, we managed to breed a fucking flock of 'em.'

Debbie Ryan was amazed when she saw the state of her friend. Vinny had knocked on her door, explained what had happened, and asked if she would be kind enough to keep an eye on Karen for him.

'Why is Mummy acting scary, Dad? She's frightening me,' Little Vinny said, clinging to his father's leg.

Debbie had never met Karen's son before and it was obvious the child was confused and upset. 'Your mum isn't well, love, but she will be better soon, I promise you that.'

'Get away from him,' Karen screamed, rocking to and fro with her head balancing on her knees.

Desperately worried about her pal, Debbie knelt down next to her. Many a time, Karen had babysat for her two kids and she was the most reliable, trustworthy and responsible person that Debbie knew. There was no way in the world that Karen would have jeopardized her relationship with her son, or her relationship with her son's father. She wasn't that bloody stupid.

'Get them away from me. You know I hate spiders,' Karen wept.

Debbie squeezed her friend's hand. 'It's OK, mate. I'm here to look after you now. There are no spiders, I promise you that.'

'Yes there are! I can see them,' Karen shouted. She then got on all fours, crawled along the carpet, and hid behind the sofa.

Grabbing Vinny's arm, Debbie led him into the hallway. 'I think we need to call an ambulance, or the police. Karen isn't drunk, and I know for a fact that apart from the odd spliff she doesn't do drugs. I reckon someone must have spiked her drink or something.'

Not expecting Debbie to be so clued up, Vinny was slightly taken aback, but still managed to hold his composure. 'There is no way that her drink has been spiked. We have only been at my mum's house with family and a few of the neighbours. Look, between me and you I think Karen has a bit of a drug problem. On a few occasions, she has got out of her nut at the club and I've got a feeling she's buying the shit off one of my other barmaids. You can't start calling ambulances, or the Old Bill, because they will put on her record that she is a druggie and stop her from seeing Little Vinny. Break her heart and his, that would. They have become so close now.'

Debbie looked at Karen's son's tear-stained face and reluctantly agreed. 'I don't mind looking after Karen tonight. My kids are at their dad's, so I can stay here with her. What if she takes a turn for the worse though? I can't sit back and do nothing then.'

Vinny asked for a pen and paper. 'I'm sure she's over the worst. Whatever she's taken is bound to wear off soon. I'm going back to the club now, and that's the phone number. If by any chance you are really worried about her, ring me and I'll pay for a private doctor to visit her. That way, it won't go on her record. I would hate to see her looked upon as a bad mother 'cause she isn't. I'm meant to be helping her move tomorrow, so I'll be back first thing in the morning. If she still isn't well enough, we'll leave moving until Tuesday.'

After she'd seen Vinny out, Debbie shut the door and leant against it. Even though Vinny had seemed sincere enough, there was something about his story that just didn't ring true.

Back in Whitechapel, Michael had finally managed to get his mother alone, and was just building up to giving her his father's letter when the doorbell rang.

'Auntie Queenie, Colleen wants you,' Lenny shouted out.

Queenie pushed past Michael and dashed down the stairs. Colleen never visited the house alone, so it must be something important.

'Where have you been? I've been trying to ring you for the past two hours,' Colleen said, before bursting into tears.

'There was a bit of a scuffle and the cable got pulled out the socket. We've only just noticed it and put it back in,' Vivian explained.

Fearing that her son had lost his battle for life, Queenie clung onto the banister for physical support. 'Please God don't tell me Roy's dead,' she stammered.

Even though she was still crying, Colleen's tears were ones of pure happiness. 'Roy's come out of his coma, Queenie. He's awake!'

As usual on a Sunday, Terry Smart had spent the whole day abusing his liver. At ten p.m. he said goodbye to his pals and staggered out of the Grave Maurice pub and onto the Whitechapel Road. Seconds later, a white van pulled up, the back doors flew open and two foreign-looking men leapt out and grabbed him. 'Get off me, you cunts. What the fuck you doing?' Terry slurred, as he was bundled into the back of the van.

Instead of answering Terry's question, one of the men grabbed a cosh, smashed Terry over the head with it and knocked him spark out.

CHAPTER TWENTY-NINE

Queenie's initial joy that her son had awoken from his coma somewhat dwindled during the course of the next week. Looking at Roy was like looking at a completely different person. He was nothing like the son she had known before the shooting. Roy was now paralysed down the left-hand side of his body, and had minimal movement in his right side. He had to be spoon-fed small amounts of mashed-up food like a baby, and his face was drooped on one side which made him look like he had suffered a bad stroke. The poor mite also had no control over his bowel movements and Queenie was sure she could see the horror in his eyes every time he shat the bed. There was no way he could tell anyone how he was feeling though, as when he tried to speak, it was more like noises than words coming out of his mouth. The only plus side that Queenie could think of was Roy recognized his family. He had tears rolling down his cheeks every time Colleen spoke about her pregnancy, so he obviously understood what was going on. He had also tried to ask in his own way what had happened to him, and had understood when Vinny had told him he had been shot outside the club and Johnny Preston had been arrested for the shooting.

'You OK, Mum? You seem ever so quiet this morning,' Vinny asked, as he parked his car.

Queenie had always had a reputation for being as hard as nails, but seeing Roy in his current state on a daily basis had really taken its toll on her. In this past week, she had cried more tears than in the previous thirty years, and once again she couldn't prevent them from rolling down her cheeks.

Vinny took his keys out of the ignition, leant across his seat and enveloped his mother in his arms. The club had re-opened again now, but Vinny hadn't shirked any of his other responsibilities. He had spent nearly all day every day at the hospital since his brother had woken up and he planned to support both Roy and his mum as much as he could, whatever the future might bring. 'You got to stop getting upset like this, Mum. Every time I see you cry, it makes me want to do the same. We need to be strong for Roy's sake, and his unborn child. They are both gonna need us to be at the top of our game, aren't they?'

'I just can't bear seeing your brother as he is, Vinny. He ain't the boy I gave birth to any more. He's a fucking vegetable,' Queenie spat, her face contorted with pain and anger.

Vinny hated hearing his brother referred to as anything but normal. 'Don't say shit like that, Mum. We've got to be positive. Perhaps the scan results will give us some better news? Roy hasn't been awake for long, and the doctors did warn us that his recovery would take time and patience.'

'But, say he don't get better? Say he never walks and talks again, eh? He can't stay in hospital forever, and how am I meant to cope if he comes and lives with me? He won't be able to get up and down the stairs, will he?'

Vinny laid his mother's head on his shoulder and stroked her bleached-blonde hair. 'Let's not look too far ahead, eh?

Roy will be in hospital for ages yet, and if he's still no better when the time comes for him to be discharged, then we can look into other options. Perhaps we could hire some nurses to care for him? I would do anything for my family, Mum, and if that means paying privately for the best care possible to help Roy with his recovery, then so be it.'

For the first time that morning, Queenie managed a weak smile. 'You're a good boy, Vinny. The best a mother could wish for.'

Michael Butler felt rather nauseous as he paid the jeweller in crisp twenty pound notes. Getting hitched at his age was the last thing he really wanted to do, but since his mum had checked out Denise's pregnancy story, which her doctor had confirmed to be true, Nancy had barely spoken to him.

Michael loved Nancy more than he had ever loved any girl, and he knew he was on the verge of losing her forever, which is why he had bought the engagement ring today. It was the only rabbit he could pull out of a hat to save their rapidly deteriorating relationship. Surely marrying her was better than losing her, wasn't it?

Unaware of her boyfriend's planned proposal, Nancy was sitting on the bench in her favourite little park currently crying on her mother's shoulder.

'Oh, Nancy. Why don't you come back home, love? I can talk your dad and brother around, so don't you be worrying about them. You don't want to stay with a lad who's having a baby with another girl, do you? It's too much to take on something like that, especially at your young age.'

'I know you are right, Mum, but even though I hate Michael for doing this to me, I still love him as well. He says he will support his child financially and as a father, but he has sworn to me he wants nothing whatsoever to do with Denise. He reckons she trapped him on purpose by not taking her contraception pill.'

Mary held her daughter's hands and squeezed them. 'Only you can decide what you want to do, darling, but let me tell you one thing. Whenever you have a child with someone it creates a strong bond, and this one's a bond you won't be part of. I know Michael says he wants nothing to do with Denise, but once she gives birth to his child he will be in contact with her on a regular basis again. How're you going to feel when she is ringing up every five minutes asking for this and that or telling him the child isn't well, Nance? You've got your whole life ahead of you, and are beautiful enough to bag yourself any lad you want. I would hate to see you sell yourself short.'

Nancy nodded sadly. What her mum had just said was spot-on and deep down she knew it. 'I'll pack my stuff when I get back to Queenie's, Mum, and tell Michael I'm moving back home. Are you sure Dad will be OK about it?'

'You leave your bloody father to me, darling. I pulled the wool over his eyes to escape today. I only let him think he wears the trousers to keep him happy. He won't overrule me, because if he does then I shall leave him. Our home will always be your home, you know that.'

Nancy looked at her watch and silently cursed the time. 'I'm gonna have to go, Mum. I am already in trouble at work for taking too much time off so I daren't be late back from lunch. Can you be near the phone if I ring at dead on eight tonight? Make sure you speak to Dad first though so I know everything is OK your end.'

'I will. When will you move back in?' Mary asked, her face a picture of happiness.

'I might as well come back tonight, I suppose. Once I've

spoken to Michael, then rung you, perhaps Dad will pick me up?'

Mary grinned. 'You bet he will, and I'll come with him so you don't feel awkward.'

'Thanks for everything, Mum. I'll see you later,' Nancy said, before sprinting off.

As Mary walked back to the shop, she could not wipe the smile off her face. She had her little girl back.

At the hospital, Queenie, Colleen and Vinny had just sat down opposite the brain specialist.

'Well? Have you got the results?' Vinny asked, impatience creeping into his voice.

'Yes, I have, and I'm afraid the news isn't as good as we had hoped for. The scan shows that there has been a considerable amount of damage to Mr Butler's brain, which is the cause of the paralysis down the right side of his body.'

'But, he will get better, won't he? There must be something you can do, surely?' Vinny interrupted, now agitated.

Bursting into tears, Colleen ran from the room. She was training to be a nurse, therefore knew what the specialist was going to say next and couldn't bear to hear it.

Queenie sat frozen to her seat. Her heart felt like a lead weight and it was as though time had stood still and she was in a trance. Images of Roy in his younger years flooded through her mind. His first day at school with his little legs poking out of his long shorts. Those same legs sprinting to glory when he won the hundred-yards race at the age of thirteen. Roy dancing with her to Kenny Ball's 'My Mother's Eyes' on the opening evening of their first ever club. How could it be possible that her handsome, strapping son would never use those legs again?

'So, what can we do to get him better?' Vinny asked the specialist.

'Roy will be given extensive physiotherapy, speech therapy, and help in learning the basics once again. Unfortunately, it is highly unlikely that your brother will ever live the life that he once did. There has been too much damage to the brain, I fear.'

Vinny was in a shocked kind of stupor. 'But, he will walk again, won't he?'

'Well, obviously miracles have been known to happen, Mr Butler, but if you want my honest opinion, the answer is no.'

When his mother started to cry, Vinny held her in his arms. He could have quite easily broken down in tears himself, but as the eldest child, it was his duty to be a tower of strength, and his mother needed that from him more than ever now. 'I'll get Roy the best help possible, Mum, I promise you that. Together, we will get through this. We are Butlers, remember?'

At the nightclub, Karen had just woken up fully clothed with a thumping headache and little recollection of going to bed once again. She half-remembered falling over and Vinny carrying her up the stairs, but she wasn't sure if she was imagining that part or not.

Karen sat up, perched herself on the end of the bed and stared at her unglamorous reflection in the mirror. She looked like she had two black eyes where she hadn't taken off her make-up, and her hair stood up on end as if she had been dragged through a hedge backwards. 'What the hell is happening to me?' she asked herself out loud. She hadn't felt right since the terrifying experience she'd suffered on the night of Vivian's birthday party. The visions of spiders crawling all over the floor, the horrendous metallic taste in her mouth, then the constant vomiting she'd endured throughout the night would be with her for the rest of her life.

The truth of her scary ordeal had come to light the following day. Lenny had been given a couple of LSD tabs at the club by a customer a few weeks ago. He had been told that they would make him feel good and have fun, but frightened to take them himself in case his mum found out, he had decided to give them to Vinny and Karen so they could enjoy themselves instead. As luck would have it, Vinny's glass that contained the drug had been knocked off the kitchen top by Ahmed's elbow, so it had been only her that had suffered.

Karen had been furious at Lenny's stupidity at first, but when Vinny had made him apologize in person, she had found it difficult to stay angry with the boy. Lenny couldn't help having mental health problems, had seemed genuinely sorry, and had promised never to do anything similar to anyone ever again. Vinny had told Karen that he knew the bloke who had given Lenny the tabs and was personally going to teach him a lesson. He had also given his cousin a good telling-off in front of her too, but what Karen obviously didn't realize was it was all an act and Lenny had been paid fifty pounds for his part in the drama.

Karen had begged Vinny to tell his family the truth. She felt so embarrassed by her outrageous behaviour that she insisted she was too ashamed to face the Butler clan again unless they were aware of what had really happened.

Vinny had refused. He said he wasn't a grass and there was no way he was going to get Lenny into trouble. He had promised to one day explain that Karen had been accidently spiked up by somebody else though, but now wasn't the right time as his family had enough on their plates with the Roy situation.

Karen ran a bath, had a quick dip, and then dried herself with a king-sized towel. Her move into her lovely new flat had been temporarily delayed as there had been a hitch with the previous tenants. A family death had stopped them collecting their belongings when they were supposed to, but Ahmed had promised her that the situation would be resolved in the next few days.

Having already given back her keys to her own flat to the council, Karen had hoped when Vinny suggested she stay at the club it would bring them closer together. It hadn't though. Karen had been sleeping in Roy's room and had not even shared as much as a kiss with Vinny. He had hinted the other day that they would share a bed when she moved into her own property though, and that thought had made Karen very happy indeed.

Karen hadn't seen much of her son since the evening her drink had been spiked. Only twice Vinny had brought him to the club and both times Little Vinny had seemed quite reserved and wary of her. Karen had cried after her son's last visit when he had refused to kiss her goodbye, but Vinny had promised that this Thursday, he would let Little Vinny take a day off school and all three of them would have a nice family day out. Vinny insisted that the boy had just been scared by what he had seen and would soon forget all about it. What he hadn't told Karen was that he had told his son that his mother had a bad drug problem, and it would be better if he didn't get too close to her in case she started acting all weird again.

Karen got dressed and rang her friend Debbie. Vinny had made her swear that she wouldn't tell anybody that it was Lenny who spiked her drink, but Karen had told the two people she trusted, Debbie and Nancy. Both had been so supportive this past week, and had promised to keep what had happened to themselves.

'You all right, mate?' Debbie asked.

'No, not really. I don't remember going to bed again last night and I have a really shitty headache. I don't know what's a matter with me lately. That's twice I've somehow got drunk and blanked out in the past week and I haven't drunk any more than usual. Perhaps it is the aftereffects of that awful bloody trip?'

'Listen, don't take this the wrong way, but I think something isn't right. First, you get spiked with the LSD, then the lovely flat isn't ready for you to move into. Now you've mysteriously got drunk twice in a week without drinking much and for no apparent reason, blanked out. Something don't sound kosher to me, Kaz.'

Karen was stunned by her pal's little speech. Whatever was she insinuating? 'So, what you saying, Deb? You don't think Vinny is trying to poison me or something, do you?'

'I really don't know, mate. Look, I'm gonna have to go now, I've got to pick the boys up from school. Just be careful, Kaz, and any time you're worried just ring me and you can come and stay here.'

'Do you honestly think I'm in that much danger?' Karen asked, her heart pounding nineteen to the dozen.

'I don't know, but watch your back, Kaz, just in case.'

When Colleen's relations turned up at the hospital, Queenie and Vivian decided to make themselves scarce. Colleen had been as devastated as anyone about the scan results and seeing as her family had just arrived from Ireland again, Queenie thought it only right that they should spend some time alone together.

Queenie's earlier sorrow had now been replaced with feelings of bitterness. Her Roy had always been a good lad. He was kind and considerate, so what the hell had he done to deserve such appalling injuries?

''Ere you go, get that down your neck. I've poured myself one an' all. Think we can do with a drink after the day we've had, don't you?' Vivian stated.

Queenie snatched at the glass and knocked the sherry back in a couple of gulps. 'Can't believe how cruel life can be, Vivvy. There definitely ain't no fucking God, you know. Makes me sick that you've got all them kiddy-fiddlers and wicked bastards roaming the streets who never catch as much as a fucking cold. Why do bad things happen to decent people like us, eh?'

'I know what you mean, Queen. I was bitter for a long time after my Lenny was born with his difficulties. I thought, why me and him? Why not some other bastard's child? Look what an awful mother that Old Mother Taylor was. Dirty whore, and them poor little mites of hers were brought up in squalor. Nothing ever happens to people like that old cow though. Tragedy always strikes good souls such as you and I.'

'I wish my Roy was dead, you know. Would have been much kinder if he had croaked it as soon as he'd been shot,' Queenie said, in her usual blunt manner.

'Aw, don't say that, Queen. It is early days. With the right sort of treatment, Roy still might be able to lead a half-decent life, and he's gonna be a dad for the first time. I know it don't seem like it at the moment, but there will be a light at the end of the tunnel. It just might take a while for it to start shining your way.'

'Light! Don't make me fucking laugh. I gave birth to that boy and I can see the look of confusion and horror in his eyes. Why do you think he cries every time Colleen's pregnancy is mentioned, eh? He don't want his kid to have a fucking spastic for a father, that's why. My Roy's life is over, Viv, and the quicker we all accept that, the better. All he has got left to look forward to is endless hospital appointments, and sitting in his own piss and shit for the rest of his days,' Queenie spat.

Just as Vivian was about to reply, the doorbell rang and

she leapt up to answer it. 'What the hell! Where do you think you're going? Get out of here,' Vivian yelled.

Freda Smart barged past Vivian and marched into the lounge. She then pointed her fat forefinger in Queenie's face. 'I know it's your Vinny that's had my Terry done in, which is why I have just been to the police station and given a statement. I hope you're proud of yourself, Queenie Butler, for raising such a fucking monster. Now, where is my grandson?'

Dean had been upstairs playing records with Brenda when he had heard his grandmother's booming voice. 'What's up, Nan? Has Dad come home?' he asked hopefully, as he ran down the stairs.

'No, he ain't, and he never will come home again, boy. You dad's dead, I can feel it in my bones. It's her evil bastard of a son that's killed him. That psycho needs hanging from the gallows.'

Queenie leapt out of her chair. The gossipmongers had already been in overdrive about Terry Smart's disappearance and even though she'd guessed that her Vinny was responsible in a round-about way, she would defend her son's innocence to the hilt. 'I am sick of my family being blamed for everything bad that happens in this area, and I ain't putting up with it no more. For your information, the night your Terry went missing my Vinny was up the hospital with me. Roy had come out of his coma and we were there all night long. Ask the fucking doctors and nurses if you don't believe me, you deluded old bat. Now, get out my house and don't you ever come back.'

When his nan started to argue her point, Dean grabbed her by the arm. 'Come on, Nan, let's get you home. I'll stay at yours tonight. We haven't spent much time together recently.'

Brenda was furious. 'And what about me? I hope you

don't think once the baby is born, you can walk out every time she has a tantrum, because I won't put up with it, Dean,' she shouted, pointing at Freda.

Thinking what a selfish bitch his fiancée was, Dean led his nan outside and slammed the front door.

Wormwood Scrubs prison wasn't the best holiday resort that Johnny Preston had ever visited, but for the first time since he had been banged-up, he had a spring in his step again.

Roy waking up from his coma had been a massive weight off Johnny's shoulders. His brief had told him that he would now only be up for attempted murder, plus a firearms charge, and if he were lucky, could be out in eight or ten years. Billy One Ear being banged-up on his wing had been another plus. Billy was from his old stamping ground, and they had often drunk in the same pubs together in South London back in the day. Billy had been given a ten stretch for armed robbery, and he was the daddy of the wing. Johnny, being his pal, was now shown massive respect by the other lags which suited Johnny's ego no end. It also made prison life a damn sight easier.

The third reason why Johnny was in such a chirpy mood was because of the letters he'd received today. His daughter had written to him to apologize for speaking out about his fling. She had asked Johnny to write back to her and told him that she forgave him and would always love him no matter what.

The other letter had been a real bolt out of the blue. It had been from his sister who he hadn't spoken to or seen for years since a family argument. Judy was also keen to build bridges. She had given him her new address and wanted to visit him.

Johnny re-read his daughter's letter. He was amazed by

how mature she suddenly sounded. Joanna had always been good at English, but seeing as she had only just turned thirteen, she wrote as well as any adult he knew. Perhaps she might really make something of her life one day and become an author or a journalist?

Grinning from ear to ear as he read the PS line at the bottom again, Johnny folded the letter carefully and put it under his mattress for safekeeping. Joanna had asked for a visiting order, she wanted to see him, and while he had his daughter's love, Johnny could handle anything else that prison life might chuck his way. The old Preston spirit was back with a bang.

Feeling like a condemned man on death row, Michael trudged up his mother's stairs. 'You all right, babe? What you doing?' he asked his girlfriend. Nancy was sitting on their bed with her suitcase by her side.

Nancy had promised herself that she would not cry, but looking at the bewildered expression on her boyfriend's face, she could not help her tears. 'I am so sorry, Michael, but I am moving back to my parents. I love you and always will, but I want to have my own children. I don't want to raise somebody else's.'

Michael sat down on the edge of the bed. 'Nance, if I could change Denise getting pregnant, then I would, babe. Yes, I will have to support the child, but I swear I will have fuck all to do with her. She trapped me, why should I? It's you I love and you I want kids with.'

Nancy shook her head. 'You say all that, Michael, but I know you don't really mean it. You're not ready for us to get a place of our own, let alone get married and have kids. I might be young, but I'm not stupid. I saw the look of fright in your eyes that last time I mentioned us getting hitched.'

Michael stood and paced up and down the room. He really wasn't ready to propose, but what choice did he have? 'I don't think you know me quite as well as you think you do, Nance. If you did, then why would I have bought you this?' Michael asked, chucking the red velvet box on the bed next to Nancy.

Nancy had always been a bit of a romantic at heart. At the age of fourteen she had played Juliet in her school play and had been awaiting her very own Romeo to whisk her off her feet ever since. Picking up the box, Nancy opened it and gasped. It was a beautiful engagement ring with a big diamond in the centre and two smaller stones either side. 'Oh Michael, it's beautiful.'

Michael dropped to one knee and grabbed his girlfriend's hand. 'I still don't want to rush into anything, babe, but surely getting engaged proves how I feel about you? Please don't let this Denise crap spoil what we have.'

'Getting engaged still doesn't change the fact that another girl is carrying your child, Michael. Anyway, I've told my mum that I'm moving back home now.'

Michael placed the ring on the third finger of Nancy's left hand. 'Please don't leave me, Nance. Agree to marry me instead.'

Donald Walker was not a man to show much emotion, but inwardly he was thrilled that his daughter would be returning home this evening. He was still annoyed that Nancy had got herself involved with Michael Butler in the first place, but he was willing to forgive even if it might take him a long while to forget.

At ten to eight, Mary sat by the phone willing it to hurry up and ring. 'Go and put your jacket on, Donald, and get me a coat. We'll be leaving in a minute and it's chilly outside tonight.'

Christopher scowled at his mother. He thought his parents were being far too lenient with Nancy, considering how badly she had treated them.

The sound of the phone bursting into life made Mary jump. 'Hello, love. Me and your dad are ready. Where do you want us to pick you up from?'

Nancy took a deep breath. 'Mum, I'm so sorry. Please don't hate me, but I'm not coming home now.'

'What! Why? The Butlers aren't stopping you from leaving, are they? If they've threatened you, you must tell me, Nancy.'

Nancy felt awful as she plucked up the courage to tell her mother the truth. 'No, Mum. It's nothing like that. Michael bought me a beautiful engagement ring, so I've agreed to stay and give our relationship another go.'

As a huge racking sob escaped from her lips, Mary dropped the phone in shock.

With Debbie's stark warning still fresh in her mind, Karen felt edgy when Vinny suggested they both take a night off work and he take her out for a nice meal instead. 'Aw, thanks for asking, Vin, but to be honest I'm not that hungry and I'd rather just work.'

'Don't be daft. I'll still pay you for your shift, babe. A pal of mine has a lovely steakhouse in Canning Town and I was gonna take you there.'

Karen shook her head. 'You go with Ahmed. To be honest, I feel embarrassed because I got in a bit of a state again last night and I would rather face the staff and apologize immediately. I've made a decision. I'm not drinking any more alcohol, Vinny. I'm sticking to orange juice instead.'

Vinny was immediately alarmed. There was a very special reason why he had to take Karen to that particular restaurant this evening, and he was determined to get her there by hook or by crook. He sat down next to her on the sofa and put his hand on her knee. 'Babe, I want us to get back together properly. I've taken things at a steady pace because I wanted to be sure about us first. I am sure now, and that's why I've booked the restaurant tonight. You must have a drink. I've spent a fortune on champagne and it's waiting for us on ice.'

Any earlier doubts about Vinny's intentions towards her were banished from Karen's mind. Grabbing Vinny's hand, she led him towards the bedroom.

Vinny felt physically sick when Karen firstly stuck her tongue in his mouth, then tried to fondle his manhood. Knowing what was in store for her later, there was no way he could get a lob on. 'I'm sorry, babe, but I want you so bad it's making me feel nervous. Let's go to the restaurant and we can come back here and get it on later, eh? I've been on my own for so long, I need a few drinks to relax me first,' Vinny lied.

Feeling slightly embarrassed, Karen removed her hand from Vinny's nether regions and nodded. She had waited a long time to be intimate with Vinny again, so another few hours wouldn't kill her, would it?

The atmosphere in the Walker household was as though a death had occurred.

'I mean it, Mary. If you have any contact with that girl again after the way she has upset us all tonight, I will never forgive you.'

'I'm sorry, Donald. If I'd have known that Nancy would break our hearts like this, I would have never asked you to allow her to come back home. I'm devastated, and so, so disappointed in her. Now she is engaged to Michael, I know we've lost her for good,' Mary cried.

Donald held his sobbing wife in his arms. He loved his Mary, hated seeing her so distraught and, unusually for him, had tears in his own eyes. 'We have to let her go now, darling. Nancy has chosen to marry the enemy, and I hope on her wedding day when she looks around and sees not one member of her own family in attendance, she will realize what pain she has caused to us.'

In a restaurant in Canning Town, Karen was thoroughly enjoying herself. She had felt a little deflated earlier when Vinny hadn't been able to perform in the bedroom, but she was fine again now.

'You enjoying yourself? It's so nice to be a proper couple again, isn't it?' Vinny asked.

'Yes, it's lovely. When are we going to tell Little Vinny? Can we tell him together?'

'I thought perhaps we'd get my mum, aunt, and the rest of the family together at the weekend and tell them all at once,' Vinny lied.

'Sounds perfect. Who was that man who just spoke to you, Vinny? The one who just left with the black suit on,' Karen asked.

Vinny leant forward across the table. Canning Town wasn't his territory and he didn't want anybody to think he was gossiping. 'That was Eddie Mitchell. Him and his family run this manor like me and mine run Whitechapel. Why do you ask, babe? You don't know him, do you?'

Karen giggled. 'No. I just asked because he was handsome like you, and I could tell he was a somebody.' Vinny had been plying her with champagne all evening, and Karen hadn't wanted to be a spoilsport and refuse to drink it as they truly were celebrating something special.

'Do you want a dessert, babe? I think I'll order us another bottle of champagne. No rush to get home, is there?

Especially seeing as we'll probably be spending all night and tomorrow in bed together.'

Karen beamed from ear to ear. 'No, I don't want a dessert, but I must use the ladies' room. Where is it?'

'Upstairs, babe. The ladies' is the first door you come to on the left.'

As Karen walked away from the table, Vinny checked no-one was watching him, topped up her glass, and discreetly added the crushed tablets to it. He shoved in a very high dosage, like he had when he had spiked her drinks twice at the club, and therefore knew it wouldn't be too long before he would have to ring his special cab to come and collect her.

Vinny had planned this evening to perfection. The flat he had supposedly rented for Karen actually belonged to a friend of Ahmed who had gone on holiday and entrusted Ahmed with a key to keep an eye on it. Vinny had put that idea in place as he had wanted to keep Karen in his clutches, rather than have her disappearing back to Dagenham. His staff at the club had been shocked when Karen had made a fool of herself at his Auntie Viv's birthday party, but seeing her collapse and have to be carried upstairs twice in the club since had really sewn the seeds that she was a junkie, which is exactly what Vinny had wanted.

Vinny had also chosen this restaurant for a specific reason. The manager of it was a regular at his club and had been there both times when Karen had collapsed. Vinny had already explained to him a couple of weeks ago that Karen had a drug problem and he was at his wit's end at what to do to help her. He had also told Nick he was trying to make a go of their relationship for the sake of his son. Unbeknown to many people, Nick's brother-in-law was East End Old Bill and Vinny knew if push came to shove, Nick would back his innocence surrounding Karen's demise to the hilt.

Vinny smiled as Karen returned from the toilet. ''Ere you go, babe. To us,' he toasted, handing Karen another glass of bubbly.

Within ten minutes, Vinny saw Karen's eyes begin to droop, and soon after she began to slur her words. Excusing himself from the table, Vinny walked up to the tiny bar and spoke to Nick. 'I think Karen has taken something again, mate. She seemed fine until she went to the toilet, now look at the state of her.'

Just as Nick turned around, Karen's forehead made contact with the table. 'Jesus Christ. Do you want me to call you a cab?' Nick asked.

'It's definitely smack she is taking, that's why she keeps going all goofy on me. I spotted a couple of needle marks in her arm the other day and I reckon she has just injected herself in your khazi. Sick of it I am, Nick, fucking sick of it. I've done my utmost to help her and I find it so embarrassing,' Vinny said, sincerely.

Nick patted his pal on the shoulder. There were only about twenty other people in the restaurant apart from the staff, and none were taking much notice of Karen so it was no big deal. 'Don't blame yourself, pal. I'll call you a cab, shall I?' Nick repeated.

'Do you know what, Nicky-boy, my mate's cousin is a cabbie so I'm gonna call him at home and get him to take Karen back to the club. I'm gonna stay here with you for a bit and have a beer, if that's OK? When you lock up, why don't you come back to the club with me? I quite fancy a game of cards.'

Nick had always been a big gambler and, as Vinny knew only too well, could never say no to a game that involved money. 'Yeah, why not. Will Karen be all right travelling back with just the cabbie though?'

'Yeah, I'll ring the staff at the club and tell them to open the back door and help her up to bed. I can't deal with her problems all the time, Nick. I need a break myself.'

'I understand. Use my phone out the back, mate.'

Vinny followed Nick out the back of the restaurant. He then rang Ahmed's cousin. 'Hello, mate. Do you think you could come and pick Karen up in your cab for me? She is in a bit of a state, and I need you to take her back to the club and make sure she gets inside all right.'

Nick shut the door and left his pal to finish his conversation in peace. He felt sorry for Vinny having a junkie as the mother of his kid. What man wouldn't?

Karen had no memory of the events that followed, or the squalid flat in Poplar she was taken to.

Injected in the left arm with an enormous amount of heroin, Karen died almost immediately.

Three hours later, her body was found dumped in a nearby street behind a row of stinking dustbins.

CHAPTER THIRTY

The day after he got engaged to Nancy, Michael surprised her by renting them a house of their own. The house belonged to a pal of his and was situated in a turning just off the East India Dock Road. Nancy had been thrilled by the gesture and since they'd moved in a few days ago, the intimacy had more than returned to their relationship. The only fly in the ointment had been Karen's unexpected death. Nancy had been terribly upset and had sworn blind that there was some kind of skulduggery involved.

On the morning of Karen's funeral, Michael was awake at five a.m. He had driven up to Suffolk the previous day to visit his father. Albie seemed to be doing well living with his brother. He had cut down his booze intake, put on weight, smartened himself up a bit, and was beginning to resemble the handsome man that he had once been. He even had a twinkle in his eye once again.

Albie's twinkle had unfortunately disappeared when Michael explained that Karen had been found dead in a back street in Poplar after an overdose of heroin. 'Something not right there, boy. I spoke to Karen at your sister's engagement party, and she was a lovely girl with a fun personality and a real zest for life. No way was she a smackhead. If you ask me this has your brother's evilness stamped all over it. I bet Vinny wanted rid of the poor girl,' was Albie's take on matters.

Michael had already had similar thoughts himself, but wasn't about to admit that.

Before leaving Ipswich, Michael had given his father another couple of hundred pounds' pocket money, and his dad's parting sentence was the reason he had been unable to sleep properly. 'Michael, I know you said with Roy waking up that you haven't felt it was the right time to burden your mum with my letter, but seeing what has happened to Karen, I now feel you should give it to her sooner rather than later. Like it or not, Vinny is a loose cannon, boy.'

Nancy leaning over and kissing him snapped Michael out of his morbid thoughts.

'I didn't wake you, did I? I've had a crap night's sleep, couldn't stop tossing and turning,' Michael said.

'I was the same. I'm dreading the funeral, Michael. I know I didn't know Karen for long, but I really clicked with her. I didn't tell you this, but I went out for lunch with her last week. I was so upset over the Denise escapade, and Karen was so supportive. She even stuck up for you. She said you was a lovely person and that I shouldn't end it with you over something that happened before we even got together. She told me something else as well, but I promised I wouldn't repeat it. It was about what happened to her at your Auntie Viv's party.'

Intrigued, Michael propped himself up on his elbow. 'Tell me, babe. It might be important.'

'Only if you promise not to say anything? I don't want to cause any trouble amongst your family.'

'I swear I won't say nothing.'

'Karen said she got her drink spiked with LSD at your

337

mum's house. Vinny told her that it was Lenny that did it. He even got Lenny to apologize to her in person. Now, I don't know about you, Michael, but seeing as what has happened to Karen since, I really don't believe that story.'

Suddenly feeling nauseous, Michael's blood ran cold.

Vinny gestured to Ahmed to follow him into his office, then shut the door and poured them both a large Scotch. The Old Bill had been sniffing around like there was no tomorrow since Karen's death, making Vinny feel both anxious and cautious.

Vinny and Ahmed had foolproof alibis for the night of Karen's death. Vinny had stayed at the restaurant until one a.m. and had then gone back to the club with Nick. As planned, Ahmed had been at the club all evening and he also stayed all night to participate in a card game with Vinny, Nick, and four other regulars. Two of the regulars were not only respected businessmen but also Freemasons, which was a bonus in Vinny's eyes.

Ahmed's cousin, Burak, had been the cab driver who had picked Karen up and driven her to Poplar on the night she had died. She had then been handed over to two pals of his who had been paid three thousand pounds between them to carry out her murder. Burak was actually a cab driver who was employed by a firm in Canning Town, so he had gone straight to work from Poplar, therefore also had a rock-solid alibi. The police had questioned Burak, and he insisted that Karen had woken up in his cab and demanded to be dropped off along the Westferry Road near the Anchor and Hope pub. Burak had also informed the police that Karen was abusive, and seemed to be either drunk or drugged up. Vinny knew Burak was to be trusted, as it had been he who had employed the men who had killed Terry Smart.

Ahmed knocked back his Scotch in one. 'Well?' he asked Vinny.

Paranoid that the Old Bill might have bugged his phone, Vinny would only discuss the situation with Ahmed in person now. Karen had told him when she had first come back on the scene that she'd made a statement to the police in case anything untoward happened to her. She'd admitted to Vinny a few weeks afterwards that she had only been bluffing, but Vinny didn't want to take any chances. 'Sniffing around again they were yesterday. I rang Geary last night and he rang me back this morning. Apparently, that nosy cunt of a neighbour of Karen's has been making herself busy. She has been to the Old Bill and made a statement saying she suspects foul play.'

'Look, we have a firm alibi, so no need to panic. What about the nosy neighbour? Shall I speak to Burak and make her disappear?'

'No. We need to lay low, mate. What with Terry Smart going AWOL and now this, we definitely need to rein it in a bit. As much as I would like to see the nosy neighbour propping up a flyover somewhere, we are just going to have to let her do her very worst. As you said, our alibi is water-tight so what can the pigs do? They have questioned Nick again as well, and he has vouched that Karen was fine in the restaurant until she disappeared into the toilets alone.'

Vinny jumped as he heard a knock on his office door. 'Who is it?' he shouted.

'It's me. The police are at the door, Vinny. They want to speak to you,' Edna, the cleaner, informed him.

Cursing the fact that the bastards had turned up yet again, Vinny ordered Ahmed to stay in his office. He then composed himself and went to greet the boys in blue. 'And what can I do for you today, gentlemen?' he asked, half-politely, half-sarcastically.

One of the officers had been at the club the previous day, and it was he who answered Vinny's question. 'It's about Karen's funeral. Her mother has requested that under the unusual circumstances neither you nor your family attend. They agreed that if you want to pay your own respects, then you can do so after the service.'

Vinny knew that the nosy neighbour must have spoken to Karen's mum. Maureen had been fine with him when he had rung her the other day. He also knew he had to put on an act to show his innocence. He smashed his fist against the wall, then turned back to the two police officers. 'Karen was very dear to me and also the mother of my only child, as you well know. If you think that myself, my son, and my family will not be attending her funeral, then you have another think coming. What have we done wrong, eh? And what do you mean under the unusual circumstances? Karen had a drug problem and was found dead due to a heroin overdose. What the hell has that got to do with me or my family attending her funeral?'

The officer doing the talking immediately tried to pacify Vinny. Like most East End Old Bill, he hated Vinny Butler with a passion, would love to see him banged-up for life, but was also slightly wary of the man. Vinny was clever, too clever for his own good, and one day he would take an almighty tumble was the overall feeling down at the station. 'As far as we are aware, you haven't done anything wrong, Mr Butler, but Karen's family are very upset over her death and would rather her service be kept small and personal.'

'Well, I am very sorry, officers, but you can tell Karen's family to go fuck themselves. My son has been in bits all week. He loved his mum very much and if I told him he couldn't say goodbye to her, it would break his little heart even more. Now, if you'll excuse me, I have work to do. We are holding a small wake here afterwards, so we can toast Karen's memory. Me and her may not have been properly together when she died, but I will always love her. She gave me the most wonderful son, so how could I not?' Vinny explained, his eyes brimming with fake tears.

When the officers said they would also be attending the funeral to ensure that there was no unpleasantness, Vinny thanked them, shut the door, leant against it and smirked. He was far too clever for the likes of the Old Bill. Always had been and always would be.

As was to be expected, Karen's funeral was a sad affair where plenty of tears were shed. Karen's mum and aunt sobbed uncontrollably throughout the whole service, and when Karen's Uncle Pete got up to say a few words, he got halfway through his speech, then broke down and was unable to continue.

Michael surreptitiously studied Vinny throughout. He genuinely looked as upset as anyone. If he was guilty of organizing Karen's murder, Michael couldn't help but think what a bloody good actor his brother was.

Michael put a comforting arm around Nancy, then handed her his handkerchief to dry her eyes. 'Oh, Michael. It's so sad. Karen was such a nice girl,' Nancy whispered in his ear.

'I know, babe,' Michael whispered back, while clocking his cousin. Little Vinny's face was devoid of any emotion. If anything he looked extremely bored. Perhaps he was too young to understand the finality of it all?

Knowing that the police were bound to have their beady eyes on him when the mourners left the church, Vinny made a beeline for Karen's mum, Maureen. 'I know you wasn't particularly keen on my family attending the service, but we all thought the world of Karen and there was no way we could stay away. I just wanted to say how sorry I am

341

for your loss. My son has been denied many happy years with his wonderful mum and I am as gutted about Karen's death as anybody.'

'You lying bastard. You killed her, I know you did,' shouted Debbie Ryan, who happened to be standing just behind Maureen.

'Don't spout such rubbish. I wasn't even with Karen when she died. I was playing cards at the club, and I have many witnesses to prove that,' Vinny spat at the nosy neighbour.

'How very convenient for you, Vinny. My brother is a known tea-leaf, so I do know a thing or two about having the perfect alibi,' Debbie spat back.

When Maureen screamed at both Vinny and Debbie to stop arguing, the police stepped in and led Vinny away by the arm. 'I think it would be better if you and your family left now rather than attend the actual burial,' an officer urged Vinny.

'My son has done sod all wrong, so why should we have to leave?' Queenie yelled, waving her umbrella dangerously close to the policeman's face.

When Vivian and Brenda both joined in the argument, Michael chucked his keys at Dean and ordered him and Nancy to go and sit in his car while he calmed the situation down.

'Hold my arm in case you slip in those heels, Nance. I don't want to have to scrape you up off the floor,' Dean joked.

Nancy smiled and took his arm. 'Never a dull moment being part of the Butler family, is there?'

'Nope. Congratulations on your engagement by the way. Michael is a lucky guy,' Dean said, sincerely.

'Thanks. We are not looking to get married just yet though. What about you and Brenda? Have you arranged yours?'

'Well, originally Bren wanted to get married before the baby was born, but she reckons she will be too fat now and wants to leave it until next summer. I'm easy, so I'll just leave it up to her. Organizing weddings is definitely girlie stuff, so as long as Bren gives me the date and time, I'll just make sure I've got a new suit and turn up,' Dean chuckled.

'Michael's the same. He has told me to arrange whatever I want when the time comes and he will foot the bill. Changing the subject, any more news about your dad's whereabouts, Dean? I meant to ask you earlier.'

'Nope. He is still on the missing list. My nan has been in bits, but I wish she would stop blaming Vinny. It makes it so awkward for me being with Bren, if you know what I mean?'

'I know exactly what you mean. I'm in a similar position with my family as you are with your nan. My dad and brother hate the Butlers and have completely washed their hands of me. At least your nan is still talking to you and you can visit her. I'm barred from visiting my family for good,' Nancy explained, her eyes brimming with tears.

Being a gentleman, Dean put his arms around Nancy and gave her a hug. 'If you ever need a shoulder to cry on, and you feel awkward discussing your family with Michael, you know where I am.'

Absolutely furious at what was happening not twenty feet in front of her, Brenda broke into a run, caught up with the cuddling couple, then punched her boyfriend hard in the side of his head.

'What do you think you are doing?' Dean yelled, letting go of Nancy.

'What do I think I'm doing? It should be me asking you pair that question. Didn't know I was walking behind you, did you? Are yous two at it behind my back, or what?' Brenda screamed, her face bright red with fury.

'Don't be so fucking stupid. Nancy was upset over the fact that she no longer has contact with her family, and I just gave her a friendly hug,' Dean explained.

'Honest, Bren. We've just been talking about our weddings. I love Michael, and Dean loves you,' Nancy added, feeling as awkward as hell as she saw Michael running towards her.

'What's a matter?' Michael asked, putting a protective arm around his fiancée's shoulders.

When Dean explained what had happened, Michael ordered him and Nancy to walk to the car while he spoke to his sister alone. 'Are you mental, or what, Bren? I've seen you throw your jealousy tantrums in the past which was why Dean probably dumped you in the first place. If you ain't careful, you will lose him one day for good. Also, don't you ever insult Nancy again in such a manner, do you hear me?'

Suddenly feeling sorry for herself, Brenda began to cry. 'I'm sorry, Michael. I just feel so fat and ugly. Nancy is stunning and I can't help feeling that Dean must wish he was with somebody slim and pretty like her.'

Michael gave his sister an awkward hug. 'Well, that's just your own insecurities. Nobody else sees you that way. You need to get a grip and discard that green-eyed monster for good. Jealously is the root of all evil, Bren.'

Vinny had organized a small wake to be held in memory of Karen at the club after the service. He had invited his family, all the staff, and a few regulars to attend. Lenny had been very quiet all day. He had sobbed as loudly as anybody throughout the funeral service and, worried about his cousin, once back at the club, Vinny had taken him into his office to have a quiet word. 'What's up, Champ? You haven't been your usual bubbly self today. Is it the funeral that's upset you?'

344

Lenny's lip wobbled like a small child's would. 'Did I kill Karen by giving her that drink, Vinny? Will I go to prison?'

Vinny chuckled and ruffled his cousin's hair. 'Of course you didn't, you daft apeth. Karen died of an overdose of heroin, Champ. That has nothing to do with the drink you gave her at the party. Now, how about you put a big smile on your face and jump up on the DJ stand and play some records in memory of Karen, eh? Karen loved your music, and she would like that, wouldn't she? She is bound to be looking down from heaven like all dead people do.'

'Will my dad be looking down and watching me play my records too, Vinny?'

'Yeah, course he will. Your dad will be well proud of you, like we all are.'

As Lenny stood up, then went to dart out of the office, Vinny called him back. 'And remember, Champ, you must never mention that drink you gave to Karen to anybody apart from me, OK? If the police, Michael, Nancy, your mum, or anyone else ever mentions what happened to Karen at that party, you know nothing, yeah?'

'Yeah. I know nothing. Love you, Vinny. Going to play my records now.'

Vinny smiled. 'Love you too, Champ.'

Unable to face going to the club or Karen's wake after visiting Roy, Queenie and Vivian decided to head straight home.

'I will never feel the same about that club again, Vivvy. Every time I set foot in it now, it reminds me of the last time I saw my Roy as a normal human being. So happy he was the night of his engagement party. Him and Colleen were like love's young dream. Anyway, Vinny popped round early this morning, and I told him how I felt about the club. And so he said he would sell it and buy the old one back just for me. He's a good boy deep down, ain't he, Vivvy?'

'Heart of bloody gold. I liked that old club much better, Queen, and I can keep more of an eye on my Lenny there. I used to like popping in there in the daytime to see the boys, didn't you?'

Surprised to see Michael's car sitting outside her door as they turned the corner, Queenie didn't reply. 'I wonder what my Michael wants? Hope he hasn't fallen out with Nancy again. Didn't you say your Lenny saw them arguing earlier or something?'

'Lenny said Michael looked like he was arguing with Brenda. I'll come indoors with you. I could do with a large glass of sherry after today, couldn't you?'

Queenie nodded in agreement. She was parched. 'You all right, boy? Why haven't you and Nancy gone to the wake?' she asked, relieved to see Michael sitting on her sofa holding hands with his wife-to-be.

'Because I needed to speak to you, Mum. Could you keep Nancy company, Auntie Viv, while me and Mum have a quick chat upstairs? It won't take long.'

'Course I will,' Vivian said, sitting down next to Nancy and squeezing her hand. Like Queenie, Vivian was a big fan of Michael's fiancée.

'Whatever's wrong?' Queenie asked. She had known by the look on his face that whatever he had to tell her was important, which is why she had poured herself a glass of sherry to take upstairs.

Michael took a deep breath and then did what he had been dreading for the past few weeks. He handed his mother Albie's letter.

Queenie glanced at the envelope. 'That's your father's handwriting. Don't tell me you've been in contact with that

346

old bastard, Michael, 'cause I won't be happy. Where is the lying old toad living?'

Michael stood up. 'I think you should just read the letter, Mum. I'm gonna wait in my old bedroom while you do so, then give me a shout when you're done.'

Queenie nodded, waited for Michael to leave the room, then opened the envelope.

Dear Queenie,

Firstly, I would like to apologize about the terrible cancer lie that I told. It was a stupid thing to do, but I swear from the bottom of my heart, I only made such an awful story up to be close to my family once again.

Secondly, I would like to say sorry for cheating on you, but I would like you to know the reasons why I ended up doing the things I did.

When I first met you, Queenie, I felt like the most luckiest bloke alive. I remember you took my breath away on our first date when you wore that smart black dress and red pill-box hat. I knew then that I wanted to spend the rest of my life with you, but it took me a good six months to build up the courage to ask for your hand in marriage.

I was ecstatic when you said yes and we finally wed, but I always felt like there was three in our marriage and not two. Vivian was always at our house, which meant we never got to spend much time alone, and I could tell that Vivvy never thought I was good enough for you. She spoke to me like I was a piece of dirt.

When Vinny was born, things seemed to go from bad to worse. You and Vivian wanted to bring my son up between you, and I felt terribly pushed out, which is when I first started to hit the bottle. As each child followed, the more of a spare part I began to feel. I got the impression that you only married me because you wanted to have children, and you had never loved me at all. You turned me from a strong, strapping confident lad into a weak drunken man, Queenie, and you turned my children against me, which is something I will never forgive you for.

Queenie put the letter down beside her and reached for her glass of sherry. There was still another page to read and she needed to pause before she did so. Had she really made Albie feel like that? She had never enjoyed sex much, and unless she was trying to get pregnant, had never really wanted it, but that was usual for a woman, wasn't it? Vivian had said the same. She didn't like doing it with her Bill. The pleasure was all the men's. All the woman could do was lie there and think of bloody England.

Knocking back her drink in three large gulps, Queenie picked the letter up again.

And lastly, but certainly not least, the reason I am writing this letter is because of my concerns about our eldest son. It is my belief that not only is Vinny a time-bomb waiting to explode, but there is a very good chance he will blow everybody else up around him.

Prior to Roy's engagement party, Vinny paid me a visit in the Blind Beggar. He had found out about my cancer lie by speaking to a doctor who he knew at the hospital. He then proceeded to blackmail me. He insisted that unless I told Colleen's parents that Roy had cheated on her many times and had been responsible for beating me up and putting me in hospital many years ago, he was going to blow the whistle on me.

At first, out of fright, I agreed to do such a terrible

thing. Then, I looked around at the party and saw Roy and Colleen gaze into one another's eyes like I once used to gaze into yours, Queenie. It was then I decided I could not go through with it.

When I told Vinny my decision, he tried to bribe me with money, and it was when I still refused that he leapt on the stage and told my secret to everybody. Michael will vouch for my story if you do not believe it. I have told him everything.

As a massive favour, I ask that you do not share the contents of this letter with Vinny or anybody else. I just wanted you to be aware of what type of person our eldest son is, so you can guard the backs of yourself, Michael and Brenda in the future. Our grandson needs to be protected too, because if he isn't, chances are he will grow up to be evil just like his father.

I hope you take heed of my warning, Queenie. As we both know, Roy's bullet was meant for Vinny and I would hate to see any more casualties. I cannot come back to Whitechapel ever again, as I know my son will have me killed if I do, so it is left to you to sort out this mess. You created a monster, so best you deal with it.

Good luck,
Albie.

Cursing under her breath, Queenie tore the letter into shreds and put it in her bedside drawer. How dare that drunken old bastard not only refer to her wonderful son as a monster, but also have the cheek to blame her for it? Yes, she had encouraged Vinny to make something of himself like the Kray twins had, but that was only because she didn't want him to have the shit life that she'd had to endure.

Wanting to cry through temper, Queenie forced herself

not to, and instead repaired her windswept hair in the mirror and put on some more red lipstick. If Albie was telling the truth about Vinny wanting to split up Roy and Colleen, and that was a big 'if' with Albie's track record, then Vinny must have had good reason to do so.

Her first-born was the heart and soul of the family. He was the one who had put food on the table when Albie had been squandering every penny they had in pubs and on whores. Vinny had always treated and respected her like a shortened version of her name. He had looked upon her as a queen, and no way would Queenie ever turn her back on him. He was even buying his old club back just for her, for Christ's sake.

With her head held high, Queenie opened the bedroom door. 'You there, Michael?' she asked, sprightly.

Michael sheepishly appeared from his old bedroom. 'Did you read it, Mum?'

'Yes, and I've now ripped it up and thrown it away. Now, this letter never existed, do you understand? And I also forbid you to ever have contact with that bitter, twisted old bastard ever again, OK?'

Feeling sick to the stomach, Michael nodded glumly.

CHAPTER THIRTY-ONE

Summer 1976

Queenie Butler got off the District Line train at East Ham and began the fifteen-minute walk that she had become so very used to. Vivian usually accompanied her to visit Roy if she didn't travel in Vinny or Michael's car, but today was Lenny's twentieth birthday, and Vivvy had wanted to take her son out for the day.

Dripping with perspiration due to the sweltering heat, Queenie decided to stop at the White Horse pub for a drink to cool herself down. Usually, she would never venture into a pub alone. In her opinion, the only women that did that were the ones she referred to as Old Toms, but as she and Vivian had got chatting to the landlord on a few occasions, Queenie felt it was OK to pop in there.

'Hello, love. Can I get you your usual? Where's your sidekick today?' the landlord asked chirpily.

'It's me sister's son's birthday, so she's spending the day with him. Yep, and I'll have my usual, please,' Queenie replied. She and Vivian had become very partial lately to a half of lager and lime. It especially went down a treat in this hot weather.

'Another scorcher, isn't it? Bloke came in earlier who has one of them temperature thingamabobs in his house. Ninety-two degrees he reckons it was,' the landlord informed her.

Queenie was now thoroughly sick of the heat. Her grass was parched, her petunias had wilted and the bastard flying ants made her want to scratch until she bled.

'Well, it doesn't look like it's letting up soon. The man on the news last night said not only was a drought on the horizon, but this summer was destined to become the hottest since records began,' she replied.

When the landlord disappeared to make a phone call, Queenie sat down at the table by the window and turned her thoughts to Roy. It still broke her heart to think that her son would never walk again. The doctors had said he had no stability in his trunk, and because of the paralysis down the left-hand side of his body, it was impossible for him to get about any other way than in a wheelchair. When Roy had first left the hospital, he had stayed in a rehabilitation centre for six months that specialized in the aftereffects of brain trauma. The staff had tried to see if Roy could walk or stand with the aid of parallel bars, but he hadn't been able to. Queenie had hated the few occasions she had watched her son attempt to walk. Roy had cried with frustration every time he was let go and fell to the ground.

On being told that he would never walk again, Roy had kind of given up on himself. His speech had improved somewhat, although his words were still quite slow and slurred, but one side of his face still resembled that of a bad stroke victim. The only other positive that Queenie could gather from Roy's treatment was that the right side of his body had strengthened somewhat. He had learned how to feed himself again, write, hold a newspaper, brush his own hair, and wheel himself about in his chair.

The worst part of Roy's condition in Queenie's eyes was mentally he was still quite sharp. He was very aware of what had happened to him and the kind of man he had once been. This seemed to cause him terrible anguish as any time stories from the past were told, Roy would sink into the depths of depression for days on end. He was the same when the club or any of his old pals were mentioned. Apart from family, he wouldn't allow a soul to visit him, and even Queenie found having a conversation with him awkward because she had to vet everything in her mind before she could say it out loud in case it caused him distress. It was like permanently treading on eggshells.

After leaving the rehabilitation centre, Roy had moved in with Queenie. Vinny had employed two private nurses, but the situation hadn't worked out. Roy had despised living back in Whitechapel, and had become angry, resentful, and sometimes even violent towards his family and the nurses. He had been particularly nasty to Colleen who had also moved into Queenie's with their beautiful daughter, Emily-Mae. Things had finally come to a head when Roy had lashed out one day with his good arm and given Colleen a black eye. Queenie had been furious with her son at the time. Colleen had given up her nursing career just to help care for Roy and bring up their child, but Roy had cancelled their engagement. Colleen had still wanted to go ahead with their wedding, but Roy was having none of it.

When Colleen had held her bruised face in her hands, sobbed like a baby, and asked the man she loved if he still loved her, Roy had shaken his head and told Colleen to go back to Ireland and bring up their daughter there.

Colleen had left Queenie's house the following day and then it had been Roy's turn to sob. Queenie had held her son close to her bosom as in his slurred speech he had explained why he had been nasty to Colleen and sent her packing. 'I feel so useless, Mum, like a burden to her. Colleen deserves better than that, and I don't want Emily-Mae to grow up and see her dad as some bitter cripple. I would rather Colleen describe me as the man I used to be when she is old enough to understand.'

Queenie could no longer be angry with her son after he had opened up to her that day. Colleen had been back in Ireland for over eighteen months now and Emily-Mae had turned four earlier this year. Colleen still kept in contact by ringing Queenie occasionally and sending her the odd letter and photograph of the little girl, but she had now moved on with her life. She had even told Queenie in her last phone call that she had met a new man.

Roy always refused to speak to his ex or daughter on the phone, so Queenie hadn't told her son that Colleen had met a new man. What he didn't know couldn't hurt him. She hadn't told Vinny either. He would only call Colleen a slag, and Queenie knew that wasn't the case. It had been Roy who had wanted rid of Colleen, not the other way round, and the girl had every right to now get on with her life.

Not seeing Emily-Mae was the heart-wrenching part for Queenie. With her blonde mop of hair, blue eyes, and sweet nature, the child was a little angel, and there wasn't a day went by when Queenie didn't miss her. One day, she would go to Ireland just so she could see Emily-Mae once again.

Feeling rather melancholy, Queenie took another gulp of her drink and debated whether to get another. Vinny had found Roy a private care home in East Ham that catered for people with needs such as his, but Roy wasn't happy there at all. He had asked Vinny to find him a different one by the seaside somewhere. It seemed as though Roy wanted to get as far away from London and his past life as possible, which upset Queenie immensely. How the bloody hell was she meant to visit him regularly if he moved a long distance from London?

Deciding against another drink, Queenie finished the one she had, took her compact mirror out of her handbag and patched up her lipstick. She then put a smile on her face, waved to the landlord and left the premises. False smiles had now become part of her daily façade, and as soon as she walked in that care home, as usual, she would sport another to greet her beloved son. As a mother, Queenie believed it was her duty to always be upbeat and bubbly. What else did poor Roy have to look forward to?

Roy Butler opened his curtains and stared miserably out of the window. East Ham wasn't the most picturesque of areas, and because his room was situated at the back of the house all he could see was derelict buildings, overgrown gardens and rubble.

Closing his eyes, Roy pictured Colleen and Emily-Mae. He missed them dreadfully, but he knew he had done the right thing by setting them free. No beautiful young woman should have to spend the rest of her life caring for a cripple and even though Colleen had insisted that she still loved and wanted to marry him, Roy had convinced himself that she was only saying that out of pity.

Roy turned his thoughts to his elder brother. His injuries, and losing Colleen and his daughter, were all Vinny's fault and Roy couldn't help but hate him. They had been so close when they were growing up, but Roy would never allow his mind to wander back to the good old days. Why would he want to when he was no longer the man he once was? That's why he'd had to escape from living at his mother's house. His mum had been devastated when he had insisted on being moved to a care home, but Roy knew he had to leave for the sake of his sanity and the tiny bit of dignity he had left.

Vinny popping in most days had driven Roy to distraction. Seeing his brother standing on two legs, suited and booted, reeking of expensive aftershave, had just reminded Roy of all he had lost and the person he no longer was. Revenge was the only thought that kept him from total insanity these days. Because he had never remembered the actual shooting, nobody including his mother had ever mentioned the argument with Vinny that had happened beforehand. His family obviously thought that his injuries had left him unaware of the build-up to the incident, but Roy remembered everything. Vinny blackmailing their father to stick the boot in with Colleen's parents was something that Roy could never forget or forgive.

What goes around comes around was a true old saying and one day Vinny would have to pay for his sins. A cripple or not, Roy was determined to heap revenge on the brother whom he had once idolized. Only then, could he move on with his own life.

Nancy Butler breathed a sigh of relief when the doorbell rang, as she knew it would be her mother.

'Ooh, you do look stressed. Nanna to the rescue,' Mary chuckled.

'See if you can shut them up for five minutes, Mum. Done my head in all morning, they have. Every time one stops whinging and crying, the other little bugger starts. I'll put the kettle on and make us a bit of lunch,' Nancy said. As much as she loved her sons, they had the ability to drive her doolally at times.

Mary sighed, her face etched with worry. Her Nancy hadn't taken to motherhood like she had, that was for sure. Once upon a time, Nancy had been a fun, vibrant girl, but since she'd given birth to her second son, Adam, she seemed permanently depressed.

'Nanny. Come and look at my new toy,' Daniel shouted out.

Mary went into the lounge and grinned as both her grandsons clamoured for her attention. Nancy and Michael had got married on Christmas Day in 1971 and Nancy had fallen pregnant soon after. Daniel Michael Butler had been born in October 1972, so would be four in a few months' time. Weirdly, his brother Adam Michael Butler had been born on the very same day two years later.

'Whoopsie-daisy,' Mary said in a silly voice, when Adam tried to run towards her, but instead landed on his bottom. The little boy hadn't mastered the art of running properly yet.

When Nancy had married Michael in a church in Mile End, Mary had obeyed her husband's wishes and not attended. There wasn't a day that went by afterwards when she hadn't regretted that decision, which is why she had then put her foot down. Mary had not only stood up to Donald, she had left him over his obstinance.

Their separation had lasted nearly a month. Then, Donald had turned up at Mary's cousin's house, where she had been staying, and begged his wife to come back home.

At first Mary had flatly refused. Then after more pleading from Donald she had agreed to return, but only on her conditions. She had three. She was allowed to see Nancy whenever she wished; they sold that awful bloody newsagent's and bought another café; and instead of living in a cramped flat like they had done for many years, they bought or rented a house instead.

Mary had been amazed when Donald went away to think about her conditions and returned the following day to say he would honour all three. The only stipulation he made was that Mary would not mention Nancy or anything to do with her life at home, which Mary agreed to.

Since then, Mary's life had been so much better. The café they had purchased in Barking wasn't smart and trendy, and neither did it have a jukebox like the one in Whitechapel, but the customers were nice, and the annual turnover decent. The flat above, Donald had rented out to a young couple which had enabled them to mortgage a two-bedroomed house themselves. Mary loved having a garden for the first time in years, and spent ages pottering about in it. She had even learned how to grow her own tomatoes.

The biggest plus point for Mary though was Nancy now living nearby. Aware that his young wife was struggling to cope with their children, Michael had done the sensible thing and moved the family to Barking so Mary could help out on a regular basis.

'Leave Nanny alone for a minute while she eats her lunch, boys. Look, there's a cartoon on telly,' Nancy said, handing her mum a plate with two ham rolls and a big Spanish tomato cut into eight pieces.

'Let's play in the swimming pool,' Daniel said, grabbing his younger brother's hand.

'Swimming pool!' Mary exclaimed, slightly alarmed.

'Oh, don't worry. It's only one of them little paddling pools and there isn't even an inch of water in it. Michael brought it home the other day. The boys have been so miserable and clammy in this hot weather, Michael said it will cool them down a bit. He also said if they don't stop driving me mad I can drown them in it,' Nancy joked.

Mary smiled. Although she had originally been very dubious about Nancy marrying Michael, Mary had really grown to like him as a person and a son-in-law. Michael was charming, funny, extremely generous, and most importantly he adored Nancy and was a wonderful father to the boys.

Nancy was now twenty-one, Michael twenty-seven, and overall their marriage was a happy one, which pleased Mary immensely. It also proved Donald wrong, which was an added bonus.

'So, how's Dad and Christopher, Mum? Are they both OK?' Nancy asked.

Every time Mary saw her daughter, she asked after her brother and father and it upset Mary greatly that Donald and Christopher never asked about Nancy. 'They're OK, love. The café's been busy and we've now taken on another girl, Tina, to help out in the mornings.'

'So, what's happening with Christopher's job? Has he arrested anyone yet?' Nancy enquired. Her brother had recently fulfilled his lifelong dream of joining the police force, and at nineteen he was currently the youngest police constable stationed at Ilford.

'You know what Christopher is like, love? Takes his job very seriously and tells me nothing. I think he speaks to your father about stuff though. As you can imagine your dad is over the moon he got in the Met. Christopher is what is called a probationer at the moment. Have you told Michael yet?'

'Yeah. He wasn't overly impressed. He don't want his family to know, he made that clear.'

'Oh dear.'

'Yes, oh dear, Mum. Michael reckons Vinny will cause us no end of problems if he finds out Christopher is a policeman, so best you never mention it in front of the boys. Daniel especially, 'cause he bloody picks up on things and repeats them all the time.'

Mary suddenly felt quite sad. Nancy had married a lad from a notorious gangland family, Christopher was now working on the other side of the fence, so a reconciliation between her two children was very unlikely to ever happen.

'You OK, Mum?' Nancy asked, noticing a faraway look in her mother's eyes.

Mary forced a smile. 'I'm fine, darling. Let's go outside and dangle our feet in that paddling pool. It might cool us down a bit.'

Michael Butler drove towards the club he part-owned with a face like thunder. When they had sold the bigger club along the Commercial Road, Vinny had pocketed the profit, bought their old club back, and made Michael and Roy equal partners. Obviously, Roy no longer had anything to do with the business, but his share was put aside to help pay for his care.

Michael had been quite happy with the new arrangement. Because Vinny and Roy had originally set up the business, he had never previously earned quite as much as they did, so the extra money came in more than handy with a family to support. Michael adored his wife and sons. Nancy's mood swings drove him mad at times, but he had not once regretted marrying her. He had been a bundle of nerves on his wedding day though. The thought of commitment had nearly made him pull out at the very last minute, but his best pal Kevin, who had also been his best man, had calmed his nerves and got him to the church on time.

Pulling up outside the club, Michael leapt out of his BMW, locked it and stormed inside.

'Fucking hell, you look happy. Nancy left you, has she?' Vinny said, grinning at Ahmed who was sitting at the table opposite him.

Michael glared at both men. Financially, Ahmed had sod all to do with the club, yet he was always turning up there like a bad penny. It was now common knowledge in the underworld that Ahmed was importing drugs into the capital, which was why Michael hated his family being

360

associated with him. Vinny swore blind he had no involvement in what Ahmed did, but Michael wasn't so sure. The pair of them were as thick as thieves and Michael wouldn't put anything past Vinny. His brother was greedy when it came to money and Michael had warned him on more than one occasion that his greed would one day be his downfall. 'I need a word, in private,' Michael spat, gesticulating for Vinny to follow him into their office.

Vinny sauntered in a couple of minutes later. 'What's up with you?'

'Graeme Bradley, that's what. He was murdered last night. A single stab wound to the heart, apparently. But, you already knew that, didn't you, Vin? Because it was you who organized his death, wasn't it?'

Johnny Preston had got a fifteen stretch for what he had done to Roy. Both attempted murder and firearms charges had stood up in court, and it was during the case that Vinny had discovered that Johnny had been living with Graeme Bradley at the time.

Vinny shook his head. 'Fuck all to do with me, bruv, and also the first I've heard of it. Where was Bradley murdered?'

'Oh, don't play the innocent with me, Vin. I know the way you tick, I'm your brother. Who did you get to kill him? Was it the same person who you got to murder Karen? Or Terry Smart? Or Kenny Jackson? Please don't take me for a fool, because I am anything but,' Michael shouted.

Vinny was furious. He might have been responsible for those deaths, but not only had he never admitted to his involvement in Karen's, he certainly knew nothing about Graeme Bradley's. Rather than punching Michael, which was tempting, Vinny picked up a chair and threw it across the room. 'Don't be acting like Billy Big Balls with me, Michael, 'cause you'll be the loser. I swear on Little Vinny's life and Mum's that I had fuck all to do with Graeme

Bradley's murder. I didn't even know about it until you just told me.'

Michael knew how superstitious Vinny was about swearing on people's lives. He also knew that their mum and Little Vinny were probably the only two people Vinny really cared about, apart from himself. Deciding to call a quick truce, Michael held out his right hand. 'I'm sorry, my mistake.'

Vinny shook his brother's hand and grinned. 'I'm glad Bradley is dead though. Whoever killed the cunt deserves a medal.'

Queenie Butler sat down opposite her son and handed him a carrier bag. Not once had she ever come to visit Roy empty-handed. She always bought him a treat. 'There's two of them chocolate éclairs you like, Roy. Why don't you eat them now? I'm worried the cream might go off in this heat.'

'Not hungry,' Roy replied.

'So, why aren't you dressed and sitting in the lounge with the other patients? Playing games in there, they are,' Queenie informed her son.

'Didn't want to get dressed today. I wanted to be alone.'

Realizing that Roy seemed even more depressed than usual, Queenie changed the subject. 'So, did Brenda and Dean visit you yesterday?'

'Yeah. They came to see me yesterday afternoon. That daughter of theirs is one spoilt brat,' Roy said, in his usual slow drawl.

Queenie nodded, not particularly in agreement, but she did know what Roy meant. Brenda and Dean had got married three years ago, and Dean now worked at the club for Vinny and Michael. Tara was four years old and was a demanding child to say the least. She had been far too spoilt by Brenda especially, and Tara knew if she wanted something, a tantrum would make damn sure she got it. 'So, did Tara play up then?' Queenie asked.

'Yes. Has Vinny found me a place near the seaside yet, Mum? I really do not like it here.'

'If you live near the seaside, boy, I'm not going to be able to visit you much. Neither will the rest of the family, will they?'

Roy's eyes suddenly welled up with tears. 'I do not like having visitors. I will be happier near the sea where nobody knows me.'

Queenie's eyes filled with tears also. 'But, I love you, boy, and I will really miss you if you move miles away.'

Roy grasped his mother's hand. 'And I love you too, Mum, but I need a fresh start away from everybody and everything to try and find myself again. You do understand, don't you?'

Filled with sadness, Queenie nodded her head. She understood perfectly.

Brenda and Dean Smart lived in a two-bedroomed council house a few streets away from Queenie's. Since giving birth to Tara, Brenda had gained a few stone in weight. Instead of walking about in hotpants as she once had, she now tried to hide her bulging stomach and bottom by wearing long baggy tops. Brenda was very paranoid about her weight gain, so much so, it had put a strain on her relationship with her husband. She was forever accusing Dean of having affairs and chasing after other women, even though she had no proof. This erratic behaviour caused nothing but endless rows, and even though her mother had warned her to sort herself out, or risk losing Dean, Brenda couldn't help flying into rages of jealousy. Nancy was her biggest bugbear. Pretty, slim, wonderful fucking Nancy who everybody seemed to adore, including her Dean.

Hearing the front door slam, Brenda dashed down the stairs. Dean had taken Tara out this morning and had told her he wouldn't be long, but they had been gone for over three hours. 'Where you been? You said you wouldn't be long.' Brenda's voice was full of suspicion.

'I popped in to see my nan. It would have been my dad's forty-fifth birthday today, and I thought seeing Tara might cheer her up,' Dean explained. It was coming up to five years since his father had disappeared, and Dean always now referred to him as dead. Terry Smart had never been seen after leaving the Grave Maurice that fateful Sunday evening, and the police had been just as baffled by his disappearance as Dean. Freda Smart still insisted to this day that her son had been murdered by Vinny Butler, but seeing as he was married to Brenda, Dean had no option other than to think of his brother-in-law as innocent.

'Tara, pop next door and see Melissa. She knocked for you earlier,' Brenda instructed her daughter. Since Dean had started working nights at the club, their sex life had become almost nonexistent and, desperate to add to their family so that Dean could never leave her, Brenda was using every available opportunity that arose to get her husband to make love to her.

Dean felt like a lamb being led into a slaughterhouse, as he allowed Brenda to drag him up the stairs by his hand. The only way he could even get an erection with her these days was by shutting his eyes and thinking of his brother-in-law's wife.

Nancy was beautiful inside and out, and even though Dean knew that she was besotted with Michael, and nothing would ever happen between them, he couldn't help his feelings for the girl who made his heart leap every time he saw her.

'Hurry up then, Dean, in case Tara comes back,' Brenda

ordered, as she took her knickers off and flung them on the carpet.

Trying not to look at his wife's fat naked body, or her miserable face, Dean got undressed, climbed on top of Brenda, closed his eyes, and pictured Nancy.

'Oi, what do you think you are doing?' Queenie yelled, as she saw a puff of smoke drift out of her nine-year-old grandson's mouth.

Little Vinny, who lived with her permanently now, was sitting on her doorstep with his best mate, Ben Bloggs. He expertly trod on his cigarette and kicked it into a nearby bush. 'Nothing, Nan. Me and Ben are just talking,' he replied innocently.

'I ain't just got off the banana boat, you know. I saw you puffing away, boy, so don't bastard-well lie to me. How long you been smoking, eh?'

Little Vinny stood up and stared at his feet. 'Sorry, Nan. Me and Ben found a couple of fags in a packet and decided to smoke 'em as we had never tried one before, had we, Ben?' he said, nudging his pal.

Queenie didn't particularly like Ben Bloggs. His gran Ivy was well-known for her pilfering, his mother Alison for being a prostitute, and Queenie couldn't help but feel that coming from such a notorious family, Ben could only prove to be a bad influence on her grandson.

'Everyone's inside, Nan. Lenny had a great birthday. He met a man with green hair and a safety pin through his nose. He had a photo taken with him and Uncle Michael said he is called a punk,' Little Vinny said.

Queenie gave her grandson the evil eye. Little Vinny resembled his father at the same age so much that Queenie found it quite uncanny. It wasn't just his looks. He had the same streetwise personality as his dad, and possessed his charm as well. Ordering Ben Bloggs to sod off home, Queenie clipped Little Vinny around the ear. 'Get upstairs to your bedroom and stay there. I had enough of your antics yesterday.' Queenie had been terribly embarrassed when Big Stan had knocked on her front door late last night to inform her he had caught her grandson and Ben Bloggs thieving items from the shed in his back garden.

'You won't grass me up to Dad about anything, will you, Nan?' Little Vinny asked. 'I swear I'll be a good boy from now on.'

Queenie knew her son would go absolutely apeshit if he knew Little Vinny had broken into the shed. Like herself, Vinny was a big believer of the rule, you never thieve off your own. It was unwritten tradition in their neck of the woods.

'I'll say nothing, boy, but if you play me up one more time, I'm gonna tell your father everything, understand me? This is the last time I save your bacon and I mean it.'

When Little Vinny strolled into the house behind his grandmother, he couldn't help but smirk. Most of Whitechapel was frightened of Queenie Butler, but he wasn't. He had his nan right in the palm of his frightfully intelligent hand.

CHAPTER THIRTY-TWO

Vinny Butler booked two big tables at Nick's restaurant for his son and Lenny's joint birthday celebrations.

Nick had once been the manager of the steakhouse in Canning Town where Vinny had taken Karen on the evening she was murdered, but he now ran his own restaurant in Stratford thanks to Vinny and Ahmed's generosity. They had provided the money to enable Nick to open, and in return demanded a fifty per cent stake in the gaff.

Nick greeted his business partners with open arms, then politely shook hands with Lenny and Little Vinny.

'Anyone else here yet?' Vinny asked. His mum and aunt had gone to visit Roy first and were making their own way to the restaurant. Michael, Nancy, Brenda and Dean were coming with their kids, and Vinny had also invited Karen's mum Maureen and her sister Rose.

Vinny was on reasonably good terms with Maureen now. She had never truly believed that he'd had anything to do with Karen's death and once she had severed contact with Karen's nosy next-door neighbour, she had been as good as gold towards him. Karen had apparently had quite a bad drug problem as a teenager, and it suited Vinny no end to learn that Maureen believed Karen's demons had resurfaced. That left him in the clear.

In the past year, Maureen and Rose had sold their respective properties and now shared a house in Hornchurch, Essex. They saw Little Vinny at least twice a month, which was OK with Vinny.

'Go and give your nan and Auntie Rose a kiss,' Vinny ordered his son. Michael and Nancy were also at the table, so after greeting Daniel and Adam, Vinny shook hands with his brother and nodded politely at Nancy. He didn't like Michael's wife at all. Nancy gave him the distinct impression that she looked down on him, and that riled Vinny no end.

Within the next twenty minutes all the family arrived and the birthday celebrations got underway with Lenny insisting that 'Happy Birthday' was sung to him first. 'It was my birthday before Little Vinny's,' he reminded everybody.

Watching Maureen and Rose both fawn over his son, Vinny smirked at Ahmed. Apart from the pest of a neighbour spouting all kinds of accusations, the police had never had anything on him for Karen's murder. They had classed it as a drug overdose, and now he had Karen's mum and aunt on side, it had shut up all the gossipmongers too. What type of man would top the mother of his child, then befriend the mum and aunt? An innocent one, that's who.

As the jovial atmosphere continued around the table, Brenda clocked Dean and Nancy share a smile and felt her stomach tie in knots as usual. When a conversation began between the two of them, Brenda dashed away from the table and outside the restaurant.

'Where's Mummy gone, Dad?' Tara asked Dean.

When his brother-in-law stood up, Michael ordered him to sit back down. 'I'll deal with this,' he said.

Queenie raised her eyebrows at Vivian.

'What happened?' Vivian whispered in her sister's ear.

'I think Bren got the hump because Dean spoke to Nancy. She'll drive that boy away one day, if she ain't careful, Vivvy. If I've told her once, I've told her a hundred times to rein her jealousy in. Only she can lose that weight and make herself feel better. She ain't gonna do that while she's stuffing packets of biscuits down her gullet like they're going out of style, is she?'

'She is turning into a big old heifer, ain't she?' Vivian replied bluntly.

'Got an arse like a fucking elephant,' Queenie added.

Seeing that both Nancy and Dean felt totally embarrassed, Queenie decided to clear the air. 'Yous two carry on talking. Take no notice of Nutty Nora. You are both part of this family and have every right to get on well.'

'Who's Nutty Nora, Dad?' Tara asked innocently.

Dean kissed his daughter on the forehead. 'Nobody you know, darling.'

Michael lit up a cigarette and handed his sister one. 'What's up with you?'

'Just wanted some fresh air. Not a crime, is it?' Brenda replied, arrogantly.

'You've got to get off Nancy's case, and Dean's, Bren. They are only friends for fuck's sake, and if it don't bother me, why should it bother you?'

'Dunno what you're on about, Michael. I haven't got the hump with Dean or Nancy. Why would I have? Haven't done anything wrong, have they?' Brenda spat.

'Look, sis, tell me to mind my own business if you want, but if I were you, I would plaster a smile on your face, get your arse back inside that restaurant, and try to be jovial. We don't go out that often, not all together, and I think our family have had enough dramas to last us a lifetime over the years, don't you?'

Brenda nodded, took a deep breath to try and calm herself down, then, knowing she had little choice, put on a fake smile, and followed Michael back inside the restaurant.

Roy picked up his address book and flicked through the pages until he reached the letter P. He was sweating like a pig today, but knew that was more to do with nerves than the freak summer England was experiencing.

It had taken Roy a lot of courage and thought to come to the decision he had, but now he had made his mind up there was no going back. Vinny had ruined his life, therefore retribution was the only answer.

Choosing the right person to help him had been Roy's biggest bugbear. There was no way he could chance his request reaching unwanted ears, that would spell disaster. After toying with involving Michael in his plan, Roy had decided against it and had opted for Paul instead. Paul had been his best pal at school, and had worked the door on both clubs of his. He still worked for Vinny now, but Roy was sure he could be trusted.

Roy wiped his brow with a tissue, then dialled Paul's number. 'Hello, mate. It's me, Roy. I need a favour, but you have to swear to me that what I ask you will go no further. I don't even want you to tell Pete. Can you promise me that?'

'Roy, we go back a long way. You can trust me, you know that. It's so good to hear from you, pal. I was gutted when you didn't want me to visit you again. Are you OK?' Paul asked. This was the first time he had spoken to Roy since he had moved to East Ham and even though it broke Paul's heart to hear his lifelong friend sound a shadow of his former self, he was still pleased to hear from him.

'I want you to visit me, Paul, but I need you to bring me a gun as well. Can you do that for me?'

'What do you want it for? You ain't gonna shoot yourself, are ya?' Paul asked, with alarm in his voice.

'No. I plan to shoot somebody else. I'm not in the mood to play games, Paul, so can you help me or not?'

Paul's mind wandered back to when he and Roy were young. His pal had always looked out for him and if it wasn't for Roy, Paul wouldn't be living in a decent house and earning the good wage he was now. 'OK, Roy. I'll sort it for you. Who are you planning on shooting though, mate?'

Roy smirked. 'Nobody you know, Paul, I swear.'

Vinny was the first to notice Denise Thompson walk into the restaurant with Michael's kid and a tall dark-haired geezer in tow. Denise had given birth to a boy called Lee. 'Fuck me. It's all gonna go off in here in a minute,' Vinny whispered in Ahmed's ear.

'Why?'

'Michael's ex and his kid have just walked in. Nancy won't have him around her or the boys, will she? I don't even think that Daniel or Adam know that Lee exists,' Vinny explained, smirking.

When Queenie walked out of the toilets and came face to face with her second-eldest grandson, she had no alternative other to pick the boy up and hug him tight to her chest. She rarely saw Lee. At the most, Michael brought him around twice a month for a short visit.

'All right, Queenie? Didn't expect to see you here. This is Glen, my boyfriend,' Denise said politely.

Queenie said a quick hello and, seeing the arrival of a birthday cake, made her excuses then dashed back to the table. 'Michael, Lee's over there with Denise and her fella. Now, whether you like it or not, Nancy, Michael is going to have to go over there and speak to his son. I won't allow him to blank him,' Queenie told her daughter-in-law.

Nancy immediately felt her hackles rise. She knew that Michael supported Lee financially, and that he saw him a couple of times a month, but there was no way she wanted her own sons confused by finding out they had a half-brother. They were too young to understand and it wasn't fair on them. She also hated the thought of sitting in the same restaurant with another woman her husband had made love to. She felt physically sick. 'I want to take the boys home now, Michael. Can you drop us off, please?'

Before Michael could even answer, he heard a child yell 'Daddy' then saw Lee run towards him with his arms outstretched.

Nancy stared at Lee. She had never seen the child before, and couldn't help but hate him on sight. Stifling a sob, she grabbed Daniel's hand, picked up Adam, and ran from the restaurant as though their lives depended on it.

'Are you going to watch me blow my candles out now, Michael?' Lenny asked, prodding his cousin's arm impatiently.

'You stay with Lee and watch Lenny blow his candles out and I'll check if Nancy's OK for you,' Dean said, as he stood up.

'No, you fucking won't,' Brenda spat.

'Shut it, you, and mind your bloody language,' Queenie said, wagging a finger of warning in her drunken daughter's face.

Brenda, who'd been necking white wine all through the meal, sat there seething as the whole of the table sang 'Happy Birthday' to Lenny. She was sure Dean fancied Nancy. She could see it in his eyes.

'Can I have me cake now, Dad?' Little Vinny asked.

'Yeah, in a minute, son,' Vinny said, snatching the bottle of wine out of his sister's grasp. Brenda had topped up her glass three times in the last ten minutes and Vinny knew if

372

she drank any more she was bound to kick off. If it had been just his own family present, he'd have found it hysterical, but he didn't want Brenda to create havoc in front of Maureen and Rose. For obvious reasons, he always liked to make a good impression in front of those two.

Seeing Dean lead Nancy back inside the restaurant with a comforting arm around her shoulders, Brenda lost the plot completely. 'You no-good fucking cuntbag,' she screamed, forcing all the other diners to look round at her.

'Brenda, sit back down now,' Queenie ordered, totally embarrassed.

Brenda was now beyond control. She picked up Lenny's cake and marched towards Dean.

'That's my cake, Bren. Give me it back,' Lenny yelled.

'Do something, Vinny,' Vivian demanded.

'Too bloody late,' Queenie mumbled, as her daughter plunged the cake into Dean's face.

When Lenny burst into tears and Nancy ran out of the restaurant again, Michael stood up. 'This is my problem and I'll sort it.'

A couple of hours later, Queenie and Vivian were sitting side by side on the sofa with a glass of sherry.

'Weren't it a terrible day, Queen?' Vivian said.

'Bleedin' awful.'

'Give them boring old trouts Maureen and Rose something to talk about, eh? Felt sorry for my Lenny though.'

Lenny had been extremely upset that his birthday cake had been ruined and in an attempt to cheer the lad up, Vinny had said he could stay at the club with him for the night.

'Did you hear what my Vinny said about Roy moving?' Queenie asked.

'No.'

'Reckons he's found him a nice place by the sea. Vinny's going to view it on Tuesday.'

'Whereabouts is it?' Vivian asked.

'Eastbourne. I don't know what I'm gonna do if he moves that far away, Viv. We ain't gonna be able to visit him much and say Roy don't like it when he gets there? It could be a shithole for all we know.'

Vivian squeezed her sister's hand. 'Why don't we go for the ride with Vinny to view it? We know a nice, friendly, clean place when we see one, don't we? In fact, why don't Roy come with us? The four of us can fit comfortably in Vinny's car. If it's Roy that's gonna be living there, he should be the one to decide if it will suit him or not.'

Queenie nodded. 'That would make me feel a lot better if we all went and I knew my Roy liked it. I can tell when he's lying, even now.'

'Well, let's do it then. Ring Vinny now. Ask him how my Lenny is as well. I hope he ain't still upset over that bleedin' cake.'

Queenie picked up the phone. The club didn't open on a Sunday evening, so it was unusual there was no answer.

'Leave it. Ring him tomorrow. I'm sure my Lenny's having a good time with Vinny anyway. He always bloody does.'

Over in a seedy bar in Dalston, Vinny grinned as he saw Lenny's face light up. 'Well, what do you think, Champ?'

'I can't believe all the women are showing their titties,' Lenny gabbled, excitedly.

When his cousin had burst out crying because his birthday cake had ended up splattered all over Dean's face, it had been Ahmed's idea to bring Lenny to his pal's strip club. 'He needs to get laid,' were Ahmed's exact words.

Vinny couldn't agree more. As much as he loved his mum and Auntie Viv, they did wrap Lenny in cotton wool and treat him like a child in some ways, and it was doing the lad no good. Ordering Ahmed to get the drinks in, Vinny led Lenny to the back of the small club. 'You see them stairs there?'

'Yeah,'

'Well, them women on stage go down them stairs a bit later. If you choose what one you like, then I will make sure you have sex with her.'

Lenny looked at Vinny open-mouthed. 'But, say my mum finds out?'

Putting an arm around his cousin's shoulder, Vinny led him outside the club. 'I won't tell no-one, but neither must you. It will be our little secret.'

'Is it like that other secret when I gave Karen that drink when I was little?' Lenny asked, innocently.

Vinny couldn't help but smirk. Lenny had never mentioned that incident to anyone since Vinny had told him not to many years ago, and he was amazed his cousin still remembered it. At least it proved the boy could be trusted. 'Yep. It's a bit like that, Champ. Now, do you want me to sort you out with a bird, or not?'

Finally making his mind up, Lenny nodded excitedly. 'Yes please, Vinny.'

Back in Whitechapel, Queenie and Vivian were in deep conversation about the family.

'I do like Nancy, but didn't she make herself look a fool when she stomped out that restaurant, Queen? I mean, she knows Michael has nothing to do with Denise, so why won't she just accept Lee as part of their lives?

'Nancy ain't strong enough, Viv. I said that to you on their wedding day. Lovely girl and all that, but she weren't meant for our world. My Michael reckons she's been struggling to cope ever since she gave birth to Adam. He says she's suffering from depression, but I think that's a load of old toffee. Look what we went through during the war. If anyone should have been fucking depressed, then we should. Soppy little mare needs to get her act together if you ask me.

Lenny was as nervous as hell when the girl sat on the bed next to him.

'I'm Layla,' the girl said rubbing Lenny's thigh. She really didn't want to be in the room any more than he seemed to, but she had just been paid fifty pounds to entertain this simple looking chap.

Lenny's erection felt as though it was going to burst through his trousers. The only naked women he had ever seen in the past were the ones in the pornographic magazines he used to buy. His mum had gone mental when she had found a stash of them under his mattress. She had been even more horrified when she tried to look through them and noticed that most of the pages were stuck together. She had told him he was a pervert, just like his father had been.

Naked, apart from a pair of tiny lacy red panties, Layla forced a smile. 'Shall I take them trousers off for you?'

'Can I touch your titties first?' Lenny asked, bluntly.

Layla put Lenny's hands on her breasts, then winced as he squeezed them roughly, poked his tongue out of the side of his mouth, and began to pant like a thirsty dog.

Just the thrill of Layla undoing his zip sent Lenny's senses into overdrive, and when she put her hand on his todger, unable to hold back any more, Lenny shot his load.

Relieved that it was all over so quickly, Layla stood up. 'What you doing?' Lenny asked, when Layla put her panties and bra back on.

'Getting dressed, love. Why don't you do the same?'

'Because my cousin paid you a fifty quid so I could bang

you, and I haven't banged you yet. Have you heard of my cousin? His name is Vinny Butler.'

Layla all but froze. Vinny had a terrible reputation on the circuit. One brothel in Soho had even banned Vinny from their premises, and had then had their property mysteriously burnt to the ground a few weeks later. Lenny sat up with another massive hard-on and a big grin on his face. 'Well?' he asked.

Too scared to now refuse, Layla got undressed again and sidled up next to Lenny on the bed. When his sloppy mouth connected with hers and his tongue nigh on shot down the back of her throat, Layla couldn't help but gag. What followed was the worst shag and the longest ten minutes of her miserable life.

CHAPTER THIRTY-THREE

Johnny Preston excitedly ripped open his letter. He knew it was from his ex-wife as she had such distinctive handwriting.

When Johnny had first got banged-up, he and his wife had fallen out big-time. Appalled by his affair and the crime he had committed, Deborah had divorced him, but over the past couple of years, they had become really good pals once again. Deborah even came to visit him once a month now.

In prison, letters were the main link to the outside world, and Johnny liked to take his time reading his so he could savour every word and imagine every event in them. Johnny Junior was sixteen now and had just got his first job in a restaurant in Colchester. He was a trainee chef, and Johnny knew that he got his love of cooking from his mother's side of the family, as he himself could barely boil an egg.

Johnny's relationship with his son was an awkward one. The boy had very few communication skills, dressed like a freak, and walked about in eyeliner at times to emulate his hero, David Bowie.

When Johnny got to the part of the letter where Deborah

described how his daughter Joanna was having the time of her life, he smiled but then frowned.

Joanna had gone to a holiday camp for an Easter break earlier in the year with her best pal Chloe, and Chloe's parents. The girls had fallen in love with the place and had decided to give up their boring jobs working side by side in a factory to work at the holiday camp for the summer season. They had wanted to be bar staff, but were too young. So instead, both girls had taken jobs as cleaners.

Joanna working at a holiday camp miles away from home worried Johnny greatly. With her long blonde hair, piercing blue eyes, ample breasts and tall, lithe figure, Joanna was a real head-turner. In prison, your mind tended to work in overdrive, mainly through boredom, and many a night Johnny had lain awake tormenting himself with the thought of young lads trying it on with his pride and joy. He was at it like a rabbit when he was seventeen and he just hoped Joanna had more sense than to fall for the spiel like he used to dish out on a regular basis.

Joanna had had a boyfriend before leaving Tiptree, but that had now fizzled out, thankfully. Deborah was adamant that their daughter had her head screwed on and he was worrying unnecessarily, but Johnny couldn't help the way he felt. What father wouldn't worry about his stunning young daughter living miles away from home in a chalet with three other young girls?

Vinny woke up with a head that felt like lead and a mouth as dry as sandpaper. Ahmed had started importing cocaine a few months ago and Vinny had become a silent partner in his new enterprise. What Vinny hadn't anticipated was he and Ahmed snorting a chunk of the profits themselves.

Vinny had never been a drug-taker in the past. He saw himself as far too cool to go down that rocky road, but there was something about cocaine that he liked. It was a social drug, and from the moment Vinny had first tried it, he hadn't been able to leave it alone.

Walking gingerly into the bathroom, Vinny turned on the tap, doused his face in cold water, and stared at himself in the mirror. He was thirty-one now, and with his jet-black hair and piercing green eyes was still a handsome bastard. 'You need to sort yourself out, Vinny boy. Don't wanna lose them good looks of yours, do you now?' he mumbled, trying to talk some sense into himself.

'Vinny, your mum and aunt are here, and a man called George has rung three times this morning. He wants you to ring him back, says it's urgent. I'm going now,' Vinny heard his cleaner shout out.

'OK. Tell my mum I'll be down in a tick,' Vinny said.

Vinny opened his address book and, with adrenaline pumping through his veins, rang George Geary's number. Even though George had retired as chief inspector a while back, he was still fond of a bung. 'George, it's me. You got 'em?'

'Yes, I have. Very pretty girl. Now, where shall we meet? It took my contact an extra day to get these, Vinny, so I'm afraid the price is higher than we originally discussed.'

'How much?' Vinny asked, in a bored tone. George had always bled him dry when he was in the force, and nothing had changed since.

'Seven fifty, instead of five hundred, that OK? He had to stay down there an extra day.'

'Yep, that's fine. Bring the goods here in about an hour, and I expect them to be clear for that kind of dosh.'

'As clear as a freshly polished pane of glass, they are. That Turk isn't there, is he, Vinny? You know how I like to keep our business private,' George remarked.

'Nope. Listen, me mother is down stairs, and I can hear

her calling my name. Say one o'clock, eh? Apart from me, no bastard will be here then, I promise.'

George Geary only had to pay his contact a third of what he had charged Vinny, so it had been a nice little earner for him. 'OK. See you at one.'

Vinny felt his heart race as he replaced the receiver. He had bided his time on his quest for revenge until the fruit was actually ripe.

Dean Smart had not had the best of mornings. His lovely wife had spewed her guts up in the night, and had left a trail of it all over the bedroom carpet and bathroom floor. Tara had been playing up something chronic for the past couple of hours and now, to top it all, his nan had just rung him in floods of tears mumbling something about cancer and having to go into hospital for an operation.

'Dad, I'm bored. Play a game with me,' Tara whinged.

'I can't love. I've got to go out. Your nan isn't well, so you'll have to stay here with Mummy.'

Looking extremely dishevelled, Brenda sat up. 'Where you going? And why can't you take Tara with you?' she asked suspiciously.

Focusing on his wife, Dean felt nauseous himself. Her hair was matted with sick, her mascara had run, she looked as fat as a bull, and her left tit was hanging out of her nightdress. 'If you don't sort yourself out and get off my case, Bren, I swear on Tara's life, I will leave you.'

'No, Daddy. You can't leave us,' Tara screamed.

When Dean left the room, Brenda chased after him. 'Well, we will see what my brothers have to say about that, won't we, Dean? Don't think Vinny will be too happy when he finds out you are threatening to leave his sister and niece.'

'Go fuck yourself, Brenda,' Dean yelled, as he flung open the front door.

'No, you go fuck yourself. You will never be allowed to leave me, Dean Smart, and you know it,' Brenda shrieked.

Another couple currently at war was Michael and Nancy. Michael had not been happy at all when Nancy had made a show of him the previous day. 'Look, Nance, can't we sort this out? Why aren't you talking to me? If anyone should have the hump, then that should be me. You made me look a right prick in front of my family. I saw Vinny and Ahmed fucking laughing at me.'

'Aw, poor you. Do you honestly think I give a damn about your psycho of a brother and his slimy Turkish friend, Michael? How do you think I felt, eh? There I was sitting in a restaurant with my two children and in walks your ex and your first-born. To say I was embarrassed was putting it bloody mildly. I felt a complete and utter fool.'

Unaware that Daniel was ear-wigging outside the door, Michael gave it to Nancy. 'Fucking sick of this, I am. You knew the score with the kid when we first got wed, and you knew all about Denise. I binned her for you, for Christ's sake. You can be so immature at times, Nancy. Why shouldn't Lee be part of the family and get to know his brothers, eh? Daniel and Adam are better learning the truth now, than when they are older.'

The conversation was interrupted by Daniel bursting into the room with Adam in tow. 'Have we got another brother, Dad? Can we meet him?' Daniel asked excitedly.

Calling Michael every name under the sun, Nancy picked up her handbag and fled the house.

Vinny opened the back door of the club and ushered George Geary inside. Geary was a funny one. Years ago when he was chief inspector and on the make, he would knock at the front door as bold as brass. Yet now he had retired, he would only use the back entrance as he was afraid of being seen. 'Where are they then?' Vinny asked impatiently.

'Hold your horses, boy. What's the rush? Sweating me cobs off in this poxy heat. I could kill a nice Scotch on the rocks to cool myself down a bit. Never known a summer like this before. Bleedin' hosepipe ban now. Can't even water my garden.'

Not in the mood to make polite conversation about the weather or George's garden, Vinny grunted, walked behind the bar and poured two large Scotches. ''Ere you go,' he said, putting the drinks down on a table. 'Well?'

Geary took a piece of paper out of his pocket. 'That's it. The girl is in chalet number twenty-five. She works there as a cleaner.'

Vinny stared at the address. Kings Holiday Park, Pevensey Bay, Eastbourne. He had known the girl had been living in Eastbourne, had even visited the area twice to try to track her down himself. That's how he had spotted the nice care home that he was taking Roy to view tomorrow. 'And the photos?' Vinny mumbled.

'Money first,' Geary demanded, holding out his right hand.

Vinny handed Geary an envelope. It amazed him that the man still asked for the money up front when he had dealt with him for almost thirteen years and had never once knocked him for a penny.

'Pretty girl, isn't she? I hope you're not planning on doing anything too nasty to her,' Geary stated, feeling slightly anxious.

Vinny didn't answer. The girl looked a bit like Nancy, but her hair was more strawberry blonde, her figure more voluptuous and she had far bigger breasts. 'I'm not sure what I'm going to do yet, George, but you won't be involved, will you? I have to get some sort of revenge for my brother, but don't worry, it will all be handled discreetly.'

Feeling himself shudder, Geary stood up. 'Give me that piece of paper back so I can dispose of it. It's my handwriting.'

Vinny handed it to him, then followed Geary to the back door. 'Thanks, mate. I'll be in touch if I need anything else.'

Geary nodded. 'And a word of advice, boy. Take a step back from that Turk. He is bad news.'

Not wanting to get into a conversation regarding Ahmed, Vinny nodded, closed the door, and leant against it. He stared at the photos again. Joanna Preston certainly was a pretty little minx, and what he would do to her only time would tell. The one thing he was sure of was that whatever he did, it would upset her bastard of a father greatly.

CHAPTER THIRTY-FOUR

The following morning, Vinny picked up his mother, aunt, and son at nine a.m. then drove to East Ham to collect Roy. He usually loved a family outing, but not today. The plan had been that he and Ahmed were going to take a drive down to Eastbourne to check out the care home. Then, on the same day, they were going to take a good look around Kings Holiday Park and see if they could spot their victim. Now his plan had been scuppered by his mother's insistence that the whole clan should travel down to Eastbourne, Vinny would have to return again tomorrow with Ahmed.

Even though he had a top-of-the-range Jaguar XJ6 which was roomy, travelling with Roy in the back was a task in itself. His brother couldn't seem to get comfortable and was complaining constantly. When Roy suddenly shouted at his nephew for asking how long it was before they arrived at Eastbourne, Vinny couldn't help but react. 'For fuck's sake, Roy, give us all a break, will ya? You've already had a go at Mum twice. We are all here to support you, you know. You wanted to move near the sea and I've worked my bollocks off to find you somewhere decent. Can't you just be grateful for once?'

Roy could only show emotion on one side of his face, so

curled his lip, and glared at Vinny. He might have suffered major brain trauma, but he still had his marbles. Roy knew exactly what a liability Vinny was years ago. What he hadn't expected was to end up a cripple because of his brother's mistakes. Roy had tears rolling down his face as he forced his words out in his usual slow tone. 'You expect me to be grateful to you, Vinny. It's your fault that I have lost Colleen, my child, my ability to walk, talk properly, and my life. I don't even class you as my brother any more.'

Queenie and Vivian were in the back either side of Roy, and after glancing at one another, it was Vivian who broke the ice. 'Now, don't be like that, Roy. Vinny loves you, we all do. You're just a bit low at the moment, but wait until you get some of that seaside air down you. My old neighbour used to go to Eastbourne for her holidays every year and said it was a lovely place.'

Sitting in the passenger seat, Little Vinny looked around and stared at Roy. He had never liked his uncle even when he had been normal. Little Vinny had a memory like an elephant and even though he had only been young at the time he could remember having a feeling that his Uncle Roy didn't like him much either. 'Don't talk to my dad like that,' he spat.

Vinny felt a warm glow inside of him. His wonderful son had just backed him like a true Butler should. 'Can we stop all this nastiness now, please? We are meant to be family and I'm trying to drive,' he said, treating his son to a wink of approval.

Queenie got a tissue out of her bag and wiped the perspiration from Roy's forehead. She loved both her sons and felt torn between the devil and the deep blue sea.

Vinny turned up the volume on the radio. 'Mum, Auntie Viv, it's your favourite record. Let's have a sing-a-long, eh?'

Demis Roussous was currently topping the charts with a

song called 'Forever and Ever' and as his two favourite women in the world started to sing it at the tops of their voices, Vinny grinned. He loved his family, Roy included, and why should he feel guilty? His brother had got shot, he hadn't, end of.

Brenda was absolutely livid when Dean rolled home at lunchtime. Never had he stayed out all night before, and when his key went in the lock, Brenda began punching her husband before he could even get his foot over the threshold. 'Where you been? You've been with another woman, haven't you?'

When Tara started sobbing and screaming at her mother to leave her father alone, Dean grabbed Brenda's wrists. 'You're upsetting our daughter. I stayed at my nan's house if you must know. She has cancer, Bren. She might die.'

About to call her husband a liar, Brenda stopped herself. Dean loved his nan. She had almost single-handedly brought him up, and Brenda knew there was no way he would say she had cancer if she didn't. 'I'm sorry about your nan, and I'm sorry for hitting you. I'm sick of all this arguing, Dean, aren't you? Can't we just make up and forget all about this stupid row? You do still love me, don't you?'

Dean had no choice other than to lie. 'Yeah. Course I do.'

Nancy opened the front door and hugged her mum as though she were a child again.

'Whatever's happened now? I didn't want to ask you on the phone because your dad was lurking nearby. Don't want him to have anything to gloat about, do we now?'

'Mum, where has Dad gone? Do you hate him?' Daniel asked innocently, tugging at Nancy's skirt.

Nancy picked Daniel up and kissed him. Her sons were

so much like Michael. Both had inherited his jet-black hair and green eyes. 'Of course I don't hate your dad. All mummies and daddies row sometimes. Now why don't you take Adam into the garden and play in your swimming pool while I have a chat with your nan?'

'Have I really got another brother, Mum?'

'No, not a proper brother, love. Now, go outside and cool yourself down. You're all hot and sweaty.'

When Daniel and Adam ran outside, Mary sat down on the sofa and urged her daughter to do the same. 'So, how does Daniel know about Lee? Did Michael tell him?'

Explaining what had happened at the restaurant and since, Nancy was rather surprised by her mother's reaction.

'I really do feel that now it's all out in the open, you should perhaps let Daniel and Adam meet their brother. They're only nippers, Nance, and I bet they'll get on well with Lee.'

'No, Mum. It's not right. Michael knew from the start that I didn't want Lee to be part of my life, so I don't see why I should suddenly welcome the child with open arms. I have enough on my plate with Daniel and Adam, without looking after a third.'

'But, you won't have to look after him, Nance. Michael won't just dump him on you, will he?'

'Why are you on Michael's side, eh, Mum? You're meant to be on mine.' Nancy's voice was bitter.

'I'm not on anyone's side, love. I just don't want to see you ruin something special. Relationships need working at. I should know, I've suffered your father for years. Sometimes, you have to learn to give and take to make things work. Where is Michael by the way?'

Nancy shrugged. 'We're not talking. When the boys overheard his comments about Lee yesterday, I stormed out and went round Rhonda's house. I didn't get back until just before Michael was due to leave for work last night, and I stayed in bed this morning until I heard him leave. I've got a feeling he might have driven up to Ipswich to see his dad. I remember him saying something about visiting Albie the other day.'

Worried about her daughter's mental state yet again, Mary sighed. 'Oh well, it's up to you what you decide to do, love, but Lee is Michael's son, and there isn't anything in the world that's going to change that. If I was you, I would allow Lee to be part of yours and the boy's lives.'

'But you're not me, Mum, are you?'

Queenie and Vivian had never been to anywhere like Eastbourne before, and they couldn't help but comment how different it was from London.

'Ain't it clean, Queen? Look at the pavements. Spotless they are,' Vivian said.

'Beautiful clean fresh air as well. I can actually smell the sea. Brings it home to you just how putrid our own area is, don't it?' Queenie replied. Whitechapel had never been the sweetest-smelling of places, but the long hot summer had made it even worse. The stink of refuse and rotting fruit hung heavily in the air back in their native East End, and Queenie had taken to shutting her windows and using air-fresheners.

'This is it here on the right. You wait until you see the beautiful grounds,' Vinny said. 'Mum, do you mind if I drop you, Auntie Viv and Roy at the home, then pick you up in a couple of hours? Little Vinny will be well bored otherwise, and there is a place not far from here where I can get him some lunch. The staff said it would take quite a while to show everything to you, and I'm no good with stuff like that. I'm sure Roy would be happier if just yous two stayed with him.' Vinny said.

'Yeah, I would,' Roy added.

When Vinny pulled up in the car park, Queenie grinned. There were beautiful gardens, tweeting birds, and a real sense of tranquillity. 'You're gonna adore it here, boy. It's the nuts.'

Having just arrived at his destination in Suffolk, Michael greeted his dad, Dorothy, and Uncle Bert fondly. Since moving to Ipswich, his father had really sorted himself out. He had cut his booze intake down to just a few beers every evening, and had also met a lovely lady who now lived with him and Bert, and cooked and cleaned for them. Albie even had his own greenhouse and allotment now, where he grew his own vegetables and fruit.

'Sorry I didn't get down here last week when I said I would, Dad. Something cropped up at the club, then it was Lenny and Little Vinny's birthdays. You know how it is.'

Albie cherished his relationship with his youngest son. Michael was the only link to his past. 'Not to worry, boy.'

'Right, I'm going to leave you men to talk while I go out into the kitchen and prepare lunch. I've cooked us a nice lamb stew, Michael.' Dorothy said.

Albie grinned with pride as his woman left the room. Dorothy wasn't his usual type. She was fifty-five years old and had worked as a librarian for many years. She had a heart of gold though, and made Albie very happy. Cuddling up to Dorothy every night was much more satisfying than all the meaningless bunk-ups he had had over the years.

'I'll leave you to it as well. I need to see to my green-house,' Bert said.

'Shall we have a beer, son? I rarely drink in the day now, but you look like you could do with one and I shall use the hot weather as an excuse to have one myself.'

'Yeah, I'd love one, Dad.'

'So, what's wrong then? You're not your usual chirpy self,' Albie said, handing his son an ice-cold can of Heineken.

Michael wasn't usually one to spill his guts, but today he felt the need to, so he told his father all about Nancy's behaviour in the restaurant. 'We're not even talking now, Dad. I love her so much, but Lee is my son and it puts me in such a fucking difficult position. Nancy hates me having any contact with the boy, and I feel so bloody guilty about it. I only see him twice a month.'

Albie nodded understandingly. He knew all about difficult relationships after living with Queenie for years. 'You've just got to go with your heart, boy, and do what you feel is right. Why don't you bring Lee down here to meet me? I'd love to be a proper granddad.'

Apart from Nancy, Michael had never told any of his family that he visited his father regularly. Nobody would approve, so he had kept his relationship with his dad as his little secret. 'I will introduce you to Lee one day, but I can't bring him down here at the moment, Dad. I only have him for a few hours at a time. Nancy would go mental if I had him any longer. She goes into a deep depression every time I mention the child.'

Albie took a sip of his beer. He was a docile man now, didn't like to get involved in debates or speak out of turn, but he knew as Michael's father he had to point him in the right direction. 'Sometimes, son, you have to put your foot down in life with women. Don't let Nancy call the shots like I let your mother, because if you do you'll lose her respect. If I could turn the clocks back I would do things so differently. Your mum and Auntie Viv ruled the roost, and me being a weak man, I just let them shove me out. I should have stood my ground, asserted my authority, but I didn't and look where it got me. I see myself in you, boy. You're not like Vinny. You're a kind lad with a big heart. Don't make the same mistakes that I did, eh?'

Michael nodded. His father might have been a drunk for years, but he spoke more sense at times than the rest of the Butler clan put together.

Little Vinny's eyes lit up as his dad drove into Kings Holiday Park. 'Look, there's an amusement arcade over there. Can we go in and play the machines, Dad?'

Vinny stepped out of the car. Children's laughter filled the air and was accompanied by the strong but pleasant smell of chlorine.

'And there's a swimming pool. Can we go swimming?' Little Vinny had never been to a holiday camp before, and he loved it already.

'No, we can't go swimming because we haven't got any towels or our trunks with us,' Vinny replied. The holiday park certainly seemed to have a buzz about it. There were lots of chalets, with adults sunbathing and children playing happily outside. There was a big clubhouse, and a shop that had rubber rings, beach balls, and buckets and spades on sale outside. Vinny had never been to a holiday park before either, and he was quite surprised by how upmarket it all seemed. 'Shall we get something to eat then, boy?' he asked. He had wanted to drive around more, see if he could find chalet number twenty-five, but there just wasn't the time today.

'Yeah. Can I have burger and chips, Dad?'

Vinny nodded, and smiled at a holidaymaker walking past. 'Excuse me. Could you tell me where we can get something to eat, please?'

'In the clubhouse. Have you only just arrived?' the lady asked, ruffling Little Vinny's hair.

'Yes.'

392

'Oh, your boy will love it here. They do so much for the kids. My grandson's favourite is the donkey derby. You must do the Treasure Island trip too. It's a wonderful camp. Much better than Pontins where we used to go.'

'Sounds great. Enjoy your holiday,' Vinny said, gesturing at his son to follow him towards the clubhouse.

Vinny had imagined the clubhouse on a holiday camp to resemble a big shed with poor entertainment, but this one was the exact opposite. It had a large modern bar, a massive stage, and top-class lighting. It also had band equipment on stage and a DJ stand. Scanning the club to see if he could spot Joanna Preston, Vinny noticed there was a darts competition going on, and also a grey-haired man sitting in the corner painting a portrait of a child while the kid's parents looked on proudly.

'Wait here, son, while I get us a drink. Kids aren't allowed up the bar,' Vinny ordered, after clocking the sign.

Two lads marched over to Little Vinny. The one with the football under his arm spoke first. 'All right? I'm Gary and this is my cousin, Steve. Do you wanna play football with us? We are one short on our team. What's your name?'

'I'm Vinny, and I'll have to ask my dad. He's up the bar at the moment.'

'Hello, lads. Do you want a glass of Coke as well?' Vinny asked, handing his son his drink.

'Yes please, Mister.'

When Vinny returned from the bar, Little Vinny asked if he could play football with Steve and Gary.

'You haven't got time today, son. We need to get back to pick the others up shortly.'

'But I like it here, Dad. I don't want to go home,' Little Vinny whinged.

Sitting down at a nearby table, Vinny urged the lads to

393

do the same. 'So where do you come from, boys? You here on holiday?'

Steve explained that his and Gary's parents owned chalets on the site, and told Vinny that they were cousins who came from Plumstead in South London. 'You should get a chalet here too, Mister. It's well nice. They have all the big stars sing here at weekends, and all the famous comedians. My mum says Butlins is shit compared to Kings. She says it is the best holiday camp ever, and we love it here too, don't we, Gal?'

Gary nodded. 'My nan made my granddad go in for the knobbly knees competition earlier this week and he won,' he chuckled.

'Dad, can't you book us a holiday here?' Little Vinny pleaded.

Vinny couldn't help but smirk. Why hadn't he thought of that? Booking a holiday was the best way possible to get to Joanna Preston, surely? 'Yeah, I don't see why not. I wonder where I can book it?'

'There's an office not far from the entrance. They'll book it for you. A man called Ray King owns the camp, he is friendly with my dad and granddad. If you see Ray, just tell him Gary Fletcher sent you. He knows me too.'

Chuckling, Vinny ruffled his son's hair. 'We'll have something to eat, then I'll book us a holiday. But, we'll need to get our skates on. Go and order some food while I get another pint. I'll have whatever you're having, and get your mates whatever they want.'

Vinny snatched the ten-pound note out of his father's hand and ran towards the food counter. His dad was the best dad ever, he really was.

Queenie and Vivian could find no fault with the home, staff, or surroundings. Roy had been shown the room that would be his, and it was spacious, nicely furnished, with its own TV and a wonderful view from the window. The food was fairly decent, they had just all eaten lunch, and the staff said that in the summer the patients that were well enough to go were regularly taken to the beach.

'Look at that flowerbed, Queen. Not seen roses like that in years. What a beautiful place, much better than that shithole in East Ham, eh?'

Nodding, Queenie looked at her watch. The staff had told her and Vivian to have a walk in the grounds while they took Roy into the dayroom and introduced him to some of the other patients. They said initial introductions always went smoother without any family present. 'Come on, let's go back in and see how Roy's getting on. Do you think he likes it? Hasn't said much, has he? He did wolf that quiche and salad though. Wasn't eating sod all in East Ham. He said the food was rotten.'

'I'm sure he will be happy here, Queen. He seemed to like his room and was chuffed it had its own TV.'

Queenie sighed. 'I do hope so, Vivvy. I really do. If he's happy, I'm happy. If he's sad, then so am I.'

Vinny liked things to go to plan, and when the lady in the office informed him that they were fully booked for the next six weeks, he was pissed off. 'But, you must have one chalet spare?'

'Not until September. Kings is ever so popular with families, and the school holidays really do get booked up months in advance. I can offer you a caravan though.'

Vinny glared at the woman. 'Do I look like a pikey?'

Little Vinny's eyes filled up with tears. He had met two nice mates, thoroughly enjoyed his burger and chips, won three pounds in the amusement arcade, and he wanted to stay at Kings forever. 'Can't you just buy a chalet, Dad, like Gary and Steve's dads did?' he asked, hopefully.

'Are there any chalets for sale?' Vinny asked the woman.

'Yes. Would you like to view one this afternoon?'

'I can't. I need to be somewhere else. I'll have to come back another time.'

'Well, the office is open all day, every day, sir. This is our phone number. Give us a call, and we can talk through prices and arrange any viewings for you.'

'Can't we do it now, Dad? Please,' Little Vinny begged in desperation.

Vinny dragged his son from the office. 'We haven't got time, boy, and I haven't much money on me.'

Little Vinny started to cry as soon as he got in the car. It was his actual birthday today, and it was now the worst one ever.

'Don't cry. Only sissies cry. Think on the bright side, you can go for a ride on that present of yours when you get home.'

'Don't wanna go for a ride on it. I want to go on holiday to Kings,' Little Vinny wept.

Vinny turned the volume up on the stereo, then hearing Dorothy Moore singing 'Misty Blue', he quickly turned it back down again. He hated that bastard record, and every other soppy love song that somehow wormed its way into the charts.

Mulling over what he should do, Vinny mentally calculated the pros and cons. He knew the chalet was going to set him back thousands, but he could easily afford it. His mum, aunt, and Lenny would all be sure to love Kings.

The downside was, sodding off to Eastbourne for days on end was not something he was comfortable with. Yet Michael and Dean were both quite capable of running the club, and he had some good staff as well. Pete and Paul were ultra-trustworthy and had been working for him for donkey's years.

Glancing at his distraught son, Vinny mounted the car onto the nearby kerb. 'Right, I'll do you a deal.'

'What?' Vinny mumbled, his lip protruding sulkily.

'Well, your nan ain't happy I bought you that scrambling bike for your birthday. She is paranoid you are going to fly off it, break your neck, and end up in a wheelchair like your Uncle Roy. So, this is the deal. I take the bike back to the shop, then I'll drive back to Kings tomorrow and buy one of them chalets instead. What do you reckon?'

Vinny's face lit up in a split second. 'You got yourself a deal, Dad.'

CHAPTER THIRTY-FIVE

To avoid any rush-hour traffic, Vinny picked Ahmed up at the crack of dawn. 'Did you bring any gear with you?' Vinny asked. He didn't like to keep a stash of his own, as it was too tempting to snort it.

'It is breakfast time,' Ahmed replied, pretending to be appalled.

'I know that, you nutter. Just thought we might perk ourselves up a bit later. I didn't get rid of all the punters until after three so I've only had a couple of hours' sleep-feel fucked I do.'

Grinning, Ahmed pulled a small see-through bag out of his pocket. 'Good job I had the brain to bring this with me then.'

Little Vinny was like a cat with two tails. All he could think and talk about was having regular holidays with his new pals Steve and Gary down at Eastbourne. 'Nan, you and Auntie Viv are really gonna love it at Kings. They have bingo, and a glamorous granny competition. I think you should enter that. I'm sure you are pretty enough to win.'

Queenie didn't want to dampen her grandson's enthusiasm, but there was more chance of hell freezing over than her standing on stage with a load of old dears who wore Crimplene dresses and stank of piss. 'Aren't you going out with Ben today?'

'Not until Dad's rang. He promised he would ring me as soon as he'd bought the chalet. I want to know what number it is.'

'Well, you're gonna have to find out later, boy. Me and your Auntie Viv are going to visit your great-nan's grave, then we have to go and see Roy. You can't stay here on your own, so if you're not going out to play, then you'll have to come with us.'

'But, why can't I stay here? I know how to look after myself, and as soon as Dad rings I'll go out.'

'Nope. You ain't staying here, Vinny, and that is final.'

Within two hours of arriving in Eastbourne, Vinny had spied through the window of chalet number twenty-five, and purchased what was referred to as a bungalow because it was newly built with bricks rather than wood. He was now sitting by the swimming pool with an ice-cold lager in his hand.

'That man's face was a picture when you handed him seven and half thousand pound in a carrier bag,' Ahmed chuckled, unbuckling his jeans.

'What you doing? You can't strip down to your pants. There's children present.'

'Which is why I put trunks on,' Ahmed said, letting go of his jeans to reveal a bright green pair of extremely brief Speedos.

Vinny couldn't help but laugh as he clocked women staring at his pal. Ahmed was six foot two, golden brown, and really did have muscles in all the right places. He had a bit of a hooked nose which seemed to suit his face, and with his mirrored sunglasses on, plus the enormous bulge in his trunks, was certainly turning some heads. Vinny had thought he had been gifted with an enormous penis until he had stood next to his pal in the toilet one day. That was a story he and Ahmed often joked about.

'I could eat a scabby horse. Where do I buy food?' Ahmed asked.

Vinny didn't answer. He was transfixed by the girl in the bikini who was walking towards him with her pal. He knew immediately it was Joanna Preston, and he nudged Ahmed's arm. 'Our prey has just arrived, and she's heading our way.'

When Joanna smiled at him, then asked if the sunbeds next to them were free, Vinny could barely believe his luck.

'I go to get my friend and I drink and food. Would you like anything, beautiful ladies?' Ahmed asked, winking at Joanna's pal. Ahmed always liked to sound more Turkish when chatting up English birds. A foreign lilt, plus a few cheesy compliments always equalled great success. Over the years, it had ensured him many a bunk-up and his beloved British passport.

'No, we're fine. But thanks for asking us,' the girl replied politely.

When Joanna took some sun oil out of her bag and began to rub it all over her body, Vinny watched her out of the corner of his sunglasses. Joanna was easy on the eye, and nothing would give him greater pleasure than fucking the arse off Johnny Preston's daughter. He could get an erection just thinking about it.

Little Vinny couldn't think of anything more boring than spending the day at his great-nan's grave and Roy's care home, so he had allowed his nan to march him round to Ben Bloggs' house. He had then knocked on the door, waved goodbye, and gone inside. What his nan hadn't realized was as soon as she had walked off, he and Ben had gone back to her house and were currently trying to get through the kitchen window.

'I'm stuck. It's hurting my arms. I can't get in there,' Ben complained, as he managed to wriggle back out, with the help of his pal pulling his legs.

'Well, we're just gonna have to get the ladder, then you can stand on the conservatory roof and get though my bedroom window,' Little Vinny suggested.

'Why me? You're better at climbing, Vin, so you do it.'

Little Vinny was like his father in more ways than one, and one of the worst traits he had inherited was impatience. He was so desperate to receive the phone call confirming that his dad had purchased a chalet at Kings that he would have done almost anything to get inside the house.

'Be careful. That roof is only plastic,' Ben said, as his mate went up the ladder.

'I'll be fine. I ain't fat, am I?'

Little Vinny slithered across the roof like a snake. But as he stood up to heave himself through the bedroom window, the shrill voice of Mouthy Maureen who lived next-door-but-one made him lose his balance.

Seconds later, the roof gave way and with a deafening crash, Little Vinny fell through to the conservatory.

Back in Eastbourne, Vinny had just got Joanna and her pal a drink and was currently laying on the charm. 'So, where-abouts do you come from, girls?' he asked, propping himself up on his elbow.

'Tiptree,' Chloe replied.

'And you?' Vinny asked, fixing his most penetrating stare on Joanna.

'I come from the same place,' Joanna replied. She'd been young when her father moved them out to Essex, and he had always warned her never to tell anybody where she had lived beforehand. Even though many years had now passed, the warning had stuck in Joanna's mind. She wasn't silly. She knew her dad was into bad stuff which was why he was locked up now, but she had never really learned the full truth of why they'd had to leave London in such a hurry. Her parents had both seemed reluctant to talk about the move, and had virtually told Joanna not to mention the subject again, which she hadn't.

'I very hungry again, ladies. Would you be so kind to join me and my friend for lunch? We can leave towel on sunbeds and eat inside club,' Ahmed suggested.

Chloe shrugged and looked at Joanna. Neither of them earned much money in their cleaning jobs, and the two men did seem quite charming. 'Shall we, Jo?'

'Go on, be a devil. Our treat of course,' Vinny said, winking at his prey.

Joanna was rather taken with Vinny. Since she and Chloe had been working at Kings, they had met and snogged a few lads. Joanna had even let one touch her breasts, but nobody had really rocked her boat. Most were just holiday-makers out for a good time. Vinny was different. He was older, extremely handsome, very sophisticated, and he had told her he owned a place at Kings. That had impressed Joanna because he had said it was a brick-built bungalow, and because they were relatively new, only rich people could afford them. Smiling at Vinny, Joanna stood up.

'Lunch it is then.'

Because of their hectic lifestyles, Donald and Christopher Walker spent very little father-and-son time alone. Either Donald was busy in the café or Christopher was on the beat, and when the two were together, Mary was usually in her armchair joining in with their conversation.

Today, however, Christopher was off duty, the café had

been quiet, and Mary had suggested that father and son go for a lunchtime pint together. 'Me and Tina can manage OK, and you could do with a break, Donald. I often pop out during opening hours, and it isn't fair that you are always stuck here,' his wife had insisted.

'Some of the lads at work drink far too much, you know, Dad. They finish their shift and go straight to the pub. Even if they are on a late shift, they go to this pub called the Spurstowe Arms where the landlord gives them a lock-in. They stay in there most of the night sometimes, and you can tell that they aren't as on the ball in work the next day as they should be,' Christopher informed his father as they walked towards their local.

'Christ! That's disgusting. No wonder there are so many bloody crimes committed if half of the Met are permanently pissed. I really have never understood why people enjoy getting drunk. It's a complete waste of money, and surely it is better to be in control of yourself. I got drunk once, son, when I was about your age, and I vowed never to allow myself to do it again. Do these colleagues of yours invite you to go drinking with them?' Donald asked, worriedly. He had thought the police force were the crème de la crème of the human race, but obviously not.

Christopher didn't answer. He hadn't seen his sister for years, but he was sure it was Nancy who was walking towards them. She was with another girl, both were pushing buggies, and there was also a dark-haired child walking alongside them. 'Dad, is that Nancy?'

'What! Where?'

'Walking towards us.'

Donald recognized his daughter immediately even though she was a good fifty yards away. She was still as slim as ever, and with her long blonde hair and beauty, Nancy was unmistakeable. And even though the child beside her looked nothing like Nancy, he knew it must be one of his grandsons.

'Where we going, Dad?' Christopher asked, when his father yanked him by the arm and dragged him across the road.

'We're avoiding your sister, son. You don't want to see her, do you?'

'No. Not really. I wouldn't have minded seeing what my nephews look like though.'

'Those children aren't your nephews, Christopher, neither are they my grandsons. They are Butlers. Never forget that, will you?'

Christopher glanced over the road and, aware that Nancy was looking his way, quickly turned back to his father. 'You're spot-on, Dad. Those kids are bound to turn out to be scum just like their father and uncles are.'

Roy Butler felt the happiest he had in ages. Paul had just turned up with the gun he had asked for, and he was moving to Eastbourne.

'How much do I owe you?' Roy asked his pal.

'Two hundred including the bullets. I wish you would tell me what you are planning though, Roy, in case it backfires my way. Vinny and Michael aren't gonna be happy if they find out I am involved, are they?'

Roy wrapped the gun back in its cloth, wheeled himself over to his bedside cabinet and hid it at the back of the drawer.

'You can't leave it there! Say one of the carers finds it?' Paul said, feeling more anxious by the second. He had a wife and two kids to support, therefore could not afford to lose his job at the club. He was also worried about repercussions from Vinny. His boss certainly wasn't a chap you'd want to get on the wrong side of.

Roy wheeled himself over to where Paul was sitting and stared him in the eyes. 'I swear on my Emily-Mae's life that your name will never crop up, Paul. I am a man of my word, as you well know.'

'But, won't you go to prison, Roy? I mean, you can hardly shoot someone and get away from the scene of the crime easily, can you? I ain't being nosy, I'm just worried about you, that's all.'

Roy tried to smile on the one side of his face that would still allow him that pleasure. 'Please do not fret or ask me any more questions, mate. My plan is infallible. Crippled I might be, but stupid I'm not.'

Back in Eastbourne, Joanna and Chloe were getting along like a house on fire with the two generous gentlemen they had met.

'Well, do you fancy Ahmed?' Joanna asked her pal, as they went to the toilet together just so they could have a girlie discussion.

'I'm not sure. I think I do, but he's a bit too old for my liking. What about you? I can tell you like that Vinny, so don't make out you don't.'

'Yeah, I do really like him, but as you said, they are a bit old for us. Then again, they are good fun and I think they are loaded, so we would be mad not to see them again if they asked us. Them lads we went out with last week made us go round for round with them, Chloe. I can never imagine Vinny and Ahmed making us buy them a drink, can you? Surely we are better to date real men than silly bloody boys, eh?'

'Yeah, you're right. We came to work at Kings to have some fun, so we might as well let Ahmed and Vinny show us a good time,' Chloe agreed.

Joanna giggled and linked arms with her pal. 'I bet they

are both good in bed too. Vinny has the most mesmerizing eyes I have ever seen, and did you see the size of Ahmed's thingamajig in them Speedos? It looked like he had a snake tucked in there.'

Chloe playfully punched her pal on the arm. 'Stop it,' she ordered.

Queenie and Vivian weren't even halfway down their road when Mouthy Maureen came running towards them. Maureen had only moved in next-door-but-one to Queenie just over a year back, and although her curtains and house were kept spotlessly clean, she did like to poke her trunk into other people's business which is why Queenie and Vivian liked to keep their distance from her.

'What's this fucking trappy cow want?' Vivian mumbled, when Maureen started to wave her hands frantically.

By the time Maureen reached Queenie and Vivian she was so out of puff she could barely speak or breathe, so leant on a nearby wall.

'Whatever's the matter?' Queenie asked.

'It's Little Vinny. I had to call an ambulance for him. He fell through your conservatory roof and I think he's broken his arm. Took a bang on the head as well,' Maureen panted.

'Where is he now?' Vivan asked, alarmed.

'London Hospital. He isn't alone though. His mate Ben Bloggs was with him, and Big Stan went in the ambulance with them. Stan wanted to take him in his car, but I told him no. I watched a programme recently, and it said if anyone has had a bad fall you shouldn't move them until the experts get there.'

Queenie could feel her hands shaking, such was the shock. 'So, was he conscious?'

'Oh yeah. He had to stand up to unlock the door, but then I made him lie back down again. Lucky he fell on that flowered sofa that you bought recently. Flattened it, he did, but it would have been a lot worse had he hit the concrete floor.'

'OK, well, thanks for all your help, Maureen. Best me and Vivvy get up the hospital now,' Queenie said, grabbing her sister's arm and marching off in the opposite direction.

'Don't worry too much, Queen. You know how Maureen likes to exaggerate, and if Little Vinny stood up to unlock the door himself, he must be OK,' Vivian said comfortingly.

'Well, I'll tell you something, Vivvy. If that little bastard hasn't got any broken bones, he soon will have if he has ruined my beloved conservatory. I'll break his fucking neck.'

After having lunch and a few drinks in the clubhouse, Vinny and Ahmed suggested they take the girls for a drive so they could explore more of Eastbourne.

Joanna and Chloe were extremely impressed when they saw Vinny's flash-looking Jaguar, and even though the men had told them very little about what they did for a living, apart from describing themselves as businessmen, the girls saw no danger in going for a drive with them. Usually Joanna and Chloe just chilled by the swimming pool every day after finishing their cleaning, so it was nice to do something different and more exciting for a change.

Vinny took a drive around some of the coastal roads and then stopped at a pub called the Moorings that overlooked the beach. 'Fancy another drink, ladies?' he asked.

'I thought you had to drive back to London this afternoon. What time do you have to leave?' Joanna asked.

Ahmed chuckled. 'We don't. Our mums say we can stay out late.'

Vinny allowed his mind to wander. Many a night he had

lain in bed virtually salivating, such was his desire to get even with Preston, and now that time had come. He had asked George Geary to track the bastard down years ago, and when Geary had failed, Vinny had surmised Johnny had changed his name. That wasn't the case though, and Vinny was now sure that Geary had purposely not even tried to find Preston in case it ended up in a bloodbath and he was implicated.

Vinny had toyed with hiring a private detective at one point, but he was too wary of who he could trust. Loose lips sink ships was a true old saying and one that his mother had drummed into him since childhood.

Vinny glanced into his interior mirror and grinned as Joanna locked eyes with him. The buzz of retribution was already in his system, and it was a bigger high than cocaine. 'Well, we was going back to London this afternoon, but that was before we met you two beautiful young ladies. Have you and Chloe got any plans for tonight? If you have, please don't think of cancelling them on our behalf, but if you haven't, Ahmed and I can stay in my chalet tonight, then drive back to London tomorrow morning. We would love to take you to a nice restaurant later. Or a club? It's your call,' Vinny said.

Joanna and Chloe immediately nudged one another excitedly. Tiptree had never been the most stimulating place to live, and the majority of the lads there were quite dull. Vinny reminded Joanna of her dad in some ways, but with a lot more going for him. Joanna's mum had always described her dad as a Vinny-type when they had first met and were living in South London, but she'd said he had changed when they had moved to Tiptree.

'Well?' Chloe asked her pal.

'It's up to you,' Joanna giggled. She wasn't a virgin, had already slept with two lads back in Tiptree, but there was something about Vinny when he looked at her with those eyes and that stare that made her feel naïve again.

'OK. Seeing as my mate can't make a decision, I say we should go to a nightclub,' Chloe told Vinny.

'I hope you good dancer. I the best. Turkish man know how to move and groove,' Ahmed cheekily informed Chloe.

'Well, that's settled then. You go get the drinks, Ahmed, while I phone home. I promised Little Vinny I would ring him earlier, then forgot. I'll be back in a minute, ladies,' Vinny said, courteously. As he turned his back to walk away, he couldn't help but smirk. He already had Joanna Preston in the palm of his clever hand, and he knew it.

Queenie Butler screamed when she saw the state of her once-beautiful conservatory. Vinny had paid for it as a birthday present last year, and now it looked like it had been a casualty of one of Hitler's bombs. The roof was ruined, the panel in the middle had completely caved in, and her lovely flowered sofa with the carved wooden arms and legs, was as flat as a pancake. 'Aw, my gawd, Vivvy. He's even flattened me best plant. I'll swing for the little bastard. Where is he now?'

Little Vinny had escaped his ordeal with just a broken left arm and a small graze on his forehead. The nurse had said that there were no signs of concussion, so he was allowed to go home, but if he were to be sick later, or complain of a bad headache, Queenie should bring him back to the hospital just to be on the safe side.

'He's gone upstairs to his bedroom. He's a bit subdued, ain't he?' Vivian said.

'I'll give him fucking subdued! I told him he wasn't allowed in this house alone, and what does he do, he breaks in, the little bastard. Couldn't even successfully do that, could he? I wouldn't have minded so much if he had smashed one of me windows, but ruining my conservatory is the final straw, Vivvy. He ain't my responsibility no more. I can't handle the child.'

'I'll get that,' Vivian said, when the phone rang. She was hoping it might be her Lenny. She always worried when he worked at the club alone during the day, but Vinny insisted he was fine. He reckoned responsibility was just what the boy needed. 'It's Vinny, Queen,' Vivian shouted out.

Absolutely livid, Queenie snatched the phone out of her sister's hand. 'Where the fuck are you? You need to get your arse back here, boy. Your son is driving me totally doolally.'

'I'm in Eastbourne, Mum. You knew I was coming here to buy a place. I've had a few beers now, so have decided to stay here for the night. I'll be home first thing in the morning, then I'm coming back here at the weekend and bringing you, Auntie Viv, and Champ with me. Guess who are appearing at the clubhouse on Saturday night? Showaddywaddy. You like them, don't you?' Vinny said, trying to smooth over his mother's obvious bad mood.

'Fuck Showaddywaddy! That little bastard you've lumbered me with has broken his arm and smashed up my conservatory. Fell through the bastard roof, he did. Now you get your arse back here a.s.a.p. I am too old to handle that child, so best you pick him up before I break his scrawny neck, or shove him in an orphanage. I've had a gutful of him. I can't hack it no more.'

Vinny sighed with pure frustration. He had been desperate to fuck Joanna Preston's brains out this evening, and by the way she had been looking at him, he had known his ultimate shag had been on the cards. 'Calm down, Mum. I hate to hear you this upset. I'll leave Eastbourne now, and hopefully, traffic permitting, will be back in three hours. Where is Little Vinny now? Is he OK?'

'In his bedroom. The nurse put plaster on his arm, then said to bring him home. I'm stressed up to me eyeballs. Not only does he worry the bloody life out of me, I now have no fucking roof on my conservatory. What with Roy now moving to Eastbourne, I'm at the end of me tether, son, I really am.'

Assuring his mother he would sort everything out including his son and her roof, Vinny ended the call, plastered a smile on his face and walked over to the table where Ahmed and the girls sat. His quest for revenge would just have to wait that little bit longer.

CHAPTER THIRTY-SIX

Mary Walker walked towards her daughter's house with slight trepidation. Like any decent mother, Mary knew her Nancy inside out, and not only was it out of character for her to ring the café, it was also the tone of Nancy's voice that had warned Mary something was dreadfully amiss.

'What's wrong, darling? Are the boys OK? I know you always wait for me to ring you unless it's urgent,' Mary said, when her daughter answered the front door.

'Oh, it's everything, Mum. Daniel and Adam both have stomach bugs. Michael has to be at the club all this weekend because Vinny has bought some bloody place on a holiday camp in Eastbourne and is taking most of the family there, and I just can't get over what Dad and Christopher did to me. How could they be so heartless?' Nancy sobbed.

Mary looked at her daughter in astonishment. 'What're you on about? Where did you see your dad and Christopher?'

'When I was walking to the park with Rhonda yesterday. I had the boys with me, and as soon as Dad and Christopher spotted us, they crossed the road. I don't care about them wanting nothing to do with me, but how could they ignore Daniel and Adam like that? I'd already told Daniel that his granddad and uncle were walking towards us and he burst into tears when they avoided him.'

Mary was absolutely furious. She had thought Donald and Christopher seemed a bit sheepish when they'd returned from the pub the previous day and now she knew why. 'Are you sure they saw you, love?'

'Of course I'm sure. Christopher even looked at me from the other side of the road, until Dad probably told him to stop. Really spoilt my day it did, and now I feel depressed again. Rhonda was appalled by what happened. She said any granddad who crossed the road to avoid his own grandsons needed stringing up.'

'Oh, you wait until I get home. I'll string him up all right. In fact, if Michael is working all weekend, shall I pack a little case and come and stay with you? That will teach the pair of heartless bastards a lesson, won't it?'

'That would be great, Mum. The boys will love it.'

'Bleedin' hell, Nance. A police car has just pulled up outside. They're looking at your house, love. Where's Michael?' Mary asked.

'Taken the boys to the doctor's. Oh my God! Please don't let nothing terrible have happened to them,' Nancy said, running to open the front door.

Mary's heart was beating like a drum as she followed Nancy into the hallway.

'Nothing has happened to my husband and sons, has it? They only went to the doctor's. It's just around the corner,' Nancy gabbled, her voice full of panic. She could tell by the serious looks on the two officers' faces that it was bad news.

'It's actually Michael Butler we've come to see. Are you his wife?' the male officer asked.

Nancy felt relief seep through her veins. If they were looking for Michael then he and the boys were obviously

OK. 'What do you want to see Michael for? Has he done something wrong?'

'No, he hasn't,' the female officer replied.

'Here's Michael now, love,' Mary informed her daughter, pointing towards her son-in-law crossing the road.

With Adam in his arms, and Daniel by his side, Michael's face whitened as he saw the two coppers standing at his front door. 'What's up?' he asked.

'I'm afraid we have some bad news for you, Mr Butler. Shall we speak inside?' the male officer suggested.

'Babe, go in the front room with your mum and the kids while I speak to the officers in the kitchen,' Michael ordered his wife. He waited until the lounge door was shut. 'Hit me with it then.'

'I'm afraid your son Lee was involved in a car accident in the early hours of this morning.'

Michael felt the colour drain out of his face. 'Oh Jesus! Please tell me he's OK?'

'Apart from slight concussion and a few cuts and bruises, Lee is fine. But, I'm afraid his mother, gran, and the driver of the car were not so lucky. There were also two fatalities in the car they collided with,' the female officer told Michael.

'What do you mean exactly? Are Denise and her mum both dead then?' Michael asked, dumbly. His brain and body were numb with the shock of it all.

'I'm afraid so, Mr Butler. Your son was incredibly lucky to survive according to the firemen who cut him free from the wreckage.'

'So, where is Lee now?'

'He is in Oldchurch Hospital in Romford. I spoke to the doctor there earlier and he said Lee should be well enough to be discharged in a couple of days. He hasn't been informed that his mother or gran are dead yet though. We thought that might be kinder coming from you rather than us.

Children usually adapt to news of that kind far better if it comes from a relative.'

'I'll go straight to the hospital after you leave. Where is he going to live though?' Michael asked, worriedly.

'With you surely, sir? You are his father after all,' the female officer said.

Michael felt embarrassed. 'Yes, of course. I'm sorry, I didn't mean it like that. I'm just not thinking straight what with the shock of it all.'

The male officer handed Michael a piece of paper. 'We understand, sir. This is the ward Lee is on and that is the name of the doctor we spoke to earlier.'

Too astounded by the bombshell that had been dropped on him to even ask where the accident had happened or who was driving the car, Michael thanked the police officers for their time, and showed them out.

Nancy and Mary appeared in the hallway as soon as they heard the front door slam. 'Whatever is it, Michael?' Nancy asked. Her husband looked like he had seen a ghost.

'It's Lee. He was involved in a bad car accident last night. He's OK, but Denise is dead and so is her mum. I've got to go to the hospital and break the news to the poor little sod. How do you tell a four-year-old kid that his family have all been snuffed out, eh?' Michael asked, rather hoping that Nancy would offer to accompany him.

Nancy didn't. Instead she said, 'Oh my God! This is so awful. Who is Lee going to live with?'

'Us, Nancy. He doesn't have anyone else now, does he?'

Nancy shook her head vehemently. 'He can't live here. No way! I have enough on my plate with Daniel and Adam, Michael. Lee must have other relatives. He will have to live with those.'

Michael had always loved his wife dearly, but for once he looked at her with hatred. How could Nancy be so bloody selfish? 'Well, like it or lump it, that boy is coming to live here, Nance. No flesh and blood of mine is going to be brought up by some stranger or in care when he has me as a father. Can you imagine the light people would see me in when they find out my son has just had his family wiped out, and I dumped him like a bag of old rubbish too? No way, darling.'

'I couldn't give a shit what people say or think, Michael. I am telling you now, I cannot cope with the two I already have, so no way I am taking on another one. Lee will have to live elsewhere,' Nancy screamed.

'I want Lee to live here, Daddy,' Daniel said, excitedly tugging his father's arm.

'Well, Nance, the choice is yours. If you don't want to help look after my son best you pack your bags and leave, love,' Michael spat. He then picked up his car keys, stormed out the front door, and slammed it so hard it nearly flew off its hinges.

Vinny Butler was not in the best of moods. Even though he had given his son the telling-off of his life, sent two blokes around this morning to mend his mother's conservatory roof, and replaced her furniture and plants that had been crushed, his mum was still refusing to allow his son to live with her any more.

'Vinny, when will you take me to see Layla again?

'Champ, you've asked me that same question at least ten times already today and you're beginning to do my nut in. I promise I will take you to see Layla again soon, OK? Now just leave the subject alone. I've got enough on me plate with your Auntie Queenie refusing to let Little Vinny live with her any more. Your sex life is the least of my fucking problems at the moment.'

'Hey, big boss man. You don't look happy. What is the matter?' Ahmed enquired, sauntering into Vinny's office.

When Lenny sheepishly left the office, Vinny kicked the door shut, took a bottle of Scotch out of his private drinks cabinet and poured a large quantity into two glasses. 'You got any gear on you?' he asked Ahmed.

'I always carry a supply, but it's a bit early, my friend.'

'I don't give a toss how early it is. I'm stressed, so just give it 'ere, mate,' Vinny demanded.

Two fat lines and three large Scotches later, Vinny felt able to deal with life once more. Ahmed was a good listener, and sometimes saw things far more clearly than he did. 'Your mum's hardly going to throw her grandson out on the street. What you need to do is what I did. Find a good woman. It's their job to look after kids. You want one that asks no questions and lets you get on with your life like my Anna. Karen was a very good mum. I told you at the time you should have kept her on the firm,' Ahmed reminded his pal. After his initial wedding to an older woman, Ahmed had then married a younger model with whom he had another two children.

Vinny's sense of humour always escalated after a couple of lines of cocaine and he couldn't help himself. 'So, what do you suggest I do? Dig Karen up and try and resuscitate her?'

Ahmed chuckled. 'You should move Joanna Preston in with you. She can be Vinny's new mum. Did I ever tell you I actually dug a corpse up once and hid it? A man owed me money and I said he could have his father back when I got my dosh. He paid me the next day.'

Laughing, Vinny poured another Scotch, put his hands on top of his head, and rocked to and fro in his chair. If Joanna Preston had been some fat ugly bitch he would have probably just had her murdered and been done with it. However, once he had seen her photograph, and met her in person, he had decided to gain revenge in a different manner. Vinny had links to Wormwood Scrubs. An old friend of his, Scottish Pat, was on the same wing as Johnny

Preston. Scottish Pat said Preston was always banging on about his beautiful daughter to the other lads, but rarely spoke about his son. Pat described the boy as a weirdo, which is why Vinny had decided to target the daughter in the first place.

Ahmed indulged in a line of cocaine himself, then grinned. 'Well? You're not saying much.'

Vinny was still mulling over things. Surely being stuck in a cell twenty-plus hours a day knowing that your daughter was being shagged senseless by your very worst enemy was enough to make Preston lose the plot completely? 'I dunno, mate. I'm sure I can get Joanna into the sack, but that don't mean I want her to move in with me and bring up my kid, does it? I barely know the fucking bird, and I can't stand tarts around me at the best of times.'

'But, there is no need for her to be around you much. Set her up in a flat or house. She can look after Little Vinny while you work and party. You need to knock her up. That way, she is trapped and has no choice but to do as you say. Be nice for you to have one more child, and imagine how upset her cunt of a father will be? That is what you call the ultimate payback, my friend.'

Vinny sipped his drink and contemplated Ahmed's idea in silence. It seemed madness even to consider trying to impregnate, then move in with, a bird he had only met once, but Vinny had always had an insane, impulsive nature, and the fact that the girl was Johnny Preston's pride and joy was what made the set-up seem so attractive. That would be the perfect revenge for ruining Roy's life. 'Do you know what, I quite like your suggestion now. When do you reckon holiday parks shut down for winter? Gotta be end of September, beginning of October, surely? That gives me at least eight weeks to charm the tits off Preston's daughter. Then, if all goes to plan, instead of moving back to Tiptree, she can move to London. I might even offer her a job at the club. That should help her make her mind up. She ain't got no job in Tiptree to go back to, has she?'

'Her friend will probably want a job too,' Ahmed stated.

'Well, if that's what it takes to get Joanna properly into my clutches, then a job her mate shall have. I can't just dump Little Vinny on her from day one anyway. The core of a perfect plan is always patience.'

Ahmed laughed. Vinny was the only person he had ever met whose mind was on exactly the same intelligent, evil wavelength as his own.

Under strict instructions from his father to be on his best behaviour, Little Vinny had spent the past few hours tidying up his nan's back garden. The sun was at a blistering heat, the lawnmower heavy, and by the time he had finished cutting the grass, Little Vinny felt thoroughly exhausted. Trying to mow the lawn with two arms was hard enough, and using just one had really taken its toll on him.

Queenie sat in her conservatory and eyed her grandson suspiciously as he flopped onto the grass. The roof was now mended, and she actually preferred the slightly different design of the new sofa Vinny had bought her. It stood out more than the old one. 'What's the matter with you? You're meant to be cutting it, not sunbathing on it,' Queenie shouted, in a brutal tone.

'I've finished it, Nan. I don't feel well now. I'm hot, thirsty, and hungry.'

'You haven't got a headache, have ya?'

Knowing his nan was obviously worried that he might have concussion from his fall, Little Vinny decided to tell a small white lie. 'Yeah, a bit, but I think it's just because I'm really hungry.'

Queenie pursed her lips. 'Get your arse in here and I'll

do you some lunch then. Do you want one roll or two? I've got boiled bacon, luncheon sausage, or cheese.'

'I'll have two boiled bacon rolls, a bag of salt and vinegar crisps, and a can of Coke please,' Little Vinny said, as he darted past his nan and flopped on the sofa in the lounge.

Queenie's lip curled into a snarl. Her lounge had recently been redecorated, and she was now the proud owner of a posh brown leather three-piece suite and an expensive Persian rug. Both items were a gift from Vinny and there was no way Queenie was allowing her ragamuffin of a grandson to tarnish the new look.

'You'll get upstairs, have a wash, and change out of them dirty clothes before you get any lunch,' Queenie barked.

'OK, Nan,' Little Vinny said, dashing up the stairs.

Queenie was buttering the rolls when she heard the front door open. 'Want a boiled bacon roll, Viv?' she shouted.

'No! Get me a brandy, Queen, quick. I've just had the most terrible shock.'

'Whatever's wrong? You look like you've seen a ghost,' Queenie remarked, as she hurried to pour her sister a drink.

Vivian snatched the brandy out of her sister's hand and knocked it back in one. 'Oh dear Jesus, it was worse than a ghost what I've just seen, Queen. I didn't know my Lenny had come home from work early. He must have got in when I popped around the corner shop. Anyway, I've opened his bedroom door because I thought I heard a funny noise, and there he was, standing opposite the mirror, stark bollock naked with his dingle-dangle in his hand. He had his eyes shut and was rambling on about some girl called Lola or Layla.'

'Oh dear,' Queenie said, pouring herself a brandy and giving her sister a top-up. 'What did he say when he saw you standing there?'

'Well, he opened his eyes, screamed, then started shouting

at me to get out of his room. And, he had a great big, you know. No mother should have to see that. It was disgusting.'

'Erection?' Queenie enquired.

'Yes, one of those. Dirty little bastard! Pervert, just like his father was. How am I ever meant to look at him in the same way, eh? And whose bloody Lola or Layla? I don't think it's good for him working at that club, you know. Too many women showing their flesh in there. It's giving him unhealthy ideas.'

'I shouldn't think it's got anything to do with him working at the club, Viv. I mean, he is twenty now, he's bound to get urges. My Michael used to when he was younger. I remember seeing terrible stuff on his sheets. Your Lenny is bound to feel far more embarrassed than you do. Why don't you pop back to yours, act like nothing's happened, and tell him to come in here for a boiled bacon roll?'

'No way is that filthy little sod coming in here to eat. I bet he ain't even washed his hands. Made me feel so ill it has, Queen. Wouldn't pour me another brandy, would ya?'

Queenie nodded. Usually, she knew the best words to appease her sister, but Vivian catching Lenny masturbating was a difficult one, and for once Queenie was slightly lost for words herself.

Back in Barking, Mary was desperate to clear her head and had decided to walk home from Nancy's house rather than jump on a bus like she usually did. It was only four stops anyway, and she wasn't ready to face Donald just yet. She wanted to work out exactly what she was going to say to him first.

Nancy had been in a terrible state all day, and Mary was dreadfully worried about her. Mary hadn't started her own family until she was twenty-two. Her daughter wasn't even twenty-one yet, and how she was going to cope with three little boys all under the age of five, Mary did not know. Nancy wasn't a bad mum by any means, but she hadn't exactly taken to motherhood. She seemed to handle the boys all right when Mary or Michael were there to give her a hand, but when Nancy was home alone, she seemed to get extremely stressed. Daniel and Adam then ran rings around her and, being so young herself still, Nancy allowed the boys to do so, then got depressed about it.

Thinking back to their earlier conversation, Mary sighed anxiously. She had managed to persuade her daughter not to leave Michael, but she wasn't sure if she had done the right thing. It was one of those six of one, half a dozen of the other situations. Nancy would not be able to cope with Lee and that was a fact.

'Hi, Mary. You OK?'

Mary had been so deep in thought she hadn't noticed Dederick and his two brothers crossing over the road.

'I'm fine, thank you, boys. How are you today?'

'Yeah, we cool. Going over the park to meet our friends. You gonna to be in that café tomorrow? Food never as good when you not there,' Dederick said, treating Mary to a cheeky wink.

Mary smiled as the three brothers walked away. They were all wearing tight-fitting white T-shirts and flared faded jeans, and with their identical Afro hair, they reminded Mary of members of the pop group the Jackson Five. Dederick and his brothers were lovely people, so was their mother Joyce, but a lot of regulars in the café didn't see them that way. England had become far more multicultural over recent years, and many local people couldn't get their heads around it. Both Mary and Donald believed there was good and bad in every race, but many English people didn't share their liberal views. The majority opinion of the natives of Barking was that England should stop immigration immediately, otherwise their beloved country would be one day taken over, and white people would become the minority. Donald referred to these people as small-minded bigots, and Mary couldn't agree more.

Mary took a deep breath as she walked up the path that led to her house, and put her key in the door.

'Hello, love. Dinner is ready,' Donald said jovially. He didn't feel at all jovial inside, he felt uneasy. He knew that his wife had been to see Nancy, and was now waiting for the backlash. He didn't have to wait long.

'You disgust me, Donald, you really do. How any man could cross over the road to avoid his own grandsons is beyond me. Nancy had told them that their granddad and uncle were walking towards them, and poor little Daniel was beside himself when you walked the other way. What type of man are you?'

Donald knew he had no option other than to stick with his beliefs. 'Mary, I told you when Nancy married into that family, I wanted nothing to do with her, or any children she might have in the future. I am a man of my word, that's what type of man I am.'

'Oh, and don't I bastard-well know it. Not wanting Nancy in your life is one thing, but crossing over the road to avoid them two little boys is another. Would it have really hurt you to stop and say hello to them? What was you frightened of? Did you think that you might actually feel some emotion for once in your life?'

'I refuse to have this conversation with you, Mary. We had a deal when you returned home after our minor break-up that if I allowed you to see Nancy, you would not mention anything about her or those children in this house. You are the one in the wrong here, not me. It is you, Mary, that has broken your part of the bargain.'

'Fuck you, Donald, and fuck your bargain,' Mary spat.

423

Stunned that his usually well-mannered wife had used the F-word twice in the same sentence, Donald followed her as she stomped up the stairs. 'Where are you going?' he asked in a bewildered tone, when he saw her pull her small suitcase out from under the bed.

'To stay with our daughter for a while.'

'But what about the café? And what about your sausage and mash I've cooked you?'

Mary threw a few bits into her case, zipped it up, then glared at the man she had married. 'You and Tina can manage the café OK, and as for the dinner, you can stick your sausages where the sun don't shine, Donald.'

CHAPTER THIRTY-SEVEN

'How was he? Did he settle in all right?' Vinny asked, when he picked his mum and aunt up from Roy's new care home at two p.m. as pre-arranged.

'He seemed OK, didn't he, Viv? I think he quite likes his new room,' Queenie replied, hopefully.

'He loves the view there as well. Where's my Lenny? Why didn't you bring him with you?' Vivian asked, worriedly. Neither she nor her son had mentioned the awkward moment they had shared again, but Vivian couldn't forget it. What she had witnessed would probably haunt her for the rest of her living days.

'Champ's with Ahmed and the boys. They were playing the machines in the amusement arcade when I left and I guarantee they will still be there when we get back. I just changed 'em up a tenner's-worth of two- and ten-pence coins. Why you worried anyway, Auntie Viv? Champ's twenty now. He's a man not a boy any more.'

Vivian pursed her lips and glanced at her sister.

'Tell Vinny what happened, go on. He won't say nothing,' Queenie urged her sister.

'Have you noticed my Lenny acting inappropriately with

any girls at the club? And do you know someone called Lola or Layla?' Vivian asked her nephew.

Vinny froze momentarily. If Lenny had blabbed and his mum and aunt found out he had paid for his cousin to sleep with a prostitute, it would cause murders. Doing what he did best, Vinny decided to bluff it. 'Yeah, there's a barmaid at the club called Lola, but I've never seen Champ act inappropriate towards her or any other girl. Why do you ask?'

'I can't tell him. You tell him,' Vivian ordered, putting her hands over her ears. She couldn't bear to be reminded of her terrible ordeal.

How Vinny kept a straight face when his mother told him what had happened, he would never know. At one point he started to laugh, but managed to cover it up with a coughing fit.

'Take your hands off your ears now, Vivvy. I've told him,' Queenie said, in all seriousness.

Trying not to laugh again, Vinny cleared his throat. 'Champ is just a normal twenty-year-old lad who hasn't got a girlfriend. Just because he isn't like the rest of us, doesn't mean to say he don't get urges.'

'Standing in front of a mirror with your dingle-dangle in your hand while spewing obscenities is not what I call fucking normal, Vinny. I bet you don't bastard-well do it,' Vivian spat.

'Well no I don't, but you really are worrying over nothing, Auntie Viv. Now, can we talk about something else please?'

When his mum and aunt started to talk about Roy again, Vinny turned up the volume on the radio. His brother hadn't uttered one word to him on the whole of the journey down to Eastbourne, and Vinny was getting very poxed off with his behaviour. He could understand Roy feeling bitter and depressed, he would if he was in the same boat, but anyone would think by the way Roy was acting that it was Vinny who had actually shot him.

Over in Barking, Mary saw Michael's car pull up outside and gave her daughter some last-minute advice. 'Now, just keep calm and remember that poor little mite has lost his mum and his gran.'

'Is our brother here, Nanny?' Daniel asked, jumping up and down excitedly.

'Yes, love. Now don't forget to share your toys with him like I told you to.'

'I won't,' Daniel said, running towards the front door. Adam toddled after his brother, but wasn't quite as clued-up as to what the excitement was all about.

'Come on. You can't sit there,' Mary said, nudging her daughter and following her grandsons.

When Michael opened the door, both Daniel and Adam flew at Lee as kids do and hugged him. Lee hadn't really understood what had happened to his mum and nan. He was too young to grasp the fact that both were dead and he would never see them again.

'Hello, Lee. I'm Mary and this is Nancy. It's lovely to meet you,' Mary said, crouching down to hug the child. Her heart went out to the poor little sod, it really did.

Michael had been thrilled when Nancy had mellowed, agreed not to leave him, and had said that it was OK for his orphaned son to live with them. 'Say hello to Lee then, babe,' he urged his wife.

Nancy stared at the child. Lee had blond hair and, apart from having green eyes, looked nothing like Michael or her own sons. She obeyed her husband's orders and awkwardly hugged the child. She felt nothing, just as she knew she would. Why should she? Lee wasn't her flesh and blood.

Within an hour of arriving at Kings Holiday Park in Pevensey Bay, Queenie and Vivian had both fallen in love with the place. 'Ain't it grand, Vivvy? I thought my Vinny was winding me up when he said Showaddywaddy were appearing here tomorrow night, but he weren't. Look, it says so on that poster.'

'And look at this brochure. They have loads of famous acts here. Jim Davidson is here in a fortnight's time. Makes me laugh, he do,' Vivian replied. She was ever so impressed by the whole set-up.

'Look, bingo tonight at seven. Shall we have a game?' Queenie suggested.

'Yous two coming in the club? Or you gonna stand in reception all day? Your lager will go flat if you stand out here any longer,' Vinny said, gesturing for his mum and aunt to follow him.

'Dad, can me and Ben go and find Steve and Gary now?' Little Vinny asked, keen to see the two lads he had met on his last visit.

'Yep, off you go. You do know what one our bungalow is, don't you?'

'Yeah. Come on, Ben, let's go,' Little Vinny said, before gulping down the last of his drink.

'Dunno why you invited that Ben Bloggs down here if Little Vinny has already met some mates. Bad influence, that boy is,' Queenie said curtly.

'Ben's OK, and I invited him in case them other lads ain't about. This is a holiday for all us, and as long as Little Vinny has a pal to knock about with, he can roam free. I'm sure you and Auntie Viv don't wanna be saddled with him, and neither do I.'

'Did you win any more?' Vivian asked her son, as Lenny walked over to the table alongside Ahmed.

'Yeah, loads of two-pence pieces fell out the bottom, but then I lost them again.'

'I told him not to put them all back. He should have saved them for later,' Ahmed said, ruffling Lenny's hair.

'Right, me and Ahmed are gonna love and leave you now. Take that fifty quid, get yourselves whatever you want to drink, and can you get a few bits from the shop for dinner tonight, and we need some breakfast stuff for the morning.'

'Where you going?' Queenie asked suspiciously.

'To spend some time with two birds we met here last week.'

'Can I come too?' Lenny asked.

'You're going nowhere, you. Now, sit down and drink your lemonade,' Vivian ordered her son.

When two youngish-looking girls appeared at the back of the club, Queenie sat open-mouthed as her son dashed towards them with Ahmed in tow. 'Well, I never,' she muttered.

Michael Butler sat on the edge of his wife's sun-lounger and smiled as he watched Lee splashing about in the paddling pool with his two half-brothers. 'Seems to have settled in well, doesn't he?' Michael remarked, as he cracked open a can of cold lager. He really wished he didn't have to go to work tonight, but with Vinny away, he couldn't leave Dean to run the joint on his own. It wasn't fair.

Realizing her daughter wasn't going to answer Michael's question, Mary did so instead. 'Yes, he has. Poor little mite. Thank God he has you, Michael. How did you tell him the news? Did he understand?'

'Not really. I just said that his mum and nan had gone to live in heaven, but I would take good care of him from

429

now on. He did ask if his mum and nan would still be able to see him, and I told him if he looked at the sky of a night, two of the stars shining down would be them watching him. I didn't really know what else to say.'

'Aw, that was a lovely thing to say, Michael, wasn't it, Nancy?'

'Did you find out if Denise's bloke was drunk?' Nancy asked, in a none-too-sympathetic tone. It had been Denise's boyfriend, Glen, driving the car when the accident had occurred.

'He wasn't drunk. It was the guy in the other car who was pissed out of his brains by all accounts. A witness came forward. Said they had seen the driver of the Ford Capri weaving all over the road a few minutes beforehand, and had had to swerve to avoid being hit themselves. Denise and her mum were just in the wrong place at the wrong time. A fucking tragedy, especially for Lee. I've spoken to the funeral directors and I'm gonna pay for their funerals. I want Lee to have nice graves to visit with proper head-stones where he can remember his mum and nan. That will comfort him, especially as he gets older.'

When Lee and Daniel ran over to Michael together, and it was Lee who her husband picked up and swung in the air above his head, Nancy couldn't watch any more. Not only were they footing the bill for the funerals, the child was obviously now more important in Michael's eyes than the two sons that she had given birth to.

'Where you going, love?' Mary asked her daughter.

'Upstairs for a lie-down. I don't feel too well. I think it's the heat.'

In a pub called the Beach Tavern, Vinny and Ahmed had just had a bite to eat and a few bevvies with Joanna and Chloe.

Vinny turned to Joanna. 'That food was smashing, but I feel bloated now. How about me and you take a little stroll? I'd like to spend a bit of time alone with you.'

Vinny's eyes mesmerized Joanna. Ever since he had swiftly left earlier in the week saying he had a family crisis to deal with, Joanna had thought of little else. The only time she could ever remember feeling slightly like that before was with Jamie Draper, her first love, but that was nowhere near as intense as the feeling she secretly harboured for Vinny. 'Yes, I'd like that,' Joanna replied.

'Where're you going?' Chloe asked, when Joanna and Vinny both stood up.

'They go for walk, but you no need worry. I will stay to keep you company, beautiful one,' Ahmed said, laying on the accent and schmooze.

'How long are you going to be?' Chloe asked, directing the question at Vinny.

'An hour, tops. See you in a bit,' Vinny said.

Joanna experienced a massive surge of excitement as she felt Vinny's hand envelop hers. It was a lovely feeling, and one she had never ever encountered before.

Queenie and Vivian were keenly waiting for the bingo to start. Both women loved a game, but rarely ever ventured to their local bingo hall any more. It was full of nosy old bats that always wanted to ask questions about family members. Vivian smiled at her son. She still didn't feel quite the same about him since she had caught him masturbating, but knew for the sake of their relationship, she must try to put the awful experience behind her. 'You all right, boy? You seem a bit quiet tonight.'

'I wanted to go out with Vinny and Ahmed, Mum. I don't know how to play bingo. It's a woman's game and I feel like a wally.'

Vivian suddenly felt a bit guilty. She did baby him a bit. 'How about you go up the bar and get yourself a pint of lager? You can get me and your Auntie Queenie another drink while you're up there as well.'

Lenny grinned. 'I don't need your money, Mum. I earn my own. Men buy women drinks.'

Watching her son walk up the bar, Vivian turned to Queenie. 'I still can't believe that Denise and Madge are dead, can you? Don't get me wrong, I never liked Madge, but I wouldn't wish death on the woman. What a tragic way to go, eh?'

'Yep, bloody awful. Now pick your pen up, the bingo is about to start.'

In a nearby chalet, Joanna Preston was all of a fluster. Vinny had kissed her earlier as they had returned to the pub, and even though it wasn't a proper tongue-in-mouth kiss, it had been on the lips, and had sent her in a bit of a manic state. 'What do you think then, Chloe? Shall I wear this? Or do you think the red dress looked better?'

Chloe sighed. Joanna had already tried on six different outfits, and was beginning to get on her nerves. 'Look, Jo, I'm not trying to burst your bubble here, but don't you think that we should be a bit cautious with Vinny and Ahmed? We don't even really know them, and I can just tell by the way you are acting that you have got it bad.'

'No, I haven't,' Joanna replied.

'Yes, you have! In all the years I've known you, I can't remember you ever being like this over any boy or man.'

'Well, so what if I like him? I thought you liked Ahmed as well?'

'Yeah, I do, but not in the way you seem to like Vinny. Look, it is nice to go out with blokes who want to wine and dine us for a change, but we shouldn't be reading too much into this, Jo. Let's just have a laugh with them.'

Joanna sat down on the bed next to Chloe and squeezed her hand. 'Look, I know you are worried about me, but there really is no need. I know my own mind, mate, and I'm far from bloody stupid.'

When Michael went to work, Mary Walker bathed her grandsons and Lee then, once they were all tucked up in bed, decided to have a heart-to-heart with her daughter. 'I'm gonna have one of them nice cold lagers that Michael put in the fridge earlier. Do you want another glass of wine, love?'

'Yes please.'

'I phoned your dad today just to check everything was OK at the café. He asked when I was coming home, and I told him I wouldn't be back for a while. I told him you weren't very well and you needed me here. He was quite polite and even asked what was wrong with you. Perhaps he is starting to mellow a bit, eh? Leaving him always seems to knock some sense into him. I reckon he will want to build bridges with you, and have a relationship with the boys before too long, you know.'

'Well, I don't want to build bridges with him, thank you. Not after he crossed the road to avoid my sons. Dad's a fucking arsehole and so is Christopher. I wonder if Chris has told his superiors in the police force that he once witnessed a murder and lied at the identification parade to protect Vinny, eh? I bet that would go down a storm with his boss.'

Shocked by the bitterness in her daughter's voice, Mary glared at her. 'What are you raking up the past for? And don't ever mention that story to anybody, for goodness' sake. Nobody has spoken about it for years, and Christopher was only a kid at the time so has probably forgotten all about it now.'

'I very much doubt it, Mum. Witnessing a murder then lying to the police is hardly something that is going to be erased from the memory, is it? Christopher just wants to forget about it, like he has managed to forget about me and my sons. Sanctimonious little shit, he is.'

As Nancy gulped down her wine, Mary stared at her daughter. She was usually such a sweet, mild-mannered girl and it was obvious something was very wrong with her. 'I think you should book an appointment at the doctor's, love. I'll come with you to see him.'

'What for?'

'Because you're not yourself, Nance. You sound depressed and bitter and that is so not like you. Perhaps he can give you some tablets, or a tonic or something.'

Nancy's reply was full of venom. 'Well, unless they have designed a pill to make you like and want to bring up another woman's son, then it's a waste of time.'

Vinny stopped his car in a secluded spot, turned off the ignition, and grinned at Joanna. 'Alone at last, eh? Shall we sit in the back, babe? It's much more roomy for us to drink our bottle of bubbly.'

Joanna's heart was beating ten to the dozen as she firstly nodded, then got into the back of the car.

Vinny popped open the bottle of champagne outside the car, then got in the back too. 'Ladies first,' he said, handing Joanna the bottle. They had gone to a nightclub earlier in Eastbourne town centre but it had been absolute rubbish, which is why Vinny had suggested Ahmed and Chloe go for a drive alone, and he and Joanna do the same. 'I can't believe how different the clubs, people, and fashion are in London to round here. The women who drink in my club wouldn't dream of wearing any of those terrible outfits those birds had on tonight. You was the only one in that place who looked sensational, babe.'

Glad it was dark so Vinny wouldn't be able to see her blush, Joanna took a large gulp of champagne just to calm her nerves. 'What do you mean, your club?' she asked.

'I own a nightclub in the East End of London.'

'Wow! You never said that before,' Joanna replied. Her heart was beating even faster now. Not only was Vinny tall, dark, handsome, and the perfect gentleman, he also owned a bloody nightclub.

'I didn't want to tell you until I was sure of you. The amount of birds that throw themselves at me just because they know what I own, you would not believe.'

'That's terrible, Vinny. Some people can be so shallow. There was a girl in my school like that. She went out with this lad who was a really good footballer for years, then when he didn't make the grade at Ipswich Town, she dumped him.'

'So, what you gonna do when Kings shuts down for the winter?' Vinny asked.

'Well, I'm coming back here next year with Chloe. We've already been offered jobs as barmaids because we'll both be old enough then. I'm not too sure what I'll do in the winter. Tiptree is just so bloody boring compared to Kings, but I will have to find a job of some kind there. I've got used to earning my own money now.'

Vinny squeezed Joanna's hand. 'Why don't you come and work at my club with me? You'll love it. It won't be boring like Tiptree, I can assure you of that.'

'Really?' Joanna asked, gobsmacked.

Vinny smiled. 'Yeah, really. I dunno if you have noticed, but I do like you a lot, babe.'

Joanna Preston could not believe her luck. Vinny was

435

like the dream man that you read about in one of those corny books. 'I like you a lot too, and I would love to come and work at your club, Vinny.'

When Vinny kissed her properly for the very first time, Joanna felt as if she had died and gone to heaven. Unlike the boys she had been out with in the past, who stuck their tongues straight down the back of her throat, Vinny kissed her lips sensually and teased her mouth by just flicking his tongue inside every now and again. It was the most sexual, amazing feeling that Joanna had ever experienced, and when Vinny put his hand up her dress and inside her knickers, she groaned with ecstasy as his finger made contact with her clitoris.

Vinny took his mouth away from Joanna's. He hated kissing, it made him want to vomit. That's why he had rarely slept with any birds other than prostitutes. 'Oh Jesus, babe. You are just so fucking gorgeous,' he panted, as he undid the zip of his trousers and expertly shoved his rock-hard penis inside Joanna.

What followed was the quickest yet most pleasurable bunk-up that Vinny had ever experienced in his entire life. Johnny Preston was at the forefront of his mind as he shot his load inside Joanna. Retribution was such a wonderful feeling.

CHAPTER THIRTY-EIGHT

Six weeks to the day since Joanna and Vinny first made love, Joanna's mum turned up at Kings for an unexpected visit with her pal, Sandy.

'Oh my God! What are you doing here?' Joanna asked, when she opened the door of the chalet.

'Well, that's a nice welcome. We're on holiday. Aren't you pleased to see me?' Deborah asked her daughter.

'Yeah, it's just a bit of a shock, that's all,' Joanna replied, glancing at her watch. Vinny was due to pick her up in half an hour to take her out to lunch, so what the hell was she meant to do now?

'Aren't you going to invite us in then?' Deborah asked, rather put out. She wasn't silly. She knew her daughter had met someone special, and it was Johnny who had insisted she turned up in Eastbourne unexpectedly to find out who the mystery lad was.

It was very unlike Joanna to keep a relationship secret. Even when she was at school, she had always been extremely open about any boys she liked or dated. It was Johnny's idea that Sandy accompany Deborah to Eastbourne. He said it was best to make the trip look like a holiday, rather than Deborah turn up there alone.

'Mum, the chalet is a tip, and all the girls are here. Go over to the clubhouse and I'll meet you there in a bit. I won't be long,' Joanna said, shutting the door.

Deborah trudged dejectedly towards the club in an even more worried state than when she had driven down. She and Johnny were getting on like a house on fire just lately, and Johnny was even making noises about them getting back together. Deborah didn't know if that was just prison talk, but what she did know was that Johnny was her first love, she still adored him, and probably always would. 'I told you Joanna was up to no good, didn't I, Sandy? Virtually slammed the door in our faces. I am so glad that we booked a week here so we can find out exactly what she is up to.'

Sandy linked arms with her friend. They had been best mates and neighbours ever since Deborah had first moved to Tiptree. 'I agree, Jo is acting very shady. She looked horrified when she opened that chalet door and saw us standing there. But, don't you worry because I was born a detective, me. We've got a week to find out what she is up to, and you can bet your bottom dollar I will suss out who her mystery man is. Now, let's have half a cider and forget about our woes for today. We are on a pretend holiday too, remember?'

Michael Butler cracked open a beer and smiled as he watched his three sons happily playing football together. Even though it was now September, the weather was still warm, and 1976 had now been officially announced as the hottest summer since records began.

'Dad, can I have an ice cream, please?' Lee asked, flopping down on the grass next to his father.

'You can later, but you've got to eat your lunch first, boy. You need goodness inside you if you wanna be a big strong man one day,' Michael replied, ruffling the boy's hair.

Considering the traumatic change in Lee's life, he had

adapted exceptionally well to his new surroundings. Daniel and Adam both adored him, and vice versa. They really were one big happy family, bar Nancy, who just lately barely spoke.

'Why didn't Mum come to the park with us, Dad?' Daniel asked innocently.

'Because your mum needed to do the housework, Son,' Michael lied. The truth was, Nancy seemed to be becoming more mentally deranged by the day. She had never been much of a drinker in the past, but now preferred wine to food. She also had trantrums for no particular reason, spent hours in bed, and refused to participate in family days out of any kind.

Michael was at his wits' end as to what to do to help his wife. She refused to book an appointment with the doctor, and had another tantrum every time he suggested she do so. He had thought that Lee starting school a fortnight ago might have improved Nancy's behaviour, but it hadn't. She seemed so unstable right now that Michael dreaded leaving the boys with her when he went to work, but what else could he do? He had a club to run, needed to earn a living, and with Vinny gallivanting down to Eastbourne every chance he got, there was no way Michael could shirk his duties. Dean was a good lad, but wasn't capable of keeping a steady ship without his help.

'Dad, am I going to see my mum and nan again today?' Lee asked.

Last week the headstones had been put in place on Denise and her mother's graves, which were side by side. Michael had taken Lee there and armed with a bunch of flowers, his son had sat happily in between the graves, and told his mum and nan all about his new school, and his form teacher, Mrs Brown. 'Not today, boy, but we can go there in the morning, if you want?'

'Can I come too?' Daniel asked.

Lee held Daniel's hand. 'Yeah. Course you can come. You're my bruvver.'

Having enjoyed a ploughman's lunch in the Moorings pub, Vinny and Joanna took a stroll along the beach hand in hand. They had spent a lot of time together in the past six weeks, and Joanna especially enjoyed the times when Vinny drove down to Eastbourne on a weekday on his own. She then got to have a romantic evening in his bungalow with him. Ahmed and Chloe's relationship hadn't worked out. A fumble was as far as they had got in the end, which had resulted in Chloe giving Ahmed a wank, then announcing she was no longer interested in him because she didn't like the way he kissed and found him a bit creepy.

'You all right, babe?' Vinny asked.

'No, not really. I shouldn't have stormed out the club earlier and been so rude to my mum and Sandy. I feel really guilty now, but I was just sick of my mum interrogating me. Do you think Chloe might have rung my mum and tipped her off about us? I can tell Chloe hates me spending lots of time with you. It's obvious she is jealous, if you ask me.'

Vinny sat down on the sand and urged Joanna to do the same. He knew she had now fallen for him hook, line, and sinker and was positive if she was forced to choose between him and her parents, he would win. 'Look, babe, I think you need to tell your mum about us a.s.a.p. You're coming to work at my club next month and you haven't even told your family I exist yet. You're a big girl now, Jo, you're not a little kid any more. I'm beginning to think you're ashamed of me or something.'

Joanna squeezed her boyfriend's hand. 'Don't be daft! I could never be ashamed of you. The only reason I haven't said anything to my mum is because of your age. You are only two years younger than her, Vinny, and if my dad finds out, he will go absolutely ballistic.'

'But, I thought you said your mum and dad were divorced?' Vinny said. Joanna still hadn't told him that her father was banged-up. In fact, she rarely mentioned him at all. She hadn't even told him that her dad's name was Johnny.

'My mum and dad are divorced, but I think they might be getting back together. It's a long story, and I will tell you about it one day.'

Vinny turned his back on Joanna so she couldn't see him smirk. He knew more about her shitcunt of a father than she seemed to. Joanna had asked him his surname weeks ago, and hadn't flinched at all when he had told her it was Butler, so it was obvious she knew very little about her dad's trial or past.

'Are you OK?' Joanna asked anxiously.

Vinny sighed. Wooing Joanna was becoming a bit tedious now. The sex between them had been mind-blowing at first, but Vinny knew that had only been because of his lust for revenge. Now he had Joanna firmly in his clutches, he was getting bored with her, so the quicker her father found out about their relationship and the shit hit the fan, the better. Deciding to give Joanna an ultimatum, Vinny propped himself on his elbow and turned to face her. 'I'm gonna book a table at a restaurant tonight and I want you to invite your mum and Sandy. I'll explain the situation to your mum, and I'm sure once she meets me she'll be fine about the age gap.'

'Noooo! I can't just drop a bombshell on her like that, Vinny. I'll tell her myself soon, I promise. Where you going?' Joanna asked, as Vinny stood up and started to walk away from her.

'Back to Kings. I've had enough of this, Jo. Treated you like a princess I have, yet still I'm deemed not good enough to be in the company of your mother. Perhaps you are right about the age gap between us being too wide. I can't be doing with immaturity. I'm too long in the tooth for it.'

Petrified that the man of her dreams was going to dump her, Joanna burst into tears and grabbed Vinny's arm. 'OK, book the restaurant then. I'm sorry. I want my mum to know about us, honest I do. Please don't say the age gap is too big, because it isn't. I think the world of you, you know I do.'

Vinny turned around and held his distraught young girlfriend in his arms. She was a begging wreck and he quite liked that. 'I'll book a table for eight o'clock at that restaurant in the town centre. Give your mum the address and tell her we'll meet her there. Me and you can have a drink in town first to calm your nerves a bit. Don't tell her you are meeting your boyfriend though, I'll do all the talking, OK?'

Relieved that Vinny had given her a second chance, Joanna nodded. 'I will just tell mum that I'm bringing a friend and I'll leave the rest to you. Tough shit if she thinks you're too old for me. It's my life and I know my own mind.'

'That's my girl,' Vinny said lovingly. He then ordered Joanna to wait inside the car while he ran inside the pub to make a quick phone call.

Even though Ahmed owned a house where his wife and kids lived, he also had what he referred to as his bachelor pad, and Vinny guessed that was where his pal would probably be after a late night. 'Vinny! My prick is still very sore from our session, and I woke up with a bad hangover. How are you, my friend? Did you make it to Eastbourne OK?'

Vinny chuckled. He and Ahmed had sort of had a foursome for the very first time, and even though there hadn't been any form of sexual contact between the two men, both had got off on watching the other abuse and shag two prostitutes. 'Yep. Made it to Eastbourne OK, and my cock's still a bit sore an' all. Listen, I can't stay on the phone long because Joanna is outside in the car, but her mother has turned up out the blue with her mate this morning. I've arranged to take them all out for a meal tonight, and I can't wait to see Mummy's face when she finds out who her darling daughter is being shafted by.'

'Do you reckon she will tell Johnny immediately?'

'Well, Jo reckons they are now on really good terms, so I should imagine so.'

Ahmed started to laugh. 'I wish I were a fly on the restaurant wall.'

Vinny grinned. 'Let the fun begin, eh?'

Nancy Butler stretched out on her sun-lounger, then nigh-on jumped out of her skin as she heard the doorbell ring. Michael had gone to visit his dad down in Ipswich, and she always made him take the boys with him now. They hadn't been told that Albie was their granddad, as Michael was afraid of his sons telling the rest of the family he was in contact with his father.

Nancy felt anxious when she tiptoed into the hallway. Her mum had moved back home a couple of weeks ago, and even though she was due to pop around later, she had her own key. 'Who is it?' Nancy asked, cautiously.

'It's me, Dean.'

If it had been anybody else knocking at the door, Nancy probably would have made an excuse not to let them in. However, she liked Dean. He was a nice lad, and she could always sense his discomfort at family gatherings, and knew he could sense hers too. 'What're you doing here? Michael's not in,' she said, as she opened the door.

'It's not Michael I've come to see. It's you, Nance. I heard through the grapevine that you've been feeling a bit low, and seeing as I've been feeling exactly the same, I thought a good chat might do the pair of us good. I bought you these to cheer you up,' Dean said, handing Nancy a big box of Milk Tray.

'Aw, thanks. Come in then. Do you fancy a glass of wine? I was just about to pour one for myself.'

Dean grinned. 'Yes please. I'd love one.'

Albie Butler had adored every second of all three previous visits he had spent with his grandsons and today was no different. Obviously, the only downside was he could not tell the boys he was their granddad, but he still enjoyed spoiling them nevertheless.

'So, have the boys mentioned me in front of the family yet? You know how suspicious Vinny and your mother can be,' Albie said.

'I've got it covered, Dad. The boys think you're Nancy's uncle. Anyway, I've not seen much of the family since Vinny bought that place in Eastbourne. Mum and Auntie Viv haven't even come home at all for the past week or so.'

Ablie took a gulp of his pint of bitter. 'How is Roy? Have you visited him lately?'

'No, I haven't had a chance, Dad. Nancy isn't right still, and what with running the club, I've had a lot on my plate. Mum has been visiting him regularly.'

'Did you ever give him that letter I wrote him, son?' Albie asked.

'No. The time has never seemed right, Dad. As much as I will always love Roy, he is a hard fucker to visit. He is just permanently miserable, and nothing I say can cheer him up. I'm quite relieved he has moved to Eastbourne actually. I found going to see him too upsetting. He is nothing like the old Roy.'

Albie waved at his grandsons who were playing happily together on the slide, and then grasped his youngest son's hand. 'Your brother needs you, Michael, especially if he is unhappy. I want you to go and visit him and read or give him my letter. Will you do that for me?'

About to make an excuse, Michael clocked the anxiety in his father's eyes, and found himself agreeing to the task. 'OK. I'll drive down to Eastbourne on Monday.'

Nancy Butler had a smile on her face for the first time in ages. Not only was a day without the kids heaven in itself, Dean Smart was ever so comical and she had thoroughly enjoyed his company. Both had spoken about the problems in their lives and marriages, and Nancy had found it extremely theraputic to be able to chat to someone that, like her, had married into the clan, but wasn't a Butler by blood.

'I'd best be getting going. I left Tara with my nan. She wanted to spend some time with Tara before she goes in for her operation next week.'

'What is actually wrong with your nan, Dean?'

'She has stomach cancer. I've been so worried about her. She's lost tons of weight.'

A bit merry from the amount of wine they had drunk, Nancy felt quite comfortable throwing her arms around Dean's neck to give him a big hug. That was soon torn away when Dean suddenly locked lips with hers. 'What're you doing? I'm Michael's wife and you're Brenda's husband,' she reminded Dean, pushing him away.

Mortified that he had got the wrong end of the stick, Dean stood up. 'I'm so sorry, Nance. I've liked you for ages, you must have known that?'

The knock on the door saved Nancy from any more embarrassment. 'Hello, Mum. Dean's here, but he's just about to leave,' she said bluntly.

445

'Hello, Dean. How are you? Are Brenda and Tara keeping well?' Mary asked.

'Brenda and Tara are fine, thanks, Mrs Walker.'

'Go in the lounge, Mum,' Nancy ordered, pushing Dean towards the front door.

'You won't say anything to Michael, will you?' Dean asked, sounding as anxious as he felt.

'No. Michael would kill you. Now, just go, and don't come round here any more.'

'I am really sorry, Nance,' Dean whispered, before running down the path.

Nancy slammed the front door, and leant against it. For a split second, she had very nearly responded to Dean's kiss, and was so thankful she hadn't. Whatever had she been thinking?

After visiting Roy, Queenie and Vivian headed back to Kings and were currently sitting outside the bungalow sipping a cold lager each.

Vivian nudged her sister. 'Look, the notrights have just pulled up.'

The people who owned the bungalow next door but one were an odd couple to say the least. 'Look at them fucking sandals and long socks he's got on. What does he look like?' Queenie mumbled.

'Looks like silly-boy-got-none. I'm sure he's a fucking pervert. He's got them tight swimming trunks on again,' Vivian replied.

'She's scoffing a bag of chips again, an' all. No wonder she's so fucking fat. I've only ever seen her get out of that car once when she hasn't been stuffing her big moon face,' Queenie added.

'Oh Christ. They're waving now. Quick, let's go inside and pretend we ain't seen 'em. I'm sure he gets a thrill out of standing in front of us with his cockalockie on show,' Vivian said, grabbing her sister's arm.

Giggling like two naughty school girls, Queenie and Vivian darted inside their bungalow, and quickly locked the front door.

Vinny could feel pure adrenaline running through his veins as he sat down in the restaurant next to Joanna. He had purposely got there a bit early, and he could barely wait for the fun to begin. 'You OK, darling?'

'Not really. My stomach is churning. Shall we pretend you're a bit younger? How about if you say you're twenty-eight?'

'No, we can't lie. Honesty is the best policy in life, always remember that, Jo. Anyway, if we're gonna have a future together, then lying to your mum is a definite no-go.'

'So, will I be living at the club with you when I move down to London?' Joanna asked, absolutely thrilled that Vinny had mentioned them having a future together.

'I don't want you living at the club, babe. It's no place for a stunning chick like you. I was thinking of pushing the boat out and buying us a trendy house nearby. That way, Little Vinny can move in with us, and you can take care of him while I go to work in the evenings.'

'But I thought I was going to be working at the club with you?' Joanna asked, clearly dismayed. She hadn't spent much time with Little Vinny, and certainly wasn't ready to become his full-time guardian yet.

'You will be working at the club with me, but in the daytime. I want you to be my personal secretary. Gotta have someone I can trust, and who better to hand such a pres-tigious position to than my girlfriend, eh?' Vinny said, planting a gentle kiss on Joanna's lips.

'Oh my God! My mum's just walked in. I hope she didn't see us kissing,' Joanna gabbled seconds later.

Seeing the look of shock appear on the faces of Joanna's mum and her friend, Vinny stood up. 'Hello. I'm Joanna's boyfriend. It's a pleasure to finally meet you. Joanna has told me lots about you, all good may I add. Now, what would you two beautiful ladies like to drink? They do a good selection of wines here. Shall I order us a bottle of red and white?'

'Yes, that would be nice, wouldn't it, Deborah?' Sandy replied, nudging her pal. Vinny looked about the same age as them. He had a dark suit on, was very handsome, and reminded Sandy of something out of the movies.

Deborah glared at her daughter as she sat down opposite her. The boyfriend had a London accent and was dressed and looked like a bloody gangster. 'Kept this a bit quiet, didn't you, dear?'

Vinny put an arm around Joanna's shoulders. He was enjoying himself now. 'We wanted to make sure that our relationship was going to work before we made a big song and dance about it. We are now completely sure that it will, so we thought the time was right to tell you. Joanna is moving to London next month. We are going to live together, and she will also be working as my secretary. I can assure you I will look after your lovely young daughter, Mrs Preston, and you are welcome to visit us whenever you wish.'

Deborah gulped back the glass of wine she had just been poured as though it were water. 'I think you should slow down a bit, mate. My daughter is seventeen years old, and if you think I'm letting her go off gallivanting around London with some shady-looking stranger who looks double her age, you can bloody well think again.'

'Mum, don't be so rude. I am old enough to do exactly what I like, and there is nothing you can do to stop me.'

'We'll see about that, young lady. I'm sure your father

will have something to say about this. He isn't going to be very happy, I can assure you of that.'

''Ere you go, mate. Have another drink,' Sandy said, topping Deborah's glass again. She wasn't family, so felt a bit awkward and unable to comment on her friend's obvious distress.

'I'm sure once your husband learns of my assets he will be more than happy for me to take care of your daughter,' Vinny said, with a hint of playful sarcasm in his voice.

'I couldn't care less if you own the crown jewels, mate. How old are you? And what exactly do you do for a living? You haven't even told us your bloody name yet,' Deborah replied, treating Vinny to an evil stare.

Vinny grinned. He had been waiting weeks for this precise moment and wanted to savour every second of it. 'I am thirty-one years old, and I own a very popular nightclub in Whitechapel. Oh, and my name is Vinny. Vinny Butler.'

As the realization of who Joanna's new boyfriend was hit home, Deborah opened her mouth wide, but no words would come out. She suddenly felt sick, dizzy, and the restaurant seemed to be spinning around before her very eyes.

Aware that her mother had gone a deathly shade of white, Joanna clasped her hand. 'What's the matter? Are you OK, Mum?'

Deborah was anything but OK. Her body went limp, as the shock made her lose consciousness and she hit the floor with a thud.

'Oh my God! Mum, are you OK? Do something, Vinny,' Joanna cried out.

'Do you want me to call you an ambulance?' asked one of the waiters.

'No. It's OK, mate. She's fine now,' Vinny said, when he saw Deborah's eyes flicker open.

With Sandy's help, Deborah sat up, and the waiter held a glass of water to her lips.

'What happened, Mum? Have you been ill?' Joanna asked, clutching her mother's hand.

Deborah snatched her hand away, and scowled at Joanna. 'You stupid, stupid girl. He doesn't love you. He's just using you as bait to get back at your father.'

Joanna looked at Vinny, her face a picture of confusion. 'Why is Mum saying that, Vinny? You don't know my dad, do you?'

'Of course he knows your father, you naïve fool. And I thought I'd raised you to be intelligent,' Deborah hissed, as the waiter helped her onto a chair.

'How would I know who your dad is? You have never even told me his name,' Vinny said, holding his arms outwards to signal his innocence.

'My dad's name is Johnny Preston. He comes from London originally. Well, do you know him?'

Clocking the contorted look of anger on Deborah's face, Vinny wanted to laugh out loud. Instead though, he feigned surprise. 'I can't believe it, Jo. Yeah, I do know your dad and we're hardly what you can call the best of friends. I swear on my own father's life that I didn't know who your father was though. You'd barely even mentioned him. It's just pure coincidence. What a small world we live in, eh?'

'You lying no-good cunt,' Deborah screamed.

Feeling embarrassed because every other diner in the restaurant was now looking their way, Joanna begged her mother to calm down.

'Calm down! You want me to calm down? You are sleeping with the man who put your father in prison, you daft little mare.'

'Come on, babe. Let's go. I'm not having you spoken to

like this. You don't deserve it,' Vinny said, grabbing Joanna's arm.

'If you choose that lowlife over me and your father, I will never forgive you, Jo,' Deborah spat.

Vinny leant towards his girlfriend and spoke softly in her ear. 'Please, Jo, let's get out of here. Everybody is staring at us and it's a proper show-up. You can talk to your mum in a few days when she's got over the shock. She'll be calmer then. It's pointless trying to have a sensible conversation with her while she's ranting and raving.'

Frightened if she didn't do as Vinny said he might finish with her, Joanna turned to her mother. 'I have to go now, Mum, but I promise we'll speak again soon.'

CHAPTER THIRTY-NINE

Donald and Christopher Walker were on their way to the pub for a pint when they heard a lady scream and a commotion going on over the other side of the road.

'It's a robbery. He's got a gun,' somebody yelled.

Even though he was off-duty, instinct kicked in and Christopher ran across the road to try to foil what seemed to be a raid on a betting shop.

Fearing for his son's safety, Donald dashed across the road as well. 'No, Chris! Be careful,' he shouted, as he saw his brave son tackle the man brandishing the gun. The gun flew out of the man's hand along with a cloth bag stuffed with money and Christopher looked to have saved the day until the man's accomplice leapt off a motorbike waving a large knife.

'Oh my God! Call an ambulance. My son's been stabbed,' Donald screamed, as the men made their getaway.

Within minutes, both police and ambulance services had arrived. Christopher had been stabbed in the thigh, but was conscious and seemed jovial enough. As he was lifted into the ambulance on a stretcher, a big cheer and much clapping surrounded his departure. The robbers might have got away, but Christopher's bravery had meant that they had left the scene without their ill-gotten gains and minus their gun.

Donald squeezed his son's hand as he sat beside him in the ambulance. He had tears of pride in his eyes. Unlike his daughter who had turned out to be a massive disappointment, Christopher was not only a son to be proud of, but also a bloody hero.

Dean Smart's head was all over the place. He knew that Nancy had been tempted to respond to his kiss before she had frantically pushed him away and he couldn't stop thinking about her. His nan was due to go into hospital today, and he was worried about that also. He was petrified her heart might not withstand the operation.

'So, where was you the other day then, Dean? I thought you couldn't wait to get rid of me. Have other plans, did you?' Brenda asked, marching into the room holding Tara's hand.

'What you on about now?'

'Tell Daddy what you just told me, love,' Brenda urged her daughter.

'I said that I stayed with Nanny Freda and you went out with a friend,' Tara mumbled. She knew she had said or done something wrong, but didn't know what.

'So? What, is that a crime then, is it?' Dean asked, glaring at his miserable-looking wife. She had obviously been interrogating their daughter as per usual. The woman was a psycho.

'Of course it ain't a fucking crime, but why keep it secret, eh? I know you, Dean Smart, you're hiding something from me. Out with one of your fancy women, was you? I might ring Michael and see where Nancy was that day.'

'You're mental, you are, Bren, and I really have had a gutful of it. I did tell you where I'd been when you came in Saturday night, and I told you that Tara had spent a few hours with my nan, but you were that pissed out your brains yet again, you obviously don't remember.'

'Liar,' Brenda shrieked, picking up the plant pot and throwing it at her husband. She could recall the conversation she'd had with Dean, and not once had Dean mentioned dumping Tara at his nan's house while he went out gallivanting alone.

'You're hurt, Daddy,' Tara screamed, as Dean crouched down clutching his bleeding head.

'It's OK, darling. Daddy's OK,' Dean said, feeling a bit dazed.

Aware that her husband's hands were covered in blood, Brenda began to worry that she had crossed the line. 'I'm sorry, Dean. I didn't mean to hurt you.'

Dean stood up, pushed past his wife and stomped up the stairs.

'Where you going?' Brenda yelled, when minutes later Dean came down with a big sports bag in his hand.

'I'm going to stay at me nan's house while she's in hospital. She's worried about her cats. It'll do us good to have a break anyway. Oh, and for your information, I had a drink with my cousin Del the other day. Ring him if you don't believe me,' Dean said. He had already rung Del to cover his back if need be.

'You're not leaving us, are you, Daddy?' Tara sobbed, clinging to her father's legs.

'No, darling,' Dean lied. As soon as Vinny returned from Eastbourne, Dean had decided to have a man-to-man chat with him. He was going to explain in detail just how unbearable life was with Brenda. Along with Micheal, Dean was virtually running the club now, so Vinny needed him on side, and as long as he got the OK from Brenda's big brother, Dean planned to leave his bitch of a wife for good.

Overcome by worry, Deborah Preston had rung Wormwood Scrubs and booked an emergency visit to see Johnny. The prison was quite strict about hastily arranged visits, but when Deborah had explained that there was a terrible family crisis and she needed to break the news to her ex-husband gently and in person, she had thankfully been granted permission to visit Johnny at short notice.

Deborah could not get her daughter's welfare out of her mind. Her Johnny might have been a bit of a villian and done some stupid things in his time, but he had a kind face and a good heart deep down. Vinny was a different breed, Deborah knew that. He had been smirking at her as she was helped back onto her chair by Sandy, and Deborah would never forget the pure look of evil in his eyes.

'Are you ready to make a move, mate?' Sandy asked, putting the last of her things in her case.

'Yeah, I'm ready. You can change your mind and stay here, you know. I don't mind, honest.'

'Nope. I'm coming with ya. Birds of feather stick together, mate. Do you wanna take another mooch over to Jo's chalet and see if she's back yet? I mean, surely she can't have gone to London for long if she wants to keep her job here?'

'No point going looking for her again. That wolf in sheep's clothing will make damn sure Jo doesn't return to Eastbourne until we're well out the picture. Why do you think he dragged her off to London the following day? Because he don't want the whole fucking truth coming out, that's why. Oh well, Chloe has promised me she will make sure Joanna reads my letter. Chloe hates the bastard too. She reckons Jo is like a different girl since Vinny's been on the scene. I mean, he must have a real sick mind, Sandy. What sort of grown man preys on a seventeen-year-old slip of a girl just to get revenge for something her father did? The thought of that bastard mauling my baby makes me want to vomit.'

'Try not to think about that side of it, Deb. Let's just hope when Jo reads that letter and knows the full story she will see Vinny in a different light. I mean, you only told me everything yesterday, and I was shocked to the core. Surely your Jo will feel the same as I did, eh?'

'I hope so. If not, Johnny will have to sort it. He knew a lot of heavy people back in the day, so I'm sure one of his old pals can step in and help him out in his hour of need. I just hope he can handle the news being in prison. I hope it doesn't fuck his head up completely.'

Sandy gave her friend a comforting hug. 'Everything will turn out just fine, mate. I know it will.'

With Nancy refusing to look after the kids yet again, claiming she had another migraine, Michael had no option other than to ask his pal Kevin to accompany him to Eastbourne. He needed someone to keep an eye on and entertain the boys. Kevin was now a married man himself with a two-year-old son.

Michael couldn't help but chuckle at the way his pal's life had turned out. When Kev was young he used to take the piss out of his mixed-race roots by putting on a fake Jamaican accent, yet he had now ended up marrying a Jamaican girl and made his living out of selling black music to black people.

The journey to Eastbourne went quickly as Michael and Kevin chatted about old times. 'Right, this is the care home. My mum said the beach is literally five minutes from here, so you take the kids there, and I'll come and find yous when I'm done. Wish me luck. I think I'm gonna need it.'

Roy was sitting in his bedroom staring out of the window when he heard a knock on his door. 'You have a visitor, Roy,' one of the carers said, in a silly singsong voice.

Wheeling himself over to the door, Roy opened it. His mum had said she was going back to Whitechapel. Little Vinny was due to have the plaster off his arm, and he had already missed the first two weeks of his new term at school. 'I'm not expecting any visitors. Who is it?' Roy asked.

'A man called Michael. He says he's your brother, and it's urgent.'

The word 'urgent' pricked Roy's interest. Perhaps one of the family had died or had an accident. If that was the case, then he hoped that person was Vinny. 'OK. Send Michael in here.'

Michael felt terribly guilty as he walked into Roy's bedroom. It was a cheerful-enough looking room with a nice view, but he immediately clocked that his brother had lost weight, looked slightly unkempt, and dead behind the eyes. 'Hello, bruv. So sorry I haven't got down to Eastbourne before. I've had a lot of problems, as Mum has probably told you.'

About to tell his brother to cut the niceties and get straight to the point, Roy remembered his mum telling him that Denise and her mother had died in a car accident, and Lee was now living with Michael. 'Mum did tell me bits and pieces. How is Lee getting on?'

Michael went on to explain that Lee had settled in well, but that he thought Nancy was on the verge of a nervous breakdown.

'That's a shame. I thought Nancy was a nice girl when

457

I spoke to her. She reminded me of my Colleen in her mannerisms.'

'How do you feel about Colleen getting engaged again?' Michael asked, innocently. He had no idea that his mother hadn't informed Roy that Colleen had a new bloke who had recently proposed to her.

Feeling like his heart was about to break in two, Roy wanted to cry, but instead put on a brace face. His mum obviously hadn't told him the news because she was worried about how it would affect him. 'Colleen deserves to be happy. She's a good woman. Where are the boys today? Is Nancy looking after them?' he asked, desperate to change the subject.

'I should be so lucky. Nancy can't even function, Roy. Lee has started school now, but I kept him off today so he could come to Eastbourne with his brothers. Kev travelled down with me. He's taken the boys to the beach.'

'Can you take me to the beach so I can see them?' Roy asked. He used to gabble his sentences once upon a time, but each now took him many seconds to complete, which still sometimes infuriated him.

'Yeah, course I can,' Michael replied. He was amazed his brother seemed so jovial.

'So, what was the urgent news?' Roy asked.

Michael put his hand in his trouser pocket and handed the letter to his brother.

'Who is it from?'

'It's from Dad, but you musn't tell anyone I gave it to you. Dad gave it to me just after the shooting and I promised him that one day I would give it to you when I felt the time was right. Put it in your drawer and read it later when you are alone, eh?'

'Are you still in touch with Dad then?' Roy asked, after he'd put the letter away.

'It's a long story, Roy. I want you to read that letter tonight, then tomorrow we'll speak on the phone, OK?'

Roy gave his younger brother a half-smile. 'OK.'

Johnny Preston was a bundle of nerves as he was led down the corridor by two screws. He knew something serious was occurring. There was no way Deborah would cut her trip short and request a visit if she didn't have bad news of some kind.

Every scenario of what might have happened flashed through Johnny's brain. Thank God he had only just found out about the visit, because if he'd have known about it yesterday, he'd have gone off his head through worry. 'Ain't you taking me to the normal visiting room?' Johnny asked the screws.

'No. I cleared it with the guvnor that you and your ex-wife could chat in the interview room. It's more private in there.'

Johnny got on well with all of the screws he had dealt with in the Scrubs. He had learned early on that if he respected them, not only was it handy to get a few perks, they seemed to respect him also. His mother used to say to him when he was a child, 'Johnny, always speak and treat other people how you would like to be spoken to and treated yourself.' Johnny had never forgotten that sound piece of advice, and had found it worked especially well in prison. 'Lads, can I ask you a favour? I know you are meant to stand in on this visit, but would you mind awfully if you waited outside? My Deborah has never requested a visit such as this before, so it's obvious something awful has happened. I would just rather be in the room alone with Deb when she tells me, if you know what I mean?'

Gerry, the taller screw, glanced at his colleague for approval, then nodded. Apart from a table and chairs, there was sod all else in the room, so he couldn't see the harm in allowing Johnny some privacy.

As soon as Johnny entered the room and saw the look on Deborah's face, his worst fears were well and truly confirmed. 'Whatever's wrong, babe? Is it Jo?'

Urging her ex-husband to sit down opposite her, Deborah wrapped both her hands around his. 'It's our Jo's new boyfriend. I found out who it is.'

'What is he, black? Indian? Spit it out, woman,' Johnny demanded.

'It's Vinny Butler,' Deborah said, her hands shaking at the thought of Johnny's reaction.

Unable to comprehend what Deborah was trying to tell him, Johnny looked at her as though she were stark raving mad. 'Vinny Butler! What about Vinny Butler?'

'Vinny is Joanna's secret boyfriend. She's moving to London next month to be with him. She's gonna work as his secretary.'

Letting out one almighty roar, Johnny Preston grabbed hold of the table, lifted it up and threw it against the wall so hard, two of the legs fell off of it. Seconds later, the two prison officers barged through the door and wrestled a deranged Johnny to the floor.

Nancy Butler was rocking to and fro in the armchair and crying like a baby. Her mum had just rung her to tell her that her brother had been stabbed by an armed robber, and even though Nancy no longer had any contact with Christopher, the thought of somebody sticking a knife in him had upset her badly.

Nancy thought back to when they were kids. She and Christopher had been so close once upon a time. The short spell they had spent living in Whitechapel particularly sprang to Nancy's mind. Their parents had been so busy trying to make their new business venture work, Nancy had no other option than to hang out with her little brother. Neither of them knew any other children in the area; they had left all their lifelong friends in Stoke Newington.

The thing that stuck in Nancy's mind the most was Christopher's obsession with the posh man with the posh car who owned the club around the corner. Ironically, that had turned out to be Vinny Butler of all people.

Nancy put her head in her hands. Even though her dad was a pompous prick at times and Christopher a little know-it-all shit, Nancy suddenly realized how much she missed having them in her life. She had forsaken her family just to be with Michael, and for the first time ever, she wondered if she had done the right thing. She wasn't a Butler at heart, never would be. She was a Walker.

Roy Butler ripped open the creased envelope, unfolded the letter, and took a deep breath as he started to digest the words.

Dear Roy,

I am writing this letter as you are currently fighting for your life in hospital. Realizing you had been shot broke my bloody heart, and I so wanted to be at your bedside with the rest of the family willing you to pull through. Unfortunately, that wasn't to be. I was forced to leave the area for good, and I had to tell you this, son, as I would hate you to think that I didn't care enough to be with you in your hour of need. Nothing could be further from the truth.

As you well know, I am not a man of many words, Roy, but I just wanted you to know that you are never far from my thoughts and you will always have a special place in my heart.

Love always,
Dad

Roy felt a mixture of emotions as he laid the letter beside him on his bed. Today had been a funny old day. He had thoroughly enjoyed spending time with Michael, even though his heart was broken at the thought of Colleen sharing her bed and life with another man. That hadn't stopped him going to the pub and having a decent bit of grub and a few pints for the first time since he'd been shot though, and he was proud of himself for not letting the news ruin his day. The letter from his dad was a nice surprise. It was lovely to know that his father loved him and hadn't abandoned him, but the part in the letter when his dad had informed him he had been forced to leave the area for good had made Roy really angry. The reason being, he knew his evil fucker of a brother was the only person in the world who could be behind such an act of nastiness.

Roy read his father's letter again, then put it in his bedside drawer. For once he felt quite mellow. The reason being, he just needed to add the last couple of pieces to the jigsaw, then he could do what he had wanted to do for the past five years. As the old saying states, revenge is a dish best served cold, and Roy was planning on serving his up at below zero.

Vinny Butler had just bent over his desk to snort a line of cocaine when his office door burst open and Lenny strolled in. 'What you doing, Vin?' Lenny asked innocently.

'What have I told you about always knocking before you enter, Champ? Made me jump out my fucking skin, you did,' Vinny said angrily.

'Sorry. I forgot. What's that white stuff?'

'Headache tablets I crushed up. I've still got hangover from last night and I can't swallow the bloody things. They're too big and get stuck in my throat,' Vinny lied.

'There's a man on the phone wants to talk to you, Vinny. He says it's urgent.'

'Who is it?' Vinny asked, discreetly putting his bag of gear back in his safe. He now kept his own stash at the club. There was nothing worse than fancying a livener and not being able to have one.

'I don't know, but he said hurry up because he's in prison.'

Vinny dashed out to the bar area. The phone in his office was definitely on the blink as it hadn't bloody rung again. 'Hello,' Vinny said, putting the receiver to his ear.

'It's me. Just thought you'd want to know the shit has hit the fan. He's gone mental apparently. Had to be put in solitary.'

Vinny smirked. 'Did the old woman visit?' he asked. He and Scottish Pat never used names on the phone but both knew who the other was referring to.

'Yeah. About three hours ago.'

'Thanks for keeping me in the loop. I'll get Pete or Paul to visit you with another parcel. Update me if there is any more news, yeah?'

The pips went before Pat had a chance to reply.

'You look happy, my friend. You win the football pools?' Ahmed said, sauntering towards Vinny.

'Ahmed! Can you take me to see Layla again soon?' Lenny asked, running towards the big man and giving him a bear hug.

'I don't see why not, Champ.'

'Come in the office. I have some gossip. No, not you, Champ. I need you to scrub the steps out the front and give the outside of the doors a good wash down. Looked fucking filthy as I came in this morning, they did.'

Ahmed followed his pal. 'So, where is your lovely wife-to-be today?' he joked.

'Ha-ha. Very funny. I gave her two hundred quid to go shopping with and sent her up the West End. Having her stay here with me has been doing my head in, mate. I'm me own man, like to come and go as I please. Feel like I've got an albatross hanging round me neck at the moment.

Anyway, on a brighter note, Scottish Pat has just rung me from the Scrubs. Preston has found out. Gone off his head apparently and has been put in solitary.'

'Do you think he might send someone to the club for revenge? If so, I'll stay here with you.'

'You're having a giraffe, ain't ya? Preston is a mug. He used to hang around the Richardsons and Mad Frankie years ago. He was more of an albatross around their necks than his daughter is round mine. They used to laugh at him behind his back. I ain't worried at all about repercussions. The geezer's a nobody. None of the big guns will help him out. He ain't worth a wank.'

'So, what happens now? You going to dump Joanna?' Ahmed asked.

'Got to see how it pans out first, ain't I? Preston must be stewing sat alone in solitary with images of me sticking my big hard cock up his baby girl. I'm hoping the cunt will top himself. It will save me the task of ending his life for him when he gets out. As for Jo, I shall take her back to Eastbourne tomorrow. I shan't dump her just yet. I want that piece of shit to suffer as much as my mother has watching Roy lose the plot.'

'You still trying to get her pregnant?' Ahmed asked.

'No. I spunked up her at first, but I haven't for the past month or so. No need to be lumbered with her or another kid if there's no point. Let's see what happens with Johnny Boy first. If finding out that I'm shafting his baby girl isn't enough to make him go off his rocker, then I will do whatever it takes to torture him even more. I might even ask the silly tart to marry me. Now, that would rub salt in his wounds, wouldn't it?'

Ahmed chuckled as Vinny laid out two big fat lines of cocaine in front of him. 'You really are an evil man, my friend. That is why I like you.'

Snorting a line, Vinny handed the rolled-up ten-pound note to his pal and grinned. 'Me, evil? Never.'

Michael had only just walked indoors when the phone rang. 'Bruv, it's me. I've read Dad's letter and I would really like to speak to him. I won't tell Mum or anybody else, I promise. Can you bring him to visit me?'

'I can, Roy, but I don't know when that will be. Dad lives miles away now.'

'But I need to speak to him a.s.a.p.,' Roy replied dismally. He had been staring at his gun for the past half an hour, and now he was positive that the time was right to use it, he wanted to tie up the other loose ends in his life as quickly as possible.

'Listen, Roy, I've just this second walked in. Give me a ring back in a bit, and I'll try and get hold of Dad in the meantime. You must swear you will never breathe a word of this to anyone though, OK?'

'You have my word, Michael. I have another couple of important phone calls to make now, so I will call you back in half an hour.'

Roy put down the phone, glanced at the gun and the photo of Vinny, then picked the receiver back up. He knew his brother was in London and at the club as his mum had told him earlier. 'Hello, Vin. It's me, Roy.'

'You OK, bruv? Is something wrong?' Vinny asked. Roy had only ever rung him once since the shooting, and that was to demand he find him somewhere to live by the sea.

'No, nothing's wrong. Michael came to visit me and it got me thinking. I feel happier since I've moved, and I really enjoyed going to the pub today for a few pints and some lunch. I thought perhaps me and you could do the same? Are you busy on Wednesday?'

Vinny smirked. It might have taken many years, but finally

Roy was ready to forgive him. 'Wednesday is perfect, bruv. It's your call, so we'll go anywhere you choose. I would love to show you Kings as well though. The clubhouse is proper. You'll love it there.'

'OK, I'm up for that. Can you get here at midday?'

'I sure can. And thanks for ringing me, Roy. You've not just made my day, you've made my bloody year.'

Roy said goodbye, replaced the receiver, picked up Vinny's photo and chuckled. 'So, you fell for it, you mug. You think you're so clever, bruv, but you'll never be as clever as me.'

Back in Barking, Michael was getting angrier by the second.

'Mummy's in bed. She won't get up,' Daniel said, tugging his father's arm.

Michael ran upstairs. He'd had enough of Nancy's silly behaviour now. There was him running around like a blue-arsed fly taking the kids to school, picking them up, cooking their meals, and running a club, and all his dysfunctional wife could do was drink wine and lie in bed all day. His mother and aunt had both said recently that Nancy needed a good kick up the arse, and instead of pandering to her every whim, it was about time she got one. 'Time to get up, Nance. The boys need some dinner, and seeing as I have to go into work tonight, I think it's time you learned how to use the oven again.'

'Go away. Leave me alone,' Nancy mumbled. Michael could tell she was pissed. She was slurring.

Crouching down next to their bed, the stench of wine hit Michael tenfold. 'I am fucking sick of this idiotic behaviour, Nancy. You need to get a grip, else me and you are finished.'

'What a matter with Mummy?' Adam asked, toddling into the room.

When Nancy began to sob like a newborn, Michael strolled out with his youngest son in his arms, and slammed the door. To say he was furious as he walked down the stairs and spotted three empty bottles of wine in the lounge was an understatement. How could he go to work and leave Nancy with the kids in the state she was in? He couldn't.

The home in Eastbourne had two mobile payphones that were wheeled into the patient's room so they could speak privately, and when one of the carers knocked on his door to inform Roy that he had hogged the phone for too long, Roy told her that he would need it for at least another half an hour.

At his request, Michael had stopped at an off licence and brought him a bottle of brandy on the way back from the pub, and Roy took a large gulp of it before he dialled the next number. He just hoped she was in. When the phone was answered, he recognized her voice immediately. She had such a beautiful Irish lilt that it almost brought tears to his eyes. He took a deep breath and did his best to pull himself together. 'Colleen, it's Roy. How are you? And how is Emily-Mae?'

When Colleen burst into tears, Roy held the phone away from his ear. He knew they were tears of sympathy rather than love.

'Oh, Roy. It is so wonderful to hear from you,' Colleen said, before going on to explain how well their daughter was doing at nursery, amongst lots of other stories about the child he barely knew.

Roy grinned as he listened to his daughter's antics. She sounded a right little character, just like he had once been.

'Have you rung because you are ready to see Emily-Mae now, Roy? I will bring her to see you whenever you want,' Colleen said.

Feeling embarrassed because his speech was so slow and slurred compared to when Colleen had been with him, Roy felt compelled to apologize for that before telling his ex he didn't want Emily-Mae to visit.

'So, why have you rung then?' Colleen asked.

'Because, I just wanted to check my daughter was OK and that you were happy.'

When Colleen assured him that everything was fine, Roy forced himself to smile. She hadn't told him about her new chap, but she sounded bubbly enough for him to know that her new fiancé must be an OK kind of guy who was obviously treating her well. 'I have to go now, Colleen, but I just want to tell you something before I put the phone down. I will always love you and Emily-Mae, but I want you to promise me you will move on with your life, meet a nice man and be happy. Can you do that for me?'

When Colleen burst into tears again, Roy ended the call. There really was no need for her to feel guilty. Colleen was truly a wonderful girl. She had sat by his bedside day and night when he had been in a coma, and even when he had woken up as a different man, Colleen had been willing to give up her own life to care for him. She had even still wanted to marry him. Roy took another swig of brandy, and smiled. He was so glad he'd had the guts to set Colleen and his daughter free. The reason being, they both deserved better.

Back at the club, Dean Smart sat down nervously opposite his boss.

'And what can I do for you, Deano? Do you need time off because of your nan?' Vinny asked, with a hint of sarcasm. He couldn't put on a sympathetic voice, as he hated Mad Freda with a passion.

'No. It's nothing to do with my nan. I need to speak to you about Brenda.'

'Go on, and there is no need to gabble. I don't bite, you

468

know. I'll pour us both a drink,' Vinny replied. He liked Dean, and thought his little sister had done quite well for herself considering what a pain in the arse she was at times.

Dean gratefully accepted the Scotch, and necked it in two gulps. He was dreading this conversation, but he was so unhappy, it couldn't be put off any longer.

Vinny listened in earnest while Dean explained how awful life was with Brenda. 'So, what do you want me to do about it?' he asked, when his brother-in-law finally came up for air.

Dean took a deep breath. 'Nothing. The reason I have spoken to you is I wanted to ask your permission to leave Brenda. I can't take any more, Vinny, I'm at the end of my tether.'

Vinny leant across the table and stared Dean straight in the eyes. 'You got a bit of fluff on the go? And don't lie to me, because I will find out if you have.'

Dean held his hands up in a surrender poise. 'I swear on my Tara's life I am not having an affair and I never have since I married Bren. I wouldn't do that, Vinny. I have too much respect for her and your family.'

'Good! Glad to hear it. Look Dean, I'm sorry to hear how bad things are for you but, I'm afraid leaving Bren is totally out of the question, boyo. My dear old mum would be so upset if that were to happen, and you know how I like my mum to be happy, don't you?'

About to argue his point, Dean noticed the dangerous glint in Vinny's eyes and quickly shut his mouth. He was doomed to a life of misery and unfortunately there was no way out whatsoever.

Roy took another swig of brandy as he re-read his father's letter. Michael had given him his dad's phone number approximately twenty minutes ago, and he was still building up the courage to make the call, fearing he was probably about to hear things that would upset him greatly.

Roy picked up the receiver and held it between his chin and cheek while he used his only able hand to dial.

'Hello, Son. I can't tell you how happy I am that you want to speak to me. I've been sitting by the phone since Michael rung me earlier willing you to phone me,' Albie said sincerely.

'It is good to speak to you too, Dad, but you must be patient with my speech. I talk very slowly now as you can probably tell.'

'I don't give a damn how you speak, or if we are on the phone all night, Roy. It is just so wonderful to hear your voice again. How are you doing? Michael tells me you've moved to a lovely place near the sea now?'

'To be honest, Dad, my life isn't so great, so I would rather hear about yours, if that is OK with you?'

Albie took the hint, and told Roy all about his new life in Ipswich. He didn't mention his new lady friend though in case it upset his son. He went on to describe how living with his brother Bert had been a godsend and spoke enthusiastically about his allotment, and how much healthier he felt for having cut his drinking down immensely.

'I am really pleased you are happy, Dad,' Roy said. He was genuinely thrilled that his father had turned his life around and seemed so content.

'Son, I must apologize about that terrible cancer lie I told. I wasn't thinking straight at the time, but I swear on the Bible that the only reason I said it was because of my desperation to have contact with you, Michael, and Brenda again. I missed you all so much, I would have said or done anything to be part of your lives once more.'

'Why haven't you mentioned Vinny, Dad? I want to know the truth of what has happened.'

'I really don't want to talk about your brother, Roy. I have nothing nice to say about him.'

'Dad, I will forgive you for you lying about your cancer if you tell me the truth about Vinny. I hate him with a passion, and I swear whatever you tell me I will take to my grave with me. On my Emily-Mae's life, I will never tell another living soul any of this conversation that we have tonight.'

Trusting his son completely, Albie then spilt the beans. He told Roy all about how he had been pushed out of his children's lives the moment they had been born, and then went on to describe in detail how Vinny had tried to ruin the engagement with Colleen by bribing him to tell her parents a pack of lies. 'I just couldn't do it to you, son. I looked around and saw you and Colleen kissing and cuddling, and I refused. That is why Vinny jumped on the stage and told everybody I had lied about my cancer. He then threatened to kill me if I didn't leave the area immediately. I was scared of him, son. You know what he did to me all them years ago when he found out about my affair with Judy Preston. You was there.'

Roy was gobsmacked. He had always known that Vinny had an evil streak, and had remembered how his brother had tried to ruin his engagement party. But, how could he threaten to kill his own father? Roy had thought Albie had left Whitechapel because his cancer lie had been exposed. Vinny really was the lowest of the low at times.

'You OK, son?' Albie asked anxiously. He had necked a couple of cans while talking to Roy. His nerves were frayed just relaying the story, and the past brought back awful memories.

Still in a state of shock, Roy decided to change the subject completely. 'Did you ever find out if Judy Preston kept your baby, Dad?'

'No, Son. I did hear a rumour that she was living not too many miles away from where I am now, but I doubt that is true. I swear, I have never seen or heard a peep out of her since the day she visited me in that hospital and your mother turned up.'

'I am so glad we had this chat, Dad. I always wondered why you spent so much time at the pub when I was a kid, and I never knew that Mum and Auntie Viv pushed you out of the family circle the way they did. Don't get me wrong, I love my mum. She has always been good to me, but I do believe you, as I know how domineering her and Auntie Viv can be at times.'

Albie rubbed the tears away from his eyes with the sleeve of his jumper. It had been both lovely and emotional talking to Roy, but it broke his heart that his son sounded like a shadow of the man he once was. 'When can I come and visit you, boy? Michael said he will drive me down there.'

Roy took a deep breath to stop himself from crying. 'Soon, Dad. I hope you don't think I've turned into a softie for saying this, but I want you to know that I forgive you for everything, and I love you very much.'

Unable to stop himself, Albie then burst into floods of tears. 'And I love you too, Son, much more than you could ever imagine.'

Choked up beyond belief, Roy knew it was time to end the call. 'Dad, somebody else needs to use the phone now, but I'll speak to you again soon, I promise,' he lied.

Nancy Walker walked over to the wardrobe and put a coat on over her nightdress. The long hot summer had now come to an end, and she didn't want to get wet. She could hear the torrential rain banging against the window.

Her handbag with her purse inside was in the lounge, and there was no way Nancy was venturing in there. She could hear Michael laughing, and her sons joining in with whatever stupid game they were playing. Then, she heard Lee's voice. The boy who had been dumped on her even though he wasn't her bloody child.

Tiptoeing down the stairs, Nancy opened the front door as gently as she could. Christopher had been taken to Upney Hospital which wasn't that far away, and even if it took her an hour or so, she would be able to walk there.

When Nancy quietly shut the front door, she suddenly realized she had her carpet slippers on rather than her shoes. Cursing herself for being so dipsy, she had no choice other than to walk on. Her key was in her purse.

CHAPTER FORTY

When Vinny arrived in Eastbourne, he decided to take Joanna for a bit of lunch in the Moorings before dropping her off at Kings. Jo had been worryingly quiet throughout the whole journey and he needed to find out why. 'I just need to make a quick phone call. Order what you want, and I'll have the scampi, and a pint, babe,' Vinny said, handing over a twenty-pound note.

'Where the bloody hell you been? Three times I rang that club yesterday, and three times Lenny said you were busy. Ain't you got time for your poor old mum now you've got some young tart on the firm?' Queenie asked coldly.

'I'm sorry, Mum. I barely had a moment to bleedin' breathe yesterday. I meant to ring you back last night, but it totally slipped my mind.'

'So, where are you now? Me and Vivvy have decided we want to go back to Kings until it shuts for the winter. When can you drive us down there?'

Vinny usually spoke to or saw his mother every single day, and he could tell she had the hump with him. Telling her he was currently in Eastbourne would only make her even more cross, so he had no option other than to lie. 'I'm in the West End, Mum. I have a business meeting arranged with an old pal of mine. I promise you faithfully I will pop round to see you later today, and I will drive you and Auntie Viv back down to Eastbourne on Wednesday morning. What about Little Vinny though? I ain't got no-one else to look after him.'

'He can come to Kings with us. Teaching him a load of old bollocks at that school anyway,' Queenie said bluntly.

'I've got some really good news, Mum. Roy rang me yesterday and he wants to build some bridges. We're going out for a drink on Wednesday.'

Queenie's eyes welled up with tears of pure joy. She had been thrilled when Michael had informed her that Roy had seemed bubbly and had enjoyed a few pints in the pub, but that was nothing compared to how she felt about Roy and Vinny going out together. Her eldest two had been inseperable as kids and throught their teenage years and it had broken Queenie's heart that they no longer communicated. 'Oh Vin, I'm so bloody pleased. What exactly did Roy say then?'

Aware that Joanna was staring at him, Vinny decided the details could wait until later. 'I've got to go, Mum. My pal's just turned up. I'll explain all when I come round,' he said, as the pips started to bleep.

'Who was that you were on the phone to?' Joanna asked, when Vinny returned to the table.

'Only me mum. I've been so wrapped up with work and you, I had forgotten to ring her. What's up, babe? You've not been your usual jovial self today. Is something bothering you?'

Joanna stared at her hands rather than look Vinny in the eye. 'My period is two weeks late. I think I might be pregnant.'

Michael Butler was beside himself. He hadn't realized his wife was missing until late last night, and she still hadn't returned. He had scoured the streets for approximately four hours in his car looking for Nancy, but he hadn't been able to find her. He had also rung his wife's best friend, but Rhonda had sworn to him that Nancy hadn't been in contact and she had no idea where his wife was.

At his wits' end, Michael had now driven to Nancy's parents' café. He knew if Donald was there, he would get anything but a warm reception, but for once he didn't care. Surely his wife's safety was more important than her father's shitty attitude?

Over at Wormwood Scrubs, Johnny Preston was pacing up and down his cell muttering expletives and threatening to murder Vinny Butler. They had kept him in solitary for twenty-four hours, and he'd had to pretend he had calmed down to be allowed back onto his wing.

'Sit down, John. You're making me feel dizzy,' said Phil, Johnny's cellmate.

Johnny punched the wall. He hadn't told Phil why he was in pieces; he couldn't bring himself to tell anyone. If he was on the outside, he would have marched straight down to Butler's club and killed him stone dead. Doing life would be preferable to allowing that bastard to touch his baby girl again. 'I'm going off my head here, Phil. That shit you inject, does it chill you out?'

Phil nodded. He had done two long stretches in prison now, and had got through both thanks to heroin. He now provided a service and supplied to other inmates too.

'Give us a bull's-eye's worth,' Johnny demanded, putting his hand inside his pants to pull out some damp pound notes.

'Take it steady, John. You ain't used to it. I'll inject some for you if you like?'

'Just give us the gear and the needle, Phil. I ain't a fucking child, you cunt.'

*

476

When Michael walked into the café, he was relieved to see Mary standing behind the counter rather than Donald. Because of the seriousness of his visit, Michael had felt it innappropriate to ring ahead. He was hoping Nancy might be there, but if she wasn't, then he really didn't want to shock poor Mary by phone.

'Michael! What are you doing here? Is Nancy with you?' Mary asked, rather bemused. Her son-in-law had never visited the café before, and Mary was relieved that Donald had left ten minutes ago to visit Christopher in hospital.

'Have you seen Nancy, Mary?' Michael asked.

'No, not today. Why? Did she say she was coming here?' Mary replied, now anxious.

'No. Nancy didn't say she was coming here, but she went out last night and she hasn't come back yet, so I was rather hoping she was with you. I'm worried sick about her, Mary, she didn't even take her handbag or purse with her.'

Mary put her hand over her mouth and totally ignored the customer who had just walked up to the counter and asked for an egg and bacon roll. 'Oh my God, Michael! We need to find her quickly. Nancy really hasn't been well lately.'

Alan Briggs lived in Upney and rarely used the alleyway that gave him access to the back of his house. However, he was having a new sofa delivered today which would probably not fit through his small hallway so, along with his dog, Spot, Alan trotted down the alley to check there were no obstacles blocking the delivery men's paths.

Spot bounded on in front of him and began barking manically, but it wasn't until Alan chased his Dalmatian that he spotted the girl lying curled up in a foetal position in the long grass. She had on what looked like a nightdress with a jacket over the top, and she was barefoot with grazes,

477

blood, and dirt covering the soles of her feet. Alan felt his whole body shake from head to foot. His first impression was that the girl was dead, but when Spot licked her face, the girl's eyes seemed to flicker open which made Alan gasp. 'Don't try to move. I will ring an ambulance. I'll be back in one minute,' he gabbled, before grabbing his dog by its collar and running back down the alleyway. He had no idea if the girl had been raped, attacked or what, but thank God she was still alive. Finding a corpse was not something that Alan could have dealt with.

Chloe glared at Joanna as she let herself into their chalet. Working at Kings for the summer was meant to have been a once-in-a-lifetime giggle for the two best friends, and it had been until Vinny bloody Butler had turned up on the scene.

'You all right, mate? I'm so sorry for dashing off to London like I did. Were work OK about it? Did you tell them that I had a family crisis to deal with like I told you to?' Joanna asked awkwardly. She could tell she was in the doghouse just by the unfriendly expression on Chloe's face.

'Yes, work were fine and believed your little lie. Wasn't much fun for me though. Not only did I have to work doubly hard to cover up for your absence, I've also been stuck here on my own. I think you owe me a favour, so I want you to do something for me for once.'

'Of course. What?' Joanna replied.

Chloe delved into her handbag and handed Jo the letter her mum had written. 'I want you to read this. I promised your mum that you would read it in front of me.'

Guessing the letter was about Vinny, Joanna ripped it open and pursed her lips as she read the scathing words. It explained how her father's best pal Dave Phillips had been murdered by Vinny back in 1965, which according to her mother was why her dad had sought revenge and ended up in prison himself. It also informed her that Roy Butler had been shot by accident. The bullet had been meant for Vinny. The letter then ended with her mum begging her to get away from Vinny at the first opportunity and return to Tiptree. She also described Vinny as a vile piece of work who would stop at nothing to heap revenge onto her heartbroken father. The PS at the bottom told Joanna she was being used as a pawn in a very dangerous game, and would live to regret not taking her mother's advice if she chose to ignore it.

'What're you doing that for? Aren't you going to read it to me?' Chloe asked, when her pal began to rip the letter into shreds.

'It's none of your business, Chloe. Anyway, there was nothing in the letter that I found that surprising. Vinny had already been honest with me about certain stuff. I bet you're really jealous deep down, aren't you? You must be well pissed off that Vinny picked me and you got lumbered with Ahmed? I would be if it were the other way round.'

Amazed by Joanna's ridiculous accusation, Chloe shook her head in disbelief. She wasn't jealous. In fact, nothing could be further from the truth. 'Do you know what, Jo, you have changed so much since you've been with your precious new boyfriend. You're nothing like the best mate I once had. I'm not jealous of you being with Vinny. All I can put it down to is he has brainwashed you in some strange way, and now you are under his spell. Hope you don't expect me to pick up the pieces when it all goes wrong, because after the way you have treated me lately, you don't deserve my friendship.'

Sick of people interfering in her life, Joanna decided a hint of sarcasm and the shock factor was her best form of defence. 'Oh dearie me. You do have an overactive imagination at times, Chloe. Well, to put your mind at rest, I can assure you that Vinny has not cast a spell, or brainwashed me. I think the word you might actually be searching for is impregnated.'

Vinny Butler had driven back to Whitechapel as quickly as the busy roads had allowed his Jaguar to travel. Joanna telling him that she might be pregnant had been enough reason for him to want to escape Eastbourne a.s.a.p. But, he had also rung the club after dropping Jo off at Kings, and Lenny had informed him that the man from prison had rung up again, and so had Michael who apparently had a crisis going on and wouldn't be in to work for the foreseeable future.

Dean's nan had been moved to Oldchurch Hospital in Romford today to have her operation there instead of at the London, so knowing Lenny would be alone at the club, Vinny had asked Ahmed to get there at two p.m. as he had a delivery from the brewery arriving that he couldn't trust Lenny to deal with alone.

'Everything OK, Champ? Did Ahmed turn up to help you?' Vinny asked as he entered the club, feeling extremely flustered.

'Yeah. Ahmed's in your office, Vin. He's making some phone calls. Do you mind if I have a pint? I worked hard today, and I deserve one,' Lenny said, grinning cheekily at his cousin.

'Course you can, Champ. You pour yourself a drink and have a rest now. If you want you can hop on the DJ stand and play a bit of music. Not too loud though, as I have a bit of business I need to discuss with Ahmed,' Vinny said, strolling towards his office.

'Ah, there you are! I've installed your new phone, and I've tested it already,' Ahmed informed his friend.

'You sure it rings? How did you test it for incoming calls?' Vinny asked.

'I sent Champ to the phonebox around corner and he rang the number.'

'I've had the day from hell, mate. Pour us a large Scotch while I rack us up a line,' Vinny said, opening his safe.

'What is wrong?' Ahmed asked.

Vinny downed his Scotch in one, then told Ahmed about Joanna's period being two weeks late.

'Oh dear! You have super sperm. You are going to be a Daddy again. Congratulations.'

'It ain't fucking funny, Ahmed. I don't wanna be lumbered with her or another kid.'

'I'm only messing with you. If things don't work out to your liking, we can just get rid of Joanna like we did Karen. Easy-peasy,' Ahmed replied.

Vinny jumped as the new phone rang. It was much louder than his old one. 'Hello.'

Scottish Pat wasn't a man of many words, but Vinny could not wipe the smile off his face as he digested the couple of sentences that his informant had to say.

'Well?' Ahmed asked, when Vinny replaced the receiver on its cradle.

'Preston was let out of solitary and then took a heroin overdose. Rumour has it, the cunt had already been brown bread for an hour when they carried him out of his cell. Fucking love it, I do. Bye-bye, Johnny Boy, you no-good shitcunt.'

'That is wonderful news. I'm well chuffed for you. Now, we must work out how to get rid of the daughter.'

Vinny poured himself and Ahmed another drink. 'I'll dump her as soon as the dust has settled, or should I say Johnny's ashes?'

Ahmed grinned. 'I think we should celebrate Johnny's death tonight. We can go to the whorehouse, shag women, and drink champagne.'

Vinny laughed. Ahmed was so on his wavelength it was uncanny.

None of the nurses or doctors at Oldchurch Hospital had any idea what had happened to the girl or who she was. There were no obvious signs of a physical attack, but the girl refused to speak, and seemed dazed and confused.

Mandy, the young Irish nurse, was very worried about the girl. Her own sister, Hazel, had been raped by a man she had met in a bar a few years ago in Dublin, and the way the girl was acting made Mandy think that the same had possibly happened to her. 'Well?' Mandy asked, as the policewoman and the matron of her ward walked out of the room.

'Thankfully, there doesn't seem to be any signs of a sexual or any other attack. We think it is more to do with mental health, such as a breakdown of some kind has occurred. She is speaking now though, although she isn't saying much.'

'What did she say?' Mandy asked, her face etched with worry.

Mandy's matron smiled. Mandy had only been working on her ward for three months and she wished all her young nurses were so kind to their patients. 'Well, she asked me for a cup of tea, and then told DS Day that her name was Nancy.'

Unaware that his daughter was currently unwell and disorientated in a different hospital, Donald sat proudly next to his son as the news reporter started the interview.

Christopher had recovered extremely well from his stabbing ordeal, and was now well enough to be filmed by the BBC who were covering his heroic story on the evening news. Christopher's bosses were absolutely thrilled with his off-duty courageousness, and not only had the hief inspector been to the hospital to visit him personally, he had all but told Christopher he would be promoted instantly as soon as his probation period was over.

Mary had warned Donald earlier that it would not be wise for him or Christopher to be interviewed and filmed by the BBC, considering the trouble they had had in the past. She had also informed him that none of Michael's family knew that Christopher was now a policeman and also reminded him of why they had once had to flee Whitechapel.

Donald being Donald did not take his wife's advice, and when the reporter began to ask him questions, he answered them with pride. Why shouldn't he? His son was a hero, a budding police officer, and the past was now just a distant memory, wasn't it?

Having driven around for hours with Mary in the hope of finding Nancy, Michael took his mother-in-law's advice and headed home to ring the police.

'Do you mind if I have a nose through Nancy's wardrobe before we call the cops? I might be able to work out what she was wearing. The police are bound to ask,' Mary said.

'Course you can. I'll make the boys some beans on toast while you're upstairs. I really can't see the Old Bill doing much until she's been missing for over twenty-four hours though,' Michael replied, feeling dismal.

'They bloody well will when I speak to them. I shall play on the fact that Nancy hasn't been very well lately. They'll have to take notice if they think she's had mental health problems.'

Ordering the boys to go into the lounge to watch TV, Michael opened a tin of beans and was about to pour them into a saucepan when the phone rang. He dashed to answer it in hope that the caller was Nancy but it wasn't, it was his mother. "'Ere, you'll never guess what, Michael?'

'What?'

'Roy wants to make peace with Vinny. Roy rang him and Vinny's going out with him on Wednesday. Isn't it wonderful news, eh?'

Michael knew immediately that something was amiss. Roy had hated Vinny with a passion yesterday and nobody changed their tune that quickly. In normal circumstances, he would have informed his mother of this, but he was too worried about his wife to even enter into a conversation. 'Mum, I have to go. Nancy is missing.'

Vinny Butler sat mulling over his life while he waited for Joanna's phone call. He had been drinking and snorting far too much recently, and decided now he had got revenge for his brother's shooting, he should really try to sort himself out. There were lots of punters who drank in his club that were forever out of their boxes, and Vinny thought far too highly of himself to end up like them. He would have one last wild night out with Ahmed tonight to celebrate Preston's death, then get his act together from tomorrow. He had barely seen Little Vinny or his mother recently, and he needed to get his priorities back in order.

Jumping as the phone rang, Vinny snatched at the receiver. 'You all right, Jo?'

'Yes and no. I did that test you told me to do and I am definitely pregnant. Part of me is excited, but I'm also really nervous. My mum told me in the past that she was in labour with me for over twenty-four hours and had never felt pain like it in her life before.'

Being as blunt as an old unsharpened knife, Vinny just said what he had to say. 'I've been doing a lot of thinking today, Jo, and I'm really not sure we are ready for a kid,

484

are you? I mean, we haven't known one another for five minutes, and what with finding out who your father is as well. It's all too much, too soon.'

Joanna was unable to keep the catch out of her voice. 'But, I chose you over my family, Vinny. You knew that the night I left my mum in the restaurant. What are you trying to say? You don't want us to finish, do you?'

'No, course not. I just think we should wait before we have kids, that's all,' Vinny explained, suddenly transfixed by the television screen.

'Do you want me to have an abortion? Is that what you're saying?' Joanna sobbed.

'Babe, I've gotta go. Something important's cropped up,' Vinny said, as he slammed down the phone and ran towards the TV to turn up the volume.

Donald Walker was an unusual-looking man with a prominent nose and flat-top haircut which made his head look rather square. There was no mistaking the bloke, and Vinny could barely believe his eyes and luck as he realized the lad sitting next to Donald was his son Christopher, who now just happened to be Old Bill.

Vinny would never have recognized Christopher in a million years. He had been quite a cute kid when Vinny had last seen him, but now looked like a replica of his ugly big-nosed father. When the interview ended, Vinny sat on his big leather chair, put his hands behind his head, and grinned as he thought of the irony of it all. A nice little insider such as Christopher could come in well handy in the future, and Christopher could hardly refuse, could he? Not when he had witnessed Vinny kill Dave Phillips many moons ago, and lied to the Old Bill himself.

'I'm back. I had a nice bath and scrubbed my penis so it is clean for the whores to suck later. You OK?' Ahmed asked, shutting the office door behind him.

Vinny could not wipe the smile off his face. 'I'm more than OK, mate. This day just keeps getting better and better.'

Freda was too proud to go to the toilet in a bedpan, and even though her stomach was giving her a bit of gyp today, she still managed to shuffle to the bathroom in her slippers. Freda thought it was vulgar the way some of the patients would just pull the curtain around their bed and fart, shit, and stink the ward out. Most of the lazy bastards were quite capable of walking to the toilet too, but lacked the manners to do so.

The cubicle was occupied when Freda tried the handle, so she sat down on a nearby chair. At that very moment, a nurse walked out of one of the little private wards and Freda happened to glance inside before the door shut. It was Nancy Walker in there, she could have sworn it was. 'Excuse me,' Freda said, hobbling after the nurse.

'What's up, love?'

'That room you just came out of. Is the patient's name Nancy?'

'Yes, it is Nancy, and thank the lord you know her. We had no idea who to contact because she hasn't been saying very much. What's her surname? Has she any relatives we can get in touch with?'

'Her married surname is Butler, but before that it was Walker. After I've used the toilet, I'll call my son. He'll know who to contact. What's wrong with her?'

'OK, love. I shall inform the police who she is in case they need to speak to her again. Thank God we can now help her and reunite her with her family. The poor lass has obviously had a traumatic time of it.'

'Is she OK? I mean, has something bad happened to her?' Freda asked.

'We're really not sure, as the poor lass seems a little

disorientated, but I am sure once she has her loved ones around her, she'll soon perk up again.'

When the nurse walked away, Freda couldn't help but smirk. If Nancy wasn't speaking and seemed disorientated, she had obviously lost her marbles, and even though Freda didn't wish the girl any harm, it served her parents right for not listening to her warning many moons ago.

Deciding to celebrate Johnny Preston's death in style, Vinny Butler was drunk and coked-up to the eyeballs before he even got to the whorehouse in Dalston. Ahmed wasn't far behind him, but was in a fitter state than Vinny to drive, so had offered to take his brand-new black Mercedes, providing they then got a cab home and Vinny took him to collect his car the following day.

Because he already felt out of it, Vinny hadn't wanted the responsibility of Lenny tagging along tonight, but his little cousin had overheard him and Ahmed saying they were going to the whorehouse, and Vinny didn't have the heart to tell Lenny that he couldn't join them. The boy was obsessed with Layla, even spoke about her at times as though they were a couple.

'Turn this one up, Ahmed. I like this song,' Lenny insisted.

Vinny and Ahmed both chuckled as Lenny sang along to the Wurzels' 'I Am a Cider Drinker'. Some people saw Lenny as a bit dim, but he had a memory like an elephant when it came to music.

'Right, we are here now, Champ. Did you wash your penis so it is nice and clean?' Ahmed joked.

'Yep. I used my mum's Imperial Leather soap,' Lenny replied, full of pride.

Laughing out loud, Vinny put his arm around his cousin's shoulder as they got out of the car. 'Come on then, Champ. Let's get you laid.'

Mary could barely contain her emotions when she saw the haunted look in her daughter's eyes. Donald had offered to accompany her to the hospital and even though Mary had been pleased about that, she thought it was best that she visit her daughter on her own at first. Michael had informed her where Nancy was. He'd received a phone call from Dean, but Mary had insisted to Michael also that she visit Nancy alone first. She was her mother after all, and if anyone could find out what had happened, it was her.

When the nurse left the room to give them some privacy, Mary sat on the edge of Nancy's bed and squeezed her daughter's hand. 'Everybody's been so worried about you, darling. Do you want to tell me what happened?' Mary asked, gently. She had already been informed by the ward sister that Nancy had been found in an alleyway in her nightdress, and she was beside herself with what might have befallen her daughter.

'I don't know, Mum. It's all a bit of a blank,' Nancy whispered.

'But why was you out in your nightdress, love?'

'Because I wanted to see if Christopher was OK. I was worried about him, so I sneaked out.'

As Nancy burst into tears, Mary held her fragile daughter in her arms as though she were a small child once again. 'It's OK, my angel. Everything is going to be all right. Mummy's here to look after you now.'

Lenny was distraught when he heard that Layla didn't work at the club any more. 'Don't mug yourself off by crying over some slapper, boy. There are plenty more dogs in the kennel. Look at all them gyrating on the stage. You pick what one you want and I'll make sure you get her.'

'But I don't want to bang another girl, Vinny. I love Layla.'

'See if you can talk some sense into him,' Vinny whispered in Ahmed's ear. He was desperate to go to the toilet to shove some more cocaine up his already bunged up nose.

When Vinny returned after his livener, he was thrilled to see Lenny now had a grin on his face and was happily gulping down a pint of lager. 'What did you say to him?' Vinny asked Ahmed.

'I told him he can have a six-up with us. I also said I'd buy some champagne.'

'Oh no. I don't mind watching you fuck, but I can't be watching Champ. It ain't right, Ahmed. He's my little cousin.'

'Don't be so boring. Champ is well up for it. Perhaps we can teach him some new tricks? It will be fun.'

'Can we go to the room now, Vin? I want that black girl in the red bikini, and I want my champagne. Is it nice? I never tasted it before.'

'Champ, I think you should go in a room with the black girl on your own. I'll buy you a bottle of champagne to take in with you.'

Lenny immediately looked crestfallen. 'But Ahmed said we would all go in the same room and bang the girls together. I don't want to go in a room on my own, Vinny.'

Ten minutes later, Vinny and Ahmed were both shagging two blonde birds and trying not to laugh as they watched Lenny receiving a blow job. The noises he was making were hysterical, and Vinny was amazed to learn that his younger cousin was even more well hung than he was.

Feeling himself going a bit limp, Vinny ordered the slag he was lying on top of to turn over. He then inserted his penis up her arse and rammed it into her as violently as he could. He didn't look at the back of the bird's head while ripping her backside to shreds though. Instead, he stared at

Ahmed having his cock sucked. When Vinny's orgasm came, it was long-lasting and very worthwhile.

Michael Butler was relieved yet angry as he ended the phone call to Mary. His wife had told her mum to inform him that she wasn't ready to see him or their sons until she felt better.

Feeling sorry for himself, Michael cracked open a can of lager and thought back over his relationship with Nancy. Even though he had been a player back in his heyday, he had never cheated on her, not once. He had been a good husband, father, provider, so where had he gone so fucking wrong? Surely having Lee, who had suffered so much misfortune in his young life, live with them wasn't too much to ask? Lee was such a good kid, was far better behaved then Daniel and Adam in many ways, so what was Nancy's problem? Michael couldn't understand it.

'I swear, if you smash my nice new car up, you pay for a replacement, my friend,' Ahmed joked, as he got in the passenger seat. Vinny hated getting cabs, had insisted on driving, and even though Ahmed was slightly concerned because Vinny had been on the piss and sniff all day, he knew his pal would never offer to drive unless he felt he was capable of doing so.

'I really love Dionne. She is beautiful and I want to marry her. When can I see her again?' Lenny asked chirpily, when he got in the back of the car. He was now absolutely besotted with the girl who had given him his first ever blow job.

'You can see her again soon, Champ, I promise,' Vinny replied, cranking up the volume on the radio.

'We had a good time, eh? I think group sex is far more fun than just shagging a bird on your own,' Ahmed said to his pal.

Vinny turned to his friend and grinned. 'Yeah, it was a right fucking giggle.'

It was ironic that the song playing on the radio was Manfred Mann's latest chart success 'Blinded by the Light' as when Vinny glanced back at the road, he was blinded by the beam of an approaching van. Desperately trying to control a car he had never driven before was impossible when drunk, coked-up, and driving fast, and as he swerved to the left, Vinny hit a building, and his head and the steering wheel made immediate contact with one another.

Aware of the loud bang and the sound of crunching metal, the van driver put his foot on the brake, before driving off at speed.

'Ahmed, Champ, are you OK?' Vinny asked, dazed. His head hurt and he felt as though somebody had hit him across his forehead with a shovel.

When he looked at his pal, Vinny realized that Ahmed was anything but OK. The passenger side of the car had completely caved in and part of the metal doorframe was stuck in his pal's head and chest. 'Wake up, mate. Please wake up,' Vinny pleaded, as he grabbed Ahmed's wrist and checked for a pulse. He couldn't find one, so, panicking, he staggered out of the car.

Luckily for Vinny, the accident had occurred in a quiet back street that was home to a couple of disused buildings rather than houses and people, and seeing as it was four a.m. there wasn't a soul about. 'Champ, you OK, boy?' he asked, as he yanked open the back door. 'Oh my God! No, no, noooo,' Vinny screamed as he sank to his knees. Lenny's head was hanging on by no more than a thread. He had taken the brunt of the accident and was smothered in blood from head to toe.

Crying like a baby, Vinny slammed the car door and vomited. He had loved Lenny immensely ever since he had first laid eyes on him. Vinny had only been a kid himself at the time, but even at his young age, he had grasped that his cousin had been born with something wrong with him, and would need looking after for the rest of his days. Now, he had accidently killed him and how he would live with what he had done, he would never know.

Wiping his eyes with the cuff of his jacket, instinct suddenly kicked in. Lenny was all but beheaded, Ahmed had pieces of metal protruding from his body and head and the quicker he himself got away from the scene of the crime the better. Going to prison was not something he could deal with. It would break his mother's heart, which would then break his.

Taking a deep breath, Vinny opened the driver's side of the car once again. 'I'm so, so sorry. I love you, pal,' he said, as he desperately tried to move his friend into the driver's seat.

Ahmed's body seemed to weigh a ton and as Vinny tried to shift it he felt physically sick once more. This was the geezer he loved, the only person outside of his family he could trust, but Vinny knew in his heart that Ahmed wouldn't want to see him go to prison.

Doing the best job he could to make it look like Ahmed had been driving the car, Vinny kissed his pal on the forehead, shut the driver's door, then opened the back door once more. He shut his eyes. 'Champ, I love you so much, and at least you died a happy boy. Please forgive me,' he whispered.

Vinny did not open his eyes again until he had slammed the car door. He then ran down the road as fast as his legs would carry him. He needed an alibi and he needed one fast.

CHAPTER FORTY-ONE

Michael was just dozing off on the sofa when he heard the frantic banging on the front door. 'What the fuck's happened? You've got blood all over your shirt,' Michael said, shocked by the obvious distress on his brother's face.

Vinny sank to his knees in the hallway, covered his face in his hands and sobbed. 'Champ's dead, so is Ahmed. I need an alibi, Michael. You have to say I was here with you. I'll go to prison if you don't, and Mum and Auntie Viv will never speak to me again.'

'What do you mean? Champ can't be dead,' Michael whispered, his face etched with fear.

'Get me a change of clothes. I need you to burn everything I'm wearing. I must have a bath in case the Old Bill turn up here.'

When Vinny stood up, Michael grabbed his brother by the neck, dragged him into the lounge, and slammed his trembling body against the wall. 'Where is Champ, Vinny? What the fuck have you done?'

'It was an accident. I was driving Ahmed's car back from a club and a van came towards me with its full beam on. I loved Champ, you know I did. I'll never forgive myself, Michael, but you have to help me. I'd usually ask Mum for an alibi, but I can't this time. I need you to say that I came here just after midnight and we had a long chat and a few beers. Say we were discussing money.'

Michael shut the lounge door as he didn't want to wake his sons, then paced up and down the room like a man possessed. 'How can you be sure that Champ was dead? Did you even call an ambulance?'

'His head was hanging off, Michael. It was an awful sight and one that will haunt me for the rest of my living days. There was no point calling an ambulance. Ahmed wasn't breathing either. They were both sitting on the left-hand side of the car and that took all the impact. I wish it had been me that had died, honest I do. I'm gonna miss both of 'em so fucking much,' Vinny wept.

Michael shook his head in utter disbelief. He didn't give a toss about Ahmed as he had never really liked the geezer, but Champ's death was going to rip the family to shreds. His Auntie Viv and mum would never recover from it. Lenny was loved by everybody, and Michael could barely believe that he was never going to see his wonderful cousin again. 'You make me want to vomit, Vinny. I can see by the state of your eyes that you've been snorting that shit again. You reek of fucking Scotch too. How could you even drive a motor in that state when you had Champ with you? You fucking fool. I ain't giving you no alibi because you don't bastard-well deserve one. Auntie Viv and Mum are gonna be beside themselves with grief, and it's all your fault, you no-good cunt.'

'Michael, you have to give me an alibi. I've no-one else to ask. I ain't just thinking of me, I'm thinking of how much worse it will be for Auntie Viv and Mum if they know I was driving the car. It's better they think it was Ahmed, trust me on that one.'

'Where did this fucking accident happen? And what club did you go to?'

'It happened in that little road that Stan's garage used to be in. I'm so sorry, Michael. I had taken Champ to a strip club, he'd been with me and Ahmed before. He loved it there. It was the only time he ever got laid. Please back me up on this one? Say I got round yours just after twelve if anybody asks. We're fucking brothers, you can't dob me in it.'

Michael felt physically sick. 'How did you get here? I mean surely the Old Bill are gonna know that somebody else was driving if the driver's seat is fucking empty?'

'I ran back to my car and drove here. I could hardly get in a cab covered in claret, could I? I put Ahmed in the driver's seat, I had to. I feel so bad, Michael. I loved Champ like a son and Ahmed like a brother. Please give me an alibi? You have to. If not, I am finished around here and our business will be finished too. I couldn't bear it if Mum and Auntie Viv hated me. I know I've done wrong, but it was an accident. Stand by me, bruv, please?'

Michael looked at the state of his usually well-groomed and composed sibling, then reluctantly found himself nodding. Vinny might be top of his hate list right now, but he was still his sibling. 'Run a bath, get them clothes off, and I'll get rid. Wear something out of my wardrobe. Don't think I'm doing this for you though, Vin, I'm doing it for Mum and Auntie Viv's sake. Finding out Champ is dead will be tragic enough for 'em, without 'em finding out you fucking killed him while out of your nut. That would finish the pair of them off. I know it would.'

The knock on the door woke Vivian up at six in the morning. Putting on her dressing gown, she shuffled down the stairs. Her Lenny had a habit of losing his key, but surely he hadn't come home this early? He often stayed with Vinny at the club now, but never came home for his fry-up until at least ten a.m. the following day. 'Who is it?' Vivian asked cautiously.

'It's the police, Mrs Harris.'

Vinny had recently had chain locks fitted for her and Queenie, and when Vivian opened the door and peered around the side, she could tell that they were real policemen. She even recognized one from bringing Little Vinny back to Queenie's house a year or so ago. 'Whatever's wrong?' Vivian asked, taking off the chain. She hated being seen with a hairnet on and without her make-up, but what could she do? 'Well?'

'Can we come in, Mrs Harris?' one of the policemen asked, removing his helmet as a mark of respect.

'Oh dear God! What is it?' Vivian gasped, as the other policeman also removed his helmet when he walked into the hallway.

'I'm so sorry, Mrs Harris, but your son was involved in a fatal car accident earlier. We need one of your family to identify the body, but we feel it is best if one of your nephews do it rather than you. Lenny suffered major injuries.'

Letting out an almighty scream that woke up nigh-on the rest of the street, Vivian's legs buckled from under her and even though she tried to save herself by grabbing the banister, she couldn't stop herself from falling. 'Not my baby. Not my Lenny. You must have got it wrong. It can't be him. Not my fucking baby,' she shrieked.

Queenie Butler always slept with one ear open, and she heard the scream immediately. Leaping out of bed, she looked out of the window and spotted the police car parked outside her sister's house. Queenie was another proud woman who slept in a hairnet and despised being seen without full make-up, but she decided not to be so pretentious for once. She was sure that scream had belonged to her sister, so darted down the stairs.

'What's up, Nan? I heard someone,' Little Vinny said, opening his bedroom door and rubbing his tired eyes.

'Bring me my dressing gown, boy. I think the police are at your Auntie Vivian's house,' she said, flinging open the front door.

Queenie's very worst fears were confirmed when she heard her sister wailing like a critically injured animal. Not even waiting for her dressing gown, Queenie ran outside in her pale-blue flannelette nightie and up her sister's path. 'It's me, Vivvy. What's wrong?' she called, hammering on the door.

When a policeman answered, Queenie flew into the hallway followed by Little Vinny who had chased after his nan.

'Is everything OK?' Queenie heard Nosy Hilda shout out. The noise must have woken her up too. Slamming the front door shut, Queenie crouched down next to her sister who was sitting on the hallway carpet, hugging her knees to her chest, and making strange noises like foxes did in the mating season.

When she realized she wasn't going to get an answer out of Vivian, Queenie stood up and faced the two policemen. She recognized one immediately. He had brought her grandson home after catching him shoplifting a while back.

'I'm so sorry to be the bearer of bad news, Mrs Butler, but Mrs Harris's son was involved in a car crash earlier. Unfortunately, her son never survived, and the driver of the vehicle is in a bad way also.'

'Noooo! That can't be right. Lenny was at the club working. He don't go out in cars,' Queenie gabbled, her voice a mixture of hysteria and dread.

'We have every reason to believe that the deceased is Mrs

497

Harris's son, but we do need somebody to formally identify the body. Perhaps one of your sons could do this, Mrs Butler?' one of the officers suggested. The Butlers and their relations were notorious to the East End police force, and the officer who had turned up at the scene of the crash, after it had been reported by a passer-by, had immediately recognized young Lenny Harris. Ahmed was a well-known character too, because of his connection with Vinny, and when a faint pulse had been found in his wrist, he had immediately been rushed off to the nearby London Hospital.

'It weren't my dad driving the car, was it?' Little Vinny asked, petrified of the answer.

'Oh no! Please God, no,' Queenie stammered. If this was true, it must have been her Vinny driving the car. Lenny wouldn't have been out with anybody else.

'No. The driver, who is now critically ill in hospital, was Ahmed Zane. We believe him to be a good friend of your family.'

'I want my Lenny. I need to see and hold my baby boy,' Vivian screamed hysterically.

Absolutely shell-shocked, a sobbing Queenie crouched down and held her wonderful sister in her arms. She was truly lost for words for once. Lenny had been the apple of all their eyes, and to think they would never see him again just didn't make sense. Life was cruel at times, it really was.

Vinny Butler hadn't slept a wink. When Michael had gone to bed an hour or so back, all Vinny could think about was his beloved cousin partially decapitated and the shocked expression in Lenny's big brown eyes.

Vinny sat on Michael's brown leather sofa and put his head in his hands. Not only had he killed his cousin, he had also wiped out the life of his best mate too. How he would ever recover from such a traumatic experience, Vinny would never know, but he had to try to act as normal as possible, else his mother would suspect that he was involved. Obviously, he could express his grief, but other than that, he had to be the strong one of the family, like he always had been. He knew his mother and Auntie Viv were bound to ask why Lenny was out with Ahmed alone, and Vinny didn't have a story prepared yet. He must think of something soon, but it was so difficult when he had just watched two of the most important people in his life die before his very eyes.

Not quite ready to face the music, Vinny crept upstairs and went into Michael's bedroom. 'I thought you'd be asleep,' he whispered.

'And how the fuck do you expect me to sleep when I know what you've done and I'm the cunt who has to cover up for you,' Michael replied.

Vinny knelt down next to his brother's bed. 'I'm gonna shoot back to the club now. You burnt my clothes properly, didn't ya?'

'Of course I fucking did. Not the first time I've burnt clothes for you when you've got yourself in the shit, is it, Vin? The difference, though, is you never wiped out any members of our own family before, did you?'

'Listen, Michael, I'm so fucking sorry. My heart is literally broken in two. Just stand by me with the story, please. I need your support. We're brothers.'

Michael sat up in bed. 'I won't grass, don't worry, but don't you dare leave me to deal with Mum and Auntie Viv's grief alone. I have enough on me plate with Nancy and the boys.'

'I'll be there for Mum and Auntie Viv, I swear I will. I'll shut the club until after Champ's funeral as a mark of respect, and as soon as I get that dreaded phone call, I will go straight round Mum's house.'

When Vinny had left the room, Michael fiercely wiped away the lone tear that ran down his cheek. Lenny was going to be immensely missed, but the thing that Michael thought about the most was how his Auntie Viv and mum would survive such a tragedy. They would never get over it, surely?

After a restless night's sleep, Mary Walker ordered her husband to open the café while she went to visit Nancy again. She had made her daughter a selection of sandwiches in the hope Nancy would eat them. Nancy had always been such a pretty, healthy-looking girl, and Mary had thought how skeletal she'd looked yesterday. The hospital nightdress had been far too big for her daughter and the bones in her wrists and ankles were protruding through her skin.

'Hello, my darling. How are you today? I've bought a bag full of goodies with me, including some sandwiches I made you myself,' Mary said chirpily, as she sat down on the chair next to her daughter's bed. Mary had spoken to a doctor on the way in, and he had said that Nancy had definitely suffered some kind of nervous breakdown. He had asked if Nancy's behaviour had changed since the birth of her youngest child, and implied that the breakdown might have been caused by a severe case of post-natal depression.

'I'm really not hungry at the moment, Mum, but I will have a sandwich later,' Nancy said, doing her best to force a smile.

'Christopher's been asking about you, and your dad wants to visit you too. We're all so worried about you, love. I spoke to Michael last night. He is desperate to bring the boys up here, but said he will come alone if you would prefer him to.'

'I don't want to see Michael, Mum. It's all his fault I'm in hospital. He was the one who made me take on a child that I didn't want. I could barely cope with Daniel and Adam, without him dumping a stranger's kid on me as well,' Nancy mumbled, her eyes welling up with tears.

Mary squeezed her daughter's hand. 'Don't upset yourself, darling. I shall tell Michael you're not ready for visitors yet, OK?'

Relieved, Nancy nodded. 'I would like to see Dad though. But, not today. Wait until I feel a bit better.'

'Whenever you're ready, love, but I know Dad will be thrilled that you want to see him. Life's too short to hold grudges, eh? I think your dad finding out that you were found in an alleyway after trying to walk here to visit your brother was a real wake-up call. Christopher had tears in his eyes when I told him as well. Can you remember anything more yet? You know, about how you ended up in that alley?' Mary asked gently.

'I remember feeling tired and my slippers had fallen apart, so I had to take them off. Then, I just remember my feet hurting and I think I sat down for a rest. I'm not sure what happened next.'

'Well, you're safe now, sweetheart. I reckon you just fell asleep in that alley, you know. The police and doctor said there is no sign of any injuries other than the cuts on your feet. Nothing of a sexual nature either, thank God. Now, will you do me a big favour?'

'What?'

'Eat a sandwich for me. You've lost so much weight over the past couple of weeks, Nancy, it's worrying the life out of me.'

Deciding to oblige to stop her mother from further worry, Nancy nodded her weary head.

Vinny felt terrible when he ended the phone call to his distraught mother. She hadn't mentioned Lenny. She had just told him she needed him to get to the house immediately as something dreadful had happened. About to leave the club, Vinny heard the phone ring again and he answered it in case it was Michael. It wasn't. It was Scottish Pat calling from the Scrubs. 'What's up?' Vinny asked.

'He ain't dead. They saved him.'

A chill ran down Vinny's spine. He had only gone out on a wild one to celebrate Johnny Preston's death. If he'd have known the cunt was still alive, then Lenny and Ahmed would have been too.

Unaware of his younger cousin's death, Roy Butler was in exceptionally good spirits. Vinny was due to visit him tomorrow and Roy was ready and waiting for him. Everything was now in place. The bullets were inside the gun, the phone calls had all been made, and he had explained his need for revenge in separate letters to his family. His mother would be devastated by his actions, Roy knew that, but for once he had to put his own feelings first. Vinny deserved the little surprise that Roy had planned for him tomorrow. In fact, he more than fucking deserved it.

When Vinny arrived at his mother's house the rest of the family were already there. Brenda, his mum and aunt were all huddled together on the sofa crying their eyes out. Dean was on an armchair looking as awkward as ever, and Michael glared at him as soon as he entered the lounge. 'Whatever's wrong?' Vinny asked.

Little Vinny flung himself at his father and hugged him. 'Champ's dead, Dad.'

Having no alternative but to put on the act of all acts, Vinny stood rooted to the spot with his mouth wide open. 'Dead! Course he ain't dead. Champ was working last night at the club with me.'

Unable to stop herself, Queenie flew off the sofa and began pummelling her fists against her eldest son's chest. 'I told you that fucking Turk was a wrong 'un, didn't I? How comes you let Lenny out with him on his own, eh? You were meant to be looking after him, you stupid bastard.'

When Tara began screaming, Michael ordered Little Vinny to take her and his three sons out in the garden to play. 'But I wanna stay here with me dad,' Little Vinny whinged.

'Do as your Uncle Michael says, boy,' Vinny ordered. He was crying himself now. Tears of grief and guilt poured down his cheeks when he clocked his Auntie Viv rocking to and fro on the sofa, mumbling incoherently.

'Answer my fucking question,' Queenie yelled at Vinny.

When Vinny came out with some cock-and-bull story about him having a terrible shock yesterday, which is why he had allowed Lenny to go off with Ahmed to stay the night at his pad, Michael looked at his brother with hatred.

'So, what was this terrible shock that was so bad you couldn't look after your own cousin?' Queenie asked.

'Yeah, what was it?' Brenda chipped in, hugging her distraught aunt at the same time.

'I was at the club and received a phone call from Joanna yesterday. Not only did she tell me she was pregnant, but I also found out that her father was none other than Johnny Preston. I wanted Champ to go home, but he loved Ahmed, and Ahmed loved him, so when Champ pleaded with me to stay at the club, I said only on the condition that when Ahmed went home, he took Champ with him. Ahmed wasn't drunk when I left, honest he wasn't. I needed to get my head straight and talk to someone about what I'd found out, so I drove straight to Michael's gaff and we sat up all night talking, didn't we, bruv?' Vinny explained tearfully, while glancing at his brother with pleading eyes to back up his story.

'Yeah, we did,' Michael mumbled, staring at his feet and feeling physically sick. How he was ever going to look his mum and Auntie Viv straight in the eyes again he did not know.

'It can't be my baby. I know it can't be him. There must be a mistake. I need to see him,' Vivian suddenly shrieked.

Queenie sat down, held her heartbroken sister in her arms, and glared at Vinny. 'The police need somebody to identify the body. It's best you do it.'

'Noooo! I want to see my baby. I have to know it's him,' Vivian sobbed.

'But the police said it's better that one of the boys do it, Vivvy,' Queenie reminded her sister.

Vivian's top lip suddenly curled into a snarl. 'I don't care what the cunting police said. Lenny is my baby and if I want to see him, then I will.'

'I'll go and identify the body,' Vinny offered awkwardly. He was dreading seeing his beloved cousin in the morgue, but at least he could apologize once again and say a proper goodbye to him.

'I want to see my son,' Vivian screamed.

'OK, darling. You and Vinny can go together,' Queenie told her sister. She couldn't face seeing Lenny herself. She had loved him too much to see him battered and lifeless.

'Shall we go now?' Vinny asked, sitting on the arm of the sofa so he could hug his mum.

Queenie pushed Vinny away. 'Let's hope that cunt of a mate of yours dies as well, 'cause I'm telling you now if that Turkish piece of shit survives, I will kill him with my own bare hands.'

'What? Is Ahmed not dead?' Vinny blurted out, his voice filled with panic.

'Critical, but not dead yet. He soon fucking will be though if I have my way,' Queenie spat.

Vinny felt his legs nearly buckle beneath him when he tried to stand up. What the fuck had he done? And if Ahmed survived what the hell would he think of him, or say to the police? Ahmed was no grass, Vinny knew that, but if he had bad head injuries, he could be capable of saying anything.

As Michael stomped out of the room with a look of disgust, Vinny put his head in his hands. He hated wishing his pal dead, but what choice did he have? If Ahmed lived, there was a good chance he was up the creek without a fucking paddle, and Vinny had always been a man to put his own welfare and happiness before others'. Saving his own bacon was probably the only trait he had inherited from his father.

CHAPTER FORTY-TWO

'I need to see my boy. He can't be dead,' Vivian repeatedly mumbled, rocking to and fro once again like a madwoman.

Unable to face going to the morgue after learning that Ahmed was still alive, Vinny turned to Michael. 'Can you take Auntie Viv to see Champ? I'll stay here and look after Mum.'

Desperate to get out of the house and away from his deceitful brother, Michael readily agreed. He knew Vinny like the back of his hand and guessed his brother must have known that Joanna Preston was Johnny's daughter before he had made a move on her. Vinny was a weirdo when it came to women. He only shagged whores, and apart from the teenage romance with Yvonne Summers, Michael had never known Vinny to properly date any other bird in his life. 'Come on, Auntie Viv. Look after the boys for me when Dean brings them back,' Michael ordered his sister. He wouldn't trust Vinny looking after a dog at the moment, let alone his beloved sons, and his mother was certainly in no fit state to do so.

After Michael and Vivian left the house, a bitter Queenie turned on Vinny. 'I know you better than you think. You must have realized that young girl was Preston's daughter, and I bet getting together with her was a revenge tactic.'

'I swear I never knew, Mum. Do you honestly think I would ever have entertained Preston's daughter after what happened to Roy? Give me some credit, please.'

'So, what you gonna do about that baby? I don't care if that girl is Adolf Hitler's daughter, don't you dare make her abort that child. Our family is dropping like flies as it is,' Queenie stated, as blunt as ever.

'I won't, Mum. In fact, I think I should still drive down to Eastbourne tomorrow to see Roy. He has to be told in person about Champ. Breaking the news to him over the phone just isn't right. I need to speak to Joanna as well. I told her on the phone I didn't want her or the baby after I found out who her father was. It was all such a shock.'

'That child will be a Butler, not a Preston. Oh Vinny, what is happening to our wonderful family? What have we ever done to deserve all this heartbreak, eh? And as for Eastbourne, I would rather you drove down there now and told Roy. You know how he gets a cob on these days when he thinks we are keeping stuff from him? I'll look after Vivvy and you look after Roy.'

Vinny gave his mum a cuddle and was thrilled when for the first time that day, she hugged him back.

'Sorry I was a long while. The kids were hungry and Little Vinny insisted I treated them all to a burger. I hope that's OK? The front door was left open, so I shut it behind me,' Dean said, as he walked into the lounge.

Brenda smiled at her husband. 'That's fine, and Mum, while we're on the subject of grandchildren, I've got some news too. I haven't even told Dean yet, but my period is nearly a week late. I know with everything that's happened, it's probably not the perfect time to tell you, but you seem so pleased that Vinny is having another child, that I thought the news might cheer you up a bit.'

Feeling as though he had just been told he had a terminal illness, Dean mumbled something about leaving his wallet in a shop, then bolted out of the front door as fast as he could.

Deborah Preston had tears rolling down her cheeks as she put her arms around her ex-husband's neck and held him close to her bosom. He had just asked her to marry him again.

'Well?' Johnny croaked, as he tried to sit up in his hospital bed.

'Only if you promise me two things, Johnny. The first is you will never, ever touch drugs again and the second is you don't go all-out for revenge against Vinny Butler. I've nearly lost you once and I'm not going to chance losing you again. Joanna has made her own bed, so it's up to her to lie on it. Anyway, I doubt very much she and Butler will last that long. Once she gets over her silly schoolgirl crush, she's bound to see Vinny for what he really is, which is why I don't want you getting involved. If we remarry, I want us to have a quiet life when you're released.'

'Deb, I only took that heroin because I wanted to dull the pain of that bastard mauling our daughter. I ain't no druggie, you know that and I swear to you, I will never touch another drug as long as I live,' Johnny replied.

'But, what about Vinny?'

'Deb, I just want to finish my stretch and have a quiet life too. Like you said, Jo won't last long with Vinny, she's only a kid and she'll see the light before too long.'

'But, say Jo is still with him when you're released? I need you to promise me, Johnny, that whether she is or isn't, you will let sleeping dogs lie.' When Deborah had first found out that Joanna was with Vinny, she had wanted Johnny to intervene, but him nearly dying had changed her views completely.

In desperate need to have something to look forward to while he finished his time in prison, Johnny had no option other than to lie. If he told Deborah that he planned to kill Vinny Butler within a week of his release, whether he was still with their daughter or not, then she would never agree to marry him. 'They'll be no payback from me. I can promise you that, babe.'

As luck would have it, there wasn't much traffic on the roads and Vinny arrived at his brother's care home only a couple of hours after leaving London.

'Hi, I'm Roy Butler's elder brother, Vinny. I wasn't meant to be visiting him until tomorrow, but I wondered could I see him now? I have some rather important news,' Vinny said to one of the carers.

'Your brother is in his room and isn't usually a fan of surprise visits. I will try to entice him out, but Roy can be an obstinate one at times.'

'OK, but just tell him it's very urgent, will you?' Vinny replied, in a rather agitated tone. He was dreading telling Roy that Lenny was dead, but was hoping his brother would still go out for a beer with him so they could grieve together and toast their wonderful cousin's memory.

'Who is it?' Roy asked, as he heard the knock on the door. He had spent the morning tidying his room, and knowing that tomorrow Vinny would finally receive the wake-up call he was long overdue, Roy was in an exceptionally good mood.

'Your brother Vinny is here to see you, Roy. He says he's a day early, but he insists you speak to him as he has some very urgent news for you.'

Roy smirked. Ever since he could remember, it had been Vinny calling the shots, but not any more. 'Tell Vinny I am sleeping now, but tell him to return at six o'clock this evening. I will be ready to see him then. Tell him to come straight to my room though, won't you?'

The carer sighed. Roy was by no means the most difficult patient she had ever looked after, but he certainly wasn't the easiest either. 'OK, I'll tell him, but I have a feeling that your brother isn't going to be too pleased.'

'Well, that's tough shit, I'm afraid,' Roy replied. Hearing the carer's footsteps walk away, he allowed himself a little chuckle.

Dean Smart was perched on a barstool in the Grave Maurice. He liked this boozer. It reminded him of his dad.

Ordering another pint and a chaser to go with it, Dean knocked back the spirit in one. Brenda's possible pregnancy was an absolute nightmare, but he had other stuff on his mind too. Heavy shit which he just couldn't stop thinking about.

A few nights back, Dean had overheard things that perhaps he shouldn't have. It had been the early hours of the morning, and he'd been about to knock on Vinny's office door to ask something when he'd heard his father's death being joked about. Vinny and Ahmed were both quite vocal when they were pissed and coked-up, and, intrigued to see if they mentioned his old man again, Dean had bravely stood outside ear-wigging. Karen's death had been the next topic of conversation, then finally Dean had heard Vinny slagging off his new girlfriend, and saying he couldn't wait to heap revenge on her father.

Dean had no doubt as he crept away that not only had Vinny done away with Little Vinny's mother, but he had also been the perpetrator behind his own dad's disappearance. It was obvious to him now that his father had been murdered, and all Dean could currently think about was how badly had his old man sufferred?

Getting involved with Brenda and her dysfunctional family was the biggest mistake of Dean's life, and he knew he had to get away from them now. No longer could he work for a man that had murdered his dad, neither could he raise another child with his nightmare of a wife. Dean might have committed a couple of armed robberies back in his youth, but the Butlers were a different breed. The bastards were pure evil.

Dean ordered another drink and gave his fucked-up life some serious thought. He loved his nan dearly, and Tara, but he knew he had to scarper. Tomorrow, he would get all his savings out of the bank, say a discreet goodbye to Tara, tell his nan why he had to leave, and hopefully be able to say goodbye to Nancy at the same time. Staying around Brenda and her repulsive family wasn't an option any more.

Having been rebuffed by Roy, Vinny drove straight to Kings Holiday Park. He had upset his wonderful mother too much recently and if she wanted another grandchild by him, then Vinny was keen to oblige. He didn't love Joanna, but he didn't hate her either, and he was determined to make his dear old mum happy once again.

Parking near Joanna's chalet, Vinny jogged across the grass and banged on the door.

'What do you want? Jo doesn't want to know you any more,' Chloe spat viciously, when she opened the door.

'Look, I made a mistake. I love Jo and I really need to see her,' Vinny replied, in an extremely loud voice. He could tell by the way that Chloe was behaving that Joanna was inside.

Having been mortified by Vinny's rejection of their child the previous day, Joanna crept out of her bedroom. She had heard Vinny say he loved her and deep in her soul, she had known what they'd shared between them was real. Apart from confiding in Chloe, she had told nobody else about what had happened. 'It's OK, Chloe. Vinny and I need to speak,' she said, in almost a whisper.

'Well, he's not coming in here,' Chloe replied bluntly.

'Babe, let's talk in my car. I'm so sorry,' Vinny said. The tears in his eyes were real, although more to do with his cousin's death, and the thought of Ahmed waking up.

As they walked towards the car, Joanna allowed Vinny to hold her hand. 'Have you changed your mind about the baby? I'm so sorry for what my dad did to your brother, but I need to know where I stand, Vinny.'

Vinny gave Joanna his most intense stare. 'I was a fool, babe, to say what I said. I want to be with you, and I want us to have this baby. Can you forgive me?'

Holding Vinny tighter than she had ever held him before, Joanna smiled. 'Of course I can forgive you.'

Michael's feet felt like lead bricks as he bravely held his Auntie Viv's hand and escorted her into the morgue. They had already been warned that Lenny's injuries were not a pretty sight, and Michael had begged his aunt to let him identify the body alone, but Vivian was having none of it. 'I will never believe my wonderful boy is dead unless I see it with my own eyes,' she had snapped.

When the sheet was pulled back, Michael couldn't help but retch, then turn away. Lenny's head looked as if somebody had tried to saw it off and had then stopped halfway.

'My baby! My beautiful baby boy,' Vivian screamed. Seconds later, she threw herself on top of her son's corpse, and began kissing him.

'We have to go now, Auntie Viv. We know it's definitely Champ,' Michael said, tears rolling down his cheeks.

'Noooo! I can't leave him. I'm his mother. He'll be lonely here all on his own. I'm taking him home with me,' Vivian sobbed, as she tried to lift her lifeless son's body.

It then took ten minutes, two extra men, and Michael to finally drag a hysterical Vivian out of the morgue. She was one hundred per cent inconsolable.

Queenie paced up and down willing the phone to ring. She needed to know how Roy had coped with the news. Little Vinny was bored and miserable, so Queenie ordered him to go out and play, before heading into the lounge and sitting down opposite Brenda and Tara, who were hugging one another and crying. 'Dry them eyes now, come on, else you'll start me off again,' Queenie urged.

'Mummy says Daddy don't love us any more and he might not come back,' Tara sobbed.

Queenie looked at her daughter in disgust. 'Whatever are you saying silly stuff like that to her for?'

'Well, Dean didn't seem very overjoyed about my period being late, did he? He couldn't get out the door quick enough and he hasn't come back.'

Queenie shook her head in utter disbelief. 'Do you know what, Bren, I often wonder if the hospital gave me the wrong baby when I brought you home. Your cousin has just been killed in a car crash, and all you can think about is you, you, you. You really are one self-centered little mare. You make me fucking sick.'

Pleased that he had managed to talk Joanna around to keeping their baby, Vinny stopped at a phonebox. He knew the news wouldn't exactly cheer his mum up, but he wanted to give her hope of some kind. 'Mum, it's me. How's Auntie Viv?'

513

'Awful, boy. Michael said she tried to take Lenny out the morgue with her. Nearly did by all accounts. I can't get no sense out of her at all now. I gave her a brandy to try and calm her down, but it's as though she's on a different planet. Do you think I should call a doctor?'

Vinny had never felt guilt like it before, but what could he do? He had to try to act normal. 'Mum, don't call no doctor or do anything rash until I get home. The last thing we need is Auntie Viv to be carted off to a nuthouse.'

'OK, love. Have you spoken to Roy yet?'

'No, but I am on my way to see him now. He was sleeping earlier. I've spoken to Joanna though and she's gonna keep the baby. I will buy a house for her to live in near yours.'

'Good lad. I've been thinking today about that Turk. Broken all our hearts, he has. If he survives, I hope you're going to sort it? Because if you don't, I will.'

Vinny was relieved when the pips saved him from answering his mother's difficult question. He loved Ahmed like a brother and there was no way he could kill him. If push came to shove then Michael would have to do the deed.

Roy unscrewed the bottle and took a large gulp of the brandy. He wasn't nervous, he was more excited than anything.

Glancing at his watch, Roy laid the letters on the bed, then took his gun out of its cloth. Vinny would be here any minute and he was good and ready for him.

At six o'clock exactly, Roy felt a flutter in his stomach when he heard the tap on his door. 'Who is it?' he asked, putting a jumper on his lap to hide the gun.

'It's Vinny. The carer told me to come straight to your room.'

'Come in then.'

Vinny entered the room and was just about to tell his brother about Lenny's death, when Roy pointed a gun at him. 'What the fuck you doing, bruv? Put it down,' Vinny said, in a shaky voice.

Roy stared at his brother. He could see the fear in his eyes and that pleased him greatly. 'Sit on the chair, Vin. It's me giving the orders out for once, not you. If you disobey me, I will shoot you.'

Vinny's heart was beating like a drum as he did as Roy ordered. He knew his brother had problems with him, but he had never imagined he hated him this much. 'Please don't do anything stupid, Roy. Think of Mum and Little Vinny. Both will be devastated if you kill me. I'm sorry that it was you who took that bullet, but it wasn't my fault, it was all Preston's doing,' Vinny pleaded. Telling Roy that Lenny was dead and admitting that he had got revenge on Preston by getting his daughter up the duff was totally off limits now that his brother was pointing a gun his way. Either of those revelations might topple Roy over the edge.

Roy chuckled as he clocked Vinny's hands shaking. 'Not such a big man now, are you, bruv? And it's not the bullet in the head that's made me hate you so much. It's the fact that you tried to ruin my engagement to the only woman I've ever loved. That was a truly despicable thing to do, you wicked bastard.'

Vinny stared at the gun and the tears began to roll down his cheeks. He had visions of never seeing his beloved mother and son again and that thought terrified him. 'I'm so sorry, Roy, and you are right. Trying to split you and Colleen up was a truly despicable thing to do. But, I only did it because I loved you so much and was afraid of losing you. Me and you had always been inseparable ever since we were kids, and that all changed when Colleen came along. I was bang out of order, I know I was, but please don't kill me. Who will look after Mum and Auntie Viv if I ain't around, eh? Michael won't. He's too busy looking after that lunatic he married.'

Roy smiled on the one side of his mouth that he still could. He then lifted the gun up and pointed it towards his own head.

'No, bruv. Stop it, please,' Vinny whispered, his face a picture of shock.

'I have explained everything in a letter to you, Vinny. There are also letters on my bed for the rest of the family, including Dad. My life is horrendous and I can't live like this any more. Having your looks, your legs, and your dignity swiped from you in one fell swoop is something that no man should have to go through.'

'Roy, don't. Mum will never get over it if you do. Neither will I. Please don't. I love you, bruv.'

'And I once loved you too, Vin, but not any more. Did you know that when you supposedly get to heaven any injuries or illnesses you might have had disappear? One of the other patients in here told me that, and I am hoping that if God accepts me at those pearly gates, I will regain the use of my legs and forgive you. Doubt we'll ever meet again though, not with your track record, but if you take the advice I have given you in my letter, I hope we will. If you don't, you will definitely end up in hell.'

'No, Roy, noooo,' Vinny screamed, as he saw his brother's finger put pressure on the trigger.

A split second later, Roy was dead.

As the evening wore on, Queenie knew she had no choice other than to call the doctor out to her sister. There was no way Queenie would allow Vivian to be hospitalized, she needed her family around her, but Viv's way of dealing with grief was like none Queenie had ever experienced.

'Stop it, Viv. What you doing that for?' Queenie asked,

when her sister began ripping up the photos she had demanded Queenie give her of Lenny.

'Because he's fucking gone, ain't he? Cunting God has taken him away from me,' Vivian screamed.

'Michael, get them off her. She is really gonna regret tearing them up when she feels better,' Queenie urged.

'Let me take them, Auntie Viv,' Michael said, gently trying to coax the photographs out of his aunt's firm grasp.

'Noooo! Lenny was my son, so I can do what I bastard-well like with them,' Vivian yelled.

'It's OK, Michael. The doctor's here now. His car's just pulled up. Go and answer the door,' Queenie told her son.

'Dad, we're hungry,' Daniel said, tugging on Michael's sleeve.

'Take your brothers upstairs and I'll be up in a bit. Your Auntie Vivian isn't well,' Michael replied, opening the front door to let the doctor in.

'But, we can't go to bed yet. We haven't had no dinner,' Daniel complained.

'When's Mummy coming home?' Adam asked innocently.

Michael ushered the doctor into the lounge, shut the door, then crouched down and hugged all three of his sons. 'As soon as the doctor has gone, I'll go round the chippy and get you some dinner, OK?'

'OK. But, when is Mum coming home, Dad?' Daniel asked.

Feeling as though his head was about to burst, Michael bit his lip to stop himself from breaking down. 'Mummy will be home soon, and she told me today to tell you she loves and misses you all very much,' he lied.

Vinny arrived back in Whitechapel at ten p.m. but instead of heading straight to his mother's house, he went to the club first. He had told his doorman to put a note on the entrance

517

saying that the club was closed until further notice, but he went in via the back just in case there were any punters milling around. After seeing his brother's brains splattered up the walls, he couldn't face anybody else at the moment.

Vinny poured himself a large Scotch. How he was going to tell his mother that Roy was now dead as well as Lenny, he did not know. Worried about saving his own skin, Vinny picked up the phone. 'Hello. My best pal was admitted to your hospital last night after a bad car crash. His name is Ahmed Zane. Could you tell me how he is, please?' he asked politely. Vinny had debated whether to put on a fake Turkish accent and say he was a relation, but he guessed Ahmed's wife would be at the hospital, and he didn't want to do or say anything suspicious in case the Old Bill were sniffing about.

'I'm afraid I cannot give you any information over the phone unless you are a relative,' the receptionist replied.

'But I am his family. I was like a brother to him,' Vinny informed the cold-hearted bitch.

'I'm sorry, sir, but it is hospital policy that we cannot divulge any information over the phone unless you are an actual relative of the patient.'

'Well, fuck you, and fuck your stupid rules,' Vinny yelled, before slamming the phone down.

Knowing he had to get to his mother's house as quickly as possible to break the terrible news to her, Vinny stared at Roy's letters. There were nine in total, addressed to Mum, Dad, Michael, Brenda, Auntie Viv, Champ, Colleen, Emily-Mae, and himself. Ripping his open, Vinny downed his Scotch before reading it. He was expecting the worst, but he couldn't have been more surprised.

Dear Vinny,

    Seeing as you are reading this letter means that I accomplished my task of blowing my brains out right in front of your very eyes, which is something I wanted to do. The reason being, I no longer have to suffer and seeing me die might actually be the wake-up call you need.

As I am writing this, I am thinking back to when we were kids. We were fuckers, weren't we? We had to rob just to get by, and I can remember our opening night when we first bought the club as if it were yesterday. Mum and Auntie Viv were so proud of us, weren't they? It really was an achievement for two East End ragamuffins who had come from nothing, wasn't it? And do you remember how we managed to buy the club in the first place? We stalked that lorry driver for at least two weeks before we managed to get our hands on them televisions. They were good times, bruv, and ones I am chuckling about as I am writing this letter.

Right, now to the nitty-gritty. I could never deal with ending up as a cripple. I saw people smile pitifully at me in that wheelchair and even though I wanted to leap out the bastard thing and punch their faces in, I couldn't. I was such a geezer years ago, just like you are and I found being different really hard to deal with. I couldn't bear people to see me the way I was, and the bitter man I had become, so death will be a total relief to me.

Seeing as I have written you such a heartfelt letter, I need you to do a few things in return for me, bruv. I want you to stop doing those drugs, drinking so much, and get rid of Ahmed out of your life. I still hear lots through the grapevine, and I know what you've been up to. I also know that Ahmed is a heroin and cocaine dealer, and he will be your downfall, trust me.

I also want you to look after Mum, Auntie Viv, and Champ for me. Michael is strong enough to cope with my death, Brenda is self-centered, but Mum, Auntie Viv, and Champ will need you to be there for them. My last wish, is that you will make up with Dad. I spoke to him recently and he had really turned his life around. He isn't a bad man, Vinny, he is our father.

Well, I must end this letter now, but I promise you faithfully, if you carry out all my wishes, I will always smile down on you from above. Heaven is meant to wipe away all the bad stuff, so hopefully I will be running about in no time again once I arrive. I might even open a nightclub up there!

Putting the letter on the bar, Vinny cried like he had never cried before.

Queenie was lying in bed cuddling her sister when she heard the front door open, then shut. Dr Baker had been the family GP for many years and, on Queenie's insistence, he had given Vivian a strong injection to calm her down, which thankfully had worked wonders.

Little Vinny had rung up earlier to say he was staying at Ben Bloggs' house. Daniel, Lee and Adam had all been tucked up in bed hours ago and, as far as Queenie knew, Michael was still downstairs.

Creeping out of bed so she didn't wake Vivian, Queenie tiptoed down the stairs. As soon as she saw the look on Vinny's face, she knew it was bad news. 'Please tell me Roy is OK, Vinny?' she pleaded, her eyes brimming with tears.

Hugging his mother, Vinny led her into the lounge. 'Michael, pour us all a brandy, please,' he ordered.

Michael wanted to tell his brother to fuck right off, but

decided he could do that later, when his mum wasn't present. She'd had enough upset in the last two days to last her a lifetime, and Michael could also tell by Vinny's face that things hadn't gone too well with Roy. 'Well?' Michael asked, handing round the brandies.

Vinny held his mother in his arms and looked deep into her eyes as he broke the terrible news. 'Roy's gone, Mum. He'd had enough of suffering and he wanted to go. I didn't even have time to tell him about Champ. Roy's mind was already made up.'

'Gone! Gone! What do you mean he's fucking gone?' Queenie asked, her lips twitching with anxiety.

'Roy's dead, Mum. He shot himself. He wasn't alone. I was there with him when he died. I tried to stop him, but he wasn't having none of it. He was ready to go,' Vinny explained, with tears running down his cheeks.

With her voice a mixture of hysteria and anger, Queenie flew at her son. 'Why didn't you grab the gun off him? You could have stopped him, why didn't you try?' she screamed, pummelling her fists against her eldest son's chest.

'It weren't my fault, Mum, honest. Roy already had the gun in his hand when I got there. He even pointed it at me first,' Vinny explained, trying to hug his distraught mother.

Queenie slapped Vinny hard around the face. 'Get away from me. I don't want you anywhere near me. This is all your fucking fault. I'll never forgive you for this,' she sobbed, before running out of the room, then up the stairs.

As Vinny mumbled something about a letter and went to chase after her, Michael grabbed him to stop him. 'Well, I hope you are happy with yourself now, Vin. That's two you've killed off.'

'Michael, I know you hate me at the moment, and you have every right to, but please read the letter Roy left for me. He has left letters for the rest of the family as well,'

Vinny said, handing his own letter to his brother.

Michael sat down, read it, and to his surprise found he had tears in his eyes. 'It still don't make it right what happened to Champ, though, does it, Vin? And Roy hasn't exactly forgiven you. He's just asking you to change.'

'Please, Michael, forgive me. I swear I'll change.'

'I don't think you are capable of changing, Vin. You've got too much of an unpredictable nature and a nasty temper.'

Vinny knelt at his brother's side and grabbed him by the head so he would have to look him in the eyes. 'Michael, I loved Roy and Champ with all my heart. I did everything for them in life that I could. Johnny Preston misfiring was not my fault, neither was the van that came towards me with its full beam on. I swear, I had sobered up at that club, and I would never have driven Champ home if I didn't think I was capable of doing so. I have taken in every word Roy said in that letter, and I swear I will abide by all his wishes. I have been drinking and snorting too much recently, but it was only since I met Ahmed. Roy was right. He is a bad influence on me. As for Dad, Roy is right about that too. I have treated him terribly, and at the end of the day, he is our father.'

Michael stared his brother in the eye. 'I want to believe you, Vin, but I don't know if I can.'

'I will make myself become a better person, I promise. Mum needs us to be united, not at each other's throats. Don't you remember Mum's old saying when we were kids? She always used to say that Butlers stand strong together through thick and thin. Well, I have just been through a thin patch, and I really need you to forgive me for my sins. Now Roy and Champ are dead, we need one another, Michael. Watching Roy blow his brains out right in front of me will haunt me for the rest of my days. It was horrific, bruv,' Vinny said, his eyes filling up with tears.

Michael held out his right hand. 'Vin, I'll stand by you for now but if you don't keep to your promises and change, I swear your life won't be worth fucking living.'

Vinny hugged his brother and smirked as he did so. Michael was a gullible chap and had always been easy to talk around. Good job really, because if Ahmed woke up and started talking, Vinny needed Michael to silence him.

Ahmed Zane opened his eyes. The smell of disinfectant and the sight of tubes poking out of his arms and his wife Anna sitting by his bedside immediately alerted him that he was in some kind of hospital. But, the mystery was, how did he get there?

'Ahmed, can you hear me? Thank God you are awake. I must go and get the nurse,' Anna said, both tearful and relieved.

'No. No nurse. Just tell me what's happened?' Ahmed croaked.

'You were involved in a bad car accident. I've been so worried, Ahmed. Your friend Lenny didn't make it, and the police said you were driving. Had you been drinking? They won't send you to prison if you were drunk, will they?'

The mention of Lenny immediately jogged his memory and Ahmed shut his eyes again as he tried to recall exactly what had happened. He could remember going to the whore-house in Dalston with Vinny and Lenny, but Vinny had insisted on driving home, he was sure of that. 'You no-good cunting motherfucker,' Ahmed mumbled to himself.

Anna squeezed her husband's hand. 'Whatever's the matter? Have you remembered that night? I've asked the police loads of questions, but apart from saying that you were found in the driver's seat of the car, they won't tell me anything.'

Ahmed felt physically sick as he pictured Vinny Butler's

face. He remembered everything now, including trying to grab the steering wheel when Vinny dramatically swerved after being stunned by the beam of an oncoming vehicle.

'Ahmed, are you OK? Talk to me,' Anna pleaded.

Ahmed was anything but OK. Not only had Vinny left him for dead, his so-called best friend had obviously tried to cover his own tracks by moving his body into the driver's seat.

Angry and appalled by such an act of betrayal by someone he had trusted so much, Ahmed felt the bile rise to the back of his throat. If Vinny Butler imagined that he was going to get away with the stroke he had pulled, he really did have another think coming.

Grassing to the police was a nonstarter. Ahmed would rather seek his own revenge. Two could play at Vinny Butler's games, and nobody played them quite as well as he did. Ahmed Zane was the fucking master of games.

EPILOGUE

Mary Walker was thrilled when she received an early-morning phone call from her daughter saying she was ready to see her dad now. Nancy sounded so much chirpier than she had the previous day. 'Oh Donald, I'm so happy. Don't you dare say anything to upset her, will you?' Mary warned her husband.

'Of course not, dear,' Donald replied, with a hint of sarcasm. He was actually just as worried about their daughter as Mary was, but Donald had always had difficulty in expressing his feelings.

'Now, go and put your nice shirt and trousers on. The hospital said Christopher can be discharged today as well, so perhaps we can all visit Nancy together? Tina can handle the café alone,' Mary assured her husband.

'OK, my love. I will go and get changed right now.'

Nancy Butler felt happier than she had in ages. The old lady who was opposite her had befriended her and, although she seemed slightly crazy, had cheered Nancy up no end. 'So, where do you live, Freda? I'm sure I've seen you somewhere before,' Nancy remarked.

'Whitechapel. Lived there all my life. Where do you live,

darling?' Freda asked, acting as though she didn't recognize the girl. She actually quite liked Nancy. She was a sweet girl, and nothing like her parents. Freda remembered them as well, especially the father. He was right up his own arse he was.

About to reply, Nancy was left open-mouthed when Dean Smart strolled into the ward. 'What you doing here, Dean?'

'I need to speak to my nan in private for five minutes. I will speak to you afterwards, Nance, if that is OK?'

'Oh my god! Is that your nan?' Nancy exclaimed. She had thought Freda looked familiar, but she'd had no idea she was Dean's nan.

Dean nodded, sat on the edge of his grandmother's bed and tenderly hugged her. 'Nan, I have to go away. I cannot be part of that Butler family for one minute longer. I have already spoken to the doctors, and they say you are going to be just fine. I will keep in touch with you always, and when I sort myself out somewhere to live and you are back on your feet again, you can come and visit me.'

Freda held her grandson's head in her hands and cried with relief. 'That is the best news I have heard in ages, boy. Get away from them no-good fuckers while you still can. I had visions of you one day propping up a flyover like your poor old dad probably did.'

Dean hugged his nan tightly and kissed her on the forehead. 'I love you, Nan. I'll be in touch soon, OK?'

Dean reluctantly turned his back on the old woman who had raised him and meant the world to him, and walked over to Nancy's bed and sat down beside her. 'I've been so worried about you, babe. Are you OK?'

'No, Dean. I've been ill. I was found in an alleyway by a man, and I don't even know how I got there. I feel like I'm going mad.'

Dean held Nancy in his arms and stroked her beautiful

blonde hair. 'I know I shouldn't be saying this, Nance, but I love you and I always will. I know we can never be together, but I can't help the way that I feel about you. Now listen, I have to go away. I can't spend one minute longer with Brenda, or her family. If you've got any sense, you should do the same. Your Michael is the best of the bunch, but the core of the family is rotten. If I were you, I would run for the hills. You were never cut out to be part of the Butler clan, and neither was I.'

'Where are you going?' Nancy asked, with tears in her eyes.

'I don't know yet, but get my nan's phone number, and I will keep in touch with you via her, OK? I know I can trust you never to repeat this conversation.'

Nancy nodded. 'But what about Tara?'

'I would love to take Tara with me, Nance, but I can't. If I do, the bastards will hunt me down. I have lived a life of hell with Brenda. Having sex with her turned my stomach, but I did it on the odd occasion just to keep the peace. She has just announced she is pregnant again, which is another reason I need to get away. Leaving one child is bad enough, and if I stayed to love the other, I would be stuck with Bren for life. Look, I really do have to go now. Take care of yourself, sweetheart,' Dean said, giving Nancy a short but tender kiss on her lips.

When Dean ran off down the ward, Nancy got out of bed, and walked over to Freda's.

With Christopher now formally discharged from Upney Hospital and desperate to visit his sister as well, Mary gave her husband and son one last warning not to say anything that might upset Nancy.

'I won't, Mum, I promise. I'm just glad to have Nancy back in our lives again,' Christopher replied, honestly.

527

'I feel the same way too,' Donald admitted.

Mary Walker was horrified when she walked into the ward. Mad Freda had one of those faces that was impossible to forget. She also had her arm around Nancy's shoulders. 'Leave my daughter alone. What have you done to her?' Mary shrieked.

Freda grinned. Nancy and Donald had always seen themselves as the perfect parents, but they were sadly mistaken.

'Get away from Nancy now, you mad old bat,' Donald demanded.

'Calm down, Dad. Let's not make a scene,' Christopher said, grabbing his father's arm. He had also recognized Freda immediately.

'Well, well, well. If it isn't the know-it-all couple who I warned about the Butlers many years ago. You thought I was mad when I walked into your posh café in 1965 and told you the score, didn't ya? Bet you don't think so now? Told you those bastards set a trap for people like us, didn't I? They caught my Dean in that trap and your Nancy. Do you still think I'm mental now?'

Donald Walker glanced at his wife before answering. 'No, you are not mad, Freda. In fact, I would describe you as anything but. You were right about everything. Smart by name and even smarter by nature.'

When loyalty is everything, betrayal can have deadly consequences...

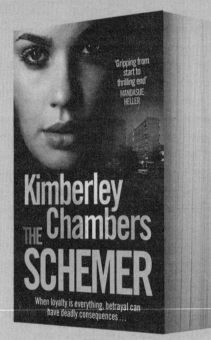